Peter Blanchard was blinded by the plane crash that killed Carl Morris.

Now fate had dealt him a second hand, and second sight—the eyes of the man who died . . . and the love of his beautiful wife.

Was it chance? The power of love? Or something beyond that drew them together?

What terrible bargain has been struck for the eyes of Carl Morris?

*And who is going to pay . . . ?*

# A STRANGER'S EYES

## BETTIE WYSOR

A JOVE BOOK

Requests for permission to make copies of any part
of the work should be mailed to: Permissions,
Jove Publications, Inc., 200 Madison Avenue,
New York, NY 10016

First Jove edition published March 1981

10  9  8  7  6  5  4  3  2  1

Printed in the United States of America

Jove books are published by Jove Publications, Inc.,
200 Madison Avenue, New York, NY 10016

For: N.J.G.
With Affection

&

E.E.F. with
Thanks

# Chapter One

The big jet was only twenty minutes out of John F. Kennedy Airport in New York when the pretty blond flight attendant stopped the beverage cart beside seat number 12B.

"Would you care to purchase a drink, sir?"

"You bet," replied Peter Blanchard, who was seated in number 12B on the aisle. "Make it a double Cutty Sark and soda, please." He lowered the fold-down table on the back of the seat in front of him and the attendant placed two small bottles and a split of soda on it. He had the exact change ready before she asked, and she smiled appreciatively. Peter was an old hand at drinking in the air, and he always tried to establish a rapport with the flight attendant.

When she leaned across him to speak to his seatmate in number 12A by the window, Peter noticed that she wore Balenciaga's Quadrille, the same fragrance worn by Jeannie Wharton. He was seriously thinking of asking Jeannie to marry him after he got the French project out of the way.

"And you, sir?" she asked the man next to Peter.

"Oh, maybe a beer. Any Heineken?"

"Yes, sir," she answered cheerfully. "We have all the imported beers on our trans-Atlantic flights."

"Heineken will be fine."

She uncapped the bottle and again leaned across Peter to place it on the other man's table.

1

"Like your perfume," said Peter offhand; he didn't want to give a wrong impression of flirtatiousness.

"Thank you." She smiled and moved off down the aisle. Peter opened the first little bottle and poured it carefully into the glass, then added soda. The other man sipped his beer and stared out the window. They'd leveled off from the steep climb out of New York and were cruising evenly now at an altitude of approximately thirty-seven thousand feet.

"You've got guts drinking beer on a trans-Atlantic flight," Peter said to his seatmate.

"Oh? How's that?" the man asked.

"Too many trips to the head," replied Peter, and the other man chuckled quietly.

"Yeah. If you stick with it." He paused to sip his beer. "I seldom have more than one. Not much of a drinker."

"Can't say the same for myself. Flying scares me."

"That so?"

"Yeah. Usually stay tanked all the way across." Peter laughed nervously. His dread of flying was not something he was proud of.

"Well, that's one way of handling it," the other man commented.

"Here's to Dutch courage," Peter laughed again and tossed off the remainder of his drink. "By the way," he said, "my name's Peter Blanchard."

"Carl Morris," his seatmate replied.

"So flying doesn't bother you, Carl?"

"Nope—enjoy it."

"Lucky." Peter began to open the second bottle of Scotch.

"Fact is," said Morris, "I do some flying myself. Have an ancient Cessna. Enjoy it a lot."

"I never used to mind flying until I lost two friends in a crash. A flight to Atlanta."

"That's rough." Morris actually sounded sympathetic, and Peter felt encouraged to continue. It helped to talk about his fear.

"Actually, I was supposed to be on that trip, but I had to go to the West Coast instead—and, uh, my assistant replaced me." That was always the hardest part for him to tell, but it was the part he needed most to tell. Peter never forgot he could have gone to Atlanta himself and sent his assistant to the Coast, but he had decided to take the San Francisco trip

2

because he wanted to spend the weekend with a woman he knew out there. "So, uh, I kinda feel like I'm—well, kinda on borrowed time."

"I can understand how you might feel, but there's another way of looking at it, too."

"How's that?"

"It wasn't your time, and it *was* his." Carl Morris spoke earnestly; Peter could tell he actually believed what he said.

"I keep telling myself that, but somehow it doesn't really *take*." Peter sipped his drink. "You see, Adams, my assistant, had a wife and kids."

"Well, that is a little rough to have to think about, but the theory still applies. You shouldn't take on that responsibility; you didn't deprive them of their father."

"You see, I was single—" He let the sentence die, recognizing it as part of his guilt trip.

"Married now?" asked Carl.

"Nope. Been thinking about it, though. There's someone I've been seeing for a while, and I've just about decided to ask her to marry me when I get back."

"Think she'll say yes?" Morris laughed softly, trying to lighten the tone of the conversation.

"Wouldn't ask if I didn't think so," replied Peter with a grin.

"Well, I wish you happiness."

"Thanks." Peter sipped his drink and Morris looked out the window. The conversation seemed to be over, but Peter didn't want it to be.

"You married?" he asked.

"Yes."

"Married long?"

"Ten years last June." Carl Morris sounded proud.

"Children?"

"No." He paused. "We haven't been that lucky." Morris grew quiet again, and Peter could tell it bothered Carl that he had no children, so he decided to drop the subject. But Peter's assumption was incorrect; Carl wasn't ready to drop it. "We've thought of adopting, but—" Morris hesitated. "We decided to wait, give ourselves a year or two more. We've got time." Morris paused again. "There's nothing *wrong* with either one of us."

"Couldn't you do both? I mean, if you're so anxious to

3

have a child, why not adopt and at the same time keep trying to have one of your own?'' Peter didn't really care one way or the other about the Morrises' problem, but he wanted to keep contact with this man; something about him had a calming effect on Peter.

"We thought of that, too, but Marcy—that's my wife—Marcy and I are very close. I mean, we're, uh, really in love.'' Morris seemed slightly embarrassed. "So we'd like to have our own child, if we can. At least one; we'd be satisfied with one.''

Peter couldn't think of any immediate response, so he sipped his drink, and signaled to the flight attendant to bring him another round. Then he began to think about Marcy and Carl Morris and the fact that they were still in love after ten years.

"That's nice,'' he said. "That you're still in love, I mean.''

"Yes.'' Morris smiled gently.

Peter watched his face and envied him the contentment of knowing he was loved. But why did he envy him? After all, didn't he have Jeannie, and didn't she love him? The question bothered him, though. Was it that he didn't believe she loved him? No, he did believe it—intellectually, anyway. But somehow, now that he thought about it, he realized he'd never felt that deep-down *knowing* he imagined one ought to feel. He wanted to hear more about how Carl Morris felt.

"Is your wife afraid of your flying?'' he asked.

"Not the Cessna, no. I don't think she's too keen on these trans-Atlantic flights.''

"Could she get along without you, do you think?''

Morris looked at him quizzically.

"I mean, you did say you were very close,'' Peter added, suddenly feeling slightly uncomfortable.

"Yeah?''

"Well, I mean, would she go to pieces if something happened to you?''

"You are a morbid fellow, aren't you?'' Morris said it good-naturedly, but Peter could tell the question had disturbed him. He thought he'd better drop that subject, too. He wondered then if he was getting drunk.

"Sorry,'' he said.

"No, don't be. It's a perfectly good question.'' Carl sipped his beer, then went on. "Marcy is a strong woman, although a sensitive one, and I imagine she'd take it very hard at first,

4

but after awhile she'd pull herself together and get on with her life. She's like that." He paused, obviously thinking about some instance of his wife's strength. "Even so, the thought of leaving her alone—that's really terrible."

"Sorry I brought it up," said Peter, seeing that he had caused Carl some distress. "Maybe you could still kind of watch over her if anything did happen to you." Carl shot him a quick look and Peter was now pretty certain that he *was* getting drunk. "I mean, don't you think it's possible that a man who's passed on could know what goes on down here with the people he loves? I mean, don't you think it's possible he would try to watch out for them if he sees them heading for danger, or something?"

"I don't know." Carl looked out the window, and Peter thought it was time for him to shut up, but Carl suddenly turned to look at him.

"You know, that's a very interesting idea you just brought up."

"You mean about looking after your loved ones?"

"Yes."

"Well, it's always kind of fascinated me," said Peter. "I wonder about a lot of things like that."

"Do you believe it's possible?"

"I don't know. I guess I think it's possible or I wouldn't be thinking about it. What do you think?"

"I don't know either. But I do know if anything happened to me, I'd sure do my damnedest to try and look after Marcy."

The flight attendant interrupted them with Peter's second round. "Want another beer, Carl?" asked Peter.

"No thanks. You've given me a lot to think about. And I still have some work to do before we arrive in Paris."

"Me too, but I can't settle down until I get the butterflies in my gut quieted down." He opened one of the little Scotch bottles. "Hope this does the trick because I've got a manuscript to reread before I arrive in Paris. Got a meeting with a French author and his publisher—important book, lot of money involved. Want to be able to discuss it intelligently."

"I suspect you'd be able to do that quite well under any circumstances," laughed Carl.

"Thanks for the vote of confidence, but I have a funny

5

feeling this deal isn't going to come off exactly the way I'd like it to.''

"Is it a good book?"

"Fair. A natural for films—got a big deal lined up already."

"If it's only fair, why buy it?"

"Sales. It'll sell like hot cakes, especially with the movie tie-in."

"Sales and movie possibilities; that's your criteria for buying?"

"It's not mine exactly, but it is my publisher's. He's in business to make money, and it's my job to see that we do. That's the name of the game—a fact of life, and publishing today."

"You're a realist?"

"Got to be if you're going to survive in this business."

"Why don't you think this deal will come off the way you want it to? If you don't mind my asking—"

"Don't mind at all, but don't know the answer. Just a feeling I have."

# Chapter Two

They were several hours out over the Atlantic when Peter noticed a change in the rhythm of the plane's engines. Because of his anxiety about flying he was always subconsciously listening for any indication of a change in the flight pattern. He glanced at his watch and saw that they were less than forty-five minutes out of Charles De Gaulle Airport.

"Guess we're beginning to descend for Paris," he said to Carl.

"Right on schedule, too." Carl had glanced at his watch and then gone back to his work. Peter resumed reading the manuscript.

"Ladies and gentlemen, this is your captain." There was a pause, and it was that pause that always caused Peter's stomach to contract into a tight knot of fear. "Uh—we're beginning our descent for Charles De Gaulle Airport and should be on the ground in about thirty minutes—depending, of course, on air traffic. It has been a pleasure to have you aboard flight 421. We hope you've enjoyed the flight, and that you will fly with us again. Thank you." The "fasten seat belts" sign flashed on, and Peter quickly clicked the belt into place and prayed for a safe landing.

"Well, won't be long now," said Carl. Peter interrupted his prayer, opened his eyes, and looked at Carl's cheerful, smiling face.

"Yeah. But to tell you the truth, that's when I get really uptight. I've been told that takeoffs and landings are the most dangerous."

"Well, technically speaking that's when the most can go wrong, but these trans-Atlantic pilots are really seasoned old hands at this job. The odds are good for a safe landing."

"You know something? I'm not a religious man, but just put me in an airplane and I start praying like a son of a bitch!" Both men laughed.

"Well, that's a kind of religion, I guess. An existentialist one, if there is such a term."

Suddenly Peter, whose senses were still attuned to every nuance of the plane's performance, noticed that the ship's nose had suddenly begun to rise and the engines had accelerated. "Hey, what's going on?"

"Probably stacked up at De Gaulle." Carl's voice was even and calm and Peter felt silly.

"Yeah. Probably," he agreed, but a double Scotch would have made him feel better. He recognized the sound of the hydraulic landing gear and assumed the pilot was raising the landing carriage if the plane was going to join a stack-up. He hoped the stack-up wouldn't turn into a long wait; he'd waited two hours to land at JFK once, and anxiety and claustrophobia had given him the worst two hours of his life.

"Guess they're retracting the landing carriage," he tried to remark casually, hoping for some reassuring words from Carl.

"Yeah," replied Carl.

Peter didn't know whether his imagination was overactive, but it seemed to him that Carl didn't sound quite as calm as he had before. He shot him a quizzical look. "Isn't that what that sound is?"

"Yes, it's the landing gear all right." Carl was listening intently, and Peter's stomach contracted.

"Something's wrong, isn't it?"

"Not necessarily. Probably just like you said. If they are stacked up, he's retracting the landing carriage so we can climb back up and circle."

"You don't believe it, though, do you?" Peter was getting a strong intuitive message from somewhere, and it told him that something was wrong.

"Hey, curb that imagination of yours," Carl laughed.

"You'll have yourself in a lather, and the bar is closed." Carl opened his case and took out the folder he'd been working on. He seemed unconcerned, and Peter relaxed. If Carl wasn't worried, he wasn't going to worry either. He made an effort to concentrate on something else. Suddenly, however, he noticed a lot of activity among the flight attendants toward the front of the plane. They had all gathered around the purser.

"Excuse me, Carl, but uh—uh—" His sentence was cut off by the captain's voice.

"Ladies and gentlemen, this is the captain again. You may have noticed that we've altered our course for landing." There was another of those disturbing silences, and then the captain continued. "We've gone back up to work on our landing gear. We're experiencing some difficulty with it at the moment, but we hope to have it corrected shortly." Another pause. "There's no cause for alarm at this time. We're confident we will correct the difficulty and make a routine landing at De Gaulle. We'll keep you informed, but I repeat, there's no reason for alarm."

"Jesus Christ!" said Peter. "I knew it, damn it. I knew it, and so did you. Didn't you?"

"I had some idea—yes." Carl still sounded calm.

"You're a pretty laid-back guy, Carl Morris."

"Not much I can do but have faith in the pilot and crew, is there?"

"What happens if they can't get that gear working?"

"You really want to talk about it?"

"Yes. I don't like surprises. I like to be prepared for any eventuality."

"Well—to put it simply, if they can't get it down, we go in on our belly."

"Swell! Nice, comforting thought—riding on top of all that jet fuel."

"I don't imagine there's a lot of fuel left after crossing the Atlantic, but if there is, he'll most likely jetison some of it."

"Which means he probably doesn't have a lot of time to get that gear working either way, right?"

"Maybe." Carl shrugged and put the folder back into his attaché case.

"May I have your attention please." It was another voice on the intercom.

"Oh, Christ!" Peter muttered and closed his eyes.

"The captain has asked me to inform you that in case of any emergency condition, it is routine practice to advise you of safety procedures. You will please note that all exits from the aircraft are shown on the card in the pocket of the seat in front of you. Please familiarize yourself with these exits now. Your flight attendants will be there to assist you in exiting should it become necessary. Your flight attendant will also instruct you in other safety measures when, and if, they seem necessary. I repeat, however, this is only a precautionary action." He paused, then went on. "We will pass the beverage cart, and all drinks will be courtesy of the airline. Please relax and try to keep calm. Captain Johnson will keep you informed. Thank you."

"Well, that's that!" said Peter. "They're being very casual about it all, but I'm not convinced." Peter was thinking of his assistant who had gone down in his stead. Had his time finally run out? "I've been scared out of my mind of something like this for years, and now—here it is," he said aloud to himself. He slapped his knees with the palms of his hands to relieve the anger he suddenly felt coming to the surface.

"Scared now?" asked Carl.

"Bet your ass!" Peter wondered what in hell Carl expected him to be, but when he thought about it a moment, he realized that something very strange had happened to him. "It's weird," he said. "I can't really feel anything all of a sudden. It's like all my circuits have gone dead."

"Know what you mean. When the thing we fear happens, we can't really take it in." Carl's voice was still quietly even, but Peter realized that Carl was afraid, too, and that made him feel calmer. Peter knew that he had always been good in emergencies, taking charge when others panicked. He hoped that strength would serve him well this time.

"Would you gentlemen care for a drink?" asked the attendant, stopping her cart beside Peter.

"And how! I'll have a—"

"Double Cutty Sark and soda," she said, smiling.

"Right! Except skip the soda. I'll take it straight this time." She gave him the two small bottles and a glass.

"How about you, sir?" she asked Carl.

"I think I'll have the same as my friend this time," Carl replied. She passed the Scotch and a glass across to Carl and moved off down the aisle.

"Well, here's looking at you, pal," said Peter, doing a halfhearted imitation of Humphrey Bogart.

"Luck and all that," said Carl, taking a slug of the Scotch and shuddering as it went down. "Man, that stuff bites!"

"How bad could this be, Carl?"

"Let's keep an open mind. They'll most likely correct the landing device. It's not an uncommon happening, you know."

"No, I don't know." Peter wondered about what could happen and fought back a feeling of panic. "What are the odds if they don't get that carriage down and we go in on our belly?" He had to ask, knowing the facts, no matter how grim, would be less awful than his imagination.

"You sure you want to know about it now?"

"That's why I asked. Like I said before, I don't like surprises."

"Well, I'd say the odds are pretty good. De Gaulle Airport will have time to lay a blanket of foam on the landing strip to minimize fire, and they'll be standing by with emergency equipment."

"Terrific! But what if she blows on impact?"

"She blows! That's all."

"Pow! So long, *finis*—we all go bye-bye, huh?"

"Well no. There's still a chance some of us will survive."

"Law of averages?"

"No. Just your time or it isn't."

"Ladies and gentlemen, may I have your attention, please." It was Captain Johnson. "Uh—we will be heading out over the English Channel to jettison some of our fuel. This is only a safety precaution, in case it should become necessary to make an emergency landing at De Gaulle. I'm going to ask you not to smoke from here on in, and to remain in your seats. If you will just be patient, we'll try to have you safely on the ground as soon as possible. Thank you."

"That belly landing is looking closer and closer."

"Not necessarily. I think it's just what he said—a precautionary action. Makes good sense."

"Well, jettisoning fuel shortens the time they've got to work with the gear. Sounds to me like he already knows we've run out of luck."

"You may be right." Carl's voice had turned flat.

"Gentlemen." The flight attendant stood beside Peter, offering a pillow. "Safety procedure requires that I give each of you a pillow, may I?'' She did not wait for an answer but pushed the pillow into Peter's lap and handed one across to Carl.

"What do our chances look like to you?" asked Peter.

"I don't fly the airplane, sir, but I have complete faith in Captain Johnson. I think you should, too." She smiled sweetly and moved off. Peter felt a little like a small boy who had been nicely scolded, but he made no reply. She was right, of course. He sipped his drink and watched the other attendants checking luggage racks, stowing all carry-on luggage such as attaché cases, etc. Both he and Carl surrendered their cases reluctantly, but the attendant assured them the cases would be quite safe.

"Well, I guess we wait it out now," said Peter.

"We should be out over the Channel any minute," said Carl, turning to look out the window.

"Ladies and gentlemen, Captain Johnson here." His matter-of-fact tone filled the cabin—and the pockets of fear in each passenger. "We are approaching Le Havre, and will be out over the water in a few minutes now. I'd like to remind you again that there must be no smoking or moving about the cabin until further notice. And, uh—let me again assure you this is only a precautionary action. We are still hopeful of correcting the landing-gear malfunction and making a normal landing. Please remain calm, try to relax, and I'll report to you again just as soon as our jettisoning operation is completed.''

"So now the big authority figure has told us there's nothing to worry about, and we're going to believe him, because we've got to." Peter looked around the cabin and saw that the captain's magic was still working, but he could feel tension mounting. Although everyone sat meekly in their seats, there was a ripple of uneasy restlessness. Passengers had begun to whisper to one another. It was almost as if they were afraid to hear the mortal sound of their own voices. Peter closed his eyes and leaned back in his seat; it was time to deal with his own thoughts.

Had he come all this way, worked like an idiot to succeed, finally found a woman he liked enough to marry, only to wind up a statistic in France? It wasn't fair; he hadn't done half the things he wanted to do, and he hadn't had nearly enough fun in his life. He thought of Jeannie; how would she take it if he didn't survive? He opened his eyes suddenly and gulped the rest of the Scotch. Here he was, almost assuming he wasn't going to come through whatever happened; expecting, even accepting his own demise. That was defeatism, and he'd always despised defeatists. He turned to look at Carl, but he was looking out the window again. Was he interested in the jettisoning operation, or was he thinking of his own life—the wife he loved, who'd be left behind without the children they'd always wanted? Funny guy, Carl Morris.

"Where do you live, Carl?" He was probably intruding on the man's private thoughts, but suddenly he wanted to know more about him. Jeannie was always accusing him of not being interested enough in other people. Well, now he was interested in Carl Morris.

"Live in Fairfield, Connecticut."

"Nice."

"We like it."

"Don't mind commuting?"

"Sometimes I mind a lot, but it's worth it, being in the country."

"Yeah, I guess so."

"You live in New York?"

"Yep. East Sixty-eighth Street."

"Marcy and I lived in the city when we were first married, then we got the country bug. We like to ride, play tennis, sail, garden—things like that. So we made the big move, and we've never regretted it."

"I was just thinking about my—my friend Jeannie and wondering how she'd take all this. Thinking I might not come through it. Then I got mad, because I realized I was assuming, even accepting that possibility. That's bad thinking, so I decided to bug you instead."

"Helps to talk. I was thinking of Marcy. We've been so damned close. She's really my best friend. It's impossible to think of us not being together." He broke off suddenly and sipped his Scotch.

"Damn it, Carl, we're alive, and we're going to stay that way!" Peter slammed his right fist into the palm of his left hand.

"Sure we are. Just—just take it easy."

"Wonder where that damned liquor cart is? I'm stone-cold sober and I don't want to be." He craned his neck to search

*13*

the aisle for the flight attendant. They were all busy making preparations for an emergency landing.

"Better to be sober, Peter. That way you can handle whatever happens with a cooler head."

"I suppose you're right, but I wish I had another stiff slug of Scotch anyway."

"Look. I'm pretty certain we're going to have to make an emergency landing, so let's go on that assumption and make some plans for ourselves."

"Good idea."

"The main thing is to get out as quickly as possible after she comes to a standstill." Carl took out the card with the plane's emergency exit plan. "Now, our nearest exit is forward, here." He pointed to the card. "But that's over the wing, and it might not be our best exit; that depends on how the ship goes down. She could nose down, and tip over on the right or left wing. A belly landing has the same effect as a frontal impact, and the ship could break in two about midship. If that happens, there's going to be a lot of flying metal. So we'd better keep well down until she comes to a stop." Carl paused.

"Go on," Peter urged.

"Well, the lights will probably go out. We'll be pretty much feeling our way, so it's important that we keep together if we can." Carl drew a deep breath. "We may need all our strength to clear the way. The main thing is to get out as quickly as possible."

"You're afraid of fire, aren't you?"

"I'm afraid it's inevitable. But we'll probably have a few minutes before she goes. That's why I want us to get out of here fast."

"Oh boy," Peter groaned. "Whatever made me want to publish that Frenchman's book?"

"Money, remember?"

"Only too well, and from where I sit now, it seems totally unimportant." Peter thought a moment. "You know, if I come through this alive, I just may not buy that book."

"Oh?"

"No. It's really a pretty awful book. I'm not certain it deserves to be published in the U.S."

"What about your publisher's modus operandi?"

"That's his problem." Peter glanced at Carl and laughed. "Sound brave, don't I?"

"Maybe you are."

"Sure would be a switch. I'm known as a big book, big deal editor."

" 'A foolish consistency is the hobgoblin of little minds.' "

"Ah yes. 'Adored by little statesmen and philosophers and divines.' With regards to Mr. Emerson." Both men laughed, breaking, for a moment, some of the mounting tension they felt.

# Chapter Three

"Uh—ladies and gentlemen, this is your captain again. We've, uh, finished our jettisoning operation and are heading back to Paris. We've been unable, so far, to correct our landing apparatus, but we are still working on it. In the meantime every precaution is being taken for a safe emergency landing. Full emergency crews are standing by at De Gaulle. Visibility is good, the wind velocity favorable, and all traffic has been routed out of our landing area. We should be able to set down with a minimum of damage." The captain coughed and static could be heard coming over the intercom. "Now, I want to ask you all to cooperate fully with the flight crew. They've been well trained for emergency situations and have your welfare in mind. It is important that you keep calm and follow instructions—I repeat, follow instructions. Don't rush, and above all, don't panic." He paused for a moment, then went on. "I'll be speaking to you again, keeping you informed, before we land." He switched off the intercom, and the flight attendant came on.

"May I have your attention, please." All the passengers were suddenly talking at once, and a baby somewhere in the ship began to cry. "May we have quiet, *please*," pleaded the attendant with authority in her voice. That authority apparently penetrated, and the ship grew quiet. "Thank you," she said and continued. "All women passengers wearing high-heeled shoes will please remove them. All persons wearing eyeglasses should remove them and put them in a safe place on their person. Please leave behind everything not contained on your person, and remove any constricting clothing. It is essential that you be able to move freely and unencumbered in exiting the aircraft. Now, you may be wondering why you've been given pillows. Well, we will now demonstrate how they should be used." Another attendant stood at the front of the ship and demonstrated as the speaker gave instructions. "As we go in for our landing, please place the pillow on your lap, lean forward over it, and grasp your ankles tightly with both hands. No matter what happens, hold that position until the ship comes to a standstill. At that point you should proceed to the nearest exit shown on the card I told you about earlier. In the meantime try to relax, as the captain told you, and wait for his instructions."

"Why didn't I choose some nice dull profession? Teaching in a university, something like that."

"I don't know that teaching in a university would be dull," said Carl.

"Right now it seems exciting as all hell!" Peter chuckled and was surprised to find that he could muster the laugh. "Listen, what do you do, Carl?"

"Corporate law, international."

"Interesting?"

"Most of the time."

"Well, I hope we both live to practice our professions."

"Just remember what I said earlier—if it isn't your time, you'll come through."

"But what if it is?"

"Then there's nothing you can do, is there?"

"There never is on a damned airplane. You're captive. That's what gets to me."

"You might try that existentialist religion we were talking about before." Carl smiled. "That's what I'm going to do."

Peter had gone through all the prayers he could remember from the Episcopal Book of Common Prayer he'd been required to learn as a child, and he'd begun to improvise his own, being especially careful always to preface each request with: "I give thanks for my many blessings and ask forgiveness for my many sins," and to add a humble: "If it be thy will, oh Lord," after each request. But as in the tortured

Easter vigil in James Agee's *The Morning Watch*, which he'd once read, Peter found his thoughts wandering in the midst of his prayer. When that happened, he'd have to start all over again, feeling guilty for his transgression and asking forgiveness for it. He wondered if God actually heard prayers. The idea had always perplexed him. With all the millions of souls in the world calling upon this supreme being he'd been taught to believe in, how could he hear one lone individual calling out from a crippled aircraft over Paris? Reason told him it was impossible. Prayer had to be an abstract concept, a consciousness shared in some metaphysical fashion with the supreme being and absorbed through the cosmos. But whether he understood the dynamics of prayer or not, the fact remained that in times of trouble he felt compelled to call upon that being for help, and it did ease his mind to call upon him.

"Ladies and gentlemen, this is Captain Johnson." This time there was a long pause, and voices from the tower at De Gaulle could be heard in the background. "Uh—we will be making an emergency landing at Charles De Gaulle Airport." A mass gasp chorused through the cabin as the hope the passengers had been holding onto suddenly evaporated.

"Oh, my God!" someone up forward screamed.

"As I told you earlier," continued the captain, "all safety precautions have been taken at De Gaulle, and a full emergency crew is standing by. We will, uh, begin our descent now, and it will be a long, slow, gradual descent to give us time to play out power in the engines. We will, in a sense, be gliding in on the wind, and will set down as gently as possible. There will be some, uh, frontal impact—but, uh, we should sustain that without too much difficulty." The captain paused, and Peter marveled at how casually calm the man could be in delivering what was probably a death knell. "Once again I want to ask you to remain calm, and cooperate fully with the attendants as they assist you in exiting." He paused again, and when he spoke this time, his voice was lower, as if he were controlling his emotions. "With the help of God, we'll all be safely on the ground shortly." He clicked off the sound system with out any sign-off.

The attendant came on the intercom then to give instructions. The ship began its descent. People could be heard crying, praying, and somewhere a priest was loudly intoning Hail Marys.

"Well, here we go," said Peter, feeling perspiration begin to soak his clothes. "Good luck, Carl." He offered him his hand.

"Good luck to you, Peter. And—God bless," he said. "Remember, let's keep together."

"You bet." Peter loosened his tie, buttoned his wallet into his hip pocket, put his head between his legs, and locked his hands about his ankles. He felt the ship gliding slowly earthward, heard the high-pitched whine of the powerful jet engines throttling back. How unreal it all seemed, this rushing toward possible extinction. He realized that he might well pass into that unknown world within a matter of minutes, and he felt both fearful and strangely excited about the possibility. The will to survive, however, forced itself into his consciousness. Oh no you don't! he said, as if speaking to a seductive lover—the death lover. You're not going to get me.

He felt the ship falling faster now, heard the scream of the engines, so loud he was surprised he could still think. Panic grew with that scream, and he began to pray feverishly, and then came the impact of metal striking tarmac. He felt his hands being torn away from his ankles despite his strongest efforts to hold on. Suddenly his body was lifted into the air, and he felt as if he were tumbling slow motion, head over heels, through space, weightless and free. Then he was hurled against an impenetrable barrier, and the impact seemed to separate his bones—even his teeth—loose from the flesh. A heavy, suffocating darkness flooded his brain, and numbing stillness engulfed him.

Time was a dark void stretching, stretching, stretching until consciousness slowly began seeping back into his being. There were voices around him. What had happened? He heard the high whine of the jet engines and memory began to return. He'd been on a plane, there was a crash. Was he dead? He tried to summon up some awareness of himself, pull himself up out of the nothingness. Slowly he became aware of his body, and he tried to move, to rise up, but his body did not respond to his command. Instead came a rush of pain, pain so intense it seemed to ooze out of every pore. Most of all his head hurt. In fact, it seemed as if his head would burst open.

Then, he heard his name being called, but the sound was faint, as if from some great distance.

"Monsieur Blanchard?" said the voice. "Monsieur Blanchard, can you hear me?" The voice had an accent. Blanchard? Yes, Blanchard—he was almost certain that was his name.

"Yes, yes, I hear you," he answered, and his voice sounded alien to him. "Where am I?"

"You are in the American Hospital in Paris. There was an accident."

"I—I remember." Again he heard the shrill whine of the engines, felt himself floating, floating, and then there was the awful impact and assault on his body. His automatic reflexes tried to respond to the assault but he could not move. "What's wrong with me?" he asked.

"You have the broken leg, and the back, it is injured."

"I can't move. How bad is it?"

"We removed some metal from the back, just above the left hip, and we put the leg in the cast."

"Am—am I going to be all right?"

"Oh yes. You lose much blood, suffered the concussion, and contusions—some minor injuries. But you will be okay—yes. But you rest now, *oui*?"

"Dr.—"

"Dr. Pontier, I am Dr. Pontier."

"Headache—terrible headache."

"But of course! You have the concussion." Dr. Pontier chuckled.

"Pressure, terrible pressure—behind my eyes." As Peter came fully back to consciousness and grew more aware of the pain, he felt as if he might pass out again from its severity.

"But naturally. You have been unconscious for more than twenty-four hours, monsieur." The doctor's joviality irritated Peter. The pain was growing in intensity behind his eyes, in his temples and forehead, and he had to bite his lips to keep from screaming. He tried to think of something else to take his mind off the pain. He thought back to the plane, tried to remember what had happened, the conversations with Carl. Carl! What had happened to Carl?

"Dr. Pontier?" There was no answer. "Dr. Pontier," he called louder. Still no answer, and he called again.

"Please be quiet. You will disturb other patients," said a woman's voice. He thought it probably belonged to a nurse.

"I want to see Dr. Pontier."

"You will have to wait. Dr. Pontier is with another patient."

"It is all right, Nurse. I am just finished with Monsieur Fuller. Now, what is the trouble, Monsieur Blanchard?"

"Mr. Morris, Carl Morris—is he okay?"

"Monsieur Morris? Umm, let me see." Peter heard the rustle of papers. He supposed the doctor was consulting a list.

"Oh, *oui*—Monsieur Morris."

"He was sitting beside me on the plane."

"*Oui*, Monsieur Morris. Well, he was not so lucky as you."

"Is he alive?"

"*Oui*. But it is very bad. There was the fire. He is badly burned."

"Oh Christ—just what he said." Peter tried to think of Carl's words about fire, but his head throbbed so badly he could hardly organize his thoughts. "Will he be okay?" he asked finally.

"Difficult to say—very difficult at this time."

"I'm sorry." Peter pictured calm, fatalistic Carl Morris in his mind's eye. Too bad, he was a nice guy. "Is he in much pain?"

"*Oui*. Such burns are very painful."

"Doctor, my head. Can't you give me something?"

"Not at this time. You are already sedated for the back."

"Why is it dark in here? Is it night?" Peter had finally become aware of the fact that the room was in darkness. How strange that it should be.

"Night?" Dr. Pontier chuckled again. "No, it is a bright, sunny Parisian morning."

"Then why is it dark?"

"Dark? No, it is not dark, Monsieur Blanchard. The sun—see it shines there, through the window."

"No! I do not see." Peter felt an almost instant panic. Why could he not see? "Doctor, I—I can't see anything!" He heard the panic in his own voice.

"That is very strange." Dr. Pontier moved closer to the bed and touched Peter's eyelid. The moment his hand touched the lid, unbelievable pain shot through Peter, pain so intense he could not help crying out.

22

"Don't touch me!" he shouted. "Don't touch my eye."
He tried to draw away from the doctor.

"It is so painful, the eye?"

"It is unbearable. Please don't touch my eye again."

"I do not understand."

"Oh, my God, I can't see. Don't you understand?" He felt
frightened now and tried to sit up, but he could not.

"But that is impossible." The doctor attempted to touch
the eye again, but Peter put his hand up to protect his eyes.

"Get me an eye doctor, please." Peter kept his voice calm
this time, but it took all the effort he had.

"An eye doctor?" Dr. Pontier sounded confused.

"I can't see, don't you understand?" Peter tried to think of
how to say it in French, but all knowledge of the language
was blotted out by the pain and panic.

"But it is impossible. There was no injury to cause it."

"I tell you, I can't see. I want an ophthalmologist." Peter
was shouting now. And then suddenly—suddenly he knew
why he could not see. His contact lenses—they were still in
his eyes. He was sure of it! Before the accident, in the plane,
the flight attendant had told people who wore eyeglasses to
remove them, but since he wore contact lenses, he didn't
think it necessary to remove them. "Doctor, it is my contact
lenses."

"I do not understand."

"I wear contact lenses. They were in my eyes when the
plane crashed. I've been unconscious for more than twenty-
four hours, you said so yourself."

"*Oui*, that is correct."

"Contacts are not supposed to stay in that long. Mine have
been in now for more than thirty-six hours. They must come
out at once. The swelling . . ."

"But of course they must be removed at once." He heard
the doctor move toward him again.

"No, no, don't touch me!" He covered his eyes with his
arm. "They must be washed off, otherwise I'll have permanent damage. Please, please get me an eye doctor." He fell
back exhausted from the pain, sure that he would pass out,
but he struggled to hold on, knowing that his sight depended
on his staying conscious. He knew that the contact lenses
must be sealed to his eyes. The ophthalmologist had explained
it all carefully when she had prescribed them: he was not to

leave them in more than fourteen hours. Ironic that he'd planned to replace the hard contacts with the new soft lenses, which could be worn safely for a much longer period of time, when he got back to New York. "Please, Dr. Pontier, I must have an ophthalmologist."

"An ophthalmologist. I don't know if there is one in the hospital."

How stupid could the doctor be? Didn't he know anything about contact lenses? Obviously not, otherwise he would understand the urgency of the situation.

"Dr. Pontier, for God's sake *move*! Get me an ophthalmologist." He could hear the hysteria in his voice, but he no longer cared. "My eyes are being suffocated, Doctor, don't you understand?"

"Yes, yes, I will see what I can do." He heard the doctor move away.

"Get a good one, too!" he called after him, then lay quietly for a moment, trying to quiet his fear. He pressed his hands hard against his temples to try and ease the pain, but his head only throbbed harder. He felt alone, isolated, and frightened. If only there was someone he could turn to, someone who was mobile and spoke French.

He began to pray now that serious infection had not already set in, for he knew how dangerous that could be. Why hadn't he made time to go to the ophthalmologist to get the new lenses, instead of putting it off again and again? But what was the use of thinking of that now; it was more important to pray. He tried to keep his mind on prayer, but his thoughts began to wander. Carl—where was he? Was he going to live? Badly burned, the doctor had said, and in great pain. He shuddered at the thought of severe burns, remembering how he had agonized over a simple burn when he'd been careless in the kitchen. He wanted to go to Carl, but how? He couldn't get up; his leg was apparently tied to something above the bed. He tried to feel what was holding his leg, but even the slightest movement increased the pain. He tried to lie very still and to make his mind a blank, and as he quieted down, he became aware of the sounds of suffering around him. He thought he must be on a ward.

"*Pardon*, Monsieur Blanchard. Time for the sedative." It was a woman's voice, apparently the nurse.

"Are you giving me a needle?" he asked.

"*Oui*, for the pain."

"Will it make me sleepy?"

"*Oui*, perhaps you will sleep."

"Oh no! I'm not taking that!"

"Oh, but it is Doctor's orders, monsieur." Her voice sounded quarrelsome.

"I don't give a damn whose order it is, I'm not taking it!"

"I will have to report this to Dr. Pontier."

"You do that!" He had reacted too quickly. Of course she was only doing her job, and it didn't help to alienate her. He heard her start to move off. "Wait!" he called and heard her come back. "Look, I can't see anything because no one removed my contact lenses while I was unconscious. I must stay awake now—they must be removed. I could be blinded otherwise. Do you understand?"

"Then take the—how do you say—contact lenses out. I will help you."

"No!" he snapped. "Only an ophthalmologist can do it!"

"An ophthalmologist?" she echoed. Christ, what kind of hospital was this?

"Yes, an eye doctor. *Comprenez*?"

"*Oui*. But must you shout?" She sounded hurt now. Oh, shit!

"Yes, I must shout! Because I am in a great deal of pain, and because every minute is important. And I can't seem to get that through your hard French heads."

"I am sure Dr. Pontier understands the situation very well," she said with defensive hostility.

"Then I wish he'd do something—and fast!" Why did the damned French have to act so superior? He'd never discovered anything about them that justified an attitude of superiority.

"If you will not take the sedative, I cannot be responsible."

"Of course not, I'm responsible. After all, it is *my* body, and *my* eyes! And if you think the pain in my back and leg is bad, you just ought to know how my head hurts."

"I will speak to Dr. Pontier." She sniffed self-righteously and he heard her walk away, leaving her disapproval hanging in the air. Well, to hell with her! If she imagined he gave a damn about her disapproval, she had another thought coming. He hated authority, and especially he hated the Godlike superiority of the medical profession. "Hospitals!" he said aloud.

"Hey, take it easy there, man," said a voice nearby in perfectly plain American English.

"It's not easy with these jokers."

"Yeah, I know. But they got a lot on their hands right now."

"So have I."

"You on the plane from New York?"

"Yes. Who're you anyway?"

"Mike Fuller—a friend."

"I could use one." He almost felt like crying; the pain was wearing him down into exasperation and self-pity. "Were you on the plane?" he asked.

"Right. I was on the same bird." The voice sounded young, and probably belonged to a black man.

"Where are you?"

"In the next bed."

"I can't see. These idiots didn't take my contact lenses out."

"Yeah, I heard. That's heavy, man."

"What happened to you?"

"Broken collarbone, broken arm, cuts, bruises, burns— nothin' worth writin' home about."

"What happened, exactly? I was knocked out. Don't remember anything."

"We hit the ground, man. I mean that big bird set down and went crazy! There was a big varoom—just like breaking the sound barrier—and she spun like a top. Then she tipped over on the left wing, busted it off, and broke open like a turkey egg. I mean, people was spewed in every direction. Then comes the fire—flames leapin' everywhere. I tell you, it—was—a—*mess*!"

"Very graphic." Despite the pain, Peter couldn't help listening to the description with a kind of horrified fascination. The man seemed to relish telling it, too. "Were you thrown out?" he asked.

"Damn right. Flew out of there like a supersonic turkey." He laughed a rich full laugh, and Peter found himself wanting to laugh, but he knew it would make his head throb harder.

"You were thrown free?"

"I think so, but man, when I hit that tarmac, was my tail feathers singed!" The man's vitality was reassuring to Peter.

"Did the plane explode?"

26

"Not exactly. The flames just whooshed up, but them emergency cats got it under control pretty fast—fast for Frenchies, that is. I mean we was all swimming around in foam, like one great big bubble bath."

"Did many survive?"

"Yeah, but a lot of 'em are in bad shape." He paused. "The captain and front-end crew didn't make it." He sounded sad about that.

"Too bad." Peter shared Mike Fuller's sadness. The captain had tried so hard to reassure his passengers, but not even all his skills could beat the big machine.

"The crew was great. A lot more people would have died without them. They pulled people out of there with flames leapin' everywhere. Man, I mean that took guts!"

"The doctor told me the man who sat next to me was badly burned. He may not make it."

"Rough. I got scorched some, nothing really serious, but it hurts bad enough for me to know how bad real burns has got to be."

"I wish I could get up and go to see Carl. We talked a lot on the way over. I got to like him."

"They sure got you trussed up there. I mean that leg is hiked up in the air, and they got your arm hooked up to that bottle—must be uncomfortable."

"Even if I could get up, I couldn't go anywhere. I can't see anything, not even light."

"That a fact?" Fuller was quiet for a moment. "When you get this ophthalmologist dude you been asking for and get them shades out of there—you gonna be okay?"

"Hope so. Depends on how much damage there is, and how good he is at getting them out."

"Tricky, huh?"

"Yes." It was hard to talk, the pain was so excruciating, but he needed the human contact.

"Say, what's your name?"

"Blanchard, Peter Blanchard."

"From the Big Apple?"

"I live there, yes."

"Born there?"

"No. Born in Massachusetts."

"Born in Harlem myself. Lived there all my life, exceptin' when we're on the road. Play drums in a rock group."

"Come over here to play?"

"Meant to. Two-week gig booked here, then one in Rome, and Berlin—even London town."

"First trip?"

"You guessed it. Nearly the last, too." He was quiet a moment. "Come to think of it, it may be the last. We lost our guitar player, and the rest are pretty cut up. 'Course we got no instruments; they all went up in flames. Some group—no instruments and a banged-up bunch of musicians!"

"Sorry," said Peter.

"Me, too." Mike laughed. Peter groaned out loud, unable to hold it back. The pain was getting worse, and he had already thought it was as bad as he could stand. Where was that fucking doctor, anyway? Had he really understood the urgency? And if he hadn't, what was going to happen to his eyes?

"Say, this cat that was sittin' next to you on the big bird, what's his name?"

"Carl Morris."

"Know where he is?"

"No. But listen, maybe I can go find out something. I can get around pretty well."

"Think you could?"

"Why not. I mean, you'd like to get word to him that you're alive and kickin', wouldn't you?"

"Yes, I would."

"You're on, brother. I'm going to see if I can find him—this sittin' around is killing me." Peter heard Mike getting up and he could tell that moving wasn't all that easy for him.

"You sure it's all right for you to get up?"

"I've been up before, checking out this sick pad. Bores my ass off sittin' here." He laughed. "What do you want me to tell this Morris guy when I find him?"

"Tell him I'd like to come and see him but I can't. Tell him—tell him I've got the existentialist religion going for him."

"Existentialist religion? Man, that's a mouthful!"

"He'll know what I mean."

"Glad he does, 'cause I don't. But listen, you keep buggin' these medical types 'till you get that ophthalmologist."

"Don't worry."

"If you ain't got some action by the time I get back, I'll stir up things some for you."

"Thanks."

"Just take it easy, and I'll see you around."

When Mike had shuffled off, Peter fumbled for the bellcord. There had to be an ophthalmologist somewhere—all hospitals had them. He found the cord and pressed the button, then kept on pressing it. He didn't have long to wait, however, for a nurse appeared at his bedside almost immediately.

"Can I help you, monsieur?" She had a pleasant voice and sounded as though she might really want to help.

"Thanks for coming."

"But you rang, monsieur." She laughed softly.

"Is Dr. Pontier around?"

"He is not on the floor at the moment."

"I've got to have an ophthalmologist at once. I can't see."

"*Oui*, I know. Dr. Pontier has called the ophthalmologist."

"Will he come?"

"Of course."

"Is he a good doctor?"

"*Oui*. I believe so." She did not sound outraged at his question.

"Every minute counts now."

"I know. I also wear the contact lenses."

"Oh, then you *do* know." He sighed with relief. "It seems so hard to make the others understand."

"It is always difficult with the languages, you know."

"*Bon jour*, Charlotte," said a pleasant voice.

"Ah. Dr. Morel, *bon jour*. The ophthalmologist is here, Monsieur Blanchard."

"This is Monsieur Blanchard?"

"*Oui*," she replied.

"Monsieur Blanchard, I am Dr. Morel."

"An ophthalmologist?"

"*Oui*. I am an ophthalmologist."

"Am I glad to see you! I mean, I can't see you but—"

"You are in much pain, no?"

"Yes. Incredible pain. My head—my eyes—they throb with it."

"You were in the plane crash, no?"

"Yes. And apparently I've been out for over twenty-four

29

hours, and I had my lenses in all day before I left New York.''

"So, it is about thirty-six hours, is it not?"

"Yes. Apparently no one thought to remove the lenses."

"*Oui*. So many injured, so few doctors. A quick look at the eyes because you were unconcious—they would not see the lenses." Peter felt the doctor lean over him and instinctively pulled back. "Not to worry, Monsieur Blanchard, I will not touch the eyes. I can see there is much edema. So we go to surgery at once. Charlotte!" He called to the nurse.

"*Oui*, Dr. Morel?"

"Please find Dr. Pontier. I must know the extent of Monsieur Blanchard's injuries, for he must go to surgery at once!"

"Of course, Dr. Morel."

"Thank you, Doctor," sighed Peter.

"Not at all. I go to make preparations now." Peter heard the doctor's footsteps die away. He felt relieved despite the pain. Something in the doctor's manner reassured him, or perhaps it was just that at last something was going to be done. He prayed that Dr. Morel was a good doctor; if he wasn't, Peter was in trouble.

# Chapter Four

"Mr. Morris?" Mike Fuller spoke softly to the man whose body was swathed in bandages. He'd been told he could speak to him for only a moment—if Morris felt like talking. He was not heavily sedated because of the doctors' fear of complications. Should they develop, Morris would need to be conscious.

"Yes?" The voice that answered Mike's inquiry was barely above a whisper, but the eyes opened and looked at him out of a great depth of pain. His face had miraculously not been burned.

"I come from Peter Blanchard. He can't come, but he wants to know how you are."

"Okay." A faint smile showed on Morris's face. "How's Peter?"

"Well, he's got a broken leg, and they took some hardware out of his back, but I don't think it's too serious. They got his leg all trussed up in the air, and he can't get up and move around."

"I'm glad he's okay."

"Yeah, if they get them shades out of his eyes, I reckon he's gonna be all right."

"Shades—eyes? What do you mean?" Perspiration stood out on Morris's face, and Mike winced; he had some idea of the pain the man was suffering despite his efforts to hide it.

"Well, seems they left these contact lenses in his eyes too long; they didn't discover them. So right now Peter can't see, but he's raising hell to get an ophthalmologist. I reckon the blindness is only temporary, though. Anyway, Peter gave me a message for you. He says he'd like to come see you, but he can't get up—and he wanted me to tell you he's got the existentialist religion going for you. He said you'd know what that meant."

"I know." Morris tried to smile and nodded his head slightly. "Tell him I can use it." He closed his eyes then and Mike thought he better go.

"Anything I can do for you, Mr. Morris?"

"Tell Peter—tell him I'm pulling for him, too." His breathing became labored, and Mike started to back away. "Thanks, come back—tell me how Peter gets on, please?"

"You bet, be back as soon as that ophthalmologist cat shows up."

"Thanks." Morris opened his eyes again. "You okay?"

"Oh, sure. Just got a clipped wing and collarbone. Nothin' serious. Be okay in no time." Mike smiled and wanted to say something reassuring to Morris, but he couldn't think of anything that wouldn't sound trivial under the circumstances.

"Tell Peter my wife is coming. She'll come see him, too."

"Okay. You take it easy now. I'll be back." Mike backed out of the room and ran into the nurse on her way in. "Hey listen, baby, is he gonna make it?" Mike gestured back over his shoulder to Carl's room.

"Who knows?" She shrugged and smiled sadly.

"What's his odds?"

"Not good." She shook her head and moved on past him.

"Shit!" said Mike to the corridor. "That's a fuckin' damned bummer!" He made his way back toward his own ward, comforting himself with a string of street obscenities learned as a boy in Harlem.

Peter was back in his bed when Mike got there, and his eyes were bandaged. He was feeling lonely and sorry for himself. Mike eased down on the bed and sat for a moment, wondering if Peter was asleep.

"Mike?"

"Yeah?"

"How's Carl?"

"You want it straight?"

"Bad, huh?"

"The worst. Not much chance. I asked the nurse."

"Shit!" Peter hit the bed with his fist and was instantly sorry. Now that his eyes had stopped hurting so badly, he could feel his other injuries.

"My sentiments, too. I talked to him some—seems like one hell of a nice guy. I can tell." Mike paused. "He's laying there all wrapped up in bandages, out of his gourd with pain, and he's asking me about you."

"Sounds like him." Peter was remembering how reassuring Carl had been on the plane.

"He said to tell you he was pulling for you, and that his old lady was comin' over. She's gonna come see you, too."

"Hope I can see her."

"Yeah. What's the word. Did they get them shades out?"

"Yeah—wasn't easy though. They nearly drowned me trying to wash them off my eyes. They were glued on tight."

"Well, what did they tell you?"

"Nothing. They don't know yet. All I know is, the lenses are out, and the pain is almost bearable now. Nurse just gave me a shot, so I guess I'll be more human in awhile."

"Man, I tell you, if I ever need shades, I'm sticking to the outside kind."

"If I come out of this okay, I'm going to give some serious thought to that, too." They were both quiet for a while. Peter was thinking about Carl's wife. "You know, it's going to be hard on Carl's wife, seeing him like that."

"Yeah. 'Specially when he ain't gonna make it."

"I gather from him they've got a good marriage," Peter said.

"You married, Pete?"

"Holy Jesus!"

"What's wrong now?" Mike reacted with alarm.

"Jeannie! It's the first time I've thought of her since regaining consciousness!"

"She your wife?"

"No. But I've been thinking of asking her to be."

"That so?"

"She must be out of her mind with worry. She doesn't even know if I'm alive."

"Man, you are out of it! That chick must be—like bonkers by this time."

"I've got to get a nurse in here." He reached for the bellcord. "Hope I don't get that sour number. She's a charmer!"

"Know the one you mean," Mike laughed. "I'm sorta paranoid, see, and I was thinking she just didn't like blacks—but man, she don't play no favorites. It's just sick people she don't like. Don't matter what color they are."

"Probably," Peter answered absently, for he was thinking of Jeannie. "Somehow I've got to get a cable off to her."

"If you're gonna depend on Miss Charm School, forget it. You write it out and I'll see that it gets sent."

"Oh shit, Mike. How am I going to write it when I can't see?"

"Yeah—plum forgot that small fact."

"Fact is, now that I think of it, I don't know if I have any money—clothes, passport, anything! I'm sort of a displaced person right now."

"Tell you what, I'm gonna scrounge around for some paper and a pencil. You just sit tight till I get back and you can dictate your cable to me. How's that?"

"It's great, but should you be moving around so much?"

"Nothing wrong with my legs, man."

"Okay—if you're sure." Peter heard Mike ease off the bed and move down the hall, and as soon as he'd gone, a cloud of gloom and depression descended on him. He felt completely helpless: he couldn't see, walk, write, do anything for himself. Okay, Blanchard, he said to himself, don't start feeling sorry for yourself. You're alive, the pain isn't so bad, and you've got a friend in the next bed. That's a lot more than Carl Morris has at this moment. Just get on with your life. He began to try and compose a cable to Jeannie. He'd say that he was alive and okay—but should he tell her about his eyes? No, that would only worry her, and they'd probably be all right in a day or two. He could telephone her then. The only thing that was important right now was that she know he was alive. Suddenly reality hit him. No one knew he was alive: not his family, not the office, nobody. God, he had to get with it, but he didn't really feel up to dealing with all that. Maybe a cable to his secretary would take care of it; she could notify everybody. Everybody but Jeannie—he'd get the cable off to her first.

"Monsieur Blanchard. It's Dr. Morel."

"Oh, yes, Doctor?"

"You are feeling better, *oui?*"

"Yes, much better."

"*Bon.* Now, about the condition of the eyes. As you know from the discomfort you suffered, the edema was severe."

"I certainly do."

"This made it very difficult to remove the lenses."

"Yes, I know that, Doctor. Please—are my eyes going to be all right?"

"Well, there is considerable corneal abrasion as a result of the protracted length of time the lenses were in your eyes, and the stubborn adherence of them."

"Doctor, what are you trying to tell me?" The man was making Peter very nervous.

"There is damage to the stroma of the Bowman's membrane." He paused, and the hesitation made Peter anxious.

"What exactly does that mean?"

"The Bowman's membrane is the third, or last layer of the corneal membrane."

"What does that mean to my eyesight?" The doctor seemed to be justifying something, and Peter was becoming extremely anxious. He clenched his fists, waiting for the doctor's answer.

"It means that your eyes have suffered severe trauma. There is some infection, but we have given you antibiotics against it, and cortisone, and we will keep your eyes bandaged for at least twenty-four hours. Then we will have a look." He still had not actually told Peter anything, and Peter had to know something more than that to live through the next twenty-four hours with any kind of peace.

"Doctor, will there be permanent damage to my sight?"

"There is damage. I cannot yet say how much. If there are no further complications, perhaps the damage will not be serious."

"What complications?"

"Infection—we must guard against infection."

"Dr. Morel, I'm an editor in a publishing house. I use my eyes constantly reading manuscripts, and if I can't see to read, I'm dead as an editor." His anxiety was snowballing into panic.

"I did not say you would be unable to read, Monsieur Blanchard."

"What did you say, Doctor?"

"I said there is damage. But, I am hopeful the eyes will heal, and there will be a minimum of scar tissue left."

"But you're not sure, are you?"

"Monsieur Blanchard, I do not play guessing games. If I attempted to give you a definitive answer at this time, I would be guessing. My advice is—be patient, relax, and rest. Build up your strength. You've been through a most unfortunate experience. Such trauma brings the shock to the nervous system, and sometimes makes one overanxious."

"It's not easy to relax under such circumstances, Doctor."

"Naturally." The doctor chuckled, and Peter felt like punching him in the nose, if he could have seen where his nose was. "But you will try, *oui?*"

"Yes." Peter answered meekly and wondered why doctors were able to intimidate so easily even when one was determined not to be intimidated.

"*Bon.* Now I must be off. I will look in on you in the morning."

"It'll be a long night, Doctor."

"I will give you something to make you sleep."

"Thanks." Peter listened to the doctor's footsteps receding down the corridor, and then he lay in the frightened darkness of his injured eyes. Had the doctor known more than he was telling? Intuitively he felt the doctor was holding back something.

"Hey, man, I got paper and I got a pencil—and I got the word on what goes on around this sick pad." Mike sounded in a buoyant mood, and Peter felt better having him back.

"So, what does go on around here?"

"The place is lousy with fly brass. They can't do ee-nough for us poor injured bastards!"

"Like what?"

"Like you want champagne, fancy French cuisine, caviar, dancing girls, the latest flicks—you name it, you got it!"

"Terrific. What did you order?"

"Some of everything!" Mike laughed a deep, rich laugh, and Peter found himself smiling. "Shit!"

"What's wrong?" asked Peter.

"I plum forgot them four cracked ribs."

"Serves you right for telling outrageous lies to a sick man."

"No lies, man!" He laughed again. "Welll—maybe just a little exaggeration. But it's true the fly brass are all over this sick pad, and they're breaking their asses to make us comfortable. They asked me how I was, anything I needed, all that shit—"

"And what did you tell them?"

"I told them I was very uncomfortable, the food was lousy, some of the nurses were unfriendly, I wanted to go home, and I wanted one fine set of drums replaced immediately!"

"And they said?"

"Said yes sir, Mr. Fuller, sorry for the inconvenience, anything you say, Mr. Fuller. Then I told them my friend wanted to send a cable home, and needed some other information."

"And?"

"Anything—just name it. So, what do you want to say to your chick?"

"Oh—well, address it to Ms. Jeanne Wharton, 930 Park Avenue, New York."

"Ver-ry fancy address. She got lots of bread?"

"Adequate, adequate, Mr. Fuller."

"Splendid, Mr. Blanchard. I approve. Now, what kind of message you gonna send to the rich chick?"

"Oh—just say, 'Survived crash. Be in American Hospital for a few days. Be in touch soon.' "

"Very cool, man. Ain't you gonna say nothin' heartwarming?"

"Oh, yeah. Say, 'Miss you. Love, Peter.' "

"Ro-mantic! Man, you are one romantic dude. How'd you get this rich chick to hang out with you anyway?"

"Lay off. It's only a cable, not a love letter!"

"Okay. It's your life. That all?"

"Yeah. And thanks a lot. Now how do we send it?"

"We wait for the fly brass to do their magic."

"Say, Mike, as long as we've got their help—could I impose on you to write just one more cable?"

"Sure, shoot."

Peter dictated a cable to his secretary detailing instructions of everything he wanted done and promising to telephone as soon as he was able. Later a representative of the airlines came to see them, and promised Peter to send his cables as

"Could you obtain them for me, Doctor?"

"I am afraid not. Many people wait for eyes now. Perhaps in New York, when you return?" Peter's hopes died in infancy.

"It's the same in New York. I was hoping that here—" He broke off, unable to go on.

"I am truly sorry." He sounded sincere, but it was small comfort to Peter. "We will continue to give you the antibiotic until the infection is completely cleared up. We must keep the eyes healthy, and one day you will have the transplants, *oui*?"

"I hope so."

"I will visit you again this afternoon." He started to walk away, then came back. "Do not give up hope, Monsieur Blanchard. Never give up hope."

"Sure, sure." Peter wanted him to go away now; he wanted, in fact, to strike out at someone, and he didn't want it to be Dr. Morel. He was suddenly very, very angry, and very bitter. He wanted to blame Dr. Morel for doing a bad job of removing the lenses, blame the airlines for their faulty plane, blame the stupid French doctors who hadn't discovered the lenses in his eyes when he'd been brought in. He wanted to blame anyone, everyone, for the terrible thing that had happened. They'd cost him his sight, his career, and probably Jeannie. His thoughts raged on as he tried to spend his impotent anger. In fact, he wore himself out with his mental rage, and finally sank into an abyss of self-pity and depression. His life was ended; there was no way to go on blind. God! How he hated the very word! Saying the word caused his imagination to take off, and he saw himself walking in New York, tapping along the street as he'd seen others do; saw someone taking his arm to help him cross the street as he'd done many times when he saw a blind person waiting at the curb. "No, no!" he screamed. "I won't be blind! I can't!" He tried to sit up, but couldn't, and panicked with claustrophobia.

"Pete." Mike was beside him, holding him by the shoulders.

"Let me go!" he shouted.

"Pete, quiet down, you'll hurt yourself."

"Hurt myself!" He began to laugh hysterically. Mike had heard the conversation with Dr. Morel, and he knew how

Peter felt, but he also knew he had to get him quieted before the panic really got out of hand.

"Listen, Pete, if you don't quiet down, I'm gonna sock you!"

"Go ahead! That'll really help! Maybe you can knock some sight back into my eyes. Go ahead—hit me!"

"Pete, come on, we can do something. Let's think, man. In New York they can help you. Don't listen to these French quacks. What do they know? In the good old U.S. of A. we can do anything. And you can pull strings at that eye bank. Man, there's always a way! You just got to know somebody." Mike kept talking fast. "Then you can sue the hell out of the fucking airlines—sue for millions! And sue this fucking sick pad, and fucking Dr. Pontier, and Dr. Morel, sue every dude that had anything to do with it."

"Don't worry. I'm *gonna* sue everybody!" Peter shouted.

"That's it, just keep remembering it, too. You're gonna get them eyes, and you're gonna see again, and you're gonna get rich off the airlines, and—"

"I wonder if you can tell me where I can find Mr. Peter Blanchard?" It was a woman's voice.

"Who the hell wants Blanchard?" Peter shouted.

"Hey, Pete, wait a minute, this is an *American* woman." Mike was certain it was Carl's wife. He'd learned from Carl that she was due to arrive that day.

"I don't care who it is. I don't want anybody around here!"

"He don't mean it, lady. He's just had some bad news."

"Oh, I'm sorry. Perhaps I'd better come back."

"No, don't go. I bet you're Carl Morris's wife?"

"Yes, I am. How'd you know?" She smiled warmly.

"Carl—he talked about you. I'm Mike Fuller, and this raving maniac is Peter Blanchard. But don't get scared—he's usually gentle as a pussycat." Mike spoke lightly, hoping he was doing the right thing.

"Oh yes, Carl told me about you, Mr. Fuller. You've been so much help to him."

"Is that Carl's wife?" Peter asked more calmly. Mike's words were finally sinking in.

"Yeah, Pete, this is Mrs. Morris. She come to see you."

"I'm, I'm terribly sorry," said Peter. "I was a little excited. Please forgive my rudeness." He held his hand out in the direction of her voice. She placed her hand in his, and the touch was nice; he pressed it gently and held onto it. "How is Carl?"

"He's—well, he's doing as well as can be expected." Despite his own turmoil, Peter could hear the tears behind the brave voice. He felt drawn to her; she was about to lose the most important thing in her life, and he'd just lost the most important thing in his.

"How are *you*?" she asked.

"I'm—I'm okay." He couldn't tell her the truth, and it was his turn to choke back the tears. The warm contact of her hand in his, the realization of a shared tragedy, threatened to destroy what little hold he had on himself.

"How are your eyes? Carl told me about the lenses."

"Well—" He swallowed hard, but his throat ached, and he couldn't speak.

"That's the bad news he just got," said Mike quietly. "Pete's blind right now." He knew Peter couldn't tell her, but somebody had to.

"Oh. But it's not permanent, is it?"

"Fact is—" Peter found his voice. "Yes, it is."

"I'm so sorry." She squeezed his hand with feeling. "Are they positive?"

"Yes."

"There's nothing that can be done? Perhaps in New York?"

"No." He shook his head and held on tight to her hand. "Nothing—excepting cornea transplants, if I could get them."

"Then it isn't permanent—there's hope."

"Well—yes, in a way. But there's a long waiting list for eyes. And there's no chance here."

"But sooner or later, you know you can regain your sight with an operation." She paused and held his hand tightly. "I know how you must feel now, kind of lost and helpless, but you must not despair—there is hope."

"Well, maybe." He swallowed hard. "But"—his voice nearly broke—"right now it's hard. Not knowing how to get along, not knowing so many things."

"I know. It's all so new and frightening right now. It's natural that you should feel overwhelmed. But you'll find a way. The resourcefulness of the human imagination and ingenuity is amazing." Her voice calmed him, and her caring warmed him. He wondered suddenly what she looked like. Carl hadn't described her. Carl—he wanted to know more

47

about him. He was running on about himself while she must be feeling as lost and frightened as he was.

"Carl—how's he doing?"

"He's—well, he's in a great deal of pain—and he's—he's fighting so hard." Her voice broke, and it was his turn to squeeze her hand, trying to convey the feeling of sympathy he would not be able to put into words.

"I'm sorry." It sounded so empty, those words. He really wanted to say something about the living, whole Carl he knew briefly and liked so much. "You know, Mrs. Morris, I'm afraid of flying, and Carl was wonderful to me on the way over. He really helped me a lot."

"He saved several lives in the crash. Did you know that?"

"No. I was unconscious until yesterday. I was thrown clear of the plane."

"Carl got out, but he kept going back. That's how he got burned." He felt her hand tremble. "He shouldn't have gone back that—that last time." She couldn't go on.

"From what I learned of him in a short time, I know he couldn't have stood by and let others die if anything could be done."

"Yes. He's like that." He heard her sniff back the tears.

"Have faith, he'll come through." He lied to reassure her, and he knew that she was aware of that, but still—there were such things as miracles. Maybe there would be a miracle for Carl Morris.

"I pray that he will. But I'm a realist. I know how bad Carl is. And—and I'm afraid." Her voice was tight, and he knew it took all her strength not to break down and cry; he knew because he wanted to cry for his own loss.

"Sure you're afraid," he said.

"And Carl's afraid." She paused, then went on. "He's being brave for me, but I know him, and I know he's afraid."

"I'm afraid, too." He couldn't help thinking of himself again. "I don't know how to be blind, and I don't know how to go on with my life. I'm an editor in a publishing house. I have to read manuscripts, and galleys—and—" He stopped suddenly, he could not go on about himself to this woman who was losing her husband. Yet he felt so anxious and cut off from everything and everybody that suddenly he thought he might suffocate from it. He wanted to get out of the bed and run, run, run away from the things he couldn't face. But he couldn't even get out of bed. She sensed his feelings.

"You're uncomfortable. Should I call the nurse?"

"No. There's nothing she can do—nothing anyone can do now. They can't turn my mind off, and that's what I need to do for a while."

"Yes. I want to do that, too, but I can't. We've got to try, though." She held his hand in both of hers then. "I must go back to Carl now. I don't like to stay away long. Try to turn your mind off—just for now. There *is* the chance that you'll see again. Just remember that when you feel afraid."

"I'll try. Thank you for coming, Mrs. Morris."

"Marcy, please."

"Okay, Marcy. And—" He paused, then determined to say what was on his mind: "If you need somebody to talk to—or maybe cry with—I'm here. I'm not going anywhere."

"Thanks, Peter. I think I'm going to need you both during the next few days."

"We're right here, Mrs. Morris," said Mike, who had moved over to his bed during their conversation.

"Anytime you need us," Peter agreed. He didn't say how much he needed her right now, but he thought it, and he knew she would somehow make it easier for him.

"Good-bye," she whispered and shook hands with both men. Peter heard her footsteps die away, and his hand lay on the sheet where she had gently put it down with an affectionate pat. Her warmth had been so reassuring, and now he felt a rending sense of separation. Tears filled his eyes, and this time he did not try to stop them. They spilled out and ran down his cheeks. He cried silently for Carl, and for Marcy, but mostly he cried for himself.

# Chapter Six

Jeannie Wharton had hardly left her apartment since the crash, not even to report to the magazine. For the most part her time had been spent on the telephone trying to find out from the airlines if Peter was among the survivors, but she'd been unable to get any definite information about him. French authorities were being somewhat vague; they were still going through the wreckage, they said. At any rate, little information was coming out of Paris, and Jeannie was nearly out of her mind with worry.

In her frustration and fear she had raged at the airlines, raged at Peter's secretary, who didn't know any more than she did, and finally had appealed to the French ambassador to the United Nations to find out if Peter were alive. No one, however, had been able to come up with a direct answer, and she had just about decided to fly to Paris when Peter's cable arrived.

"Oh, thank God," she said aloud as the words on the paper became blurred through her tears. She read and reread it, even reading it aloud: "Survived crash. Be in American Hospital for a few days. In touch soon. Miss you. Love, Peter." In the hospital. That meant he was injured—but how badly? Maddening of him not to give a clue about himself. Still, now she knew he was alive, and where he was; that was a big improvement over the situation an hour ago. At least now she knew what to do, and went to the telephone to try and get through to Peter at the American Hospital. The international operator, however, informed her that all circuits between New York and Paris were busy and there would be a wait. Well, she'd gotten used to waiting, so she gave the information to the operator, who promised to call her the moment there was an open line. Jeannie hung up the phone and returned to the state of frustration she'd been experiencing all along. She lighted a cigarette and then stubbed it out almost instantly; she'd smoked constantly since the news of the crash had flashed over the picture while she was watching Barbra Streisand and Robert Redford in *The Way We Were* on television. She'd hardly slept, had smoked, paced the floor, cried, raged, and finally arrived at a total state of exhaustion. She tried to calm herself now, even imagined she'd try to sleep until the call came through, and finally stretched out on the sofa. She was almost certain she would be unable to sleep, but total exhaustion, combined with relief at knowing he was alive, prevailed, and she fell asleep almost instantly.

Mike was passing the nurses station on his way back to the ward from seeing Carl, when he heard Nurse Charm School talking on the telephone.

"I am sorry. There is not the telephone in Monsieur Blanchard's room. *Non*, it is impossible. He cannot come to the telephone." Mike stopped and went back to the station. He tried to catch Nurse Charm School's eye, but she ignored him, and, in fact, turned her back on him. "I am sorry that the call is from United States. It is not possible to speak to Monsieur Blanchard."

"Hey, cool it, baby," Mike said, but the nurse ignored him again.

"*Non*, I cannot give out information. Only Monsieur Blanchard's doctor is able to do that."

"Listen, sugar," said Mike, cutting her off. "You ask the party if they'll speak to me, huh?" The big man leaned over the counter and smiled at the nurse, but his intent was clear.

"The call is not for you, Monsieur Fuller," she replied frostily.

"Yeah, I know that, and it's a damned good thing it ain't, too. But I can take any message to Pete." Mike extended his hand for the receiver.

"This does not concern you!" she said with authority.

"Tough! I'm making it my business. I'm Pete's friend, and if that party is calling all the way from the U.S. of A., you can't just leave them high and dry like that. Besides, it costs a bundle of bread to call over here. Now, give me that phone!" Mike put his hand on the receiver.

"If you do not let go, I will report your conduct to Dr. Pontier," the woman threatened, trying to hold onto the receiver and her dignity at the same time.

"You do that!" Mike laughed and wrenched the instrument out of her hand. "Hello, this is Mike Fuller, Pete Blanchard's friend. Can I help somebody?"

"One moment, I will consult with New York," the international operator replied. Mike listened to the rumble and echo of the oceanic cables. "Yes, the party will speak with you, sir." Then a woman's voice came over the wire.

"Hello, this is Jeannie Wharton. Who am I speaking to?"

"Name's Mike Fuller. I'm in the bed next to Pete on the ward. I happened to overhear the conversation with the operator here in the hall, and decided to horn in when I saw you were getting nowhere."

"I'm so glad you did. How is Peter?"

"He's okay. I mean, he was a little spaced out for a while—unconscious and all. That's why you didn't hear from him."

"But are his injuries serious?" She sounded anxious.

"Don't think so. He's got a bad broke leg, and these cutting cats took some metal out of his back but he's gonna be okay."

"You said his leg was bad—"

"Oh yeah. Well, it's pretty bad, but they got it all trussed up on one of them pulleys, so he can't move around, you know. That's why he can't come to the phone. But the leg—it's gonna get well. I mean, everything is cool here. Don't you worry."

"How are his spirits?"

"Good. I mean, good as can be expected. Yeah, that's about it. I mean, it ain't no picnic crashing, and it ain't no picnic being in this hospital neither. If you know what I mean—" Mike let his sentence trail off as he smiled at Nurse Charm School.

"Yes, I suppose so." There was a pause on the other end

of the line and Mike heard the echo of the cables again. "Do you think Peter would like me to fly over, Mr. Fuller?"

"Oh, well, I don't know about that, sugar."

"Peter and I are very close, Mr. Fuller."

"Oh yeah, I know who you are, all right. And I know Pete misses the hell out of you and all. But if he's like me when I'm sick, man, I just want to be left alone to lick my wounds—so to speak—'til I get well. Tell you what, though, I'll talk to him. And—if I was you, I don't think I'd come unless he asks you to. He's uh—he's been through a hairy time."

"Yes, I understand. Would you ask him?"

"Right on. You call back later and ask for me."

"I do wish I could talk to him."

"Tell you what, let me see what I can do. Maybe if we set a time for you to call, I can con these cats into wheeling Pete out here so he can rap with you."

"Oh, that would be wonderful! Really, it would mean so much to me."

"You're on. But I don't promise nothin', you understand?"

"I understand."

"Okay! Now let's get our clocks synced up. Say you call back at twelve noon, French time, tomorrow?"

"Twelve noon, French time—perfect!"

"If you can't get Pete, at least you'll get me with a message."

"Thank you so much, Mr. Fuller. I do appreciate it." There was a pause. "Would you tell Peter I miss him—and—I love him?"

"My pleasure, sugar. Just you sit tight now." Mike handed the phone back to the nurse who had glared angry disapproval at him all through the conversation. He winked at her now and showed all his teeth in a big, exaggerated smile.

"Monsieur Fuller, you are not in charge of the hospital. I will speak to the authorities about this." Mike went on smiling and leaning forward, patting her cheek gently.

"Know something, sugar, you're one chick that's all heart!" He took off down the hall before she could recover and unload her outrage at him.

In their ward Peter lay rigid, seeming to stare straight ahead from behind his bandages, and Mike couldn't tell if he were asleep or not. He approached his own bed quietly and eased down onto it; he was suddenly feeling very tired.

"That you, Mike?"

"Yeah, Pete. Thought you was asleep, man."

"No such luck. I just lie here and stew in my own juices, trying to think what I'm going to do with the rest of my life."

"I don't know about the *rest* of your life, man, but I got an idea what you gonna do at noon tomorrow."

"What's happening at noon tomorrow? Somebody going to bring me some more good news?"

"Maybe." Mike moved over to sit on the edge of Peter's bed. "Bet you can't guess who I just spoke to via the trans-Atlantic Graham Bell?"

"I don't feel like guessing games," Peter replied irritably.

"Well, since you're so nice, brother, I'm gonna tell you anyway. I spoke with none other than your Park Avenue rich chick, herself!"

"Jeannie?"

"You got it!"

"Mike—did you call her?" demanded Peter, feeling instantly resentful. He'd been getting steadily more annoyed with Mike's attempt to spoon-feed him a positive attitude since Dr. Morel had told him he was blind.

"No way, man! Your chick called to rap with you and got Nurse Charm School on the honker. I just happened along in time to rescue her call."

"You mean that bitch was going to hang up on Jeannie?" Peter was instantly angry; he'd been flying into rages a lot.

"Hey, cool it, man! That ain't exactly the way it was. You see, your chick wanted to talk to you, but Old Charm School told her that was impossible. Then she wanted news of you, and Miss Charm wasn't giving out no news."

"And I suppose you got on the phone and spilled everything!" Peter's voice had an unpleasant tone.

"Listen, Pete, I'm in no mood to fight, so cool it, see." Mike understood Peter's bitterness and frustration, but he had no intention of becoming his whipping boy.

"Exactly what *did* you tell her?"

"I didn't tell her you was blind, if that's what's buggin' you. That's your business, man, but I did tell her you had a broke leg and a sore back, and that you was going to be okay."

"Sorry, Mike." Peter felt contrite. He realized he was

becoming short-tempered much too often, lashing out at others, slipping into fits of feeling sorry for himself; but it was maddening to lie in continual darkness, feeling lonely, frightened, claustrophobic, and lost.

"Your chick wants to talk to you, Pete. She wants to know if she can come over."

"No way!" Peter shouted, trying to sit up. "All I need is her hanging around here—"

"Hey, easy man." Mike's voice was soothing. "She's not coming over if you don't want her."

"Who said I didn't want her?"

"You did. Just now, man!"

"It's not that I don't want her—it's—"

"That you don't want her *feeling sorry* for you, right?" Mike was quoting what Peter had said on several occasions.

"That's right."

"Well, man, you're going to have to face up to the fact one of these days. You can't keep something like this from her. Man, if she digs you—I mean, give her a chance."

"Not yet! I can't handle her knowing yet." Peter was becoming highly agitated, and Mike backed off.

"Okay. Tell her whatever you want to, but I told her to call back at noon tomorrow. I was going to see if I could get one of these cats to roll your bed out to the desk where you could talk."

"No! I can't talk to her either."

"Shit, Pete!" Mike shot back, then softened his voice. "You're getting to be one big pain in the ass, man."

"Yeah? Well, I'll trade with you. You try being blind and see how you like it."

"You try being black and see how you like it, brother."

"Ah, come on, Mike—"

"I'll tell you something, Pete. I wouldn't like being blind for one motherfuckin' minute! It's a bummer. You got a lousy break, and I know how you feel, but it ain't the end of the world."

"Isn't it?" Peter said angrily.

"No, it ain't! I mean, you ain't the only turkey the lights ever went out on! I happen to know a couple of black cats blind as a bat, and they're hackin' it just the same."

"Hooray for them!"

"Yeah, right on! Takes guts! Earl Garner—blind as a bat.

Plays piano and sings better than most seeing cats. Stevie Wonder—man, he was right on top of it, then this accident comes down, and the lights go out on Stevie! But did he crawl off and hide behind his shades? No way! He picked himself up and gets back out there on the fuckin' stage, and he's better than ever. That's what you got to do, Pete!''

Mike was forceful and Peter knew he was right. He was acting weak, and feeling sorry for himself, but he just couldn't get a handle on himself. He tried, and he wanted to, but he couldn't sustain an optimistic attitude for long.

"Mike, don't lean on me right now," he said. "I know you're right, but I just can't face Jeannie yet."

"You don't even want to talk to her?"

"No, you talk to her. Tell her I'm okay but—oh, tell her something that will satisfy her, and keep her from coming over here. I've got to have some more time."

"Okay, I'll fix it. But you got to get it together, Pete. I mean, I'm gonna get out of this sick pad before you do, and I don't want to leave you in the shape you're in now."

"You're leaving?" The instant anxiety produced by the thought of Mike leaving registered in his voice, and Mike didn't miss it.

"Not for a while, but you got to get ready to go it alone. I mean, the way you are now is a heavy trip, man."

"Mike?" It was Marcy Morris's voice, and it was a good sound for Peter. He'd come to anticipate her short visits.

"Hi, Marcy!" Mike glanced up, and the look on her face told him something was happening with Carl. Jesus, don't let Carl's time run out yet, he said to himself. "What's happening, sugar?" he asked, masking the dread.

"Carl wants to see you—alone." She smiled a sad but determinedly brave smile. "I'll stay here and talk to Peter."

"Yeah, okay. I'll get right over there." Mike got up and started off, then turned back to Marcy. "See if you can talk some sense into this turkey. He's trying to give up."

"I'll try," she replied.

Every time Mike had seen Carl, he'd felt the man's determination to survive, and he'd almost come to believe that somehow he would be able to make it, but today he saw that the fight was going out of him. Carl's face was drawn and gray, and contorted with pain. When he opened his eyes at the sound of Mike's footsteps, Mike saw that he was frightened, but he tried to smile anyway.

"Hey, man. How you makin' it?"

"Not so good, Mike." He was quiet for a moment. "Thanks for coming. I—I got to talk."

"Sure, Carl." Mike pulled a chair close to the bed and straddled it. "What's on your mind?"

"Got to ask you—keep what I say in confidence."

"Right on. I promise."

"I—think you'll understand why—"

"Don't matter why. You want me to keep buttoned up, that's how it's gonna be. Promise."

"Thanks. I believe you." His breathing was labored, and he struggled to keep it even. "I know—I'm not going to—make it, Mike."

"Hey man, you've come this far. Don't give up now!"

"Not giving up—just can't beat it off this time." He tried to smile again. "Something—something I've carried with me for over ten years—never told anyone. Too heavy to take with me."

"Okay. I dig. Lay it on me."

"I—I'm not proud of it."

"So? We've all got something we're not proud of."

"It was before—met Marcy." He closed his eyes and swallowed hard. "Used to steeplechase—'til I crashed through a fence. Came unstuck from horse—went down. Two riders behind piled up, too. I got stepped on—hoof in lower abdomen."

"Ouch!" Mike exclaimed.

"Not too bad—recovered okay." He paused and struggled for breath. "I was okay—but—" He stopped again and Mike waited until he began to wonder if Carl had forgotten what he was talking about.

"You were okay but—" Mike prompted.

"Hard to say it." Carl opened his eyes. "I was sterile." Despite the pain, despite the fact that he knew he was dying, it was difficult for him to bring himself to say aloud what he'd kept to himself for so many years. Yet, as he finally said it, he felt a sense of relief.

"It was—a blow." Carl shifted in bed, trying to ease the pain. "Then I met Marcy. Crazy about her—wanted to marry her. But—another man did too. She—she couldn't decide between us.''

"And—you were scared you'd lose her if she knew about you?''

"Yes.''

"Jesus, what a fix!'' Mike grimaced, and Carl looked away.

"Finally—she said yes—to me.'' He smiled a full smile now. "So happy—couldn't believe it—didn't have guts to tell her.'' He closed his eyes again and his breath rattled in his chest. The sound frightened Mike, but he waited patiently. "We got married. It was okay—didn't want children right away—didn't say anything.'' He coughed and Mike could feel how painful it must be for him. "Time came—Marcy wanted children. By then—was in a corner—I'd waited too long to tell her.'' Carl stopped, and Mike kept silent, but minutes went by and Mike became concerned.

"Hey, Carl, you okay?''

"Tires me to talk—''

"Just—just take it easy, man. I got plenty of time.''

"I haven't. Got to get it off my conscience, Mike. I—I meant to tell her the truth—when I got back from this trip. It was eating me up—seeing her disappointment—waiting—hoping. Then—the crash—no use telling her now. Hurt her too much—maybe make her bitter.''

"I don't know, Carl—if you really wanted to, man—I think she'd understand.''

"When she didn't get pregnant, she got worried something was wrong—wrong with her. Went to doctor—he said she was okay. So she wanted me to go to a doctor—''

"That was a cool time to tell her—like you just found out. She didn't have to know about before—'' Mike had blurted it out without thinking, and was instantly sorry.

"Thought about it—couldn't do it. I lied, Mike—said I was okay too.''

"Jesus, Carl. Why then?''

"Don't know—never understood—afraid she might leave me maybe.''

"But, man, she loves you! Don't you know that?''

"Guilt maybe—got her dishonestly—not telling her before marriage. Afraid she'd be angry at me for not telling her, think less of me—just couldn't do it.'' He paused and looked away, his face was unbearably sad. "Didn't deserve her, Mike."

"You paid—having to live with the lie, man. Don't punish yourself now."

"My character—that bothers me. Vanity—couldn't tell her I was sterile. Lied to that wonderful woman, Mike—deprived her of children. Now she's all alone—"

"She's a strong woman, Carl."

"She needs to be loved—give love. Done a terrible thing to her, Mike." Tears stood in Carl's eyes, and the sadness on his tortured face brought a lump to Mike's throat.

"Shit, Carl, Marcy's never gonna want for love." As soon as he'd said it, Mike realized he'd made another blunder. How insensitive could he sound? "I'm sorry, Carl—"

"No—s' okay—want that for her. Want her to get married, have children—I couldn't give her—"

"Yeah, I can understand that, man. I mean, I guess I'd want that, too if I was in your place."

"But—right kind of man—"

"Yeah—sure."

"Mike?"

"Yeah, Carl?"

"Tell me about Peter Blanchard."

"He's hurting bad, Carl. Being blind is driving him bonkers. If he don't get it together soon, it's gonna be some heavy scene."

"I mean—is he a good man?"

"Yeah. He's all right. Got a lot going for him."

"Sensitive?"

"Oh hell, yeah! Maybe too much that way—"

"But he's got strength, too?"

"I'd say yes to that. He'll come out of this okay—just needs time."

"Marcy likes him."

"Yeah. They hit it off good."

"He could see with a transplant?"

"According to this cat, Dr. Morel, yeah." Carl was quiet for a time and Mike sat watching his face, wondering what he was thinking. He could only guess how hard it had been for Carl to tell the truth about himself; how hard it had been for him to live with his secret all those years; how much he wanted to die with Marcy's image of him intact.

"I'm leaving my eyes to him, Mike." He said it matter-of-factly.

"You are?" A strange feeling came over Mike as Carl opened his eyes and looked at him.

"Yes."

"That's—well—dynamite, man!" Mike paused. "But maybe—I mean you might—shit, Carl! Miracles do happen."

"No. Not now I know, Mike." Both men were quiet then.

"Marcy know—about the eyes I mean?"

"Not yet. When she gets back—"

"Oh, hell! That's gonna be hard for her, man."

"She'll understand. Want Peter to see—leaving something behind, too."

"That's the best thing could happen to Pete. I mean, you're saving his life."

"Don't tell him—let Marcy—"

"No, I won't." Mike scratched his head. "Man, that's some fuckin' gift!"

"Will you—will you ask Peter to do me a favor?"

"Anything."

"Ask him to go see Marcy sometimes?"

"Right on."

"You too, Mike?"

"Don't have to ask, man. I plan to."

"Thanks, Mike." He sighed heavily. "Better go now. Marcy will be back. Got to talk—not much time left—"

"Sure, Carl." Mike got up. He wanted to shake Carl's hand, make some physical contact with him, but Carl's hands were heavily bandaged. Carl seemed to read his thoughts as their eyes met.

"Thanks for everything, Mike—for listening to my confession—for being a good friend—"

"Your secret's safe with me, man, don't worry." Mike hesitated. "Been—been great knowing you—" Mike felt himself choking up again, and was suddenly embarrassed. "But I'm still hoping for that miracle—"

Carl nodded slightly. "One more favor, Mike?"

"Name it."

"Look after Marcy for me?"

"Sure will." Mike started to back out; he couldn't look at Carl anymore.

"Good-bye, Mike."

"So long, Carl." Mike turned and went quickly out the door. He started down the hall, looking neither to the right nor left.

"Mike—" It was Marcy coming toward him down the hall.

"Oh hi, Marcy."

"Is Carl all right?" She sounded alarmed, and he guessed that his own feelings were showing.

"Yeah, he's okay." He tried to sound convincing.

"You were gone so long I got worried."

"We rapped a little—" He avoided her eyes. "He's waiting for you now."

"I'll go right in." She rushed past him, and he was sure that she knew he was dying, had known all along. He dug his hands into the pockets of his robe.

"Fucking damned shit!" he said out loud and repeated it louder.

"Please, monsieur, silence," said a nurse, putting her finger to her lips as she came abreast of him.

"Silence?" he demanded of her. "A man's dying—I mean he's gonna buy a big fucking eternity of silence, and you're telling me to be silent. Lady, I am mad! And—I am going to shout fucking damn shit all I want to! Got that, sugar?" The nurse's eyes opened very wide, and he saw that she was frightened of him. She rushed off down the hall, and he resumed his journey to the ward, swearing loudly as he went.

# Chapter Seven

On the morning of the fifth day after the crash, Peter was awakened early by Dr. Morel.

"Monsieur Blanchard." The doctor shook him gently.

"Yes?" It took him a moment to get his bearings these days. Being blind, he woke up to a world little different from sleeping—it was always dark.

"Monsieur Blanchard, Dr. Morel here."

"I know. What do you want?" He felt irritation rising already; lying in the darkness, facing an uncertain future, he'd come to fix all his resentments on Dr. Morel, and to blame him for his blindness. "What do you want?" he demanded unpleasantly.

"I'm afraid I bring sad news," said the doctor, and Peter forgot his irritation.

"It's Carl Morris, isn't it?"

"*Oui*. Monsieur died at six this morning."

"Damn it! Damn it to bloody hell!"

"He was a very brave man."

"And Mrs. Morris—how is she?" Peter's thoughts went instantly to Marcy.

"Very sad, and very brave."

"Why do things like this have to happen to the best people? Tell me the answer to that, Doctor, will you?"

"I cannot, Monsieur Blanchard. I am only a doctor, I do

not speculate on such matters. I accept the decision of the higher power."

"I suppose the higher power decided that I should be blind?" he said under his breath.

"Pardon?"

"Nothing." He paused. "Don't you sometimes wonder, though, why that higher power takes a good man like Carl Morris?"

"*Non*. Because I cannot know the answer, I do not ask the question."

"Smart."

"I have come to tell you that your friend Monsieur Morris called me to his bedside yesterday. He knew that you were blind."

"So?"

"You see, he knew that he could not live."

"I'm sure he knew. So did Mrs. Morris."

"Monsieur Morris called me to his room because he wished to leave his eyes to you."

"Oh my God!" Peter began to cry. "My God, my God!" He covered his eyes and wept, unable to control himself. The news had taken him so totally by surprise, he could not assimilate it.

"His wish was that you would see again, and he wanted my assurance that you would be able to see with cornea transplants. I assured him that in all probability you would. He then asked me to bring an attorney, and he signed a paper legally giving you his eyes."

Peter could not speak; the tears ran down his cheeks and he made no effort to stop them. So many mixed emotions surged through him that he thought his heart, his being, whatever it was that lived inside his chest that was his soul, his center, would burst.

"It was his very strong wish that you see again, and go on with your life," Dr. Morel said.

"But, Marcy—" His thoughts went at once to her. "Mrs. Morris—how strange it must be for her."

"Madame Morris was a witness to the signing of the paper. It is a fait accompli." The doctor paused a moment, then went on. "Privately Monsieur asked me to give you a message."

"Yes?"

"He asks please, if sometimes you will go to see Madame Morris, to see that she gets along well."

"Oh God, yes. He didn't need to ask." Peter's voice was still choked with emotion.

"A dying man wishes to have assurances for those he leaves behind."

"Of course." Peter bowed his head and wiped the tears from his eyes with a quick swipe of his hand. His thoughts were with Marcy now. "Where is Mrs. Morris?"

"Making the arrangements. Monsieur will be cremated here in Paris, and Madame will take the ashes home to America."

"When will she go?"

"I do not know."

"I wish I could go to her, help her."

"I believe your friend Monsieur Fuller has been helpful. He was with her before Monsieur died, and Dr. Pontier told me he asked permission to leave hospital to help her with arrangements."

"Oh, that's good."

"*Non*, Dr. Pontier would not allow Monsieur Fuller to go. He did not feel his injuries were sufficiently healed."

"But he told me he'd be getting out of hospital in a few days."

"Perhaps that is so, but not today."

"Too bad. I'm sure Mrs. Morris would have been glad to have his help." Peter paused, thinking how helpful Mike had been to all of them. "Good man, Mike Fuller," he said. "He's kept me from wallowing in self-pity and depression."

"*Oui*. But now I must once again be the doctor. We should go to surgery no later than tomorrow morning for the transplant. It is seldom that one gets such an opportunity—to take an eye from the donor, and to transplant the cornea to the recipient immediately, as we will be able to do in your case. I would like, however, to give your eyes a few more hours for the infection to clear entirely. I want to give you the best possible chance, for the circumstances in all other respects are ideal."

"You're sure they will work, Dr. Morel?" Peter was beginning to feel apprehensive.

"Why not? Monsieur Morris's eyes were very healthy, totally unharmed by the accident."

"Yes, but does an eye ever reject the transplant?"

"*Oui*. Of course it can happen, but it is a rare occurrence."

"Is there a way of testing it out beforehand?"

"I'm afraid not. One can only know by trying."

"What about—I mean, what if my eyes reject Carl's corneas? Would I have another chance?"

"Of course."

A few moments earlier Peter had been facing a future of blindness, perhaps even a lifetime of it, and now he was offered an almost certain chance to recover his sight, and yet he felt hesitant. How to explain it? Did he distrust Dr. Morel? Was he frightened of rejection, and possible permanent damage to his chances in the future? Was he afraid to have his eyes operated on in France? They had set his leg, and operated on his back, but he had been unconscious and incapable of taking control of his life. Now he had a choice. His leg and his back should be all right, but Dr. Morel had removed the contact lenses from his eyes and he was blind from the scar tissue. Was that because of the damage done by overlong wearing, or by Dr. Morel's incompetence in removing them? No way to know.

Suddenly a thought occurred: why couldn't he take Carl's corneas and fly to New York, have the operation there? After all, the eyes belonged to him legally, and his ophthalmologist in New York was a highly skilled and respected surgeon; he would have no reservations about her performing the transplants. He knew from previous conversations with Dr. Morel that an eye could be frozen and kept for a few hours, but no more than forty-eight to seventy-two hours. It would be cutting it awfully close to try and fly to New York for the operation, even if his ophthalmologist in New York could perform the transplant on such short notice, and if arrangements could be made at the hospital there. He began to see how impossible the idea was when looked at from a practical point of view. After all, he was flat on his back, blind, unable to walk, unable to move out of the bed without help, and with no access to a telephone. He was isolated in his helpless darkness; alone in a foreign country where he knew no one well, and had only a limited command of the language; and had neither close friend nor trusted physician to help him make a decision that could determine the course of the rest of his life.

There was something else that caused him to hesitate to undergo the transplant, and that was the idea of giving up part of his own eyes. Even though his corneas where no longer useful to him, they were a part of him, and giving them up was like killing off a part of himself. He realized that his thoughts were unrealistic, perhaps even neurotic, but he couldn't help feeling the way he did.

"Monsieur Blanchard?" Peter suddenly realized that Dr. Morel was speaking to him, had been for some time.

"What?"

"You have many thoughts, *oui*?"

"Yes."

"May I guess some of your thoughts?"

"Be my guest."

"You are thinking about losing part of yourself, *non*?" It was as if the man had read his mind, and Peter found it disturbing, but the doctor continued. "It can also be disturbing to receive a part of someone else." Dr. Morel sat down on the edge of Peter's bed. "You see, Monsieur Blanchard, the eyes have very special psychological significance to us, and especially to a man—not all men, but some. I do not understand why, but I know it from my patients. Many men associate the loss of an eye, or loss of sight, with castration. Especially is it so when the entire eye is removed. I do not know if such thoughts are in your mind; however, I sense some apprehension, and some hesitation, and I thought I would speak about it."

"You are amazing, Doctor. I will admit to having some similar thoughts."

"It is not unusual. You have been through great trauma, and have been preparing to accept a difficult future. Suddenly I arrive and say to you—it is all over, all is saved, you do not need to fear. It is wonderful news, but subconsciously you resent it a little. You had made friends with the struggle, and now the relationship is over, you no longer have need of it. But—you don't know what is coming now—it is all new."

"Perhaps that was happening subconsciously—perhaps those thoughts were there, and I just hadn't formulated them. But you're right about the feelings of losing part of myself—"

"Ah—" Dr. Morel smiled understandingly. "Please allow

67

me to say that you are not losing your eyes, you are having the small part replaced that will restore sight." Dr. Morel paused a moment. "It is a wonderful gift, Monsieur Blanchard."

"Yes, it is." Peter sighed. "I'd better shape up and be damned grateful I've got a chance to see again."

"That is the good attitude. Now, about the operation. It will be tomorrow morning. We cannot keep the eyes longer than seventy-two hours, and I would like to use them sooner. In twenty-four hours your eyes will stabilize, and we will be using Monsieur Morris's eyes in good time."

"How long will it be before we know if the transplants work?"

"About twenty-four hours."

"Will I be able to see normally then?" Peter felt excitement beginning inside.

"You will be able to determine shapes and forms. It will take sometime longer to regain normal sight. It will come slowly, a little more each day."

"That's good enough for me."

"*Bon*! Now, please to rest and be of good cheer. The ordeal will soon be over."

"Thanks for the talk, Dr. Morel."

"Not at all, Monsieur Blanchard. I am very pleased for you."

After the doctor had gone, Peter lay quietly, trying to rethink his life. Perhaps everything would be all right again, and he could pick up his life as it had been before the crash. Before the crash? No, his life would never be the same as it had been before, he'd been through too much. Too many bridges had been crossed in his psyche to be just the same again. But to see again—that was enough for now, more than enough, and he wanted to be elated, but some protective instinct cautioned him not to expect miracles. The transplants might succeed, and they might not; anything could happen in surgery. And after all, he knew little or nothing about Dr. Morel as a surgeon: his reputation, his credentials. If he had been in New York, he would have searched for the best eye surgeon in the city, but here in Paris he knew no one to ask. Again he was isolated, captive. Then too, there was the matter of Carl's eyes suddenly being available, and the necessity of having to use them so quickly. When it came right down to it, he didn't have a choice, he was essentially helpless, and that was a difficult position for him to accept.

"Peter?" He recognized Marcy's voice.

"Marcy." He held out his hand to her and she took it. "I am so sorry," he said with feeling.

"You've heard?"

"Yes." He'd never been good dealing with death; it confused him, made him uneasy in the presence of the loved ones left behind. He wanted to say something truly comforting to her, but he couldn't think of anything that wouldn't sound like a cliché.

"He doesn't have to suffer anymore," she said quietly.

"That's the only good part."

"He suffered so terribly much—endured more than any human being should have to endure." She sighed, and he heard the tightness of control in her voice. "He—he fought so hard, but finally it wore him down, he had to give up." Her voice broke, and Peter wanted to see her face, her eyes, to tell her with his eyes that he understood her grief, and that he cared. But it was another frustration that he could not communicate his feelings in a silent way, and had to fall back on words he didn't have.

"Marcy, I'm not good at this sort of thing. I just can't say what I feel—can't think of things to say that would help. But about Carl—I liked him. I only knew him a few hours, but I wouldn't have forgotten him. He gave me something of himself that I can use all my life, something of his philosophy and acceptance of life."

"Thanks for that." She seemed under firmer control now.

"I know that he loved you, and that you were also best friends."

"He told you that?"

"Yes."

"Sounds so like him." She paused, and he knew she was trying not to break down again. "I loved him, too, and yes, we were best friends. I'm going to miss that as much as anything else."

"I'm sorry you have to be alone, Marcy." He pressed her hand.

"I've not been alone for a very long time. It won't be easy—but I'll manage."

"I wish I could help you, Marcy." He held onto her hand.

"The thought is enough."

"What will you do now?"

"I'm going to take Carl's ashes home to Connecticut, and try to pick up my life. I've always tried to move ahead with my life, and that's what I'll try to do again. But first I have to get home—to familiar territory—before I can really let my feelings come out."

"I understand."

"I just have to hold on until then."

"You will, Marcy. There's always that emergency strength that surfaces when we need it."

"Yes." She paused a moment. "But I have to go soon. I'm using up my emergency reserve. I've been running on it ever since I arrived and found out how it was with Carl."

"I'll miss you, but get out as soon as you can, Marcy."

"Peter—Carl wanted you to have his eyes." She said it so quietly he barely heard her. "He wanted you to see again."

"Yes—Dr. Morel told me." Again he didn't know what to say, and the silence between them grew.

"I'd like you to know, Peter, that I was pleased that Carl wanted to give you his eyes. It was a very strange feeling at first—after he told me—but then I realized what a wonderful thing he was doing. It was good to think that if Carl had to go, you would have a chance at seeing again because of it. And then when I thought about it further, I liked the idea that a part of Carl would go on living, living in someone I knew and liked."

"Thank you, Marcy." He was too moved to say anything more—even if he'd had anything to say.

"Well—I must be going now. I'm flying home in a few hours, and I've got to go back to the hotel and pack."

"Marcy, I'm terribly grateful to Carl—and to you. You've given me a new chance at life, and I want to make it count."

"I'm sure you will, Peter."

"I was getting pretty low before this—feeling sorry for myself, lashing out at everybody, even Mike. I was really turning into a miserable human being—"

"You were scared, Peter, and it was understandable. It was a terrible thing that happened to you."

"Just keep your fingers crossed that everything goes all right with the operation."

"When will they do it?"

70

"Tomorrow morning."

"I'll be thinking of you." She leaned forward and kissed him on the forehead. "Good luck, Peter."

"Marcy, if ever you need any help—a friend—anything—I hope you'll call on me."

"I will—and I'm sure I'm going to need that friend."

"I'll always be there."

"Good-bye, Peter."

"Good-bye Marcy." She slipped her hand out of his and walked quickly away. As Peter heard her footsteps retreat, he was stricken with panic. He couldn't let her go just like that.

"Marcy?" He called after her.

"Yes, Peter?"

"Marcy, can I come and see you when I get back home?"

"I hope you will. I'm in the Fairfield, Connecticut, telephone book."

"I'll be seeing you," he said and realized he'd never seen her. "Of course, I won't recognize you."

"But I'll recognize you." She laughed softly and walked away again. He lay in the silence of her faded footsteps and thought of Carl Morris, and what he had done for him.


"Man, this sick people's pad is to hell and gone from downtown Paree!"

"Mike, you amaze me. You always appear at just the right time, like an actor in a play."

"That's me! Man, my timing is per-fect!"

"So what's all this about downtown Paris? You thinking of cutting out after hours for a little sightseeing?"

"You got it. But, man, taxi fare to where the action is—man, it is pro-hibitive!"

"How do you know?"

"I asked this dude sittin' in his hack at the front door, I say, hey brother, how much to where the action is? And he looks at me like I'm bonkers, and tells me this fantastic number of francs without batting an eyelash. I says, you got to be kiddin', man! He gets mad!" Peter had stopped listening and was thinking of Carl again.

"Mike, Carl's dead."

"Yeah, I know. I was there." Mike's voice dropped an octave.

"Was it bad?"

"Hairy. But that Carl, he fought like a champion!"

"How about Marcy?"

"Something else. I mean that is one cool lady. She's dying inside watching him die, but she don't let on nothin' to him. She's just sittin' there, talking him out quiet and loving, like nothin's gonna separate them ever."

"I guess maybe nothing will. The kind of thing they had together stays."

"Yeah. I mean, it got to me, man. I had to cut out of there."

"What's Marcy look like, Mike? I can't visualize her, really."

"Good lookin'. Classy. Tall—maybe five nine or so, and long-legged. All the right things in the right places, if you dig what I mean."

"I think so. And?"

"Well, she's a blonde, and she's got the bluest eyes you ever did see."

"Nice."

"Real nice—on account of there's this warm, feelin' look in her eyes. You know there's somethin' special about her the minute you set eyes on her. And—pretty." Mike chuckled. "Course you realize I'm partial to the darker types. Right?"

"If you say so."

"But Marcy Morris—well I'd sure turn around and look at her if I passed her on the street. Besides, she's got this dark suntan right now. That helps." Mike laughed.

"What kind of type would you say she looks like?"

"Outdoors, rich. I mean she looks like she plays a lot of tennis, or somethin' rich. Nothin' stuck-up about her, though. I mean, in my book Marcy's the greatest!"

"You know Carl left me his eyes?"

"Yeah. I knew he meant to. He kept askin' me about your eyes, who your doctor was, things like that all along."

"Why didn't you tell me?"

"None of my business, Pete. Then there was always a chance Carl might make it. No use gettin' your hopes up."

"You know something, Mike. I never once thought about getting Carl's eyes if he died. And even after Dr. Morel told me, I couldn't really feel glad. If I had, I'd have been glad Carl was dead, and I wasn't." Suddenly he understood why it had been difficult to accept freely the idea of regaining his sight when Dr. Morel told him. On a subconscious level, the idea of profiting from Carl's death was repugnant and shocking.

"Know something else, Mike?"

"You're just full of revelations, Pete. What is it now?"

"You're one hell of a guy yourself."

"Well hell, man, I know that! Tell me something else. Like, when're they operating?"

"Tomorrow morning."

Mike nodded and eased down on his bed. There didn't seem to be anything more to say.

# *Chapter Eight*

Marcy left the hospital with a heavy feeling of sadness. She got into a taxi to go back to the Hotel Queen Elizabeth on the avenue de Serbe and found herself thinking of the first time she'd come to Paris with Carl, shortly after they were married. His job often brought him to Europe, and on this occasion she'd come with him because they'd planned to drive down through the chateaux country to St. Tropez in the south of France after his business was completed. On the second day of their stay in Paris she'd come down with a bad sore throat and Carl had insisted that she see a doctor. There had been a lot of streptococcus infection going around in New York, and he didn't want to get far from Paris with her sick. They'd gone to lunch on the Left Bank the day before they were to leave, and she'd begun to feel really rotten. He would not be put off any longer, and after lunch they'd taken a taxi straight from the restaurant to the American Hospital. At the hospital she'd encountered a woman she knew from Darien, Connecticut. The woman had brought her daughter to the hospital because she'd developed an eye infection while staying in Rome. Eyes—there it was—Carl's eyes. No, they would shortly be Peter Blanchard's eyes.

She would never be able to look into Carl's eyes again, see his love for her there. Oh God, how could she face life without him? Endless days of aloneness and missing him

75

stretched before her, as the terrible finality of death entered her consciousness and filled it with agony. Carl was gone, gone from her life forever—yet, something remained. A part of him would live on in Peter, and she wanted Peter to regain his sight. She had come to like him and had felt his bewilderment and fear at facing the future blind. His blindness had made him afraid that he would be facing the future alone, and knowing that Carl was not going to live and that she would be facing the future alone, made her able to share that dread. Aside from that, she perceived Peter as a man who was in touch with his feelings, or who tried to be honest with himself and others about them. She understood the quality of his sensitivity, and was, as far as she knew, quite reconciled to his being the recipient of Carl's eyes. So why was she aware of a persistent uneasiness? Where did it come from?

She arrived at the Queen Elizabeth to find a message from the crematorium: Carl's ashes would be ready in an hour. She decided to pick them up on her way to the airport and asked the concierge to order her a taxi in one hour. Then she went up to her room where the casement windows had been thrown open by the maid, and she went to look out on the courtyard. The garden restaurant at the far end was buzzing with activity; it was lunchtime, and although she'd had nothing to eat since the night before, she didn't feel hungry.

Marcy began to put the few things she'd brought with her into the bag. She'd left Connecticut in such a hurry she'd taken only the barest essentials. She was packed in a few minutes, and moved idly about the room looking for anything she might have missed. The exhaustion of her constant vigil at Carl's beside, and the loss of sleep suddenly came over her, making her feel faint. She eased down in a chair by the open window, and it was then that the stark impact of her loss permeated her entire being. The grief she'd been trying to hold off until she could get safely home to Connecticut, and the tears she'd kept bottled up since the phone call telling her of the crash, now moved in on her so acutely she experienced a frightening, choking sensation which brought with it a feeling of near hysteria. Finally, unable to hold back any longer, she allowed the tears to spill out and run down her cheeks, but she uttered no sound. She was not ready to let her grief take over; not yet, not here in Paris, not until she was safely home in Connecticut—if she could hold out.

But fighting it off was not easy either, and left her exhausted. She dragged herself to the bed where she huddled miserably. She closed her eyes, trying to calm herself, but the moment she closed them, Carl's face was there, and the great lump of grief was back in her throat.

You've got to accept it, Marcy. It's going to be this way for a long time, she counseled herself. Just hold on until you get home to Connecticut.

Connecticut—home. Was she ready for that? Walking into the house for the first time was going to be difficult, and being in the house where there were so many reminders— could she handle it? And yet the house was her safe haven, and she knew she had to get there to grieve. But was it too soon to go home?

If only she could sleep for a few hours, rest her mind so she could sort out what was best to do. She looked at her watch and found that it was later than she'd thought. She would have to hurry if she were going to pick up Carl's ashes and make the flight to New York. Getting up, however, seemed an impossible task, let alone going to the airport, flying to New York, getting into the city late, going to a friend's house, and then taking the train out to Connecticut tomorrow. It was somehow just too much to face. Perhaps if she stayed overnight in Paris, and flew to New York in the morning? Yes, it made more sense to do that. She picked up the phone and told the desk she would be staying over, then asked to be connected to the concierge. He was gracious and understanding and promised to try and get her on a flight to New York tomorrow. After speaking to the concierge, she telephoned the crematorium and informed them she would not be picking up Mr. Morris's ashes until the next day. That accomplished, she sighed with relief; it did make more sense to stay another day. After all, no one was waiting for her at home, not anymore, not ever.

Exhausted as she was, sleep would not come. She tried making her mind a blank, but that would not work either. Finally, however, toward midafternoon she fell into a restless sleep; a troubled sleep filled with dreams of Carl: Carl swathed in bandages, running toward her, his arms outstretched, but never quite reaching her. Dreams of Carl riding his chestnut jumper, Juniper, about to take a fence, and her calling out to him to stop; Carl taxiing down the field in his Cessna, and her running after him, begging him not to take off. Then came dreams of him in the hospital, his life slowly seeping away, and her begging him to hold on, not to leave her. There was also a dream in which a French doctor was standing by Carl's bedside, about to tell her that he was dead, but she was trying to stop him from saying the final, terrifying word.

Although troubled by dreams, her physical and emotional exhaustion caused her to sleep through the night, and shortly before she awakened came the most terrifying dream of all. It was a surrealistic horror of two enucleated eyes staring at her out of limbo. They were Carl's eyes, full of pain, and a thin, strained voice, resembling his, emanated from them.

"We're still alive, Marcy. We're here to look after you. Don't leave us, Marcy." Then slowly a face materialized around the eyes: it was the face of Peter. Marcy awakened screaming. She sat up in bed, shaking violently, and had to clasp her arms about herself to control the shaking.

"Oh, my God," she whispered and pulled the light blanket around her. She sat huddled against the headboard, her knees drawn up under her chin. "It was only a dream, nothing more," she said aloud, but she could not make the dream-picture go away. She looked at her watch and saw that it was nine thirty A.M. She'd slept for hours! Peter had been scheduled for surgery at eight. It's true, she thought. Carl's eyes are alive now—in Peter. Alive, if the operation had been successful. Suddenly she wanted desperately to know if it had been, and to look at Carl's eyes in Peter, or perhaps more accurately, to be looked at by them. But they really weren't Carl's eyes; only the corneas were his. Yet it was the cornea which gave sight, and it was Carl's sight that would look out of Peter Blanchard's eyes; sight that knew her face, knew everything about her. How did recognition happen between eyes and brain? Did the eye register the image, and the brain remember? If that were the case, Peter would not recognize her even though he had Carl's sight.

She found herself remembering how Carl had insisted on her getting to know Peter. Had Carl been thinking of giving Peter his eyes long before he'd mentioned the idea to her? Had he been looking for a way to stay alive for her—stay alive through Peter? The thought was so disturbing she began to shake again. "Please, don't let this happen to me," she whispered, for she knew that was crazy thinking, and she dared not let it infect her. She pressed her hands tightly to her temples and held them there as if to stop her thoughts. She had to do something, take some action; stop thinking.

She got out of bed and went to the bathroom to draw a bath. She stood watching the water running, trying to clear her head, then turned it off. She had to get out of Paris at once! Get away from the sudden feeling of danger that was infecting her; get safely home to Connecticut where she could deal with such thoughts. She went to the telephone and asked for the concierge, and learned from him that all flights to New York had been full for today. He'd had to book a flight for the following morning. Frustrated and anxious, she put down the phone. No, she could not wait, she had to go now. She began to pace, trying to think of a way to get out of Paris and home before she came apart. Perhaps she could fly to London and get a flight on to New York from there; anything to get out of Paris today. Now! She went back into the bathroom and turned on the water again. You're acting hysterical, she told herself. And all over a dream, too. You're not some silly, neurotic, helpless female, you're going to stay in Paris until tomorrow and come to terms with this. She got into the tub. After all, Peter was going to have Carl's eyes a long time, and she'd better get used to it now.

She sat soaking in the warm water, trying to relax. When she felt calmer, she got out and put on her robe. She went to the telephone and ordered croissants, confiture, and coffee. She had not eaten in over twenty-four hours, and she knew she had to put something in her stomach, no matter how repulsive the thought of food was.

By the time the tray came, she was fully dressed, for she meant to get out of the room as soon as she had forced some food down. She would go to Versailles, Fontainbleu, Chartres, anywhere to take her mind off the disturbing dream, and to stop thinking of Carl's eyes in Peter.

She went first to the crematorium to get Carl's ashes, then, holding the container pressed firmly against her body, she started to walk. She craved the life-renewing sunshine and fresh air, but try as she could, she could not stop thinking of the last remains of the man she had loved and lived with for over ten years. She looked at the container and marveled at how a six-foot-two-inch, one-hundred-seventy-five-pound man could be so reduced. One small container held all the tangible remains of her husband. No, not quite all, not his eyes; Peter had those. The dream came crowding back into her consciousness then, and she quickened her step. She had to get Carl's ashes back to the room and then go somewhere, anywhere, to get away from her thoughts.

Later she went to the Louvre and walked through the great halls filled with treasures. Occasionally she forgot her loss and her grief, and Carl's eyes alive in Peter, but not for long. The ache inside her was too big and too powerful to be put aside for long. But she walked the picture galleries until she tired of them, then went to stand at the top of the great staircase leading into the grand hall where she could admire the marvelous "Winged Victory of Samothrace" on the landing. It was indeed a magnificent statue. How wonderful it would have been to see it in its original natural setting on the island of Samothrace. When she had looked her fill, she slowly descended the great stairs and went on to the Greco-Roman hall. She wandered aimlessly among the statues of Diana, Apollo, Aphrodite, and the other sculptured treasures from that great era.

Suddenly she found herself staring at the eyes of the statues; some painted, some sculpted as shallow holes. As she went from one to the other, staring at the eyes, she began to feel panicky, and then began to run out of the hall, up the stairs, across the great hall, and out into the sunlit gardens. She did not stop until she came to a bench, and then dropped onto it. What is happening to me? she cried. What must I do to make these thoughts go away? Somehow it seemed that Carl's eyes were following her, calling her back to the hospital. But why? Did she simply want to know if the operation had been successful, or did she want to see Carl's eyes in Peter? Then another more disturbing thought entered her mind: was Carl reaching out to her from that other region? Was he telling her to go and see Peter? "This is insane!" she cried. A man strolling past stared at her, then smiled. He wore a tricorn hat, doublet and knee breeches, but she did not notice.

Perhaps if she tried to telephone Dr. Morel she could find out if the operation had been successful, but she did not have enough faith in her French to deal with the hospital operator. Perhaps if she went to the hospital and spoke to Mike Fuller, he would know about the operation. Or if he didn't, he would surely telephone her when he found out. Yes, she would do that. Mike would understand. But why go to Mike, rather than directly to Peter? Because she was not yet ready to face Peter.

She got up then and walked through the gardens to the boulevard, where she hailed a taxi and gave the address of the American Hospital. But as the taxi neared the hospital, she began to shake again. For a moment she thought of telling the driver to turn around and take her back to the Queen Elizabeth. The driver sensed her distress and glanced over his shoulder at her several times, and it was the look of concern on his face that finally brought her back to reality. At the door of the hospital, he turned around in his seat to look directly at her, and she smiled and got out her money. It was silly to have come so far and not see Mike. She paid the fare and got out, but the driver continued to stare as she walked away from the taxi and went into the hospital. She did not go to the ward, but went instead to the front desk. She explained to the woman on duty that she did not want to go up to the ward because her husband had died on that floor the day before, and asked her if it would be possible for his friend Mr. Fuller to come to the desk. The attendant seemed to understand and suggested she take a seat on one of the benches at the entrance and wait. Marcy did as she was told and prepared to wait. It was difficult being there; after all, she had waited night after night with Carl for death to release him from agony, and bring her a new kind of suffering.

"Hi, Marcy!" Mike stood looking down at her. He was smiling, and she knew she'd been right to come.

"Hi, Mike," she said.

"How come you still in Paris?" He sat down beside her.

"I was just too tired to leave. I'm going in the morning."

"Yeah?"

"I wanted to know if the operation on Peter's eyes was successful?"

"The operation went okay—I mean, like it should, but he don't know nothing yet. Be several days before he knows if he can see or not."

"Is he in good spirits?"

"Yeah. Still afraid though."

"I guess that's natural?"

"Hell yes! I mean, his future is riding on this."

"I don't want him to know I came to the hospital and

didn't come to see him. I mean, I'd like to see him but—''
She couldn't really say what she meant.

"You spooked, Marcy?" He spoke gently.

"Yes." She was annoyed with herself then because she felt
tears tightening in her throat.

"Hell, Marcy, that ain't hard to figure! I mean, this business of Carl's eyes is a spooky business, if you don't mind
me saying so. And I bet you Pete's gonna be a little spooked
at first, too. But you'll both get used to it. I mean, it's a fact
of life now."

"I know. I'll—I'll be okay when I get out of Paris. It's just
difficult still being here." She broke off and he patted her
shoulder gently.

"Sure it is, Marcy," he said softly. She looked up at him
then and smiled bravely. He wanted to put his arms around
her and hold her. Goddamn! Why did this have to happen to
somebody like her?

"Mike," she began, "would you—would you do something for me?"

"Anything. You know that."

"Would you let me know when Peter finds out about his
sight?"

"Sure."

She took out a pencil and paper and wrote her telephone
number in Connecticut.

"Telephone me collect when you know? I'll be at this
number by the weekend. Call me then—or whenever you
know?"

"Got it."

"You've been really wonderful, Mike. I don't know what
we would have done without you."

"Yeah, got to watch me; I kinda grow on people." Mike
laughed easily.

"Will you come and see me when you get back?"

"You can count on that!" He grinned. "I mean, you don't
think this dude would pass up a chance to do that high-class
Connecticut scene, do you?"

"You know something, Mike, you're a tonic!"

"With or without the gin?"

"You don't need the gin." She kissed him on the cheek
and stood up. "Well, I guess I'd better be going. Take care
of yourself."

They shared a quick hug and a smile, and then she was outside in the sunshine again, where her good feelings quickly evaporated. The day and the night, and the rest of her life stretched ahead of her. Suddenly she didn't want to leave the hospital—she wanted to go up and see Peter. But that was ridiculous; he wouldn't be able to see her, and she wouldn't be able to see his eyes under the bandages. She must have realized that all along. Why then had she been so determined to return to the hospital?

The truth was not easy to face. She'd come back because she'd been drawn back, as though by some outside force—a force stronger than herself. She had wanted to see Peter, yes—but it was as though the force wanted it more. Had that force been appeased? Would it leave her alone now and let her go home without actually seeing Peter? He had said he would be hospitalized for at least another four weeks with his other injuries. By the time he got back to New York, she'd have herself under control. It would be better that way.

She left the hospital and found the same taxi that had taken her from the Louvre still parked at the front door. She got into it and gave the address of the Queen Elizabeth. She didn't really want to go back to the hotel, but at the moment she could think of nowhere else to go. The further she got away from the hospital, however, the lonelier she felt, and the heavier her grief seemed to become.

She was going to have to get herself through the rest of the day. Perhaps she'd do a little shopping; perhaps go to a movie or a play, or even to the opera. The opera—yes—she'd always loved going to the Paris opera. It would make her feel better—if they were not doing anything heavy. She wouldn't be able to take one of the tragic operas; music had always been the fastest route to her emotions, and that's what she wanted to avoid for now. She asked the driver to take her to the Place Vendôme instead of the Queen Elizabeth. She'd check the opera playing at the opera house, and then browse through Le Drugstore—she'd always loved shopping there. Carl had loved it too. Carl . . . Would the ache ever stop?

# Chapter Nine

Nice Nurse Charlotte was helping Peter to eat his breakfast, and this morning he ate it with more grace then he had at any time since he'd been in the hospital. If he had not accepted his blindness well in other matters, and had been irascible to everyone in sight, he had been most difficult in the matter of eating. Today, however, he was cooperative, even jocular; for today was the day he hoped to find out he could see again.

"Eats like a normal, helpless human being today, don't he?" commented Mike as he sat on his bed and watched Charlotte feeding him.

"A man who's helpless is not normal," retorted Peter.

"Okay, I'll grant you it's been frustrating, but you're gonna have to shape up after today, man, 'cause you ain't gonna have no more reason for being a pain in the ass." Mike was trying to relieve the tension he knew Peter was feeling in anticipation of the bandages coming off.

"How do you like the way he talks to me? Is that a friend?" Peter directed his remarks to Charlotte.

"*Oui*, Monsieur Fuller is a good friend." She fed him a slice of orange. "But Monsieur Blanchard should not expect the miracle today. The sight it will come slowly."

"I know." Peter had accepted this, but he couldn't entirely stop hoping for the miracle. "How long will it be?"

"I do not know. Dr. Morel, he will tell you that."

"Well, just so long as I know I'm going to see, I guess I can be patient a little while longer."

"*Bon*! That is the good attitude."

After Charlotte had gone, Peter began to think about Carl's eyes—how clear and earnest they had been. Would his own eyes now take on some of Carl's characteristics? Technically he understood that he had only received the corneas, but he did not totally comprehend what that meant.

"Hey, Pete."

"Yeah, Mike?"

"You planning on seeing Marcy when you get back home?"

"Sure. Why?"

"Oh, just wondered."

"No, you didn't just wonder, you asked me for a reason. I know you well enough by now to know you don't make chitchat."

"No, man, sometimes I run off at the mouth just to make noise." Mike was quiet for a moment. "Shit, Pete, you're right—you know me too well. Truth is, I was thinking about that lady, and how lonesome she's gonna be when she gets home."

"Yes. I've been thinking about that, too."

"I mean, I know she's hurtin' to the quick right now, but she's putting on that brave act, and she's gonna cave in any day."

"Yeah—bound to happen sooner or later." Peter was thinking about Marcy now, about her going home to an empty house full of memories. "Be hardest when she get home, I imagine."

"You got it. That's gonna be heavy!"

"Wish I could be around to kind of help her over the rough spots."

"Ever thought about how she's gonna feel about seeing you?"

"You mean because of Carl's eyes?"

"Right. She's gonna have some curiosity about your eyes. How you reckon she's gonna feel looking at you and knowing you got part of her husband?"

"Strange, I guess. I would." He paused. "Fact is, I'm not sure how *I* feel about having part of Carl."

"Be damned glad, that's what."

"Oh, I'm glad, believe me! But—I knew the guy, Mike—and

86

I survived and he didn't. And—here I've got his eyes. I mean, I keep asking myself why him instead of me?"

"Because he was unlucky, that's all!"

"Yeah—but—well, it's just a weird feeling, and you can't help asking yourself some rough questions."

"Fuck it, Pete! Don't you go gettin' weird over this eye thing."

"No, I don't think I will. I'm lucky and I know it—and I just hope the transplants work, but still—a man wonders why he lives and someone else dies when they've both got the same chance. I mean, Carl was sitting right next to me."

"Shit, man, Carl wasn't fucked up about it. He had it straight. His time was up—period—the end!"

"I know, but that's the second time in my life that I've survived and another man has died."

"Maybe the big man in the sky's got some plans for you."

"It's a little frightening, Mike."

"Uh, oh! Here comes the little eye doc."

"Morel?"

"Yep. See him way down at the end of the ward, and he's making tracks this way." Peter heard Mike move off his bed. "I'm gonna cut out on this scene. Be back later."

"Chicken?"

"You got it!"

"Come back in time to help me pick up the pieces if I get bad news?" Peter felt his heart begin to pound.

"Hell, man! You ain't gonna get no bad news. But you sure take the cake for being pessimistic!" Mike laughed and headed off down the ward.

"*Bon jour*, Monsieur Blanchard."

"Good morning, Dr. Morel."

"Well, and how are you feeling this morning?"

"Anxious to know what miracle you've performed."

"Ah! Miracles? Perhaps. Let us have a look, shall we?" The doctor began to carefully remove the bandages. Peter tried to remain calm, but he was already drenched with perspiration, and he'd had butterflies in his stomach since awakening. Dr. Morel almost had the bandages off, and Peter kept his eyes tightly closed. Suddenly he was terrified to open them, afraid to know the truth.

"Now, Monsieur Blanchard, please open your eyes."

"I know it's stupid, Doctor, but I'm afraid to open them,"

Peter replied in a small, apologetic voice. Dr. Morel chuckled, and that annoyed Peter. The bastard had no right to treat anything so important to him lightly.

"Not to worry, Monsieur Blanchard. Come—look at my hand." Dr. Morel held his hand before Peter's face. "The light will probably hurt for a moment, but the pain, it will go away."

Peter said a quick prayer and opened his eyes slowly. The doctor was right, the light did hurt, but he didn't mind.

"I can see something! Yes—yes, it looks like the outline of a hand!" Peter felt a rush of excitement, and he blinked several times, trying to focus more clearly.

"*Bon*! Now, would you know the hand, had I not told you?"

"I—I don't know." Peter squinted automatically, trying to see more clearly. "No, I don't think so. I don't think I could identify it as a hand—perhaps just an object."

"Hmm. Now, let's have a look." Peter could see the pinpoint of light coming from Dr. Morel's ophthalmoscope as he peered through it into his eyes.

"How do they look, Doctor?" Peter spoke hesitantly, for the anxiety had not gone away; in fact, had Charlotte not warned him, he probably would have panicked; he felt very close to it as it was. He could see little more than he'd been able to see before the operation.

"Very good. Yes, everything seems fine, Monsieur Blanchard."

"But, Doctor, I can see little more than I could before the operation," protested Peter.

"That is expected. Sight will come slowly, a little more each day. But let me assure you, everything looks very good in the eyes."

"But how long will it take before I have good sight?"

"Difficult to say. The eyes should heal well—there's no indication of infection—and we will continue the antibiotics as precaution. Yes—perhaps a week, perhaps a fortnight, then you will see more clearly."

"And before I have full sight?"

"Two—perhaps six weeks. It comes slowly, Monsieur Blanchard. First the sight, it will be blurred. Of course, you will have to wear the corrective lenses."

"Glasses?"

"Yes, or contact lenses."

"Oh, I don't know about that, Dr. Morel. I think it will take me awhile to adjust to that idea. After what I've been through, I don't know if I want to take a chance on them again."

"There is no need to be frightened of the contact lenses. It was an unusual circumstance in your case. But in time you could wear them again. You will only need to be careful." Dr. Morel paused, then added thoughtfully, "You know that you should have removed the lenses when you knew the plane would make an emergency landing."

"I was afraid I wouldn't be able to see to get out without them."

"Ah, yes. That is a point."

"But I'd like to know why they weren't removed when I was brought into the hospital?"

"Who can say? So many injured people—everyone rushing to take care of the obvious: those with broken bones, those bleeding heavily, those needing emergency surgery. Your other injuries were obvious: leg, the back. The doctor would look only briefly into your eyes to see if the pupils were dilated because you were unconscious. But he would be rushed, and he would not be looking so carefully to discover the contact lenses."

"All that may be true, Doctor, but it still seems careless to me."

"Perhaps, but under the circumstances is it not understandable?"

"No, it was not in the least understandable as I lay here in darkness facing a possible future of blindness. My career, my life had gone down the drain."

"But that is all changed now, Monsieur Blanchard."

"I hope so." Peter sighed. "But what about the rejection? If my eyes are going to reject the transplants, would we be able to tell by now?"

"Hmm, perhaps not," replied Dr. Morel, and then he hastily added: "But I do not think that is going to happen. I think the transplant is going to be fine. What you must do is try to relax and be very patient. If you become apprehensive and tense, that will not be good for the eyes and will retard the healing process."

"It's always been difficult for me to relax, Doctor, and it's especially hard now. I have an enormous amount of work piling up in my office in New York. That's aside from being anxious about when and if I will regain my sight.''

"*Oui*, I understand." He began to rebandage Peter's eyes. "I do not think you need to worry, however, for I believe that you will have sight, and normal sight within a matter of time.''

"I've got to have, Doctor, that's all.''

"Now, should you experience greater pain, ask the nurse to call me at once.''

"What would that mean?'' Peter was anxious again.

"Perhaps some complication.''

"What kind of complication? Do you expect something?''

"No, no, I do not expect complications. I am only being cautious.''

"I see.''

"Of course you realize that you should not touch the bandages; should not rub the eyes, or bring pressure of any kind to them.''

"Of course.''

"*Bon*! I will see you this evening. Fortunately, because of the other injuries you cannot move about. That is all to the good, for you must rest quietly. The healing, it will be better and faster if you are quiet—and serene in your attitude.''

On the morning of the eighth day after the operation Dr. Morel removed the bandages, and Peter saw the blurred features of the doctor's face.

"Dr. Morel, do you have a moustache?'' Peter could hardly contain his excitement.

"*Oui*. A small one!'' The doctor laughed softly, and Peter let out a whoop of joy. People came running from all over the ward to see what was wrong. Among them was Mike.

"He's finally gone bonkers, huh?'' asked Mike.

"No, you ugly son of a bitch, I can see!'' Everyone laughed.

"He *can* see!'' shouted Mike. "Everybody knows I'm an ugly son of a bitch!''

"No, man, you are *beautiful*!'' shouted Peter. "Say about six feet three inches tall, and you've got a moustache, too! Does everybody around here have a moustache?''

"I do not have a moustache," said Nurse Charlotte, stepping close to the bed.

"No, but you've got the bluest eyes I've ever seen!"

"*Oui*, I have blue eyes," she replied with a warm smile.

"And—and a beautiful smile!" Peter started to laugh, and kept on laughing. He wanted to get out of bed and run and jump, do a dance for joy. His excitement was too much to contain, but contain it he would have to because his leg was still firmly elevated on the pulley. But he kept on laughing, and pointing out all the things he could see around him. It didn't matter to him that his focus was blurred, because he could see enough to give him hope, and that gave his spirits the lift they so badly needed.

After the initial excitement had subsided, and the ambulatory patients and staff had left, Peter asked Mike to see the book he'd been reading to him. Although the letters were blurred, he could almost read the large letters of the title.

"I can't read the text," said Peter, "it all runs together."

"Hey, man, slow down! You're expecting too much. I mean, you just found out you can see big ugly objects like me, and that's one hell of a lot more than you could see before."

"I know, I know, but I'm losing too much time. I've got to get back to work, and how can I when I can't read print?"

"Shit, Pete! You ain't got your glasses yet, and besides, you ain't going nowhere on that leg yet. By the time you get able to gimp around on it, you'll be able to see."

"Yeah, yeah, okay, you're right."

"I mean—"

"I said okay. You made your point!" replied Peter irritably.

"Want me to read you some more of this book?"

"No, I'm too restless to concentrate."

"Right." Mike stretched out on his bed, and both were quiet.

"What's Dr. Pontier say about you?" Peter asked a moment later.

"Maybe next week. The fuckin' airlines won't let nobody leave 'til the doc says okay."

"Any word on your drums?"

"Yeah, man, forgot to tell you. I get to pick out a brand new set. How you like that?"

"How do you like it?"

"Rather have my old skins. Had 'em all broke in good. But—no use crying over spilt milk, right?"

"Monsieur Blanchard, I have a present for you." It was Nurse Charlotte carrying a huge vase of red and white carnations. There must have been two dozen.

"Whooeee!" exclaimed Mike and followed it with a long whistle. "That is one big fancy flower garden!"

"Who sent them?" asked Peter.

"There is a card." Charlotte put the card into Peter's hand.

"Thanks a lot, Charlotte. *Merci beaucoup*," he said.

"*C'est très bien.*" She smiled, and then sensing that he wanted her to put the vase on his bedside table. "*A tout à l'heure,*" she said as she left.

"So what was all that?" asked Mike.

"She said she'd see me later."

"I'll bet she will!"

"Whatever that means."

"Means, in my expert opinion, Nice Charlotte's got the *hots* for you."

"You've got a one-track mind."

"Bet your ass." Mike laughed and reached for the card in Peter's hand. "Here, give me the card, *lover dear*, and I'll read you who sent them flowers." First, though, he read it silently to himself, grinning and shaking his head.

"Well, what does it say?" asked Peter. Mike did not answer at once; instead he fixed Peter with an amused look. "What's the matter, is it written in Sanskrit or something?"

"Oh, no, it's English."

"Then for Christ sake, read it!"

"Sure you're ready for this?"

"Mike, will you just read me the card."

"Okay, here it is: 'Darling Peter, wondering how you are? Why haven't I heard anything? When are you coming home? Longing for you. Should I come over for the weekend? Love and kisses, Jeannie.' Sweet, man, sweet!" said Mike with a chuckle.

"Ummm. Guess I ought to try and get to a telephone." He was feeling guilty because he'd been too wound up in his own problems to think of her.

"No reason why she can't come over now. I mean, with you being able to see again and all."

"I don't know. Something tells me it's still not a good idea."

"Well, in that case I'd say some communication is definitely indicated. Unless, of course, you want one angry, rich chick waiting for you in New York. Or maybe not waiting, if you don't move your butt!"

"Don't nag, Mike. Why did she have to send so many, anyway?"

"The bigger the bunch, the more she loves you, right?"

"Wonder what made her send carnations?"

"Don't you like them?"

"Don't dislike them, but they're not my favorites."

"Ever send her flowers?"

"Sure."

"What do you send her?"

"Roses most of the time."

"Romantic, but ordinary."

"She likes them. They symbolize love to her."

"Then how come she sends you carnations?"

"How the hell do I know." Peter thought a moment. "Well, maybe she thinks they're more masculine."

"Balls! Hey, Pete, you really in love with this chick?"

"I think so. I mean, sometimes I think so, and I think we ought to get married, and then I have spells when I'm not sure. But how do you really know, Mike?"

"Don't ask me, man. I never been in love. I know all about good old lust, but love—never happen to this turkey."

"I thought I was in love a couple of times before I met Jeannie, but then it just kind of evaporated all by itself. They didn't wear well. But Jeannie and I've lasted a couple of years, so I've been thinking maybe I'd ask her to marry me when I get back."

"Don't rush into anything, Pete."

"I'd hardly call a couple of years rushing into it."

"Yeah, but I'd give it some time if I were you."

"Why?"

"Oh, I don't know." Mike paused. "Got a hunch, that's all."

"About what?"

"Oh—about Marcy Morris."

"*Marcy Morris*?"

"Yes, *Marcy Morris*!" Mike mimicked Peter.

"What are you talking about?"

"Well, that's a woman to get serious about, brother."

"Mike Fuller, you shock me. She's a grieving widow!"

"She ain't gonna always be. Besides, you've got something big in common."

"We sure do—Carl Morris's eyes. And you know something? Everytime that woman looks at me, she's going to think of him. Man, you have really taken leave of what little sense you've got!" Peter was really shaken up by Mike's suggestion.

"I ain't no fuckin' prophet, but I'd lay bread on it. She's gonna come looking for you one of these days."

"And what about Jeannie?"

"Well, if you're all that damned certain, be my guest, but you don't seem so sure where you are about the rich chick."

"Mike, I don't even know Marcy Morris, not really."

"Forget it, man, it was just a hunch, that's all."

Peter felt a shiver go through him, and what that shiver really meant, he wasn't certain. All he knew was that the idea was extremely disturbing to him.

"Listen, Mike, can you get me a mirror? I want to look at my eyes, see if they still look like mine."

"Sure." Mike came back a moment later with a small mirror. Peter took it, and stared at the reflection. His eyes looked exactly the same, but they weren't. There was part of another man in there.

# Chapter Ten

On July 15, five weeks after the crash at Charles De Gaulle Airport, Peter landed at John F. Kennedy Airport in New York. He had not let anyone know when he was returning, not even Jeannie, whom he had managed to dissuade from coming to Paris. He had wanted that time alone to think things out, but after he was able to get up for a few hours a day, he had managed to talk to her at least twice a week. Now he walked off the plane on crutches, carrying one small overnight case, because he had no possessions excepting the few necessary things he'd had to buy to dress himself. He got into a taxi, gave his address, and tried to arrange himself comfortably for the ride into Manhattan, and back into his life.

He'd been cut off in a kind of limbo in Paris; in a sense his life had come to a halt. As he waited for his body to heal, he'd become introspective, especially after Mike had been released and he was alone. He'd taken stock of his life and found that he was dissatisfied with much of it, both his professional life and his personal life; some important ingredients had been missing. The realization had been disturbing to him, and he knew he had to take the time to find out where he was.

Now he was home, and all he wanted to do was get into bed and rest. The long flight had tired him, but he was not suffering great pain. As for his eyes, he was seeing pretty well with the glasses Dr. Morel had prescribed. As the taxi carried him across the Queensboro Bridge into Manhattan, the skyline came into view, and he was grateful that he could see it at all. A shudder went through him as he reminded himself that had it not been for Carl Morris, he would have come home blind. But thank God he wasn't blind, and Dr. Morel had assured him that his sight would improve with time. Tomorrow he would go to his ophthalmologist and learn what she had to say. He would also see a bone specialist to find out what kind of job the French doctors had done on his leg. Tomorrow he would begin to pick up the threads of his life, but tonight he was just tired, and very glad to be home.

He struggled out of the taxi at his apartment house, and went through the explanations of what had happened to him with the doorman, the elevator operator, and various tenants who happened to be coming or going. When he finally got up to his apartment, the place seemed almost alien. He moved around restlessly, touching objects, reading titles on the books in his bookcases, picking up photographs. One was a photograph of himself with Jeannie which a friend had taken at the Harvard-Yale game last fall. Jeannie laughed up at him, looking like the chic, attractive, well-bred socialite she was, and the man sitting next to her—himself—looked serious, almost handsome with a square, cleft chin, full mouth with laugh lines in the corners, high cheekbones, dark wavy hair, and blue eyes that smiled, making crinkles around them. He looked a long time at the picture, and both people seemed like strangers to him.

Finally he put the frame back on the table and switched on his stereo. Rock music blared out of the speakers, and he thought of Mike. After Peter got resettled into his routine, he wanted to see him; he'd grown genuinely fond of the big musician. He switched the dial and found the New York Philharmonic playing Mahler's First Symphony. That suited his mood better. He poured himself a Scotch, the first he'd had since the drinks on the plane going over to Paris. He took the stack of mail that had accumulated in his absence and went to bed to read it.

The next day Peter's ophthalmologist concurred with Dr. Morel; everything was in good shape, and she felt sure that with corrective lenses he would have completely normal sight again in a short time. He went to the office then, and submerged himself in the mountain of work awaiting him. But a restlessness had taken hold of him since returning to New York, and it stubbornly persisted. Try as he could, he couldn't get to the root of it. It was as if he were waiting for something to happen, but he had no idea what it was. He lunched with colleagues, accepted several dinner invitations, met with authors, attended editorial meetings, but he often felt as if he were walking through a play. Nothing seemed familiar or right to him anymore, and the moment he was alone, he was seized with an overwhelming feeling of unrest.

Finally he decided he was ready to see Jeannie, he was also afraid she would hear he was back and be hurt, and he didn't want to start out that way. At first she was excited at hearing his voice and knowing he was in New York, and then annoyed with him for not telling her when he was coming home. He told her there had been good reasons and he would explain everything when he saw her. They made a date for dinner at Chez Pascal, a small restaurant on East Eighty-second Street where they often dined. She asked him to come to her apartment first for a drink, and from there they could walk over to the restaurant nearby. He agreed, not telling her that he would be unable to walk that far yet. He had argued unceasingly to persuade Dr. Pontier to allow him to leave the hospital a week early, and he wasn't going to jeopardize the healing process any more than was absolutely necessary.

At seven Peter pushed the bell at Jeannie's door and waited, resting on his crutches. The door opened, and there she was, looking lovely and happy to see him.

"Hello," he said.

"Darling!" She threw her arms about him, almost knocking him off his feet, and sending his crutches clattering to the floor.

"Hey, take it easy," he managed to say as he caught onto the door to support himself.

"Oh, my goodness!" she exclaimed as she bent down to pick up his crutches. "What are these for?"

"Walking," he laughed and took them from her.

"Of course. Silly question, wasn't it?"

"Kind of."

"I had no idea your leg was still so bad."

"Yeah, well, it was a pretty nasty break, and then my back isn't so good either." She helped him into the room, and he eased into a chair. The near fall at the door had aggravated his back and started up the pain again. "Could I have a glass of water?" he asked, digging for his pills in his jacket pocket.

"How about a real drink?"

"I suppose it wouldn't hurt. Might help kill the pain quicker."

"In fact, I got champagne to celebrate your homecoming."

"That's a nice idea." She smiled and started to leave the room then came back and kissed him on the forehead.

"Welcome back, darling. I've nearly perished without you."

"Yeah, been a long haul, hasn't it?"

"And how! But you wouldn't let me come over. That was mean of you." She kissed his nose teasingly.

"There was a reason. Get us the champagne and I'll explain everything."

"You got a deal, Mr. Blanchard." She left the room, and he sat staring. It was a room he knew so well, but he felt a stranger in it now. And Jeannie—she didn't seem the same either. In fact, he almost felt awkward with her. He didn't understand any of it, and that made him still more uncomfortable.

"Here we are! Champagne for the brave survivor of flight number 421!" She raised her glass to him and there was a happy smile on her face, but her words brought an acute pain to his chest and he felt almost faint. He set his glass down on the coffee table to keep from spilling it. Seeing the look on his face, she rushed to his side.

"Peter, what's wrong?"

For a moment he was unable to speak: he was thinking of Carl Morris, Captain Johnson, and all the others who did not survive flight number 421.

"There were a lot of brave people who didn't survive, Jeannie—and one guy in particular who became my friend, and gave me a new lease on life." His voice was low and emotional, and she felt his distress.

"I'm terribly sorry, Peter. How thoughtless of me."

"You had no way of knowing." He was surprised to realize his own feelings about his survival. Was it guilt he felt at being alive when so many others had died? This was a new thought, and he suddenly wanted very much to be alone with it.

"Would you like to talk about it, Peter?" She knelt on the floor beside him, looking up at him with concern.

"I guess so, at least some of it. You see, there is something you don't know. In fact, it was why I didn't want you to come over." He told her then about Carl, and his blindness, and the transplants. When he'd finished, she did not speak for some time; she seemed to be very far away with her own thoughts.

"I'm sorry you didn't feel you could tell me, Peter," she said at last.

"It wasn't that I couldn't tell you so much as I couldn't handle it myself."

"Couldn't you have trusted me enough to let me come over and see it through with you?"

"It wasn't a matter of trusting you, Jeannie. It was a matter of me facing up to the possibility that I might have to go through life blind, and what I was going to do for a living, things like that. The world, your life, your own feelings get all turned around, and you don't know where you are. It's all you can do to try and keep yourself from falling into a pit of depression and self-pity. There's nothing left for dealing with someone else's feelings."

"I think I can understand it, intellectually, but it does hurt that you didn't at least give me a chance to try and help you."

"I guess what I meant to say is, no one could help me but myself. And frankly you wouldn't have wanted to be around me—I was a hostile bastard. I was so sorry for myself I tried to make everybody around me pay for what had happened to me."

"I find that hard to believe. It's so unlike you." She lighted a cigarette, and he saw that she was nervous.

"You can't imagine what it's like to be captive to darkness, not to be able to even feed yourself, and in my case I was confined to bed because of my leg and back injuries. I was almost completely helpless, and I went crazy from claustrophobia almost every day. Sometimes I had several attacks a day."

"My poor darling." She took his hand and kissed the tips of his fingers. "How awful for you."

"Yes, it was awful, but I was lucky to come out alive. And thanks to Carl Morris, I can see again."

"How sad that he had to die—but if he hadn't, you wouldn't be able to see."

"I keep asking myself why Carl instead of me? Why all those others had to die and I lived? Sometimes I even feel guilty about that."

"But that's absurd."

"Is it?"

"Yes, it is. All tragic disasters leave behind the living and the dead. Some are lucky and some are not, that's all."

"Carl Morris left behind a wonderful wife who loved him very much. She's sitting up in Connecticut right now, probably asking herself why it had to be Carl instead of me. But here I am—alive, and seeing with her husband's eyes."

"It's positively macabre, having someone else's eyes. Don't you feel strange?"

"Yes, I do, and I try not to think about it. Actually nothing is different in my eyes except for the corneas."

She looked up into his eyes. "You don't look any different. I mean, your eyes don't."

"Well, of course I don't." He suddenly felt slightly annoyed; the comments about his eyes seemed insensitive to him.

"And your leg, is it going to be all right?"

"Yes. It was really a mess, though. Kept me flat on my back with my leg hitched up to a pulley for a long time." He told her about his back, and then asked for another glass of champagne. When she left the room, he stretched out his leg, and leaned his head against the back of the chair. He found his thoughts going to Marcy: how was she? How was she feeling being back home? He would go and see her soon.

"Here you are." She handed him the glass and reseated herself on the footstool in front of him. "Let's drink to us this time."

"I'll drink to that." She smiled at him over the rim of the glass and he smiled back. He realized he had not kissed her, and leaned down to kiss her affectionately. Her eyes were slightly questioning when he sat back, but he pretended not to notice. He wanted to avoid any discussion of their relationship tonight, if possible. "What's been happening here since I've been gone? Anything interesting?"

"Not much. I've been going out to Southampton on weekends. We've been busy at the magazine." She sipped her champagne. "Mother and Father ask after you all the time. We were all terribly worried, of course. And I'm afraid I couldn't tell them very much. They thought that strange, and kept asking me questions. It was quite embarrassing."

"I'm sorry. It's just that I had all I could handle over there."

"Would you like to come out to Southampton this weekend?" she asked tentatively.

There it was; the old routine, the old habits. He'd always enjoyed going to Southampton, or at least he'd thought he had, but now he didn't want to go. How could he answer her in a way that wouldn't hurt?

"I don't think I should just yet, Jeannie. It's such a hassle getting around and all, and I'm rather weak and shaky from being in bed so long. I tire easily. Besides, I have a lot of work piled up."

"Why don't we just stay here then?"

Her suggestion sent him into panic. He wanted desperately to be alone, and the idea of her hovering over him all weekend made him feel as captive as he'd felt in the hospital. What was happening to him? Normally he would have been delighted with the fact that she was willing to stay in town for him.

"I think you should go on out to Southampton. There's no reason for you to have to be stuck in town. You love it out there, and I'm not going to be much fun here."

"But, Peter, I haven't seen you for six long weeks. I want to be with you."

"We've got plenty of time. Besides, it will just be hot and uncomfortable here."

"Both our apartments are air-conditioned."

"What's the use of staying cooped up inside when you can be out in the sun and sea air enjoying yourself? I'd feel terribly selfish if you stayed in on my account."

"I'd be staying in on my account, too. I want to be with you."

"I'm not going anywhere. I'll be right here when you get back."

"Peter, are you trying to tell me you want to be alone?"

"I guess I am. I've got a lot of adjusting to do, Jeannie. I lost my sight and nearly lost my life. The experience turned a lot of things upside down in me, and I'm still feeling a little disoriented. I need to sort things out, and I've got to do that alone.''

"Can't I help any at all? Can't you share it with me?''

"It helps a lot knowing you're here and that you want to help, Jeannie. But there isn't anything anyone else can do because I don't even know what some of it's about myself. That's why I need time alone—to unravel what's going on.''

"All right, if you're sure.'' He heard the hurt in her voice, and saw it on her face, and he was sorry, but he couldn't handle a weekend alone with her right now, and the fact that he couldn't was disturbing in itself. In fact, he was beginning to feel restless again.

"Come on, let's go eat. I'm starving. I spent six weeks in Paris, but the food was lousy.'' He began to struggle to get out of the chair. Sitting down and getting up were the most difficult movements for him. Pulling himself up, hanging onto his crutches, put a strain on his still painful back. Jeannie saw him struggling and gave him her hand.

"Here, put your arm around my shoulder.''

"No, it's easier this way. Just takes me a minute.''

"Your back still bothers you, doesn't it?''

"Yes. But it's getting stronger. Be good as new any day now.'' He hoped what he said was true. The mending seemed to go so slowly.

"Well, I don't need to worry about you running off with some other good-looking woman, anyway.'' She grinned and gave him a flirtatious look. He knew she was wondering if they were going to sleep together tonight, and he knew he couldn't do it, regardless of his injuries. He simply didn't feel any urge to be with her, and yet the last couple of weeks in the hospital he'd thought constantly of making love to Jeannie.

"Since when have you ever worried about me running off with another woman?'' He tried for a light tone of voice. "Maybe I'm the one who should be worried.''

"Why should you be worried?'' She laughed softly.

"Well, I don't think I'm going to be much use to you in that department for a while yet. You're apt to get very bored with me.''

"I fell in love with your mind, anyway. Didn't you know that?''

She was stylish, he thought; she was letting him off easy,

and he appreciated it, but at the same time he felt guilty about letting her down. And he was already tired.

The atmosphere had been slightly strained over dinner, regardless of both their efforts to be amusing. It was a relief to get back later to his own apartment; he had a lot of thinking to do. He felt like another person, and he knew that Jeannie had sensed his distance. She hadn't said anything, but he could read the worry in her eyes. At one point she had asked him what was wrong, and he had avoided the question by saying his leg hurt. She had accepted his answer, but he knew it hadn't satisfied her concern. Actually he had been thinking of Marcy Morris at that moment and wondering how she was making out.

As he let himself into his apartment, he heard the telephone ringing. He rushed to get it, stumbled over his attaché case and nearly fell, but he got to the phone in time.

"Hello. Blanchard here."

"Hey, man! How you doin'?"

"Mike!" It was great to hear his voice.

"So you finally got out of that sick pad, huh?"

"Yep. Been back several days now."

"How're you seeing these days?"

"Good, really good. Practically normal already!"

"And the leg —how're you gimping?"

"Gimping. In fact, I'm dynamite on crutches!"

"That's cool, man."

"How's the wing?"

"Flapping! I'm beatin' the skins. Rusty as hell, but. I'm getting there."

"Say, where are you?"

"In a joint on 125th Street."

"Feel like slumming in the Sixties?"

"Got any gin?"

"A brand new bottle!"

"I'm on my way."

"Apartment 12H."

"Got it!"

Peter hung up the phone and felt elated for the first time since coming home. Mike was just what he needed. Besides, he was also a part of all he'd been through, and a kinship existed between them.

"Brother, this is some pad you got here!" Mike walked around the apartment, looking at everything.

"I used to enjoy it. Now I feel as though I don't really live here." Peter poured Mike a gin. "What would you like in this?"

"One piece of ice." Mike had picked up the photograph of Jeannie and Peter. "This you and the rich chick?"

"Yes. Taken last fall at a football game." He held the glass out to Mike.

"She's a looker."

"Yeah. Jeannie's a good-looking woman."

"Seen her?"

"This evening."

"First time?"

"Yeah." Peter answered from the liquor cabinet where he was pouring himself a Scotch.

"What's the matter? Couldn't get it up?" Mike laughed his deep, rich laugh.

"Vulgar, but accurate." He lifted his glass to Mike. "Glad to see you."

"Same here." Mike sprawled on the sofa. "So, how's everything going?"

"I'm restless enough to orbit."

"Crutches don't help."

"I guess that's some of it, but not all. Something's eating at me, Mike, and I can't put my finger on it."

"Hell man, you been through a fuckin' war. What do you expect?"

"But I'm going to be okay. My eyes are improving every day, and my leg is going to be all right. I'm back at work, where I wanted to be. But somehow nothing is right."

"How's it with the chick?"

"That's another thing. I feel almost like a stranger with her, and I'm sexually turned off."

"She know that?"

"More or less, I think. Although I tried to blame it on all that's happened, and on my injuries."

"Could have something to do with it, you know."

"There's something else, too, but like I said before, I can't put my finger on what it is."

"I ain't no shrink, man, but maybe you're trying too hard too soon. I mean, just be laid-back for a while."

"I'll buy that, but how can you feel laid-back, as you say, when you're so restless you can't sit still?"

"Take a vacation, change the scene. Get a new chick. You came back to the same old things, but you ain't the same man, Pete."

"I'm *not* the same man, that's the trouble, and I'm not sure who I am, or what I want." Peter sipped his drink. "You know, Mike, I keep thinking about Carl."

"What about him?" Mike's eyes narrowed.

"Oh—why him instead of me. And—I keep wondering if it had been the other way around and he had my eyes—what he would do. Things like that."

"That's shit thinkin', my friend! You better get your act together!"

"I keep trying to, but I don't seem to be having much luck." There was silence between them, and Mike sipped his gin while Peter stared into his glass.

"Went to see Marcy last week," Mike said finally.

"Oh? How is she?"

"Hurting. Grieving. But she's doing all right. Started to work this week."

"Doing what?"

"Seems like the lady's got a law degree. Ain't that something?"

"Well, I'll be damned."

"Met old Carl that way. She was a law clerk, just starting out in this big dude firm where he worked. But after they got hitched up and started trying to have kids, she quit. They thought that might help. Can you beat that?"

"I've heard of things like that, yeah."

"Well, didn't do no good. Anyway, she's gone back to lawyering in Carl's office."

"She's working here in the city?"

"You got it."

"I'll be damned." Peter shook his head. Marcy was full of surprises.

"Why don't you go see her, Pete?"

"I will, I will. Soon."

"I mean it, man. Maybe she can help you with your head problems. I mean, like she thinks straight."

"I'll think about it, I really will."

"What exactly is your hang-up about her anyway? I mean, she's one terrific lady."

"I know she is, Mike. The problem is me. I want to go see her and I don't want to. I think maybe it has something to do with me being able to see because Carl died."

"Pete! You are one hardheaded turkey. She don't have nothin' against you."

"I guess it's just in my head. I'll go and see her as soon as I get things squared away a little." He started to get up. "Let me get you a refill."

"Stay where you are. I can pour just as well as you can." Mike got up and went to the liquor cabinet.

"Are you getting a group together again?"

"Yeah. Found a cool guitar man yesterday."

"How long before you're in shape to play a gig?"

"Oh, maybe a month or so."

"Looking forward to it?"

"Bet your ass! This sittin' around leads to dissipation, man!" Mike came back and sat down. "Listen, Pete, why don't you hobble uptown one of these nights and listen to us cats work out?"

"You're on!" Peter saluted him with his drink.

"Now, about this rich chick—you really in trouble with her?"

"I don't know, but I think I might be. Have to wait and see, I guess."

"Time, man, give yourself some time."

"Maybe that's not the problem." Peter grinned. "I mean, maybe it's not a matter of time." Mike laughed his big laugh.

"Speaking of that very important down-to-earth matter, you didn't by any chance make out with Nice Nurse Charlotte before you left old Parec, did you?"

"Charlotte? Hell, no. Where'd you get that idea?"

"She had the hots for you, man! Thought maybe you cashed in on it."

"Mike, this is going to come as a shock to you, but being flat on my back as I was, the thought never even occurred to me."

"That crash must've really knocked the starch out of you. Better get back in practice, man." Mike looked at his watch and suddenly shot to his feet.

"Shit, I'm late! Got a chick waiting for me. Thanks for the gin. Call me when you feel like coming uptown."

"I will. Glad you came down, Mike. You're good for me."

"Father Mike, that's me."

At the door they shook hands. Mike punched Peter on the shoulder. "Don't forget to go see Marcy. She wants to see you."

"Think so?"

"She said so." Mike was out the door then, and Peter stood for a moment watching him lope down the hall. He locked the door and picked up his drink. So Marcy was working in New York. Seeing her in the city would be much easier, and he did want to see her. He'd promised Carl. He also admitted to himself that subconsciously he'd probably wanted to see her ever since coming home. He went to his desk and looked up the number of Carl's law firm in the telephone book. He made a note of it on the desk pad, then switched out the light and hobbled toward the bedroom. He was exhausted. Maybe he would be able to sleep, and maybe he would be lucky enough not to have nightmares again.

# Chapter Eleven

Eight hours later Marcy sat at her desk, twenty-four stories up in a midtown Manhattan office building, searching in the telephone book for the number of Parthenon Publishing. She found it and made a note of the number under Peter Blanchard's name. Mike had said Peter was back, and that he was seeing well. Since Mike had told her that, she'd felt the same strong urgency to see Peter that she'd felt in Paris. She wanted to see him, at least once, to look into his eyes. Not a day passed without her remembering that a part of Carl was still alive in Peter. Something, however, kept her from placing the call to Peter. She knew that one day she would have to use the number she had just written down, but it would keep until that time.

Peter was at that moment lunching with Jeannie at Côte Basque and trying to explain once again the strangeness he'd been feeling since coming back to New York. He'd also tried several times to talk to her about how he felt at having Carl's sight, and his conflict about going to see Marcy, toward whom he felt a responsibility.

Jeannie listened patiently, then finally said: "Darling, you've talked constantly about how strange you feel having that man's eyes. Don't you think maybe you're becoming a little obsessed? I understand that it must be difficult to adjust to all that's happened, and that you might feel strange about the man's eyes, even feel a responsibility toward his wife, but what I don't understand is why you're letting it affect our relationship the way you are."

"How is it affecting our relationship?" He was instantly on the defensive.

"Peter, you are withdrawn, restless, moody, irritable. It seems as if our relationship is falling apart."

"Jeannie, darling, it's not easy to come back to the way things were when you're not the same anymore." He spoke quietly, anxious to explain, but aware that he couldn't explain what he himself did not understand.

"Yes, I know it's not easy, and I expected a period of adjustment, if that's what you want to call it."

"But it's more than that. I'm alive and I can see. I owe something for that, but I don't know what. All I know is, I can't get it out of my mind that I'm alive and a lot of other people, my fellow passengers, are dead. Why? And I can see because Carl Morris died."

"But, Peter, you're not responsible for any of those things. You're acting as if it were somehow your fault, and you're feeling guilty that you're alive and others aren't. And you even seem to feel guilty about being able to see again because Carl Morris died and chose to leave you his eyes."

"Well, I guess I do feel a little guilty, but I think you're exaggerating. I'm not letting it ruin my life, I'm just trying to get my bearings. I have to put everything that's happened to me into a perspective I can live with."

"I don't want to be insensitive to your feelings, darling, but I do wish you could make some peace within yourself about it, because our relationship is suffering. In fact, right now we don't have a relationship."

"How can you say that?" He felt indignant and misunderstood.

"Peter, you've been back two weeks, and you've—you've hardly touched me." She smoked nervously and stared down at the table.

"Jeannie, don't you think I know that? I feel badly about it, but my injuries are barely healed, and I'm still in a lot of pain. It—it just takes the romance out of me. Getting through the day is about all I can handle." He tried to keep the resentment out of his voice, but she was making him feel guilty—and trapped.

"That may be so, but what do you think it's like for me being with you? I don't feel you love me. Oh, you're polite, and attentive—but you're almost a stranger. Peter, you act more like a casual acquaintance than a lover."

"Now, that's absurd!" he protested, but what she said was essentially true. How could he admit it, though, without hurting her deeply and really putting the relationship in jeopardy.

"No, Peter, it is not absurd, it's the truth. I don't know what to do. Whatever I do, you don't seem to notice me as—as a woman." She looked at him and there were tears in her eyes.

"Jeannie, Jeannie, honey"—he took her hand. "I certainly notice you as a woman. It's just that I don't feel like a lover, but that has nothing to do with you. It's whatever is going on inside me. But I think it's a phase and it will pass, if you can just be patient with me for a little while."

"You know what I think, Peter?"

"What do you think?"

"I think you're becoming obsessed with Carl Morris—and his wife. Why don't you go and see her and get it out of your mind? You keep talking about her being alone, and the responsibility you feel toward her, but you don't do anything about it. So, go and see her. Maybe it will make you feel better."

"Yes, you're right, I will go and see her."

"You've got to do something. I see your restlessness, and your unhappiness, and it makes me feel dreadful that I can't help."

"Okay. I'll go and see Marcy, and I'll try and get my act together."

"You've got to, darling. For your sake, and for our sake. Because if you keep on this way, you're going to crack."

"Oh, come on, I'm not that bad." He was suddenly annoyed and impatient with her.

"Apparently you don't see yourself objectively. Your moods are up and down and subject to change on a moment's notice. You've never been this way before. You're always been even-tempered and sane, but since you've been back, you're almost the opposite."

"Now I'm insane, huh?" He heard the defensiveness in his voice, but he was too tired to be diplomatic.

"No, you're not insane, but you act very strange at times, and I wonder if maybe you shouldn't see a therapist to help you adjust to being alive and having Carl's corneas."

"Oh, so now you're trying to pack me off to some shrink's couch!"

"You know better than that. I'm concerned about you, and about us. But, Peter—you seem more concerned about Carl Morris's wife than you are about me."

"Now that really does it! You're jealous of a woman I've never even seen." He was getting angry, and he suddenly realized that he wanted to be angry.

"But you know her quite well anyway. You've told me about your talks with her in Paris, and the closeness you felt."

"Well, of course, we went through some traumatic experiences there and we were able to share our thoughts and help one another. Same thing with Mike. I suppose you're jealous of him, too?"

"Now you're being unreasonable and twisting what I've said." She stubbed out her cigarette. "I'm going back to work now, but I suggest you think seriously about what I've said. Because I don't think I can stand very much more of this. You're gone for six weeks and come home a stranger. Do you really expect me not to feel anything about that?"

"No. I expected you to feel disappointed and hurt, but I hoped you'd understand my confusion. I don't know what's wrong, Jeannie."

"Then I think you'd better see somebody about it." She picked up her handbag. "I've got to get back to the office." She stood up.

"Jeannie?"

"Yes?" She looked down at him, and he saw the deep hurt in her eyes.

"Don't give up on me, Jeannie. I'll do everything I can to work it out."

"I hope so, Peter."

"I'll call you tonight."

"Thanks for lunch." She turned and walked out of the restaurant. He watched her go with mixed emotions: on the one hand he was concerned about her and afraid of losing her; and on the other hand he was angry at what he considered her insensitivity to his turmoil and her superficiality in attaching so much importance to their sex life. It was true that they'd always been very active sexually, and it had been extremely satisfying, but there were more important elements of their relationship to be examined at this stage.

He signaled the waiter for the check, and while he waited for his change, he found himself sinking into a kind of depression. By the time he limped out into the sunlight, he was feeling rotten. He dreaded going back to the office. He stood on the curb trying to hail a taxi with one of his crutches and almost lost his balance. He swore aloud as he gripped a lamppost. He finally got a taxi driver's attention and painfully eased himself into the back seat. He gave the address of his office and tried to get comfortable. As the taxi turned onto Park Avenue, he suddenly knew that he was not going back to the office. He didn't feel like sitting in his office and doing the work waiting for him, but what did he feel like doing? He had no idea at the moment, and was, in fact, somewhat shocked at himself. Peter had always been the first to arrive at the office in the morning and was usually the last to leave. He loved his work and had a driving ambition to succeed, but somehow this afternoon that didn't matter at all.

But what was he going to do with his afternoon? Suddenly he thought he'd like to go to the Central Park Zoo. He wanted to look at animals that really were captive and study how they coped with their frustration. He leaned forward and tapped on the glass divider. When he'd told the driver where he wanted to go he suddenly began to laugh. The idea of going to the zoo amused him. And after the zoo he thought he would go to the Metropolitan Museum and look at the Temple of Dendur, the gift from the Egyptian government, and sit and watch the sun fade on the rough stone as it stood majestically exposed under its great glass housing. And after that he would know where he wanted to go, but of one thing he was quite certain: he would not be going back to his office that day. He couldn't remember feeling so free since he'd played hooky in grammar school.

At six thirty that evening, after a thoroughly indulgent afternoon, Peter got out of a taxi at Fifth Avenue and Fifty-eighth Street and limped toward the side entrance of the Plaza Hotel. He had decided to keep his dinner date in the Oak Room with one of his authors because the man was a science-fiction writer and it was a wonderful subject for escapists. As he crossed the street and passed by the Pulitzer Fountain, a man and woman dressed in evening clothes came out of the Plaza and stood under the marquee waiting for a taxi. The woman was exceptionally tall, deeply tanned, blond, and he could see even from a distance that she was beautiful. Also there was something familiar about her, but he was certain he had never met her; one did not forget a woman like that. Yet he felt almost irresistibly drawn to her; his pulse began to quicken. He hurried to cross the street. A taxi pulled up to discharge passengers and he knew the couple would take that taxi. He panicked and tried to run, but his leg gave way and he nearly fell.

"Marcy!" He called out to her just as she was about to step into the taxi. She turned around and looked in his direction. "Marcy Morris," he repeated, speaking her name without conscious awareness, and then he was standing on the sidewalk near her.

"Yes?"

He saw a quizzical look cross her face, and then their eyes met, and they stood paralyzed, staring at one another. He felt his heart quicken with an almost electric excitement.

"Peter?" she said softly.

"Yes," he answered.

She began to walk toward him, her eyes holding his, and his heart began to pound so loudly it almost deafened him. She stopped in front of him and they looked at one another silently.

"How did you know me?"

"I don't know," he replied, and they went on looking at one another, not speaking, searching each other's eyes. He knew what was in her mind: she was looking for Carl in his eyes, and the look reached down into his soul. What he did not know was that Marcy's excitement was equal to his own. "I've been meaning to call," he whispered. His throat was suddenly dry and full, and he wasn't certain he could speak.

"Yes. So have I."

"Marcy—" Her escort stood by the open door of the taxi. "We're going to be late."

"A moment," she replied without taking her eyes from Peter's.

"I didn't know you were so beautiful," he said.

"How are you?" she asked, and he knew that she cared about the answer.

"Okay. Still a little lame."

"Is it painful?"

"Yes."

"I'm sorry."

"How are you?"

"Getting along."

"Does it hurt very much?"

"Yes, it does." He saw tears well up in her eyes but she controlled them.

"May I come and see you?"

"Please."

"Marcy, dear." The man came over to her. "I'm terribly sorry, but we must hurry now."

"Oh." For the first time she took her eyes away from Peter. "Adam, this is Peter Blanchard. "Peter this is Adam Newhouse, my husband—Carl's law partner." The two men shook hands and made polite responses. "I'm sorry we must go," said Newhouse.

"Of course. Don't let me keep you." Peter watched her turn back toward the cab. She took a few steps, then turned and looked back at him.

"You won't forget?"

"No. I won't forget," he replied. She got into the taxi and he stood in the same spot and watched them drive off. When the taxi turned the corner onto Fifth Avenue, he experienced a sense of overwhelming loss. He shook his head almost violently to clear it, and limped up the steps and into the hotel. He went straight to the bar in the Oak Room and ordered a double Scotch. When he lifted the glass, his hand was shaking enough to cause the ice in the glass to rattle. He had felt the great love Marcy felt for her husband, felt it projected onto himself for a brief moment, and it was a powerfully moving experience.

As he began to grow calmer, reality hit him. How had he known her? For he had known her instantly and without question. Had he unconsciously been looking for her since Mike told him she was in the city every day? Still, looking for her did not explain away the fact that he had known her without ever having set eyes on her before. But it was not his eyes that had seen her now—not really; it was Carl Morris's sight that had seen her. Carl certainly knew his wife. The thought was shattering, and what Mike would call "shit thinking." He gulped down the drink and was about to order another when someone tapped him on the shoulder.

"Turning into a solitary drinker these days, Peter?" It was Robert Webber, the author he was to meet.

"Oh, hi, Bob. No, fact is I just had an extraordinary experience outside the hotel. I'm afraid it shook me up."

"Is it a secret?"

"Not really, but it wouldn't make a lot of sense to anyone else."

"Try me."

"Well, I just saw a woman I've never seen before, and I called her by name. I knew her."

"Total stranger?"

"Not exactly. I met her a few times when I was in the hospital in Paris after the crash. But I was blind then. I never saw what she looked like."

"Maybe you met in another life." Had Bob Webber not been a fine fiction writer who just happened to believe in all kinds of strange and supernatural occurrences, Peter might have thought he was being facetious.

"You're not kidding, are you?"

"No, I'm not. It's possible. It's also possible that she recognized you, and if you have very strong ESP, you may have received her message of recognition."

"No, I don't think so. She hadn't seen me when I called her name. She was getting into a taxi." Peter was quiet for a moment, thinking about what Bob had said about ESP. "Tell me, Bob, what do you know about possession?" he asked.

"Possession? What kind?"

"Where the will of someone departed inhabits that of a living person, or maybe tries to." Peter had never even voiced to himself the idea that Carl might be trying to influence his actions, but somewhere in the back of his mind the idea had begun to peck away at him.

"Heavy, Peter."

"You're telling me. But aside from that . . ." Peter let his sentence trail off.

"One hears stories. I can't give you any hard evidence of it happening, but I suppose it's possible. I think the receiver would have to be open though. I don't think it could be forced on someone. But you know, people used to believe that the devil could possess, could will someone to do his work. That's what all the witch trials in history were about. I suppose some people still believe that the devil can possess. But what's on your mind.''

"It's just an interesting idea, that's all. Thought I'd ask you. You're the expert on that sort of thing.'' Peter had decided not to discuss the matter any further. He had to work with Robert, and he didn't believe in mixing personal matters into a working relationship. He'd said enough already, and now that the Scotch had done its work in relaxing him somewhat, he wanted to change the subject. "Come on, let's get a table and sit down.'' Peter signaled the maître d'.

"How's the leg?''

"Getting better. But that's enough about me. I want to hear about this new book of yours.'' Peter knew from long experience that the best way to divert an author's attention from any subject was to ask about the writer's current book.

When Peter arrived home that evening, he was more emotionally shaken than he could ever remember being in his entire life. The experience of recognizing Marcy, and the thought that Carl might be trying to tamper with his life, were more than he could deal with. He mixed himself a drink and sat down to think about it all. He could see Marcy's face as if she stood before him. God, she was lovely, and there was something so warm and open and comforting about her face that he felt good just looking at her. But *how* had he known her? Some way, somehow, he had known it was Marcy the moment she came out of the hotel. There had to be a logical explanation, and yet there wasn't any. He thought of the old cliché about people being soul mates. That was how he felt about her, and for some reason he had the impression that she had felt the same thing: that they recognized more than each others' faces.

Had he possibly met her somewhere, sometime before all this happened? Perhaps he'd even met her before she married Carl. If that had been the case, however, he wouldn't have known her by the name of Morris. Whatever the answer was didn't matter; what did matter was that he had seen her, and recognized her, and he had to see her again soon. He had to talk to her about the meeting at the Plaza, and find out what she felt about it. What was it Mike had said about her? Oh yes, he had said she might be able to help him with his dilemma about Carl. Well, maybe Mike was right, maybe she could. After all, Mike had also said she wanted to see him.

Having seen her at last, and having made the decision to see her again as soon as possible, he felt calmer than he had since coming back to New York. Could his restlessness have been somehow related to Marcy? He didn't know, but that plaguing restlessness which had churned inside him since coming home was miraculously stilled. In fact he felt better than he had before the crash. Of course he knew that he and Marcy had been destined to meet after Paris because of Carl's eyes; yet whatever it was that caused him to know her tonight had to do only with her, not with her as Carl's wife. Somehow he knew he was on the threshold of a turning point in his life, and Marcy fitted into it in some important way.

# Chapter Twelve

Lincoln Center was festive on this warm summer evening. It was opening night of the Joffrey Ballet's season with Rudolf Nureyev dancing an *Homage to Diaghlev*. As Marcy and Adam rushed across the mall to the New York State Theater, she felt a sense of excitement. She particularly liked the ballet, and Adam, finding himself at loose ends with his wife and children at the Cape, had suggested they attend. He thought it might cheer her up, and it had. In fact anticipation of the evening had kept her buoyed up all day. But that anticipation had been overshadowed by the surprise meeting with Peter outside the Plaza.

Strange—even eerie—that he should know her. Thinking back on their meeting tonight brought an uneasy feeling along with the excitement, because there was no logical explanation for what had happened. Perhaps he might have remembered her voice and recognized it. But when she'd asked him how he knew her, he had replied that he didn't know. How to explain it? Perhaps he was a man with extraordinary awarenesses, or perhaps he was especially attuned to extrasensory perception.

"Come on, Marcy, we're going to miss the curtain and have to stand through the first ballet," said Adam, hurrying her along.

The conductor appeared just as they took their seats, and

she quickly opened the program to read the notes on the first ballet. She hadn't quite finished when the overture began and the house lights went out. She was soon caught up in the electrifying movements of Nureyev on stage. But despite the fascinating images on stage, her thoughts kept returning to Peter and the unanswered question. Finally she made a supreme effort to clear her mind and turn her full attention to Nureyev. As she watched, suddenly her eyes seemed to be playing tricks on her; Peter's face had begun to appear over the images on stage; that interesting, almost handsome face was staring at her with Carl's sight. The sudden appearance of his image caught her by surprise, and momentarily she felt disoriented; in fact she found that she was holding her breath, hardly daring to breathe. Then all the features of his face faded out, and only the eyes were left. They looked directly at her, as if trying to speak to her, tell her something, hold her captive. Slowly a familiar feeling of Carl's presence came over her, and she felt close to him, no longer alone. She welcomed the feeling, and then the image began to fade, and the dancers came back into focus.

The return of reality was unwelcome, even a frightening intrusion. What is happening to me? she thought. She remembered the dream of Carl's eyes in Paris, and she began to rub her eyes as though to do so would make her see more clearly, or make the disturbing images go away. She started to tremble, and a feeling of claustrophobia came over her. She longed to get up and dash out into the night, and run, and run, and run! But where would she run to? The answer came back immediately: to Peter Blanchard, of course. She wanted to look into his face and find Carl in his eyes. No, no! she cried silently. I must not think these thoughts.

"Marcy, are you all right?" asked Adam.

"Yes. Yes, I'm fine," she lied. How could she possibly sit through the rest of the ballet? She concentrated all her willpower on putting the thoughts out of her mind, but they would not go away. Peter's face reappeared, just as before, and his eyes seemed to struggle to communicate some thought to her. This time, however, the eyes grew larger and larger, blocking out his features. What was it his eyes were trying to tell her? Oh God, she pleaded, what is the meaning of this, what does he want of me? She told the eyes to go away, she willed them to disappear, but they remained. She became frightened, then panicked. Adam had sensed her discomfort and was watching her.

"Marcy, what's wrong?" he whispered.

"I must leave," she whispered back.

*"What?"*

"I must!" She had risen. Adam stood up. "No, you stay," she said.

"Sit down!" someone behind them hissed. Marcy moved into the aisle and began to run. She ran to the door where a startled usher tried to say something to her, but she brushed past the woman and pushed through the door. She ran down the corridor to the stairs. Finally, outside the theater, she stopped and tried to catch her breath. The warm night air, the sound of traffic, and the rushing lights helped to clear her head. She struggled to get hold of herself and fixed her eyes on the Chagall murals at either side of the entrance to the Metropolitan Opera. She felt bewildered and shocked at her own behavior.

"Marcy, what on earth is it?" Adam was standing in front of her, a look of deep concern on his face.

"Please go back," she said.

"You can't be serious."

"I'm so sorry, Adam."

"Marcy, please stop apologizing and tell me what it is."

"It's the man we saw."

"What man?"

"The man at the Plaza."

"Oh, that man. What about him?"

"He has Carl's eyes."

"Carl's eyes?"

"I never told you. Carl gave his eyes to him."

"How do you know?"

"I was there."

"You were there?"

"Yes. At the hospital in Paris. His name is Peter Blanchard. Carl became friendly with him on the plane over."

"But I don't understand."

She was beginning to feel calmer. "Peter was blinded, something about contact lenses, and when Carl found out he was going to die, he had a lawyer draw up a paper leaving his eyes to Peter. This evening at the Plaza was the first time I'd seen Peter with Carl's eyes."

"I don't know if that's legal."

"Adam, for God's sake, the man already has Carl's eyes."

"Oh, yes, I'm sorry. I forgot myself." Adam was quiet for a moment. "Well, my God, no wonder you're upset."

"I met him at the hospital but he was blind during that time. Tonight he recognized me. And Adam, he'd never *seen* me."

"That's impossible!"

"But he did, Adam."

"Yes, well—I'll be damned!"

"I kept seeing his face all during the ballet, and his eyes—Carl's eyes." She felt tears in her throat again. "I couldn't make the image go away."

"Well, no wonder you're upset. Do you want me to take you home?"

"Would you mind terribly?"

"Of course not." He took her arm and they walked across the mall, then down the steps and across to Broadway to hail a cab. The lights of the rushing traffic, the horns and the noise were all welcome distractions.

In the taxi on the way home she tried to explain to Adam how she felt about a living part of Carl being in another person. He listened, but she knew that no matter how sympathetic he was, his good, logical legal mind could not really grasp the significance of her meeting Peter tonight.

"You're overwrought, Marcy. You've been through a great deal these past few weeks, and you're still in something of a state of shock. Just try to get it into perspective, and don't let this throw you."

"I know you're right, Adam, but I can't get over how he knew me."

"Maybe you should take some time off. Go away somewhere, get away from everything that reminds you of Carl."

Adam meant well, but she knew it would be impossible to go away so soon. She would only take her grief with her. No, she had to stay here and learn to live with it, and with the fact that Peter Blanchard had Carl's eyes.

Peter made himself wait two days before telephoning Marcy. Waiting was about the most difficult thing he'd ever had to do, but he had some thinking to do before he saw her, and he wanted to take his time about it.

On the morning of the third day he telephoned and invited her to lunch, but she suggested dinner instead. She explained that it would give them more time to talk, but he suspected that she was afraid she might be upset by seeing him. He had welcomed her suggestion for dinner, as well as her suggestion that they meet somewhere other than the small apartment where she lived during the working weeks. They made a date to meet at the Café du Parc of the Stanhope Hotel on Fifth Avenue, across from the Metropolitan Museum of Art.

He arrived early at the Stanhope so Marcy would not have to sit alone waiting for him. He took a table under the canopy, ordered a wine spritzer, and made a concentrated effort to quiet the anxiety he found rising at the thought of seeing her again. He tried to occupy his mind by deciding where to take her for dinner. He thought of Tavern-on-the-Green in Central Park; that outdoor setting seemed a better place than the intimate atmosphere and confined space of a midtown restaurant. At the Tavern-on-the-Green they could look out at the trees in the park.

He checked his watch and saw that she was slightly late. He began to be afraid she might not appear, then dismissed the idea, for it didn't seem like her to stand him up. He began to study the facade of the museum across the street with its colorful exhibition banners flying, and the gushing jets of water rising from the fountains. It was a pleasant, almost peaceful atmosphere, with lovers strolling hand in hand under the trees, and men, women, and children walking their dogs along the avenue. He became so involved in watching the promenaders that he did not see Marcy arrive.

"Peter?" she said, and he looked up to see her smiling down at him. He felt a heady kind of excitement at the sight of her.

"Marcy!" He stood up, almost knocking over his chair. "I'm sorry I didn't see you come in." They stood looking at one another, and he felt the excitement building in him as her eyes met his.

"Can—can I get you something?" he stammered.

"Could we sit down?" She eased into a chair, feeling weak in the knees. He sat across from her.

"I have to tell you, I'm a little nervous," he managed to say.

"So am I."

"Why is it?" he asked.

"Because of Carl." The answer came back strong and clear.

"Yes, I suppose so."

"Peter, I have to ask you something."

"Yes, I know: how did I know you?"

"Yes." Her eyes were direct and searching.

"I knew you'd ask, and I've asked myself the same question a hundred times, but I don't know, Marcy."

"I must tell you that it was a disturbing experience, seeing you suddenly like that, and having you know me. I've thought of little else since it happened."

"Same here."

"Would the lady like something?" asked the waiter.

"Marcy, what would you like?"

"Maybe what you're having?"

"I'm having white wine and soda," he said, and she nodded approval. When the waiter had left, Peter took out a cigarette and fumbled with the lighter; his hands were shaking. She noticed and smiled sympathetically.

"I—I guess it's natural." He laughed apologetically, trying to avoid her eyes.

"It's a strange feeling—seeing your face—your eyes." She paused; her voice gave away her emotion. "I can't stop looking at you." He looked at her then, and she tried to smile. He smiled back, not knowing what to say to her and feeling mixed emotions himself.

"Do you—uh, do you see Carl's eyes in mine?" He had to ask.

"No, they don't look like his. I—I did wonder about that, though."

"So did I. I wondered if my eyes would look different to me."

"But I know that you're seeing me with his sight, so to speak, and that is rather disconcerting."

"That's disturbing to me, too."

"How?"

"Well—I don't know if I'm seeing with my own perception—or—or—"

"Or Carl's?" She finished his sentence.

"Yes. Sometimes I almost feel like a different person." It

was the first time he'd actually verbalized that thought. He shifted restlessly in his chair, suddenly uneasy.

"It must be very difficult for you. I haven't thought much about what it might be like for you, I'm afraid."

"I'm trying to get used to it. But mainly it's great to see again." He was quiet for a moment then, and she looked down at her hands on the table. He debated how much he ought to tell her about his own feelings because it might be upsetting to her to hear his thoughts about possessing Carl's eyes. "I'm trying to have a healthy attitude about the transplants, but psychologically it's a little difficult to deal with."

"I suppose that's to be expected."

"Yes." He was quiet again. "How are you doing?"

"Oh—sometimes I can forget—for about ten minutes." She looked down at her hands again. "I'm awfully restless—something I've never been before. I—I guess I'm trying to run away from grief, and there's nowhere to run."

"I'm restless, too. But oddly enough, I don't feel nearly so restless since I saw you at the Plaza. It was as though I were waiting to see you, and once I'd seen you, and knew you were in the city, the restlessness let up."

"What are you saying?" A look of concern crossed her face.

"I don't really know. All I do know is, you have a very important place in my life now. I—I feel drawn to you." He felt embarrassed, almost as though he'd confessed some dark secret.

"I feel drawn to you, too," she said quietly. "If you hadn't called soon, I would have called you." It was her turn to feel embarrassed. "I—I knew I had to see you again."

"Did you know that Carl asked me, through Mike, to go and see you?"

"I didn't know."

"Marcy, forgive me if this seems insensitive or out of line, but do you think Carl wanted us to be friends?" She didn't answer at once, and he wondered if he'd said the wrong thing after all. He started to apologize, but the waiter arrived with the spritzer. She picked up the glass and sipped it thoughtfully while he waited.

"Perhaps Carl did want us to be friends. He asked me to go and see you in the hospital, and he kept asking me if I liked you."

"Well—did you?" He laughed softly, to ease the tension building up. She looked up at him then and smiled. It was a warm, open smile, and he knew that smile was just for him.

"Yes, I did. It was such a difficult time, but yes, I must have, because I kept coming back to see you, and I like you now."

"Thank you." He lit another cigarette and was relieved to see that his hands were steadier now.

"How are your other injuries?"

"I'm walking better. The doctor tells me I'm mending well."

"And the eyes?" She paused. "You're seeing well?"

"Almost entirely normal."

"I'm so glad."

"Marcy, I've wanted to see you ever since I got back, not just since the other night at the Plaza." He was feeling embarrassed again, but he wanted to be honest with her; he felt that was the only way they might be of any help to one another. "In fact the urge to see you was so intense at times, it almost amounted to a compulsion."

"I understand. I've had something of the same kind of compulsion."

"Oh, well, good. I don't feel so embarrassed by telling you."

"Why would you feel embarrassed?"

"Well, it is a delicate area, Marcy. You see, one of the reasons I didn't go ahead and call you—well, I've been asking myself why Carl died instead of me? Why did I survive instead of him. And I'm seeing today because Carl is dead. I didn't know what feelings you might have about that."

Her eyes opened very wide and she looked at him in surprise. "Did you really think I'd resent you because of that?"

"It would be perfectly understandable if you did."

"Well, I don't. I can honestly say the thought has never occurred to me. I guess I'm too much of a fatalist. I know it was just Carl's time." She paused, then added thoughtfully, "There has to be some reason why God took Carl instead of you, and I've accepted that."

"I don't know that I'd feel so generous if our positions were reversed. But I have to tell you that I feel I ought to make my life count for something important. I have to earn this second chance at life. In a sense I've got two lives to make up for, and I can't take that lightly.''

"I'm sure *your* life counts for a lot, Peter.''

"Oh, I'm not trying to put myself down. But I've taken stock since the accident, and I think I was a pretty smug, selfish guy before. I was ambitious and wrapped up in my work. I haven't spent much time thinking about the more serious things, like what I was doing with my life, and what I really wanted out of it besides success. Or what I wanted from others, and what I myself was willing to give to others. I do know one thing: in a lot of ways I'm a different guy since all this happened. I don't know exactly why, and I don't know exactly who I am now.''

"Only a very superficial man could go through what you've been through and not be different, Peter.''

"Sometimes I wake up at night in a cold sweat, realizing how close I came to death. It does something to your insides to know that, and for some reason it's difficult to make people who are close to you understand that everything inside you is in turmoil, and you don't know how you feel about much of anything anymore.''

"I think being alone for a while is one way of bridging that difficult period—that period in which you're trying to get your balance and know where you are and who you are. It's easier being alone, because you can think better, and be still enough to hear your own feelings. And you avoid hurting another person who might feel rejected.''

"That's absolutely right. Why can't people understand that?''

"Because they don't know you anymore, and it disturbs their balance, too. They don't know how to read you, or what your feelings about them are. It's a trying time for them, too.''

"You're so sane, so reasonable. You make it seem so normal somehow.''

"I think it is normal, Peter.''

"You know, I feel very close to you, Marcy.''

"I'm glad, because I feel close to you, too.'' They looked at one another for a moment, and Peter could not read what her expression meant.

"You know, Marcy, you've not really told me very much

127

about yourself—what you're feeling, what you're going to do.''

"I don't know. I've been thinking about it, and I haven't gotten much beyond going back to work. I need to be out in the mainstream of life, to talk to people, exchange ideas, know about their lives.''

"I hope you feel you can talk to me.''

"I feel that I can.'' She looked at him and smiled softly.

"Will you let me help you if there's anything I can do?''

"Yes. I'm sure the time will come.'' Again there was the searching look in her eyes.

"You're looking for Carl again, aren't you?'' He had to ask it, and she lowered her eyes and didn't answer for a few moments.

"I suppose I am. Do you mind very much?''

"Let's say that I understand, but it's a little hard to get used to.'' The fact was, he did mind very much, but he realized that he was being selfish, insensitive, and unreasonable in feeling resentment at her looking for Carl in his eyes.

"If only we had had children. It would be easier if some part of Carl had been left.''

"Carl told me on the plane how much you both had wanted children.''

"He did?''

"Yes. In fact he was thinking about how alone you'd be if anything ever happened to him. This was when we knew the plane was going to have to make a crash landing.''

"That always bothered him. I don't know why, because it wasn't his fault any more than it was mine, that we didn't have children. The doctors assured us we were all right, but somehow we just couldn't make it happen. We hadn't given up though. We still hoped.''

"And the thing he feared most happened before you succeeded.''

"Yes.'' That searching look was back in her eyes, and he knew that she wanted desperately to make some contact with Carl. Why did he have to have the only living part of Carl left in his own head?

"Come on, let's go have some dinner.'' He was feeling uncomfortable for the first time, and he thought she must have read it in his eyes because she said:

"Are you sure you want to, Peter?''

"Why not?" He tried to sound light and easy.

"Well—it must not be very comfortable to have me staring at you."

"You're a beautiful woman, Marcy. Any man would be glad to have you look at him the way you're looking at me."

"Even if the woman's reasons are neurotic and selfish?"

"Do you feel you're being neurotic, Marcy?" His voice was gentle.

"A little, and I guess I'm afraid of becoming too attached to you. I do feel comforted by your presence, though. It—it seems like I've always known you," she said shyly.

"That's good enough for me," he replied. But was it? Was he similarly in danger of becoming too attached to Marcy? Would he come to resent her thinking of Carl every time she looked at him? "Come on," he said, getting up. "Let's go get some dinner."

# Chapter Thirteen

---

Peter allowed several days to go by before he called Jeannie again. It was becoming more and more apparent that despite all the excuses he could find for his fading interest in Jeannie, they were, in fact, facing a crisis in their relationship, a crisis that had to be talked out.

She had been delighted with his dinner invitation, but insisted on making dinner for him at her apartment. It was not what he wanted to do—a quiet restaurant would provide a better atmosphere for objective discussion—however, he had given in to her wishes. But from the moment he arrived at her apartment, he realized that it was not going to be easy to have the discussion he wanted. She was charming, seductive, and extremely affectionate, and he decided to try to relax; maybe she could rekindle his ardor. He hoped so, for he was more fragmented than ever, and Marcy was constantly on his mind. If Jeannie could make him want her again, perhaps they could work out their relationship and he could get his life back into some kind of order.

"Peter?"

"Yes." He became aware that she was calling his name.

"Penny for your thoughts?"

"Oh, I was thinking how lovely you look tonight."

"Far be it from me to turn down such a delicious compliment, but you seemed thousands of miles away."

"I'm cultivating a look of studied indifference for business purposes." He smiled his boyish smile.

"Do me a favor?" She curled up on the sofa beside him.

"Anything."

"Leave it at the office?"

"You got it."

"Have I, Peter?" She pulled her knees up under her and turned to look into his eyes. Her face had sobered from the playful smile she wore a few moments before.

"Surely you're not beginning to doubt that fatal Wharton charm?" He laughed softly, trying to keep the tone light, for he could see where she was headed.

"Well, it hasn't worked very well on you lately."

"It has nothing to do with your charm, my darling; it's strictly my battered libido." It was difficult for him to see her doubting her own womanhood, and it was all his fault: he had done that to her. Somehow he had to give her back the self-assurance his indifference had taken away for her.

"Can't I help to repair your libido?" She leaned forward and kissed him lightly on the lips, then again, more provocatively.

"Umm, you just might at that," he replied softly. She was launching her campaign, and although he felt no stirrings of desire, he pulled her head down on his shoulder and put his arm about her.

"Do you have any idea how much I missed you while you were over there?"

"Yes. I've an idea by how much I missed you."

"You never told me." She snuggled closer to him. "It would have helped to know it. I was terribly hurt because you wouldn't let me come over."

"I'm sorry, Jeannie, but you do understand why now, don't you?"

"Yes. I understand how you felt, but I'm sorry you thought I couldn't take it."

"Let's not talk about the past. It's all over and we're together again. It's more important to think about our future." Perhaps this was a good time to try and talk about their relationship.

"I don't want to think about the future right now, I just want to enjoy this moment, and this evening, and this night—if you don't mind?"

"Suits me." Well, that was that. Talk of their relationship was obviously going to have to wait. "Do you suppose I could have a nightcap?"

"Does that mean you're staying?" She turned around to look at him.

"If I'm welcome."

"Do you have to ask?"

"A gentleman never takes a lady for granted." He smiled, and she returned the smile happily.

"See how aggressive I've become in your absence!" She jumped to her feet and moved across the room toward the bar.

"A very racy female, that's what you are!" he teased. She grabbed a pillow from a chair and tossed it back over her shoulder at him. "And violent, too!" he added, catching the pillow.

Lying in bed beside her later, he felt her naked warmth against him and it felt good. He began to kiss her, and desire stirred faintly inside him, although it was nothing like the hunger he used to feel.

"Welcome home," she said and laughed softly into his ear. He felt her breasts pressing against his bare chest, and that too felt good. He began to fondle one of her nipples, and it came up taut and hard under his touch. He slid down to take it into his mouth, caressing her other breast at the same time. He kissed her breast, sucked it, teased it with his teeth; he felt her body tensing with desire and her hands exploring his own body. Again there were stirrings but no passion.

She touched him between his legs and found him limp; she stroked him but nothing happened. He knew then that is was going to be a disaster and that he should not have gotten into bed with her, but there hadn't seemed any way to avoid it without hurting her more deeply than he already had. He used every fantasy he'd ever invented to try and make it happen, but it was no use. Suddenly he felt panicky and wanted to jump out of bed, put his clothes on, and go home, but he certainly could not do that. It was devastating enough to a woman to find that she was unable to arouse passion in her lover, but for him to be unable to produce an erection was the ultimate rejection.

"Jeannie, it's my back," he lied.

"I don't think so, darling." She gave a deep sigh of resignation, and guilt came down on him like a sudden shower.

They had been lovers, and passionate lovers for two years, and now to feel nothing but affectionate regret, and guilt at failing her, was equally shattering to him. What was wrong with him? Why couldn't he respond to her as a man?

She started to move away from him, but he pulled her into his arms and held her close. He felt tears spill onto his shoulder but she made no sound. He felt more miserable then he'd ever felt in his life. He touched her between her legs and began to manipulate her with his fingers. At first she was unresponsive, then he felt her relax and she moaned softly. He moved to kiss her there, and that brought a cry of pleasure. She placed her hands on his head and pressed it deeper between her legs. He stroked her center of pleasure with his tongue; entered her with it and felt her abdomen contract. Her breathing quickened.

"Oh, Peter, yes—yes. It's so good, don't stop!" He held the pleasure bud between his lips and attacked it with his tongue until she began to move with his rhythm. Gently he put his fingers into her and kept up the rhythm. She came with a cry of pleasure and release. He moved quickly to cover her body with his own, and to hold her in his arms until the spasm subsided.

"Oh, darling, I've missed you," she whispered and locked her arms about him. The panic, the urge to escape, came rushing back in on him again. He had ceased to think at all as he'd made love to her, had concentrated only on giving her pleasure, but now his mind was churning wildly. How could he escape?

"I'm here now. Relax and enjoy it." He laughed softly, willing his mind to stop working, hoping she might fall asleep. He stroked her hair and face.

"I'm sorry about you," she whispered.

"Don't talk now." He continued to caress her, feeling a burden of guilt for his dishonesty. After a time she did sleep, but not before he'd fought down wave after wave of panic. His nerves were strung out and screaming, and he knew he would not be able to last much longer. He began to pray that she would sleep; over and over he prayed, trying to occupy his mind and control the panic. Finally he heard her breathing change, and he knew she was really asleep. He slowly eased off her and got out of bed.

He threw on the robe she kept there for him, then went into

the living room and headed straight for the liquor cabinet where he poured himself a straight Scotch. He lit a cigarette and walked out onto the terrace. Some air might clear his head. What was he going to do? He stood looking out over New York, the question hanging in the night air. Suddenly New York seemed just another dirty, hot city to him, not the city he loved. He felt like a stranger here, but he knew New York had not lost its magic for him; he still loved it, it was just that he didn't like himself right now.

He took a sip of Scotch and let it go down slowly, savoring the hot bite of it in his throat. Was it over with Jeannie? Had tonight proved that? How could something like that happen? She hadn't done anything different; she was the same warm, loving, attractive, desirable woman she had always been, yet he couldn't feel the same thing he'd felt before the accident. What kind of man was he?

"Peter." Jeannie's voice came from behind him. So she wasn't asleep. He broke out in a drenching sweat; the time for truth had arrived, but what was the truth? He couldn't, he wouldn't lie his way out of it this time; they had to face it together. He turned around and saw her framed in the doorway. She was wearing a robe, and her hair fell softly about her face. Just for a brief moment he felt a wave of love and affection for her go through him. He started to take a step toward her, and then he saw the strange, almost sardonic smile on her face, and he didn't know what it meant.

"Yes?" he asked.

"Got a cigarette?"

"Sure." She came to stand in front of him. He took out his cigarettes and lighted one and handed it to her.

"Thanks." She walked to the terrace railing and leaned her elbows on it as she looked down on Park Avenue. After a few moments she spoke, with her back still to him. "I've lost you, haven't I?" Her voice was calm, almost matter-of-fact now.

"Of course you haven't lost me; it's just that something is wrong. We just don't seem to have it anymore." He spoke sadly.

"Why?" Still she did not turn around.

"I don't know. I wish I did."

"Is it her?"

"Her? Who?" He asked it automatically, but he knew who she meant.

"*Mrs*. Carl Morris." She turned then, and her dark eyes flashed angrily. "The Morrises have done a real number on you, haven't they?"

"I don't know what you're talking about."

"Oh yes, you do! And you know what I think?"

"What?" He had never seen her so angry.

"I think Morris gave you his eyes and took possession of you."

"Jeannie!" Verbalization of his own idea plunged him into a panic of anxiety. "Please, let's keep this between you and me. That's what this is about." She was angry and hurt, but he didn't want to be drawn into an argument, especially now; he was too disturbed by what she'd said, and he was afraid if they argued now, there would be no going back. He didn't want them to end that way.

"No. No, it isn't just between us. Since you came home, you've been like a stranger. At first I put it down to the trauma you'd been through, but you've grown into someone I don't know and can't communicate with. Your obsession with Morris himself was bad enough, but now both the Morrises stand between us, and I'm not sure I can fight her, too.

"Jeannie, please."

"Please what?"

"You don't know what you're saying. You're hurt and angry."

"No, Peter, it's true—you know it yourself. You can't stand there and tell me differently."

"It's normal to be interested in the person who gave you part of himself."

"Maybe it is, and maybe it isn't—I don't know. All I do know is, you've become someone else, and you're taking on more and more of his life—including his wife."

"Now that is sheer nonsense!" he protested but without firm conviction.

"I don't think so. I think you're just as obsessed with her as you are with him. In fact you're so obsessed with her you didn't even see me walk past the Stanhope the other night when you were having a cozy drink with her."

"How did you know it was Marcy?" He was taken aback. Did everyone who'd never seen Marcy know her?

"You described her to me. You may not be aware of it, but you've talked incessantly of her."

"I have?" He hadn't realized that he was talking so much about her.

"Do you know what I think, Peter?"

"No, and I'm not sure I want to." He took out a cigarette and lit it.

"Well, I'm going to tell you anyway."

"Apparently."

"I think that paragon of virtue, that beautiful, brave, grieving widow Morris is trying to take over the rest of you. I've been squeezed out of your life by the Morrises."

"Jeannie, don't." He closed his eyes and shook his head to clear it. He wanted to be angry, but he couldn't; partly because he suspected there might be some truth in her accusation about his obsession with the Morrises, but also because he realized how much she was hurting. "Look, I'd never seen Marcy when I came home, and I'd only talked to her a few times in the hospital." He paused, then went on. He wasn't certain where he was going with what he was trying to say. "Things weren't the same between you and me right from—"

"Yes. Morris was already in control. He was there the moment you got his damned eyes."

"Would you have me be blind?"

"Of course not. But I wish they'd been someone else's corneas, someone you'd never met. I don't know what Morris wants from you, but he wants something. Either that, or it's you that's becoming obsessive."

"Jeannie, are you really serious about this, or are you just rationalizing why things aren't working with us?" He was scared, and he wanted to know the truth from her.

"Yes, I'm serious. I think it's possible Morris planned it all. He knew he was going to die, so he gave you his sight, made certain you met his wife, asked you to go and see her when you got back. He planned it all. Don't you see? He didn't want her to be left alone, so he made certain she wouldn't be by giving you his sight. A part of him is still here, not only in your sight—*he's* here. He's still alive in you."

"Jeannie, stop it!" He was becoming more frightened by the moment.

"No, you've got to face up to it. He's really succeeded—because you're in love with her."

"Now you've gone too far!" Suddenly he was angry, and he was glad because it diminished his fear.

"Peter, I saw it. I saw the way you looked at her at the Stanhope. I know that look, remember?"

"And I knew Carl Morris. He wasn't that kind of guy."

"Oh, come on, Peter! A man might do anything for the woman he loves. You said yourself that he loved her very much." She paused but Peter made no response. "You're not saying anything."

"What can I say? You're saying things I don't know how to respond to. I suppose what you say could be possible—that such things can happen—but I don't know that they've happened to me."

"But it has occurred to you?"

"Yes. Except the part about me being in love with Marcy. You're way off base there."

"Maybe you don't know it yet, but she is a part of it—that's the reason for Carl's trying to take you over. He wants to be with her through you. Don't you see, Peter?" She was pleading now. "That's why you're a different man, and that's why we're having problems."

"I don't think the Morrises are responsible for our problems, Jeannie." He spoke softly, but inside he was in turmoil. What if she *was* right? No, it couldn't be possible. Yet, if she was—it could explain a lot of things. He almost wanted to believe it, wanted to believe that he still loved her, and that if only he could unravel his confusion, things would come right again between them.

"Do you still love me, Peter?" There it was, the all-important question. How could he answer it honestly, and yet not close the door on them?

"I don't know, Jeannie. I honestly do not know, and it's tearing me apart." The look on her face told him how much that honest answer had hurt her. "Maybe I just need more time, Jeannie." He turned away then; he couldn't bear that look of pain, and he wanted to run away from the problem now. He walked back into the apartment and put his glass down on the bar, then went into the bathroom where he started to get dressed. He was buttoning his shirt when she came into the bedroom.

"You're leaving?"

"Yes. I've got to be alone. I'm just making you unhappy with all my problems."

"Do you want to break it off, or just not see each other for a while?"

"I want—" He stopped, uncertain of just what he did want at that moment. He put his tie under his shirt collar but did not tie it. "Lets just cool it for a while, okay?"

"I'm going to start seeing other men. I've got to. My ego has taken a beating in these last few weeks." It was not a threat; he heard her pain.

"Of course. I understand."

"Will you be seeing her?"

"Oh, for God's sake, Jeannie, will you come off it! It seems to me that you're the one obsessed with the Morrises." He was about to get angry again because she was pushing him into areas which made him confused and frightened. He had to get out of the apartment, and he started out of the bedroom.

"Peter!"

"Yes?" He turned back to look at her.

"Take care of yourself, please?" She smiled a tender, caring smile, and he felt about six inches tall.

"Jeannie—" He paused, not knowing what to say. "I'll—I'll call you in a few days." He did not wait for a reply but walked out of the apartment and hurried to the elevator.

Outside in the street he began to relax for the first time that evening. As he put distance between himself and Jeannie, he felt better. How odd it was—there had been a time when he couldn't wait to get to her. How did one change so quickly? He had thought he loved her and wanted to marry her before the accident. If this could happen to him now, how could he ever be certain of his feelings in the future?

He walked on at random, thinking over what had happened, trying to analyze his feelings. Suddenly he stopped short; he was standing in front of Marcy's building. Somehow he was not really surprised; perhaps subconsciously he'd intended coming. If so, that was shocking, and made him think of the things Jeannie had said. He stood in the street, looking at the building as the doorman eyed him with suspicion. He glanced at his watch; it was one-thirty A.M. He began to walk again, but when he got to the corner he saw a telephone booth. Very convenient. Why not call Marcy? He found a dime, inserted it in the slot, but did not let it drop. Should he call? Probably not, it was awfully late. Oh, what the hell? Somehow he knew she wasn't asleep, and he thought she might even be glad to hear from him. He let the coin drop and dialed the number which he had already memorized. He waited impatiently; maybe she had gone home to Connecticut tonight.

"Hello." She sounded wide awake.

"Marcy, Peter Blanchard here. I'm sorry to disturb you at this hour, but I find myself in your neighborhood, and I wondered if you're up to a little talk." He blurted it all out in one breath.

"As a matter of fact I wasn't asleep. You'd be welcome company. Come up."

"Be right there." He hung up the receiver and felt a wonderful sense of elation. His step was considerably lighter as he strode back to the building and up to the doorman.

"Help you, sir?"

"Here to see Mrs. Morris, Mrs. Carl Morris." The doorman looked at his watch.

"It's late. She expecting you?"

"Yes."

"Name?"

"Blanchard. Peter Blanchard." The doorman turned to his call-board. Marcy answered at once.

"Mrs. Morris, there's a Mr. Blanchard down here—says you're expecting him." There was a silence and then the doorman nodded to him. "Okay. You can go up. Apartment 9C." He opened the door and Peter entered, thanking him, and crossed to the elevator. The operator was sprawled, half-asleep, on a bench.

"Ninth floor, please," said Peter, speaking loudly. The man opened his eyes and looked annoyed. "Ninth floor, 9C, please." The man got up slowly.

"That'd be Mrs. Morris, right?"

"Right." They rode up to the ninth floor in silence.

"Third door to your left," he said, pointing.

"Thanks." Peter walked down the corridor, feeling happy anticipation. He rang the bell. The door opened, and Marcy stood there smiling. She wore a bright pink shirt and white cotton jeans.

"Hi. What a nice surprise."

140

"Hi. Maybe I should say good morning?" he said. She responded with a soft laugh.

"Good morning will do fine. Come in."

"Thanks." He walked into the apartment and looked around. Her apartment was almost all white, with touches of bright color added here and there by bright pillows, drapes, and a handsome Oriental rug. It was an inviting, comfortable-looking apartment.

"Would you like a drink, coffee, something?"

"I wouldn't say no to a Scotch."

"How would you like it?"

"With soda, please?"

"Of course." She moved toward the kitchen, and he watched her go, admiring the movement of her tall, trim body. As clearly as if she'd been standing before him naked, he saw her body unclothed; saw the long, lean line of her back; saw a tiny brown mole on her right shoulderblade. Oh God, he said to himself and dug into his pocket for a cigarette. His hands were shaking as he lighted it. Am I imagining this, or am I seeing her with—with eyes that already know her intimately? He fumbled with the lighter, having failed to light the cigarette the first time. He crossed to the sofa to sit down and saw Carl's face staring up at him from a small silver frame on the glass coffee table. He picked up the frame and stared at the serious face he only dimly remembered now. The eyes looked at him with gentle kindness.

"That's my favorite photograph of Carl," she said behind him. He turned around and she held out his drink. He put the photograph back on the table and took the glass from her, careful to steady his hand for fear he would rattle the ice in the glass and give away his nervousness.

"Thanks." He wanted to ask her about the mole, but was afraid to find out. If she confirmed that she did indeed have a mole on her right shoulderblade, it would mean that he'd been right, and how could he know? She would want to know how he knew, and he couldn't answer that.

"Please sit down." She motioned him to a chair and sat down on the sofa.

"I promise you I've never before burst in on anyone at this hour," he said.

"No apology necessary."

"I didn't set out to come here. I was just walking and I found myself in front of your building."

"You're upset about something, aren't you?"

"It shows?"

"Umm, slightly."

"You're very astute."

"Want to talk about it?"

"Well, yes, maybe." He debated: should he tell her about his confusion over Jeannie? Somehow that seemed minor in comparison to the significance of his knowing about the mole. If he asked her about the mole, she would understand the implications of such a question. No, it could upset her too, and he didn't want to take that chance. He decided to talk about Jeannie instead.

"If you're not sure, Peter, I'll understand."

"I guess I would like to talk about it. Maybe you can be of help to me." He paused and smiled tentatively. She thought the smile boyish and attractive.

"I'll try, but I'm not very good at sorting things out for myself these days."

"Well, I'm certainly not. But they say two heads are better than one."

"I'm not sure that's true."

"Well, neither am I." They were both quiet, she waiting, he debating how to say what was on his mind.

"What is it, Peter?" Her voice was gentle and compassionate.

"Well, the truth is, I'm wondering what kind of man I am."

"Oh?" There was the boyish smile again, and she wondered if he knew how attractive it was.

"You see, I was more or less engaged before the accident. I mean we had an understanding, and I was thinking about asking her to marry me when I got back from the trip to France." He stopped, but Marcy said nothing and he continued. "But—when I came home, I didn't feel the same about her. Jeannie is her name." Still Marcy said nothing; she was certainly a good listener. He lit another cigarette to give himself time to think how to phrase what had happened. "At first I thought it was just a reaction to all that's happened." She nodded and he felt encouraged to go on. "We had trouble communicating from the moment I got back, and I felt almost as if I were a stranger when we were together. She was really very good and understanding about it—patient—gave me space, and didn't push or reproach me. But—I knew she was hurting, and I just got more and more confused because I didn't know how I felt. It seemed that all I felt was friendship and affection." He stopped and sipped his drink. "Tonight it came to a head. I—I tried to—uh—stay with her—but—" He coughed, trying to cover his embarrassment and self-consciousness.

"But you couldn't perform?" she said softly. He looked up at her and saw that she understood entirely.

"Yes. I—I panicked. I wanted to run away, Marcy." He stopped. What else was there to say about it? "We, uh—agreed to put some time and space between us."

"Are you unhappy about it now, Peter?"

"No. No, that's what I wanted. It wasn't fair to her. She—she deserves better than a mixed-up character like me."

"Then what is it that's disturbing you?"

"I don't understand how my feelings can change so completely, and so quickly."

"I see."

"I'm concerned about the quality of my feelings, Marcy." He looked at her searchingly, waiting for her to say something that would make him feel better.

"And that's why you're wondering what kind of man you are?"

"Yes."

"Well, Peter, people do make mistakes. Sometimes they're lucky enough to find out in time to prevent themselves from making a bigger mistake."

"That's the way I looked at it, but Jeannie thinks I'm a different man."

"Perhaps you are. You've been through a lot. Perhaps your needs and values have changed."

"I know they have." Should he tell her what Jeannie had said about Carl taking him over? It was hard to know how much he could say to her about Carl, yet she was the only one who could possibly give him any insight into whether or not Carl might try to do that. "Marcy, forgive me if I overstep the bounds of friendship in what I'm about to say, but some of it concerns you—and Carl."

143

"I'll stop you if I can't handle it." Her face was more serious now. Was it apprehension he saw there?

"You see, Jeannie feels that Carl has come between us."

"Carl?"

"Yes. She thinks I've become obsessed with him because of the transplants. In fact she thinks he has taken me over, that he planned it so that part of him would remain alive." Marcy's expression did not change.

"What do you think about it?" she asked quietly.

"I don't know." He paused, looking into his glass. "There's a lot I can't explain."

"Yes." She seemed to be alone with her own thoughts then. He did not intrude, but he did want to get it all out in the open and talk about it when the time seemed right.

"There's more," he said finally.

"More?" She seemed to come back to the room, to him, and he wondered again about how much he should say. "Go on," she said, coaxing him.

"Well, she also thinks I'm obsessed with you." Marcy averted her eyes, looking down at her hands. He was instantly worried that he'd upset her. "I'm sorry. Perhaps I shouldn't have told you."

"No. You should have told me." She looked up at him suddenly. He tried to read her expression, but couldn't. "Are you?" she asked.

"Obsessed with you?"

"Yes." She went on looking at him.

"Perhaps." He was not prepared for the question. It was truth time again tonight, and he was no more able to answer her with conviction than he'd been able to answer Jeannie. "I don't know that I'd exactly call it an obsession," he began. "Maybe it's a lot simpler than that—maybe it's just plain attraction." He watched her face, but her expression did not change.

"I don't know either," she said, her voice barely above a whisper. "I've agonized over it since we had dinner the other night."

"I'm really sorry if I've caused you agony by imposing my confusion on you."

"Oh, Peter, that's not what I've been agonizing over." She looked away. "You see, I find that I—I am also attracted to you."

"You are?" He felt excitement buzz through him.

"I'm afraid so." Their eyes met, and suddenly he didn't know what to say or do; in fact he felt momentarily paralyzed. She continued. "At first I thought it was because of Carl's eyes, and then I found that I was attracted to you as a man. Still I thought the attraction was related to Carl, and perhaps it really is."

"And if it isn't?"

"Then I have a problem with myself. That's what bothers me." Her eyes were troubled now. "How can I be attracted to another man so soon after Carl's death?"

"I understand. In a way we have the same dilemma. I'm wondering how my feelings for Jeannie can change so suddenly, and how I can have such strong feelings for you."

"But my feelings about Carl have not changed. I've just added another set of feelings to them." She got up and went to the window. "I loved Carl very deeply, and I still do."

"I know." He had a compelling urge to get to her, to put his arms about her, but he knew that would upset her, and possibly spoil whatever existed between them. "My good sense tells me this can't happen, yet it seems to be happening to both of us. I don't know if there's some supernatural phenomenon taking place, or if I'm imagining it to assuage my guilt over the feelings I find growing for you."

"It almost seems like an invisible power is drawing me toward you," she said.

"That's how I feel."

"And—when I don't follow that impulse, I'm plagued—and that's the only word for it: plagued with an unbearable restlessness."

"Me, too," he answered. She turned around to face him and their eyes met; each searched the other for an answer, and at the same time showed the tension of attraction between them.

"Is it Carl that's pushing us toward one another, Marcy?"

"It's the only other answer I can come up with. Unless—"

"Unless we're simply attracted to one another and trying to find an excuse for what we feel?" he suggested.

"Yes. In either case we're left with feelings we don't know what to do with."

"Don't we?" He hadn't meant to say that, it just popped out, but he looked straight at her nevertheless; having said it, he was not going to back down. She looked at him for a moment, and both felt the electric current of the attraction. She turned away.

"Don't, Peter. I can't handle it."

"I'm sorry." Again he wanted to go to her, but he knew he could not. "Perhaps I'd better leave?"

"No!" she cried out and wheeled around suddenly, her eyes pleading with him. She seemed to crumple then; he started toward her but she caught hold of the back of a chair and steadied herself.

"Oh God, Peter. What are we going to do?" He saw the pain in her eyes.

"I'm going to get you a drink right now." He went into the kitchen and poured them each a straight Scotch. When he came back, she was seated on the sofa. He handed the drink to her and sat in a chair facing her. He thought of the brown mole. It was time to ask that question.

"Marcy, do you have a brown mole on your right shoulderblade?"

"Yes." Her hand went to her mouth. "How did you know?"

"I saw it."

"You saw it?"

"Yes. When you went into the kitchen to fix my Scotch, I looked at your back and I knew how it looked. I saw the tiny brown mole."

"Oh my God!" She covered her face with her hands. "What in the name of God is going on?"

"Perhaps it *is* Carl." He was quiet, feeling the same fear she felt: fear of the unknown. "If it is, what does he want from us?" he asked, half to himself. She did not answer. "Is it that he doesn't want you to be alone, and he's pushing me toward you—pushing us toward one another?"

"Do you believe that?" She took her hands away and their eyes met. Each saw the fear in the other.

"I don't know. I don't know what to believe, Marcy. If I accept that idea, it means I don't have a will of my own."

"If that were possible—if Carl had the power to do that—I suppose I wouldn't have a will of my own either."

"I suppose so."

"And—neither of us would know if we actually care for one another, or if we were only part of Carl's plan." She began to shiver.

146

"Yes." He gulped his Scotch; she'd summed it up for them both. "Take a sip of the Scotch, it'll steady your nerves," he advised.

"I'm scared, Peter. I don't understand this, and things I don't understand scare me."

"You lived with Carl for ten years—would he do something like this?" he asked. She did not answer right away, and he knew she was thinking back over her life with Carl.

"I don't know." She paused. "Surprising that I don't know, isn't it?"

"What can I say?" he shrugged.

"I thought I knew everything about Carl, but now I find I can't really answer that question." She paused. "I suppose one never really knows *everything* about another person."

"I suppose not. And—I guess one shouldn't. No matter how much one loves, and how close one is to another human being, we all need some private space for ourselves."

"Are you scared, Peter?"

"Yes, Marcy, I am. The implications of what we might be facing scare me very much. And the fact that I don't know what I can do about it scares me more."

"Perhaps we shouldn't see each other for a while?"

"If Carl wants us together, I doubt if we'll be able to stay away from one another." Already the idea of not seeing her made him feel frustrated and restless. "I think we've got to try and find out if it's really true, Marcy."

"But how?"

"I don't know, but I've got to find some answers somewhere, somehow. And, Marcy, I'll be very honest—I don't know if I *can* stay away from you." He looked into her eyes. "I really don't."

"Will you try?" Her eyes told him that she was just as uncertain.

"Yes, I'll try anything. But I'm going to go to somebody who knows about these things. I know I'm not capable of handling this by myself." He got up to leave, and she rose too. They faced one another, their eyes holding. She closed her eyes then. "What's wrong?" he asked.

"Just everything." She paused and opened her eyes. He saw that tears stood in them.

"I want to hold you," he whispered.

"I know—I want you to." He took a step toward her, and

she came into his arms. A tremendous surge of emotion rushed up inside him. "Oh, God, you feel so *right!*" He held her closer against him, and she clung to him as she began to cry. Despite his deep concern for her, he felt himself sexually excited, and knew nothing was wrong with him; he was perfectly capable of sexual activity. He also knew that she was aware of his excitement.

"Peter, we can't, we just can't do this. I'm so confused I feel I could get just crazy."

"I'd better go then." He loosened his hold on her, and she stepped away from him.

"Give me time to get hold of myself, Peter, will you?"

"Of course." He walked to the door and looked back at her. She was looking at him, and he knew she wanted him to go yet didn't want him to. "I'll—I'll telephone you in a few days, but if you need me, will you call?"

"Yes," she replied with a sad little smile. He turned and went quickly out the door.

As he walked down the deserted street, his hands sunk in his pockets and his mind in turmoil, he felt anger rising inside him. What a mess he'd gotten into. His life was completely fucked up now. He was cold to the woman who really loved him, and helplessly drawn to a woman who was still in love with her dead husband, and still grieving over him. That left him exactly nowhere. But Marcy wanted him, he knew that, and he also knew just as well that she would not give in to that desire. Damn it!

He kicked at a trash basket on the corner, and set off across the street, against the light.

# Chapter Fourteen

"Pete! Hiya, baby, how you doin'?" Mike bounded over to the bar and threw his arm around Peter's shoulder.

"Really great sound you got there!" Peter had come in while the group was playing a set.

"You dig?" Mike beamed with pride.

"I dig."

"Hey, listen, welcome to 125th Street, U.S.A.!" He patted Peter on the back. "You know, I never thought you'd make it up here. Congratulations!"

"Never underestimate whitey!" Peter grinned.

"Listen to the man talk!" Mike threw his head back and laughed loudly. "So, whatcha drinkin'?"

"Scotch, and I've got one."

"Okay." Mike turned to the bartender. "Hit me with a gin, Jake." The bartender nodded and Mike turned back to Peter.

"So, what's happening?"

"Everything," Peter replied.

"Like what?"

"Like I want to talk seriously with you about something."

"Whooeee, man! That sounds heavy."

"It is heavy. I've seen your secret love."

"Yeah, which one?" Mike laughed again.

"Marcy Morris." Peter said it quietly, and Mike's face sobered.

"Did, huh?" He nodded philosophically. "Good. That's good, Pete."

"I saw her by accident."

"By accident?"

"That's right. I saw her coming out of the Plaza Hotel, and I *knew* her."

"Hey, wait a minute! You *knew* her? Unless I missed something, you was blind in that sick pad when you met her."

"That's right."

"Then how the fuck did you know her?"

"I don't know, I just did. And—I spoke to her and she remembered me."

"Man, that is *spooky!*" Mike got up. "Come on, let's grab a table. I got to hear about this." Mike picked up his gin and led the way to a small table in a far corner of the bar. They sat down facing one another. "Now, let me hear this right. Are you telling me you recognized Marcy when you never laid eyes on her before?"

"That's exactly what I'm telling you."

"How?"

"I don't know. I just saw this woman, from across the street, and I *knew* that's who she was."

"Man, you must have blown that woman's mind!"

"It pretty well blew both of us," Peter said. Mike nodded. "In fact there's a lot of blowing going on in *my* mind."

"Yeah?" Mike sipped his gin.

"You spent a lot of time with Carl before he died. How well did you get to know him?"

"Pretty well." Mike's expression turned quizzical.

"Do you think—I mean in your opinion—would he try to keep on living through another person?"

"That person being you, Pete?"

"Yes."

"How come you asking?"

"Because of the weird things that keep happening—things I can't explain. Like recognizing Marcy. And—I also know that she's got a tiny brown mole on her right shoulderblade.

"Has she?"

"I asked her. She confirmed it."

"Uh-huh. You been seeing the lady?"

"Yes. A couple of times."

"Uh-huh. I'm not surprised."

"What does that mean?"

"Nothing. I just thought you would, that's all."

"You kept telling me to."

"I know, I know. Go on."

"Well, I'm so goddamned restless I can't sit still, and I can't stay away from her. It's as if some power outside me is moving me around like a pawn on a chessboard." Peter's voice gave away his inner turmoil.

"Does Marcy know about this?" Mike was serious now.

"She's got the same problem. Of course my having Carl's sight may have something to do with her wanting to see me. After all, I've got a living part of him."

"Right. Figures."

"But there's more to it than that. We're—uh—attracted to each other."

"Terrific!" Mike grinned. "Tell me something I didn't expect. I mean, any dude who wouldn't be attracted to Marcy has gone senile."

"Yes, Mike, but it's too *soon*. The lady's got problems with it."

"Oh yeah—yeah, she would." Mike shook his head.

"I—I've sort of broken it off with Jeannie—temporarily—I think."

"Oh, right. The rich chick?"

"And that's another thing. I think I told you when you came down to see me the other night that I felt like a stranger to myself when I got back."

"Yeah."

"Well, it didn't get better. It seemed to me that she was a stranger too, and I wasn't in love with her anymore." Peter paused, then added, "Not only that, but I just couldn't get it up. I didn't want her physically."

"Yeah?" Mike sipped his gin. "That's rough on her."

"I was just making her unhappy. So I thought the only thing to do was cool it before things turned really bad. There was no use hurting her anymore." He lit a cigarette. "Funny thing, though. She thinks it's all because Carl's trying to stay alive through me. She thinks I'm obsessed with him—and with Marcy."

"Are you?"

"How do I know!" Peter signaled the waiter for another drink. "All I know for certain is something is driving me up the wall. I'm nervous, restless, anxious—it's as though some force is driving me toward Marcy, and when I can't get to her, I'm wild. I'm beginning to wonder if I've got a will of my own anymore."

"You think old Carl is doing this to you?"

"I keep asking myself if he would try and stay alive through me."

"If I read you right, Pete, you want to know if I think he would try."

"That's right." Peter placed his palms down on the table and waited while Mike scratched his head and seemed to be debating with himself.

"Yeah. Could be. He just might." Mike's eyes met Peter's. "But why?"

"That's obvious." Mike shrugged. "Because of her."

"Is that why he gave me his eyes?"

"I don't think so. I mean, you never know, but I'd put my money on him honestly wanting you to see again." Mike thought of his last talk with Carl, his agony and guilt over lying to Marcy. Maybe he'd had it in the back of his head to try and push Pete and Marcy together, sort of his way of trying to make it up to her. But what was he going to tell Pete? "You know, Pete," he said, "the idea of some living part of yourself staying behind—if you've got to die—well, shit, man, that's a dynamite idea. And—maybe he did hope Marcy might get a fix on you. I mean, that don't have to be no evil trip, you know."

"All right. Let's say he is trying to stay alive through me—what does he want from me?"

"Just what's happening."

"You mean about Marcy?"

"Right."

"But it's upsetting her, Mike. Does he want that to happen? After all, he loved her, I know he did."

"You better believe he did."

"And she loved him. Still does. Something like this can tear her apart. I mean, you can have the best of intentions but—"

"Maybe he thinks it's worth it—in the long run, I mean."

"At the moment it's got her torn up, and it's getting to me."

"That's bad."

"We don't know what to do, Mike. We don't know if these feelings are our own, or if we're just tools being manipulated by Carl." The waiter brought Peter's drink and put it on the table. Peter thanked him and continued. "For a while I thought I was just imagining it all. But now—well, I'm not so sure. I think maybe I'm in for a bad time, and I don't know what in hell to do."

"If Carl's got it in his head that he wants you and Marcy together, I don't think he's gonna let go," Mike said.

"But why?" Peter hit the table with the flat of his hand. "I've got his sight, and that's all. He can't get to Marcy through me unless he takes me over entirely, inhabits my body and crowds me out. I mean, he'd have to make me a physical shell with himself inside." Mike stared at Peter in alarm.

"That's what really buggin' you, ain't it?"

"Damn it, Mike, I'm scared." He stubbed out his cigarette. "And so is Marcy."

"You know you can go really nuts this way?"

"If I could just understand why he would do such a thing, maybe I could fight it."

"Shit, Pete! How would I know?" Mike looked away; he was uncomfortable seeing Peter's distress.

"Sorry, Mike. I just hoped Carl might have said something to you to give me a clue." Peter seemed to sag and Mike saw it.

"Look, Pete. Yeah—Carl rapped a lot to me over there. I was sorta his father confessor at the end." Mike stopped and frowned; he would have to be very careful what he said now. "You see, Pete, Carl had a secret that was weighing real heavy on him. I guess everybody's got one."

"Yes?" Peter's face lighted up with hope.

"He'd been carrying a big load of guilt around with him for a long time, and he had to take it with him. There was no way he could make it right anymore—he'd run out of time—so he had to talk about it."

"Yes, go on." Peter's face was expectant.

"Can't tell you what it was, Pete. You don't break a promise to a dying man."

"Just tell me this much: did it have anything to do with Marcy?"

"Yeah, sorta, but that's all I'm tellin' you."

"He didn't have a mistress, or something like that?"

"Are you jiving me? That cat was nuts about Marcy. You know that!"

"Was it something that might make him want to bring Marcy and me together?"

"Pete, I told you—"

"That's not giving anything away. Just tell me that much, and I promise not to ask you another question."

"It could, Pete, it could! End of subject!"

"Well, I guess I really don't know much more than I did, do I?"

"No. But if Carl did want you two to get together, I don't think he'd let anything bad happen to you. I got to know him pretty well, and I'm telling you his intentions would be—"

Peter broke over him. "The road to hell is paved with good intentions. But so far those good intentions haven't panned out too well. For starters I seem to have fallen out of love with the woman I meant to marry, I'm attracted to a woman who is still in love with her husband, and is running into moral conflict because she's attracted to me. Not exactly evil, but definitely not a prescription for happiness and tranquility either." Peter looked grim, and Mike sank into a depression. "I don't know where I am, Mike. I don't want to blow it with Jeannie. I mean, I may get over my hang-up there."

"And you're thinking Marcy may not get over Carl, so you could get left high and dry, huh?"

"Something like that."

"Man, you are in a fizz, and it ain't gin neither!" Suddenly the cloud left Mike's face and he began to grin. "Listen, I got an idea!"

"Spill it, for God's sake!"

"There's this old conjure woman up on 135th Street."

"Conjure woman!"

"Hey, cool it just a minute! She's not exactly a conjure woman. I mean, the story is, she gets in touch with folks that have passed on. Now, maybe she could contact Carl—ask him what the fuck he's up to."

"You're putting me on, aren't you?" asked Peter incredulously.

"Only part way. I mean, I used to hang out with her granddaughter. She swore the old lady could to it."

"Did you ever see her do it?" Peter was fascinated despite the fact he still couldn't take Mike seriously.

"Well, sort of." Mike laughed a little guiltily. "See, a bunch of us cats was sittin' around one night, having some drinks, smoking a little grass, things like that, and Alicia, that's the lady I was hanging out with, she ups and tells this story about her grandma. So one of these turkeys, a trumpet player, gets it into his gourd he wants to talk to Ole Satchmo Armstrong. So we're all stoned enough to think that's cool, and we hop a cab and travel up to 135th Street to see Grandma Geranium Victoria. So help me that's her name! Alicia said Grandma claimed the Victoria part was after the fat English Queen Victoria who was queen when she was born. She also claimed she was the illegitimate daughter of a Scottish sea captain who came to Barbados. That's why she was named after the queen."

"Well, there's a lot of Scottish blood down there, but I never knew the Scots to favor a British ruler that much. But tell me what happened with Grandma Geranium Victoria."

"Well, first of all she's older than God, and looks it. And she hangs out in this pad that's got black walls, and it's so dark in that hole you can break your ass without half trying."

"Mike, what did she do?"

"Do you want to hear this story?"

"Yes, I do."

"Then let me tell it *my* way."

"Sorry, I didn't realize you were such a temperamental yarn spinner." Peter laughed and punched Mike playfully on the shoulder.

"Okay, we get up there in this black pad, see, and this turkey says he's got to get in touch with Ole Satchmo. So Grandma Geranium Victoria demands a ten-dollar bill before she's doing anything."

"Which you gladly paid," laughed Peter.

"Bet your ass! It was shaping up to be the best show in town. So, when Grandma pockets the bread, she starts chanting—and I mean that voice would curdle your blood—and she's rolling her eyes and throwing her body around so it actually made you dizzy."

"What was the chant about?"

"Who knows? Couldn't understand nothin' she said. Nothin'! But pretty soon she freezes, see, and opens her eyes, and you can't see nothin' but the whites of her eyes—she's got them rolled so far up in her head. Then she tells this turkey trumpet player that Mr. Armstrong is waiting to talk to him, but he'll only answer questions. So this turkey asks Satchmo if he plays his horn in heaven." Mike started to laugh.

"Well, did Satchmo answer?"

"Sure."

"What did he say?"

"Grandma said Mr. Satchmo said 'Oooohh yeeaah!' " Mike started laughing at his own imitation of Satchmo and Peter laughed with him.

"Don't tell me any more. I know Satchmo never said anything but 'Oh, Yeah!' "

"You got it! But the damned thing was—the last question this turkey asked, he got an answer in a voice that sounded like Satchmo, and not from Grandma neither—she had her mouth zipped tight. And that turkey swears to this day that he saw Satchmo smiling at him in the dark!" Mike was laughing so hard tears were running down his face, but Peter was laughing more at Mike than at the story.

"Okay, we had a good laugh. Now tell me you made the whole thing up," Peter said.

"Can't do that. I swear it happened just like I said it did."

"Do you believe this, this Grandma Geranium, uh—"

"Geranium Victoria," offered Mike.

"Yeah. Do you believe she really got in touch with Satchmo?"

"Hell, I don't know. I was stoned out of my gourd, we all was, but it don't matter what I believe. That turkey that wanted to talk to old Satchmo believes he did."

"You're kidding."

"No way!" Mike was looking intently at Peter, and suddenly he said, "You know what I think?"

"No idea."

"I think everybody believes what they wanna believe, and I'm tryin' to figure out why you wanna believe that jazz about Carl, and maybe Marcy does, too. I mean maybe you're both kidding yourselves."

"We beat you to it on that, Mike. We've both thought of that explanation."

"And?"

"No way."

"How do you know?"

"Because we're not buying it, that's why. We're not doing anything about our attraction. If we were, then you might say we were trying to use this stuff about Carl as an excuse, but we're not. In fact, we're trying not to see each other at all for a while."

"Bullshit!" Mike exploded. "That's the biggest pile of bullshit I ever heard."

"Thanks a million, pal." Peter was taken aback.

"I mean it, Pete. It's like masturbation! You're talking the hell out of it, instead of doing the *real* thing you want to do, and finding out where you are that way. I mean, ole' Carl may be powerful up there in that spook pad, but he can't make you get it up with Marcy if you ain't got it for her, and he can't give her an orgasm if she don't want it from you." Mike spoke with conviction. His dark eyes left no room for doubt that he meant what he said.

"You think so?" Peter didn't know how to respond, for Mike's sudden intensity had overwhelmed him.

"I sure do!"

"It's just not that simple, Mike." Peter had begun to recover somewhat.

"The hell it ain't!"

"All right, let's say we do exactly what you say, and it works, and we're nuts about one another, how are you going to change the fact that Marcy will feel bad about herself for turning to me so soon after Carl's death? And how are you going to eliminate the guilt I'm going to feel about being alive, having his sight, taking his wife, and hurting a wonderful woman who's done nothing but love me?"

"Look, Pete, if you and Marcy want each other, and think you've got something good going—shit, man, grab it! So, you feel a little guilty—it ain't gonna last forever. Marcy's alone—she's gonna get together with some dude sooner or later. I mean, you don't really think the world's gonna let her stay a widow long, do you?"

"I suppose not." Peter felt depressed.

"Well, she digs you, and you dig her—that puts you way ahead of all the rest. And if this rich chick is as wonderful and gorgeous as you say she is, she ain't gonna stay alone neither. I mean, that's life, man. Happens all the time."

"It's just not that simple, Mike," Peter repeated.

"Wrong! It *is* that simple. Marcy likes you, you like her, but you're both hung up on how it looks, or what the fuckin' society might think, shit like that! The real thing is you want each other and you need each other. Period!"

"You make it all sound logical and easy, but it's just more complicated than that."

"Look man, you ain't takin' nothing from Carl. He's a dead man, and he's gonna stay dead if you don't bring him back to life. You said yourself you're both wondering if he's trying to push you together. Well, hell, what the fuck do you think that means? He wants you two together. That's how I read it. So, what's all the shit about?"

"Jesus, who wound you up?" exclaimed Peter.

Mike began to smile. "Gin, I guess. But I don't take back nothin' I said. In my opinion ole Carl would be tickled to death if you and Marcy made out, and got married, and had a flock of kids."

"Hey, wait a minute—one step at a time!"

"What's the matter, you don't like kids?"

"Would you just mind if I took one step at a time? I've never even kissed the woman!"

"Tough!" Mike laughed and got up. "Listen, got to go make music, but hang around, we'll raise a few. Maybe we'll go see Grandma Geranium Victoria for laughs."

"I'll hang around awhile and listen, but I think I'll pass on the laughs at Grandma Geranium Victoria's."

"Never can tell how you'll feel later. Be back in half an hour." Mike strode away. Peter signaled the waiter for another Scotch. How wonderful it must be to see things as Mike did—so black and white. He grinned, thinking how Mike would laugh at what he'd just thought.

It was in the early hours of the morning when a somewhat unsteady Peter and Mike got out of a taxi in front of a dingy storefront on 135th Street. Mike went to the door and began to pound on it, then getting no answer, began to pound on the glass storefront.

"Hey, wake up in there!" he shouted.

"You want to wake up all of 135th Street?" Peter said.

"Nope—just Grandma Geranium Victoria." Mike laughed and gave the door another thump.

"I must be drunk, or really out of my mind to let you drag me up here," said an uneasy Peter.

"Both!" said Mike. "Come on, shake a leg, Grandma!" he shouted.

Presently the door opened a crack, and a deep, raspy voice said: "What you want here?"

"Grandma Geranium Victoria?"

"Yes?"

"It's Mike Fuller—Alicia's friend. I got a friend with me who wants to contact somebody real bad."

"You got money?" asked the voice.

"Yeah, we got the bread, Grandma."

"Price go up, Mike."

"How much now, Grandma?"

"Twenty dollar."

"Twenty dollars! That's robbery for what you do!" shouted Mike.

"No, *inflation*, Michael." She cackled. "Also harder to contact spirits now." She spoke with the cadence of the West Indies.

"Yeah? How come? Lose your touch?"

"No lose touch. Too much sputnik in space." Mike roared with laughter and the old woman cackled.

"Come on, let us in, Grandma."

"See money first," she said firmly. Mike pulled out a twenty and started to pass it through the crack. Peter caught his arm.

"Wait a minute, Mike, I don't think this is a good idea. But if I did, I'd pay for it myself."

"No way! This gig is on me!" Mike shook off Peter's arm. "Here, Grandma. Now, let us in. I'm tired of standing out here in the street." The door opened, and Mike grabbed Peter's arm and pulled him inside.

The room was as Mike had described it: walls entirely black, no light except for the large candle which burned in the center of a round table in the middle of the room. The old woman was dressed in black also, and Peter would not have been able to see her had her white hair not shown faintly in the light of the candle.

"I go to make preparation for journey to spirits. Please make confortable."

"Yeah, okay, but don't take too long, Grandma. My friend here is nervous."

"No be nervous, please. All is tranquility here." She lifted the curtain at the end of the room and disappeared. Mike fell into a chair beside the table.

"Pull up a chair, Pete." Peter did as Mike suggested because there didn't seem to be any other chairs in the room.

"What in hell am I doing here?" he asked the room at large.

"You're having an experience," chuckled Mike.

"If this is what happens when I come uptown, I think I'll stay in my own territory," Peter grumbled, but his intellectual curiosity was beginning to be aroused.

"All talk stop, please!" announced Grandma Geranium Victoria as she appeared between the parted curtains. She waited a few moments, like an actress awaiting her entrance. "All vibrations of outside world must leave your soul," she said in Peter's direction. Despite his skepticism he found her command compelling and he tried to make his mind blank. Grandma waited, and it was not until he had stopped thinking of anything at all that the old woman advanced into the room. She approached the table slowly and sat down facing Peter. Her face was deeply wrinkled and emaciated. Her eyes, however, were bright and alive, and a startling pale gray color. Peter felt his own eyes held almost hypnotically by them.

"Who to contact is it you wish, sir?"

"Carl Morris," he replied.

"When pass on to other world, Carl Morris?" she asked softly.

"About three months ago," replied Peter.

"A friend, was he?" she asked.

"Yes."

"How die?"

"From burns in an airplane crash."

"How old he?"

"I don't know. Maybe thirty-five."

"You please to think very hard about friend. No matter what happen, you think of friend." Grandma Geranium Victoria closed her eyes and began a wild chant that sounded like gibberish. Her voice soared up and down the scale, the strange words interspersed with shrieks and cries like those of wild tropical birds. Her body swayed dangerously in the chair; her arms flailed the air. Suddenly her voice slowed to a whimper, and she grew silent. Then her eyelids fluttered open, just as Mike had described, and only the whites showed. Peter stared in fascination as she raised her arms and beckoned the heavens, touching her temples with the tips of her fingers each time she beckoned. Suddenly she stopped, and blinked her eyes. When she opened them, they were normal, and she looked at Peter.

"Friend's spirit not in other world," she said. Mike stirred in his chair, and Peter felt himself break out in a cold sweat. "Friend's spirit here in this room," she said, staring into Peter's eyes with penetrating intensity. "I feel it," she said, "but it no speak." She continued to stare at Peter. "Your friend's spirit no speak. It hides because has secret." She got up suddenly, as if something had upset her. "You go now," she said and shuffled out of the room.

Peter remained seated, drenched with sweat, his heart pounding. Fear crowded into his brain, blocking out all thought. Mike got up and touched him on the shoulder.

"Come on, Pete. Let's go."

"I can't," answered Peter.

"Sure you can."

"No. Not yet," he whispered. His stomach seemed to come up into his throat then, and he suddenly sprang out of the chair and lurched across the room and out the door. He stood at the curb and threw up until nothing more would come, then he dry heaved, his stomach in convulsion. He hung onto a lamppost to keep from collapsing. Mike caught him under the arms and dragged him back against the building.

"Pete, take deep breaths. Come on now, deep as you can. That's it—just keep at it."

"How did she know, Mike?" Peter gasped between breaths.

"Shit, Pete, the old witch wasn't getting no vibes, she was faking just to earn the bread."

"No, she wasn't. She knew."

"It was a fuckin' guess, Pete! That's all it was. Come on now, let's get a taxi and get you back downtown."

"No, I have to go back and ask her what she meant."

"No way, Pete! Not tonight! She won't let you in, anyway."

"But I have to know!"

"Later, man, not tonight." Mike spoke with authority. He hailed a cab and helped Peter into it, then jumped in beside him. "Shit, Mike Fuller," he said to himself, "now you've done it! You and your big fuckin' ideas!"

# Chapter Fifteen

Peter was awakened by the ringing of the telephone. He grabbed for it and croaked into the receiver.

"Hello!"

"Mr. Blanchard, it's Grace."

"Grace! What the hell are you calling me for at this hour?" he said angrily.

"Mr. Blanchard, it's ten o'clock!" she replied indignantly.

"So?"

"Mr. Blanchard, you had an editorial meeting scheduled for nine-thirty. Everybody's waiting, and some of them are very upset!"

"Cancel it!"

"Cancel it?"

"That's what I said!"

"But what am I going to tell them?"

"That's your problem, Grace. That's what I pay you for." He slammed down the receiver and turned over with a groan. The phone rang again. He sat up, and found it was a mistake, then put his head back down on the pillow and groped for the phone.

"Hello," he said, somewhat less angrily this time.

"Mr. Blanchard, it's Grace again."

"Grace, for God's sake, what is it now?"

"Are you all right?" She sounded worried; Peter had never

spoken angrily to her in the six years she'd worked for him.

"No!"

"What's wrong?"

"I've got a hangover, Grace," he replied. "Cancel all my appointments for the day."

"But, Mr. Blanchard—"

"Grace, you heard what I said!"

"Yes, Mr. Blanchard," she replied with a patient sigh.

"And don't call me, I'll call you!" He slammed the phone down again, and slowly sat up. His head throbbed and his stomach protested against even the thought of coffee. He got out of bed with elaborate care paid to his condition and hobbled off to the shower.

After he'd soaped himself down, he stood under a strong jet of cold water, letting it pour over him until his flesh tingled. He got out finally and toweled himself off, then searched in the medicine cabinet for a headache remedy. He found a bottle of aspirin and shook three tablets into his hand. He padded barefoot into the kitchen for a glass of ice water. He took the aspirin along with a vitamin B-complex tablet, then went back into the bedroom and began to dress. Every reflex was slowed down, and it took him twice as long as usual to put his clothes on.

By the time he was dressed, however, the aspirin had reduced his headache to an almost bearable level, and he decided he'd better eat something no matter how repugnant the idea seemed. He left his apartment and walked over to a coffee shop on Lexington Avenue. When he entered, the smell of cooking food almost sent him back out into the street, but he needed fortification for the day in front of him, and his system craved protein. He slid into a booth.

"Morning, Mr. Blanchard. Little late today, aren't you?" asked the waitress.

"I'm a lot late, Dorothy, and lower the decibels, will you?" He sounded quarrelsome, and he felt quarrelsome.

"My, we're in bad shape, aren't we?"

"No, *we* aren't, *I* am."

"Okay, sport, whatcha gonna have?" Dorothy was a pro in her job and she knew when to back off.

"What have you got?"

"What we've always got, but how about some scrambled eggs and ham?"

"Can't handle it."

"Here, look at the menu while I get you a cup of coffee." She went to get the coffee, and he tried to read the menu. In moments Dorothy was back with a cup of steaming black coffee.

"Okay, what's it gonna be?"

"Everything sounds nauseating."

"Look at it this way, Mr. Blanchard. You're gonna be miserable for about eight hours, but food's gonna make it a little easier to bear, so think of it as medicine. That makes it a lot easier to get down."

"Okay. Think you could persuade the chef to make me a small medium rare steak and scrambled eggs?"

"Don't know, he's kinda cranky today."

"Well, I'm a lot cranky, and I don't need a cranky chef."

"I'll try." Dorothy disappeared, and he sat stirring his coffee, staring out the window at passersby on Lexington Avenue without really seeing them. It was time to think about last night, and what he was going to do about it.

What had the old woman meant when she said Carl's spirit was not in the other world? She'd even said his spirit was in the room, and he'd imagined that he could feel it, too. Mike said he hadn't, but he wasn't certain Mike hadn't been lying. Still Mike had spent a long time after bringing him home trying to convince him that Grandma Geranium Victoria was a fake. But he, Peter, had looked into her eyes and he thought she believed what she told him. How could Mike call her a fake when he himself had said Carl did have a secret? How could she have known about the secret?

The fact that the old woman had seemed shaken by her own pronouncement added further credibility to what she'd said. He remembered, too, the way she'd looked at him when she said Carl's spirit was not in the other world, but in that room, and it was a look of conviction and awe. He experienced again the fear and anxiety he'd felt then. Had she meant that Carl's spirit was in him, or was he imagining it because he feared Carl's power over him? And what was Carl's secret? His intuition told him that the secret was somehow related to the things that had been happening to him, and he would have to find out what that secret was. He knew that Mike would never tell him, but had Mike taken him to the old woman in the hope that she would? If so, why had Mike gone

*165*

to such lengths afterward to convince him she was a fake? When he'd questioned Mike about why he'd taken him to see the old woman if he thought her a fake, Mike had explained that he'd thought the bizarre appearance and outrageous performance of the old woman trying to raise the spirits would make Peter see how ridiculous his obsession with Carl was. Or, if not that, perhaps Grandma might just say something that would pacify him for a while.

At some point last night, when they'd both been very drunk, he had told Mike that he wasn't convinced that Carl wouldn't try to use him. He'd even told Mike that he thought *he* was the one who was faking. But no matter how hard he tried, he couldn't remember what Mike's reply had been. Well, it didn't matter, it was his problem, and he was going back to 135th Street and try to find that storefront.

"Okay, Dracula, here you are. Steak and eggs, just like you ordered!"

"Thanks, Dorothy. You probably saved my life."

"You look like you need somebody to." She shook her head. "Must have been some night!"

"You wouldn't believe it if I told you," he said, looking at the plate and having second thoughts about eating.

"That bad, huh?" Dorothy shook her head again and walked off with her body language telegraphing disapproval.

After forcing down the breakfast, he went back to his apartment and changed into jeans and a polo shirt. He took forty dollars out of his wallet and his driver's license for identification. He put the wallet into the bureau drawer and pocketed the money and license. He hoped forty would be enough—twenty of that was for Grandma, the rest for cab fare, and a little extra to spare just in case he needed it. Next he removed his watch and signet ring and put them into the drawer along with the wallet. Maybe he was being overly cautious, but a lone white man with a limp (he still had a slight limp which the doctor kept assuring him would go away as his leg strengthened with physiotherapy) prowling around Harlem was a temptation some hostile black man, or junkie hurting for a fix, might not be able to resist.

As he passed the telephone, he was tempted to call Marcy, but they'd agreed to give one another some space for a while, and he meant to do his best to keep the agreement. Instead he dialed his office.

"Hello, Grace."

"Oh, Mr. Blanchard. It's you. How are you feeling?"

"I may live. Sorry for the outburst, I'm not in a very good mood."

"Yes, I know." Grace wasn't going to thaw easily. Well, so what? He'd spoiled her anyway.

"Look, Grace, I'm going to be unavailable for a while, and if you don't hear from me in a couple of hours, call Mike Fuller and tell him I've gone to try and find Grandma, and maybe he should come looking for me."

"What's his number, Mr. Blanchard?"

"It's in my address book on my desk."

"Okay. If I don't hear from you in two hours, I should call Mr. Fuller and tell him you went to find Grandma, and maybe he should come look for you."

"Right."

"Mr. Blanchard, you're not going to get into any trouble, are you?"

"Stop mothering, Grace. Talk to you later." He hung up and picked up his house keys.

He took a taxi to the bar on 125th Street and tried to remember if they'd gone up Broadway to 135th Street when they left the bar. He couldn't remember, but the bar was open and he decided to go in on the chance that Mike might be there, but he was pretty certain the big drummer was in bed sound asleep at this hour. It was dark inside the bar, but cool, and he was glad to get out of the broiling summer sun.

A jukebox blared some hard rock number, and several men of varying ages sat around looking bored. When they saw him, however, their interest seemed to pick up. He took a seat at the bar. The bartender stared at him from down at the end of the bar where he was talking to a customer.

"Yeah? You want something?" he asked.

"Got a Budweiser?"

"Sure." The bartender moved lazily down the bar and produced the beer and a glass, which he set on the counter in front of Peter. "Dollar twenty-five cents," he said. It was a little high for that part of town, but Peter wasn't going to argue. He put two dollars on the counter and the bartender gave him back seventy-five cents. Peter took a quarter and left fifty cents on the bar as a tip. The bartender looked at it but let it stay there. He watched Peter with casual interest, and it made Peter feel uncomfortable.

"Don't suppose Mike Fuller is around at this hour, is he?"

"Ain't seen him."

"We got a little tanked together last night. Guess he's sleeping it off." He was making conversation, using Mike's name to legitimize himself.

"Yeah? You a friend of Mike's?" The bartender's expression did not change.

"Yes. I was on the plane that crashed in Paris."

"Yeah?" The bartender's interest picked up slightly.

"Mike and I were in beds next to one another in the hospital."

"That so? What happened to you?"

"Broken leg, back injuries, things like that."

"Oh. For a minute I thought maybe you was that cat that was blind and got new eyes." The bartender looked disappointed.

"I am," said Peter casually.

"Yeah!" The bartender stepped closer to the counter and peered at Peter's eyes. "Uh-huh. Same color as yours?"

"You don't get that part, you just get the cornea. That's the transparent part that covers the iris and the pupil—it admits light and images."

"Uh-huh. Make you feel kinda weird?"

"Sometimes." He wished some of his friends would be as candid and direct as the bartender. He could see the same question in their faces, but they never came out with it.

"Can you see good?" The bartender was still peering at him.

"Yes. See just fine now. It took a little while though."

"Bet you was scared, huh?"

"Damned right!"

"I don't know as I'd trust the French. I was in France in World War Two. Didn't like 'em."

"I'd rather have been here, but I didn't have any choice."

"Well, turned out okay anyway. Guess we oughten to be so suspicious of them just because they're foreign."

"You've got a good point there."

"Uh-huh." He leaned his elbows on the bar and lowered his voice. "None of my business but you got some reason for being up here? I figure you live downtown right?"

"Yes. I have a reason. I'm looking for somebody Mike and I met last night. Just thought I'd stop in for a beer to cool off."

"Uh-huh. Know your way around, do you?"

"No." He looked the bartender in the eye.

"They's some neighborhoods up here not too safe for a lone white man now. Didn't used to be that way, though. Seems like people's just all stirred up and mad. It's the unemployment, and the drugs, things like that, you know."

"I know."

"Just watch yourself. I mean, you're okay around here on 125th Street. Nobody's goin' bother you here, but if you're aimin' to go wanderin' around, well, best keep your eyes open. That's all."

"I appreciate the advice." Peter sipped his beer. The man's advice hadn't increased his self-confidence. "How's 135th Street?"

"Depends on where on 135th Street. Some of it's fine—up around City College that is—that's okay. And if you go way on over, there's the police station. But some areas in between—kinda rough." He scratched his chin. "If you don't mind me asking, where you goin'?"

"I don't know exactly. Hope I'll recognize it when I get there." He got down off the barstool. "Thanks a lot. Maybe I'll stop in for another on my way downtown."

"You do that." The bartender smiled, showing a gold tooth in front.

"Nice meeting you—"

"Sam."

"Nice meeting you, Sam."

"Uh-huh. What's yours?"

"Peter. Peter Blanchard."

"Yeah. Nice meeting you, too, Pete." He picked up the bottle and glass. "Just remember what I told you."

"I will. See you later." Peter squared his shoulders and walked out into the steaming street. The bright light hurt his eyes after the darkness of the bar, and he shaded them with his hand for a moment, then spread his fingers to let the light filter through more slowly. When his eyes had adjusted, he set off up Broadway.

At 135th Street and Broadway he turned right and walked two blocks east into a dead end. City College students were milling about, and he spotted the bright yellow umbrella of a hot dog vendor's cart in the middle of the block toward 136th Street. Peter headed for the cart. A short, stocky man with huge, square hands was tending it, and around the cart several students stood eating.

"Excuse me, but can you tell me what becomes of 135th Street?" he asked. The vendor, in the midst of stuffing a frankfurter into a bun, looked up, squinted at him, and pointed east.

"Across park," he said with an Italian accent. Peter looked in the direction he pointed and saw green behind the buildings. He felt disoriented for a moment, for Central Park stopped at 110th Street.

"How do I get there?" he asked.

"138th Street," he answered.

"Go up to 138th Street, that'll take you around the park. You come back to 135th Street then," offered a young black woman waiting for the hot dog.

"Thank you," said Peter and set off again, but more slowly now; his leg had begun to hurt. He spotted a taxi cruising near the CCNY gates and whistled for it. The taxi stopped and he continued walking to it. Normally he would have run to catch up to it, being conditioned as New Yorkers are to someone else snatching a taxi before they can claim it, but now he took his time. He knew he couldn't make it running.

"Can you take me around the park to 135th Street?" he asked, getting into the taxi.

"Sure," said the driver.

"It's a short haul, but I've got a sore leg, and I didn't know 135th Street was divided."

"Yeah. Strangers always making that mistake." New York was an amazing city, thought Peter; he'd lived here for ten years, and he was constantly discovering areas he never knew existed.

He sat back in the cab and tried to organize his thoughts to remember everything he could about the storefront. The cab rattled along—it seemed about to fall apart—and Peter suspected the fleet owners gave the worst cabs in the garage to the black guys who cruised Harlem. Although he'd ridden in a few heaps downtown, he couldn't remember riding in any that had been quite as bad as the one which bore him now.

170

He watched the neighborhood worsen as they got away from the CCNY area. The taxi stopped at the corner of 135th Street, and he paid the fare and got out. He looked around for anything that looked vaguely familiar, but nothing did. It was miserably hot and humid, and his leg hurt a great deal now, but he began to walk.

One hundred thirty-fifth Street turned downhill, and he knew the store wasn't on that block, it had definitely been on level ground. Run-down brownstones lined the block, and residents were hanging out windows or sitting on stoops, obviously trying to get a breath of air. They regarded him with little or no interest; it was too hot to care what a white man was doing there in the heat of the day. Further on down he could see that the street leveled out, and neighborhood youngsters were playing stickball in the street. When he came up to them, he saw that they were oblivious to the occasional automobile that challenged them for the right-of-way.

He crossed the avenue and passed a house where several teen-agers loitered around the stoop of a brownstone. He didn't like the hostile way they looked at him as he passed, but he kept on going, his eyes directed in front of him.

"Hey, whitey!" called the tallest boy. "You got yourself lost, man?" They all laughed, but Peter ignored the challenge and kept on walking. Out of the corner of his eye, however, he saw the boy and one of his friends get off the stoop and fall into step a little distance behind him. They didn't hurry, but strolled along nonchalantly. Peter tensed. It could be coincidence that they were going the same way he was, then again it might not be. At any rate, he thought there were too many people in the street at this time of day for them to try to take him. Still he was painfully aware of his limp, and knew he looked like a pigeon to anyone interested. Up ahead he saw what looked like some storefronts and kept on walking.

He came to the first glass front in the block and stopped. It didn't look like Grandma Geranium's. He glanced back up the street and saw that the two teen-agers had stopped in front of a brownstone and stood against the stoop watching him. Okay, they were watching him, but that didn't mean they meant to mug him. He walked on, keeping well out to the curb. He had no intention of being hauled into a doorway and having his money removed from him at knife point; for it was likely the other boys who'd been on the stoop with the two

171

behind him might have run on ahead. They could be waiting for him in some doorway. He'd read somewhere that muggers often worked that way.

He passed another storefront and it looked vaguely familiar. There was a streetlamp in front of it, too, so he walked over to the curb and saw that what he'd thrown up the night before still lay there stinking and collecting flies. This was undoubtedly Grandma's place. He felt his pulse quicken; he wanted to rush up to the door, and at the same time he wanted to run away from it. He looked back up the street to see where the boys were, and saw them watching him. He tried to estimate the time, and thought it probably around twelve-thirty. Grandma might very well be asleep, and it might take some time to get her to come to the door—time enough for the teen-agers to trap him in the doorway. Further down the street he saw several blue and white patrol cars of the New York Police Department parked nose in to the curb. That would be the station house the bartender had mentioned, but it was two blocks away. He looked back again and saw the boys still in the same place, but clearly watching him.

He debated: he could pound on Grandma's door, then step back to the curb and wait for her to answer. Then again, he might have trouble persuading her to let him in, and the boys could rush him and be on their way before she had realized what was happening. Being streetwise, as he was certain she was, she might very well slam the door in his face. After all, hadn't she been very careful about opening her door last night—keeping the chain lock on the door while she identified Mike to her satisfaction? He didn't want to bring her any trouble, and he was certain the boys would welcome a chance to get into her place.

He decided to walk on ahead to the police station, if necessary, and maybe put them off. He began to walk again; purposefully now, even though his leg was protesting more seriously. He stopped at the light, and glanced back over his shoulder. The boys were still in the same place. Perhaps he had been wrong; perhaps they were just curious as to where a white man was going. Or maybe they were afraid of coming closer to the police station. The light changed, and he crossed the street. There was a phone booth on the corner, and he stepped into it. His two hours were nearly up, and he thought he should call his secretary; otherwise she would be calling

Mike in a panic. He dropped a dime into the slot and looked up the street while the call went through. The boys were still on the stoop. After he'd assured his secretary that he was all right, and that he'd check in again in another couple of hours, he hung up.

It really irritated him to be so close to his destination and have two boys keep him from doing what he'd come to do. But now that he knew exactly where Grandma Geranium Victoria lived, he could take a cab right to her door later on in the afternoon. In the meantime he decided to take a taxi back to the bar on 125th Street and wait an hour, then come back. He stepped out of the booth and waited on the corner for a taxi. He had to wait several minutes. Taxis were evidently not plentiful in this neighborhood. Just before he got into the taxi, he looked up the street and saw the two boys still watching him. It gave him a small sense of satisfaction, being able to thwart them.

At three o'clock Peter arrived back at the storefront and asked the taxi driver to wait until he was admitted; if no one let him in, he'd be going back downtown. He gave the driver an extra two dollars to wait. He looked up and down the street: it was almost deserted this time. The sun had finally driven people indoors, and the teen-agers were nowhere in sight.

He went to the door and knocked. There was no response, and he looked back at the taxi driver who was watching. Peter shrugged, and knocked again, this time more vigorously. He heard someone stir within and knocked harder.

"Who knocks?" asked a muffled voice.

"It's Mike's friend, Grandma. I'd like to see you." There was a silence inside, and then the door opened slightly. He could see it was dark inside.

"What you want, mon?" It was Grandma Geranium Victoria all right, for he could see the strange gray eyes.

"I want to talk with you for a moment."

"Talk? What you talk about?" she asked.

"What you told me last night."

"What I told you last night?" she asked.

"About the spirit of my friend."

"About Michael?"

"No, about my friend who died from the airplane crash." He was beginning to have a sinking feeling. Was it possible she didn't remember? "Look, Grandma, may I come in?"

"You got money?"

"Yes. Twenty dollars, isn't that right?" Peter took out the twenty and pushed it through the door toward her.

"Okay. You come in." She took the money and removed the chain on the door. Peter looked back at the taxi.

"Okay, you can go now. Thanks." The driver waved and drove off. Peter stepped into the dark room. He could just make out Grandma's figure moving toward the curtained doorway.

"You take seat, please. Think very hard about friend. I go to prepare for meeting spirit."

"Grandma Geranium Victoria, please, you contacted my friend last night."

"Why you come back then?" She sounded quarrelsome.

"Because you said he was not in the other world, he was here."

"Here?"

"Yes. You said he would not speak because he had a secret. I want to know what you meant about him being here, and what his secret was."

"I not tell you secret?" It was obvious now: she remembered nothing of the previous night's revelations.

"No. You said his spirit would not speak."

"You want to know secret?"

"Yes. Very much."

"If spirit no speak, cannot know secret." She stepped close to him and looked into his eyes. He met hers directly. She opened her eyes very wide then and backed away from him. "Remember now. No can help." She seemed suddenly very agitated and held out his twenty dollars. "Please, you go now!"

"Wait, please. What is it you see that disturbs you?" Frustration was beginning to rise in him.

"No can help!" She pushed the twenty at him again, but he did not take it. "Please, you go now." He had to think of some way to make her talk.

"Can you try to contact my friend again? Perhaps this time he will speak?" He was getting frantic. "I will pay more."

"Is wrong to disturb spirit when hides."

"Do you know the secret?" He moved closer to her.

"No! Twice I tell you spirit no speak!" Her eyes flashed

with anger. She dropped the twenty on the table. "You no have the honest eyes. Go now!" He was stunned by her statement. How to explain to her?

"Let me explain. I was blind. My friend gave me his sight when he died. I had an operation."

"Is possible?" Her voice betrayed her disbelief.

"Yes. They took a part of his eyes—the corneas—and put them into mine." Fear came into her eyes, and she held up her hands, palms outward, as if to push him away from her.

"Shame!" she hissed. "You steal friend's eyes. Go! Go out of my house!" She moved forward, pushing the air with her hands. "Evil thief! Devil thief!" she shouted.

"No, no! You don't understand!" he protested frantically as she forced him back toward the door.

"Understand plenty now. Spirit speak through eyes. Friend have no more eyes, no can speak. You steal eyes, steal spirit, now want to steal secret, too!"

"No, please—"

"You have the big devil's curse!" she screeched.

"No! He wanted me to have them, he gave me his eyes!" cried Peter.

"Go! Go away, evil man!" Her face contorted with fear and hatred, and despite his anguish Peter realized that he was looking into the face of primitive superstitions; her origins had taken command. It would be no use to try to explain further; she would not hear him. He had no choice but to leave.

She flung open the door, and the bright sunlight burst into the room. "Never you come back here!" she screamed. He hurriedly backed out the door, and she slammed it in his face.

He stood in the street, shaking with impotent rage and awe. He had never encountered pure, raw superstition before, and it totally unnerved him. He tried to compose himself as he began to walk away, oblivious to everything around him. Her charge of evil, the pronouncement that a curse was upon him, echoed in his ears. Ravings of a crazy old woman! he rationalized. No more! And yet. . . .

# Chapter Sixteen

Peter was aroused by a loud knocking at the door. He started to get up, but his leg gave way under him on the first try. He had fallen asleep sitting in the chair he had collapsed in when he got home from Harlem. He finally got up on the second try and limped to the door.

"Jesus Christ! Where the hell have you been?" Mike burst into the room.

"Mike? What are you doing here?"

"Looking for you, you clown!"

"Looking for me? I don't understand."

"You don't understand?" Mike threw himself into a chair. Peter remained standing, uncertain what was happening.

"Look, man, I've walked my shoe leather off looking for you, right?"

"So you say." Peter eased into a chair, he was feeling confused.

"So I say!" shouted Mike. "Pete, I'm sleeping peacefully in my pad, and the telephone starts ringing off the wall, right? Finally I answer, right? So this lady lays on me that one Peter Blanchard has gone to see Grandma, and ain't been heard from in *too* long. This sweet chick lays on me that one Peter Blanchard has told her to call me, right?"

"Oh, my God!" Peter slapped his forehead with the heel of his hand.

"This Peter Blanchard says I should come looking for him, right?"

"Mike, I forgot to call in—" Peter started to apologize, but Mike cut him off.

"So I go chargin' up to 135th Street, and I find Grandma Geranium Victoria with blood in her eyes, ready to kill. She's got it into her crazy gourd that I sent this devil with stolen eyes to tempt her!"

"Mike, I am so sorry."

"I barely get out of there with my life, right? Then I go asking everybody I can find if they've seen a crazy white cat prowling around. And they've seen one all right, but a lot earlier in the day. Man, I turn that neighborhood upside down, but I don't come up with nothin' on that white cat. So I go back to 125th Street to do some thinking. But Sam tells me this cat's been in there three times: once in the morning drinking beer, and later on drinking beer, and still later on drinking straight Scotch. So I start calling this cat's pad—no answer. Then I call his office, and his secretary says she ain't heard from him, but some sci-fi scribe named Webber has, and he's supposed to meet this cat, see, but he's got to be late, and he can't get an answer at his pad either. So, I hightail it over here, figuring you've got a drunk going over whatever Grandma said, and considering the state I found her in, I reckon she's said plenty!" Mike ran out of steam.

"Yes, she got excited all right. You see, she said I had dishonest eyes, and then I tried to explain about the operation, and—"

"And she went bananas!"

"Yes."

"Man, I thought you had smarts, but was I wrong! Didn't you know that old crow was a superstitious voodoo fruitcake?"

"I just didn't think. I—I had to find out what she'd meant last night when she said Carl's spirit was in the room."

"And—what his secret was?"

"Yes."

"I never should have blabbed to you about that secret."

"But you did. And besides, she knew he had a secret."

"Guessin', that's all."

"And she picked up something about my eyes, too."

"Peter, take some advice: get off this Carl trip before you

drive yourself round the bend." Mike's face showed serious concern.

"Can't do it, Mike. Not until I find out what it is Carl wants from me."

"Jesus Christ! You're a fuckin' masochist!"

"It's easy for you to say; you're not the one being haunted."

"You're doing it to yourself, Pete. Why?"

"Oh, sure. I just love being haunted by a dead man!"

"I give up!" Mike brought the flat of his hand down on the arm of the chair and shot to his feet. At that moment the doorbell rang.

"Wait a minute, Mike!" Peter moved toward the door.

"Shit, man! I'm getting out of here," said Mike, but Peter already had the door open.

"Hi, Bob. Come in, come in." Peter held the door open, and Bob Webber walked in.

"Sorry I'm late."

"Mike, I want you to meet Bob Webber." Mike was already halfway across the room to leave. "Bob, my friend Mike Fuller. Mike was in the hospital with me in France. Also a fantastic drummer." The two men shook hands and exchanged pleasantries. "Bob's the best science-fiction writer in the country, Mike."

"Yeah?"

"Sit down. Let me get you both a drink." Peter was already at the bar. "What'll it be?"

"Listen, Pete, I got to be going."

"Come on, Mike, have a drink." Peter crossed the room and handed the glass to Mike. They looked at each other. "Come on, Mike, stay awhile." Peter didn't want Mike to leave angry: Mike had gone to a lot of trouble on his behalf, and he wanted him to know that he was grateful.

"Okay. I guess I got time for one." Mike grinned and took the glass.

"Good. Now, how about you, Bob? What can I get you?"

"Vodka tonic?"

"Vodka tonic it is."

"Were you in the plane crash, too?" Bob asked Mike.

"You guessed it." Mike sat back down in the same chair.

"From what Peter tells me, it was a horrific experience."

"Wouldn't want to do it again," laughed Mike.

"Here you are, Bob." Peter handed him the vodka tonic and limped across the room to the sofa.

"That leg's still bothering you, huh?" asked Bob.

"Overdid it today."

"You can say that again!" said Mike.

"So, did you get the name?" Peter asked Bob.

"Yeah. Had to make a few phone calls, but I got the name of the man I was trying to think of."

"Where is he?"

"He's up in Westchester."

"That's good. I was afraid he might be in California, or someplace like that."

"A lot of the psychics are out there, but the best one is here in Westchester—according to my information."

"That's what I want." Peter turned to Mike. "I asked Bob to get me the name of a topnotch, reputable psychic."

"Man, you just won't let go, huh?" Mike shook his head. Peter laughed nervously.

"Mike doesn't quite approve of my interest in psychic phenomena."

"No?"

"I got my hands full with the here and now," Mike said lightly.

"Well, Peter's always been right on top of current trends. Just one of the things that makes him one of the most successful editors in the business."

"That so?" said Mike. So the science-fiction cat didn't know why Peter wanted that name. This new development made him more uneasy about Peter than ever.

When Mike finished his drink, he made his excuses, telling Peter that he'd call him later, and left. He walked a few blocks, trying to ease his mind, but a nagging fear that Peter was getting deeper into trouble kept gnawing at him. The worst of it was, he felt part of it was his fault. He should not have told him that Carl had confessed a secret to him, and he should not have taken him to see Grandma. Too much gin, that's what it had been. But he hadn't realized that Peter was that far gone. Somebody had to talk to him, somebody he would listen to. And there was only one person he could think of who might talk some sense into him.

Mike sat across from Marcy in her comfortable apartment,

sipping a cool drink and trying to think of the best way to tell her why he'd asked to see her.

"It's a pleasant surprise to see you, Mike," she said as she brought her own drink and sat on the sofa across from him.

"Yeah. Good to see you, Marcy. But I gotta tell you I'm here for a special reason."

"What's that, Mike?" Her smile was warm, and her eyes showed genuine interest. That was just one of the outstanding things about Marcy: she was genuine—all the way.

"Well, I'm worried about Pete." He did not miss the change of expression on her face at the mention of Peter's name.

"Is something wrong with Peter?" Her voice was concerned.

"A lot could be wrong, if somebody don't talk some sense into him. I tried, but I bombed out."

"And you think maybe I can?"

"You guessed it."

"Tell me about it, Mike."

"It's this business about Carl, and his eyes." Mike paused, "I'm sorry, Marcy—"

"It's all right, go on." She smiled reassuringly.

"Well, I think he's going off the deep end over it." Mike repeated the conversation he'd had with Peter about Carl's reasons for wanting, or trying, to take him over, but he was careful to leave out mention of the secret. He also told of the visit to Grandma Geranium Victoria, again omitting the secret. Marcy turned ashen when he told her about Grandma's saying Carl's spirit was not in the other world but in the room.

"Poor Peter. He must have been terribly upset," she said.

"The trouble is, he went back up to Harlem by himself today to see Grandma, and she really laid a trip on him."

"What happened?"

"She told him he had dishonest eyes. He tried to explain about the operation and she went bananas! Grandma's from Barbados, and superstitious as a witch. So she ups and accuses Pete of stealing Carl's eyes! Then she lays on him that he's got a big devil curse on him."

"Oh, my God." Marcy stared at him and clasped her hands tightly together. "He already feels guilty that he's alive and Carl's dead—mainly because of me, I'm afraid. I've tried

181

to tell him that I feel no resentment. I know it was just Carl's time.''

"I've told him, too, but there's something else, too, Marcy.''
"Yes?''

"Well—'' Mike paused and scratched his ear, wondering if he should say it. He decided she could handle it; probably already knew. "Marcy, honey, I think the man's in love with you. He wants you, but he's got a load of guilt.''

She looked down at her hands in her lap for a long time, and when she looked up, there was pain in her face. Her voice was tight with emotion.

"We are drawn to one another, Mike.'' She paused. "It is not an easy thing for either of us.''

"Marcy, this may be out of place, but I think Carl wanted this to happen.''

"You do?'' Now her eyes were softly questioning.

"Yeah, I really do. It was a heavy thing on his conscience that he was leaving you all alone. He told me toward the last there, to ask Pete to go and see you.''

"I know. Peter told me.''

"But the far-out part is, Pete's got it in his head Carl's trying to take him over. I mean, he is bugged by that notion.'' Mike gulped his drink; he was feeling the strain of wanting to help Peter and at the same time being afraid he'd say something to upset Marcy. "Now he's planning on going to see one of them fancy *psychic* cats—find out what Carl wants from him that way.''

"He *is*?''

"Yeah. I was at his house when this science-fiction turkey, some writer, turns up with the name and address of this psychic up in Westchester.''

"He *is* upset.'' She spoke as if to herself and with a worried look.

"I mean, Grandma Geranium Victoria is a crazy, superstitious old crow, but some real smart psychic could really fu—uh, sorry, Marcy, I mean, uh—could really do a number on his head.''

"How was he when you left him?''

"Couldn't tell. He was playing it real cool, talking to this sci-fi scribe, but he was—you know—restless. Man, the vibes I was gettin' from Pete made waves in *my* head.''

"I don't really know what to do, Mike. If he wants to go to

the psychic, it's really his business. I shouldn't try to interfere."

"But hell, Marcy, the way he is right now, anything could happen to him. I mean, he wasn't this rattled when he was blind in the sick pad."

"He's a grown man, Mike." She smiled reassuringly. "You're a good friend, and I know you're worried, but we have to let him work it out for himself. We can help if he asks us for help, but if he doesn't—well, we might do more harm than good."

"Marcy, tell me something."

"If I can."

"What do you think about this fix he's got on Carl?" Mike watched her face closely, trying to read what was behind the quiet composure.

"I think it's very painful and disturbing to him. He feels and knows things that he has no logical explanation for." She was quiet for a moment, her face thoughtful. Mike waited. "Sometimes people have psychological reactions to transplants, and I think something like that is happening to Peter."

"People can get crazy that way, too."

"I know." She paused. "Of course I haven't seen him for almost three weeks."

"Maybe you could talk to him?"

"Yes. Perhaps I should, if you feel he's that disturbed." She looked away, and Mike glanced at his watch.

"Gotta bug out, Marcy. Gotta go make music." Mike got up. "Thanks for lettin' me come."

"Thank you for coming." She walked to the door with him and held out her hand. "I'll think about what you've said, Mike. Maybe there is something I can do."

"Yeah. You do that." Mike started out the door, then leaned back inside. "I'm so busy talking about Pete, I forgot to ask—how *you* doin', Marcy?"

"Let's just say some days are better than others."

"Yeah. But this thing about Pete, it ain't getting to you, is it? I mean—"

"As you would say, I'm trying to stay cool." She smiled, and Mike laughed.

"When he ain't so crazy, he's an all right cat."

"I think so," she replied. Mike leaned over and kissed her on the cheek.

" 'Bye," he said and set off down the hall.

After Mike had left, Marcy washed their glasses and puttered around the apartment thinking about what Mike had told her. Could she help Peter? What could she say to him that would help? It was difficult enough to find answers for herself. If she went to him now, would it destroy her determination not to become involved with him, and confuse them further? Actually, in the three weeks since they'd seen one another, she'd done little more than wrestle with the urge to contact him. Also she was no closer to understanding what was happening to them or to reconciling herself to the fact that she felt attracted to him. She had planned to talk to Father Spencer this weekend in Connecticut. He had been a close friend to both her and Carl, as well as being their minister, and she felt sure he would be able to help her. Perhaps she could persuade Peter to talk with him, too; after all, Peter had been raised an Episcopalian. He had told her that in the hospital. But one did not even have to be religious to find help and comfort in the wise counsel of a learned theologian.

She sat down at the desk and stared at the telephone. Why not ask Peter to come up to the country on Saturday? Perhaps in the quiet of the country she could talk to him, and maybe being at the house where Carl had lived might help him find some answers. She picked up the phone and dialed his number. The phone rang and rang but there was no answer. As she put the receiver back into its cradle, she experienced a sense of disappointment and at the same time a feeling of uneasiness. She was surprised to find that she was more concerned about him than she'd realized. She'd call again first thing in the morning.

Peter had gone to dinner with Bob Webber. He hadn't wanted to because he was tired and anxious, but Bob had insisted, and he had finally given in; he felt obliged to him because Bob had gone to some effort to get the name of the psychic and even bring it over to him in person. The evening, however, had been disastrous for him; he had drunk too much, stayed up later than he wanted to, and got home exhausted and depressed. It had taken him a long time to get to sleep.

*    *    *

"*Peter, Peter Blanchard*." A voice came to him as though from a very great distance.

"Who's calling?" he answered.

"It's me. Don't you recognize me, Peter?" Peter was staring out over a vast plain covered with a swirling fog.

"I can't see you," he replied.

"Oh no, Peter, it is I who cannot see," replied the voice.

"Carl?"

"Yes, it's me, Carl. I've come for my eyes, Peter."

"But you gave them to me!"

"No, Peter. I never gave them to you. You stole my eyes from me."

"But Dr. Morel, and Marcy—they said you left them to me."

"You imagined that, Peter. You imagined it because you wanted to take them."

"That's impossible, Carl. I couldn't take your eyes. I wouldn't know how."

"Oh, you were clever. You paid Dr. Morel to take them."

"He couldn't do that. It would be illegal."

"You got around that, too. You had a paper drawn up. I saw it. It said that I, Carl Morris, bequeathed my eyes to Peter Blanchard in the hope that he would regain his sight. But I never wanted you to have my eyes—I need them. So you have to give them back."

"But that's impossible, Carl. The corneas are sewn to my eyes."

"Oh, that's no problem, I've brought a knife." Suddenly Carl stepped out of the fog, and Peter saw him clearly. He looked as Peter remembered him, except that his eye sockets were black, smoldering holes with smoke pouring from them. Carl smiled a diabolical smile and then Peter saw it: light caught the blade of a surgeon's scalpel as Carl brandished it, advancing toward him.

"No!" Peter screamed. "You keep away from me!" Peter tried to run, but his feet would not move. Carl came closer, still smiling, pointing the scalpel toward Peter's eyes.

"No! You can't have them! They're mine now. I—I need them." Peter put his hands up to shield his eyes.

"I need them, too, and I'm going to take them back."

"I won't let you!" Peter started to scream again and tried to lift his feet off the ground with his hands. They would not move. "Oh, please, please make them work!" he cried. Carl began to laugh hysterically. Peter fell on his knees and bent his head toward the ground, covering his eyes with his hands. Suddenly a hand shot out and grabbed him by the hair of the head, forced his head back, and knocked his hands away with a powerful blow. Peter stared up at the scalpel which was now surrounded by a blinding halo of light.

"No, no, please don't take my eyes!" He pleaded as he fought, but there was no pain in his hands even though he knew he must be lacerating them as he beat the scalpel back.

Peter awakened sitting straight up in bed, screaming. As he fought his way out of the dream, he began to shake violently.

"Oh, God!" he cried, and covering his eyes, burst into uncontrollable sobs. He was still shaking when the telephone began to ring, but he had stopped sobbing and was staring straight ahead at a sliver of early morning sunlight spilling into his room through the slightly parted draperies. He let the phone ring several times before reaching for it.

"Yes?" he whispered into the phone.

"Peter?"

"Yes."

"It's Marcy."

"Marcy?"

"Peter, are you all right?" She sounded alarmed. He was slowly becoming conscious of reality.

"Oh. Marcy. Yes. Yes, I'm all right. How are you?"

"I'm well." She paused. "I've been doing a lot of thinking."

"Me, too." There was a long silence, and he couldn't think of anything to say.

"Peter, I think maybe it might be a good idea if you come out to the country on the weekend—if you don't have plans."

"Why?"

"Well, I thought it would give us a chance to talk, and I thought perhaps being in the house might help you to answer some of the questions that have been troubling you."

"I suppose it might." He couldn't completely shake free of the dream and understand what she was saying, but he was clearheaded enough to wonder whether he belonged in Carl Morris's house right now.

"Peter, what's wrong? You sound so strange." She had

186

sensed from the beginning of the conversation that something was wrong with him.

"I feel strange, too," he replied.

"Did something happen?"

"You might say something did. Listen, Marcy, I'm sorry, but I'm not operating very well right now. I—I just woke up from a terrible nightmare."

"Oh." There was a pause on the other end. "Would it help to talk about it?" Her voice was warm and sympathetic, and he wanted to talk about it, but he couldn't do it yet.

"Maybe on the weekend, Marcy."

"Then you will come out?"

"Sure. If you think it's a good idea."

"There's a train out of Grand Central at nine-thirty on Saturday morning. If that's all right, I'll meet you at the station in Fairfield."

"Okay. I'll be there." He hung up the phone and sat staring straight ahead. Saturday was three days off; maybe it would be long enough to pull himself together. He dragged himself out of bed; he had to get to the office and catch up on the work he'd let go yesterday, especially since he meant to leave a little early in order to get up to Scarsdale in good time for his appointment with Vadim. It had been difficult to get an appointment with the psychic—in fact he'd had no opening—but when Peter stressed the urgency of his need, he had agreed to see him after hours.

Peter looked into the mirror as he plugged in his razor, but instead of seeing his own face, he saw Carl's. He threw the razor at the glass and shattered it. He grabbed the towel rack with both hands to steady himself.

"Damn you Carl Morris! Leave me alone! Leave me along—do you hear!"

187

# Chapter Seventeen

It was not until noon that Peter remembered that Vadim had asked him to bring something, some object, that had belonged to Carl. Peter's anxiety level was so high that his brain was not functioning well, and it was not surprising that he had forgotten Vadim's instructions. Those instructions, however, presented a problem. How was he going to get hold of something that had belonged to Carl without asking Marcy? He didn't want to go to her because he didn't want her to know he was consulting a psychic; she might try to dissuade him from going. But if he didn't ask her, how was he going to get something of Carl's? Of course, he possessed a part of Carl, but Vadim had specifically said to bring an object. Then he remembered: Carl had given Mike his watch. That would be perfect.

He reached for the telephone, then stopped. Would Mike let him have the watch? He'd have to tell him why he wanted it, and last night Mike had made it very clear that he didn't think much of psychics. Still Mike was the best bet. Oh, he'd argue, but he'd probably give in. If he had to, Peter would pressure him by telling him that Grandma had made such a mess out of his head that he had to go see a professional to get it straightened out. That wasn't all fabrication either.

He started dialing Mike's number.

\* \* \*

Peter squeezed his car onto the East River Drive at Ninety-sixth Street and headed north in bumper-to-bumper traffic toward the Major Deegan Expressway leading into Westchester County. It was rush hour, and he'd tried to leave himself enough time to get to Scarsdale. He felt Carl's watch in his pocket and went back over the struggle he'd had with Mike to get it. Mike's argument had been much as he'd expected. At least it kept his mind off last night's nightmare, though, and away from the anxiety he felt over the upcoming interview.

Vadim lived in an ugly red brick mansion hidden behind high walls and tall trees on a quiet street in Scarsdale. Peter drove slowly up the long, winding driveway toward a columned portico. A young, muscular butler appeared even before he'd brought the car to a stop and put his head through the open car window.

"Mr. Blanchard?"

"Yes."

"Vadim is expecting you. Please leave your car here and come with me." Peter got out and followed the young man into the house and down a long red-carpeted corridor to a heavy paneled door. The butler opened the door and stood aside.

"You will go in, please."

"Thank you." Peter stepped into a softly lit room beautifully appointed with antique furniture of the periods of Queen Anne and George I. The floor was covered with a large Aubusson rug of subtle colors. Music could be heard faintly, and Peter identified it as Bach. The atmosphere was one of taste and tranquility, and immediately he felt at home.

"Mr. Blanchard?" A tall, thin man with a delicately handsome face and a shaved head came toward him. He was elegantly dressed in a dark pinstriped business suit. He held out his hand. "I am Vadim."

"Peter Blanchard."

Vadim's handshake was firm, and he smiled warmly as he studied Peter's face with dark, penetrating eyes.

"Won't you sit down?" He indicated a chair. Vadim seated himself in a chair some distance away, facing Peter. "Is this your first visit to a psychic, Mr. Blanchard?" His voice was deep and quietly resonant.

"Yes."

"You are much troubled, are you not?"

"Yes, I am."

"And you wish to make contact with a friend who has departed?"

"Yes."

"Let us hope it is possible. Did you bring an object which belonged to your friend?"

"Yes. His wristwatch."

"Excellent. May I have it?"

Peter took out the watch and handed it to Vadim. The psychic looked at it casually and closed his hand around it." Tell me something of your friend, Mr. Blanchard."

"Well, I didn't know him very long, or very well." Peter had expected to be nervous and anxious, but he felt surprisingly calm. "I sat next to him on a flight from New York to Paris. We talked a little about ourselves, as strangers will on a long flight."

"But this was not an ordinary flight, was it?"

Vadim sat with his head resting against the back of the chair. His eyes were closed, and he was rubbing Carl's watch between his thumb and forefinger. His expression was one of intense concentration.

"No, it was not," Peter replied.

"It crashed, did it not?" It was really a statement, and Peter did not feel shocked.

"Yes. We crashed at the airport. We knew for some time beforehand that we would have to make an emergency landing because of a malfunction of the landing gear. It was jammed."

"You and your friend became somewhat closer then, knowing that you might die?"

"Yes. We talked about our own lives."

"But your friend, what was his Christian name?"

"Carl."

"Yes. Carl did not die in the crash."

"No. We were both injured, and taken to the American Hospital. He died there several days later."

"He suffered much." Again it was a statement.

"Yes. He had been badly injured."

"He was a brave man, your friend?"

"Yes. He was burned helping others escape from the plane."

"Did he help you to escape also?"

"No. I was thrown clear of the plane."

"You liked him?"

"Yes, I did. He was an easy man to like. Someone you could talk to—a calm, rational man. He inspired confidence and respect."

"He gave you something, something very important."

Peter felt jolted for the first time.

"He gave me his eyes." A lump came into his throat.

"You were blinded?"

"Not in the crash. As a result of other complications. Carl heard about it and, knowing he was going to die, willed me his eyes. I had cornea transplants."

"You see well now?"

"Very well."

"Do you feel indebted to him?"

"No, at least not consciously. I do sometimes wonder why I survived instead of him. But, of course, I am very grateful for the gift."

"Of course." Vadim was quiet for a moment, and Peter watched his face. It was almost the face of an ascetic, except for the determined jaw and the slight suggestion of arrogance in the way he carried his head: they belied the asceticism. "I sense that you are troubled by this gift, nevertheless."

"I'm troubled by the change in my own perceptions and attitudes since regaining my sight. I feel restless—almost like a different person. And sometimes I know things I could have no way of knowing."

"Why does that trouble you?"

"Because I can't explain them. I don't know where they come from."

"One may cultivate one's perception, intuition, awareness to know many things that might seem impossible to someone else."

"Yes, I know that, but—" He let his sentence trail off.

"For example, Mr. Blanchard, you come to me to tell you something that presumably I do not know, and you will not be able to explain how I know. Why then are you disturbed by knowing things yourself?"

"I'm not sure. It—it just never happened to me before the operation." Peter felt slightly foolish.

"Perhaps you had the ability before, Mr. Blanchard, and never cultivated it. Since you have had a close brush with death, and other traumatic things have happened in your life, it is possible that other aspects of your personality and psyche may surface, may even begin to dominate more than before.''

"I suppose that's possible. I have always been rather intuitive. But—this is different—'' Peter felt uncertain of his ground.

"Is it possible that these things you know are things that only your friend Carl would know?"

"Yes." Peter relaxed then and realized he had been holding his breath.

"Perhaps he is sending you messages.'' Peter saw the shadow of a smile on Vadim's face then.

"Yes. Sometimes I feel he is—that he wants something from me, and I don't know what it is.''

"Is that what you came to me to learn?''

"Yes, partly. You see, sometimes I feel he is trying to take me over.''

Vadim had been sitting with his eyes closed, but now he opened them and gave Peter a slightly quizzical look.

"Is there some reason he might want to do that?''

"I'm—I'm not sure.''

"But you have an idea?''

"Well, yes. Maybe.'' Peter didn't want to reveal too much, yet he had to give the psychic some knowledge of his situation before he asked the two questions he'd come to ask. "You see, I feel drawn to his wife. They were very much in love, but had no children. She is alone now.''

"Ah.'' Vadim sighed and closed his eyes again. "And the woman?''

"She also feels drawn to me.''

"Has anything of an intimate nature occurred between you?''

"No.''

"But you think Carl is drawing you together.''

"Yes. Or—well, perhaps he is trying to take me over to get back to her.''

"Tell me, do you perceive Carl's spirit as a good or an evil spirit?''

"I—I don't know.'' He was somewhat surprised at his answer, but it was true, he didn't know. Two months ago he would have been able to answer that question with conviction, now he was not certain.

"There is something else troubling you, is there not?"

"Carl had a secret—something he felt guilty about. It was so heavy on his conscience, he had to confess it when he knew he was dying. He confessed to a man who had been on the plane."

"What is this secret?"

"I don't know. The man promised Carl he wouldn't tell anyone. But he did tell me that Carl carried a secret, and that it was heavy on his conscience at the end. My intuition tells me that it may still be troubling him—that he perhaps has some unfinished business—"

"Something that he wants you to do?"

"Yes. But I don't know what it is. I just feel that if I knew what that secret was, it might give me a clue to what is happening to me, and why."

"Ah. Then it is the secret that you wish to know."

"Yes. I'd like to know that, and what he wants from me."

"Direct questions are difficult, Mr. Blanchard. I seldom ask them, for answers seldom come that way. Let me explain how I work. You see, I associate myself with the departed spirit, and through deep concentration I make myself open to receive any message the spirit wishes to send. All knowledge is in the cosmos, Mr. Blanchard; it is we who are unable to receive it, to become one with it. I attempt to make myself one with it—to be open to it."

"I understand." Peter was fascinated, his intellectual curiosity had been piqued despite himself.

"Sometimes answers come, but they are strange, vague, even puzzling. At other times they are clear and strong and revealing. It depends on the desire of the departed spirit to convey a message, and the strength of the spirit in sending it."

"In other words some spirits have a stronger signal than others?" Peter could not resist the analogy. Vadim smiled indulgently.

"You might put it that way, yes. Let us hope your friend has a strong one, and that he wishes to send a message to you. Now I must ask you to meditate, to clear your mind of all distractions and concentrate on a tranquility of spirit. When you have rid your mind of worldly distractions, I wish you then to concentrate intensely on Carl. Visualize his face, hear his voice, relive any conversation you had with him on

*194*

the plane. Become aware of him as a spirit, a being—the essence of the man as you perceived him. I will be concentrating with you, and preparing myself to be open and receptive. Under no circumstances are you to speak to me, unless I ask you to. Is that understood?''

"Yes. I understand." Peter felt himself begin to tense up, but Vadim had closed his eyes and seemed completely relaxed. The attitude of his body seemed liquid, flowing. His face had become tranquil, unlined, almost beatific. There was no sound in the room, and the only movement was Vadim's hand as he fingered Carl's watch. Peter concentrated on clearing his mind as he had been instructed and then on Carl. The minutes slowly ticked by, but Peter had become unaware of time, or even of Vadim; he was concentrating on Carl with all his being.

"Yes. There is something there," whispered Vadim. Peter felt his pulse quicken, but he forced the excitement down and kept the picture of Carl in his mind.

"It is faint—but it is coming—" The moments ticked by again, and Peter opened his eyes and saw Vadim lean slightly forward in his chair. "Yes—" he whispered. "We are here, Carl—we await your message." Peter felt the churning of panic beginning to rise, but he tried to clear his mind and begun to pray that he would not panic. As he prayed, a kind of quiet settled over him, and he was able to direct his mind back to Carl.

"Yes—yes—" Vadim whispered softly. *"Ch—"*Peter opened his eyes and saw Vadim again leaning forward, his face intense and expectant. *"Ch—ch—ch—ild—Child!* Yes, 'child'— we hear you." Vadim continued to lean forward, straining to receive the rest of the message. Peter forced himself to concentrate again on Carl, and time ticked off. Then he heard Vadim stir, and he opened his eyes. Vadim had collapsed against the back of the chair; he seemed totally exhausted and spent. He rested that way for a few moments, then opened his eyes and looked at Peter. "The message Carl is sending you is 'Child.' ''

"Child? Is that all?"

"I'm afraid so. The message was faint, but there was no mistaking it. It came several times, but there was no more."

"But what does it mean?"

"It has no meaning to you?"

"No. As I told you, they had no children. I can't imagine—"

"Sometimes, as I said, the message is obscure, but if one searches one's own heart and mind, and asks questions of others, the meaning of the message often will become clear."

"But the word 'child'—so vague." Peter felt let down; he had to know more. "Do you think Carl's spirit will reveal more?"

"Perhaps. One never knows."

"Is it possible to contact it again?"

"Not tonight, Mr. Blanchard. The intensity of concentration required to become associated with the departed spirit, and to open myself to receive its message, is extremely exhausting." Peter believed him, for he could see the fatigue on his face, in the attitude of his body, and in his voice. In fact he felt exhausted himself.

"May I come back?" asked Peter.

"Surely. But first try to find the meaning of what he has already given you; for I must warn you, he may not reveal more. I remained in contact with him for some time hoping he would reveal more, but there was nothing.

"But if he wants me to know something, why would he withhold so much?"

"Sometimes the spirit is not strong enough to reach us clearly. Sometimes I am unable to make strong enough contact." Vadim rose and handed Carl's watch back to Peter. He held out his hand. "Good luck, Mr. Blanchard."

"Thank you." They shook hands, and Vadim escorted him to the door. "One more thing," said Peter. "Do you believe Carl would try to—well—I guess I mean *possess* me?"

"I don't know, Mr. Blanchard," said Vadim with a gentle smile. "But if you believe he is trying to do that, you must gather your strength to prevent it. He cannot possess you unless you allow it." Vadim opened the door and stepped aside for Peter to pass through.

"Good-bye, and thanks again," said Peter.

"Good-bye, Mr. Blanchard."

On the drive back to New York Peter further exhausted his brain trying to make some meaning out of the message. He felt deeply disapppointed that he had not learned more, but he did not feel cheated. He believed that Vadim had received that message, and there was meaning in it if he could just find it. But until he succeeded, the message was one more thing to torment him. He hoped to find out something that might give him a little peace; for he didn't know how much longer he could go on with tormented sleep and restless days before he cracked. He did, however, feel somewhat calmer since seeing Vadim; perhaps it was the tranquility of the man himself, and his surroundings, or perhaps it was the fact that Carl *had* sent him a message. At least he had something to go on.

He took the 125th Street exit off the Triborough Bridge. He had promised Mike to return his watch as soon as he got back. Mike was waiting for him at the now familiar bar. Peter went up to him and put his arm around his shoulder.

"Hi, Mike."

"Well?" Mike turned to look at him.

"Thanks for the watch." Peter handed him the watch, and the big man strapped it back on his wrist immediately.

"Want a drink?"

"No. I'm beat. I'm going home to try to sleep."

"Do you mean to say you ain't gonna tell me what happened?"

"Well, there's not much to tell." Peter sat on the stool next to Mike.

"What's that mean? He's a fake?"

"No. He got through to Carl."

"He did!" Mike's eyebrows shot up.

"Yes."

"Well—what the hell did he say?"

"According to Vadim, the message was one word—" Peter deliberately paused because he wanted to see Mike's face when he told him; he wanted to see what kind of reaction it produced.

"Peter, for Christ's sake! What was the fuckin' message?"

"The message was 'child.' "

" 'Child?' " Mike's eyes opened wide and he stared at Peter.

"That's it. There wasn't any more, just 'child.' "

"Son of a bitch!" Mike drained his glass and set it down hard on the bar.

"Mean something to you?"

"Hey, Joe!" Mike yelled at the bartender. "Hit me again!"

"Mike, does it mean something?"

"Shit, Pete, how would I know?" Mike scratched his head. "Mean anything to you?"

197

"Nothing at all." Peter lit a cigarette. "All I know is, I asked Vadim what Carl's secret was, and what he wanted of me. That's the message he got."

"This cat, this Vadim, what did he make of it?"

"He didn't. He just received the message and relayed it on to me."

Mike gave Peter a long, hard stare and began to drum his fingers nervously on the bar.

"Mike, it does mean something, doesn't it?"

"Pete, if you're gettin' around to asking me again what Carl told me, I'm heading you off at the pass."

"Okay, okay. But just tell me if there could possibly be any clue in what he told me, in light of what you know."

"I'm not saying yes and I'm not saying no. I'm saying nothing at all." Mike picked up his drink and sipped it thoughtfully.

From Mike's reaction, Peter guessed that he might have touched close to home. But he knew Mike wouldn't say anything more, so he was up against a stone wall again. If only he could get some little thing out of him, something to go on. But he knew Mike had a temper, and if he pushed him too hard, he could make him mad. He decided to try another approach.

"Do you think I'd be wasting my time if I went back to see Vadim?" asked Peter.

"Now how the hell would I know?"

"On the strength of the message he received, would you say I should go back?" Peter realized he was doing exactly what he'd just counseled himself not to do.

"Know something, man? You shoulda been a Philadelphia lawyer. You can think of more ways to ask the same question than any cat I ever ran across."

"You didn't answer my question."

"And I ain't going to either!"

"Okay. But would you let me have the watch again if I decide to go back?"

"Yes. Now leave me alone, will you?"

"I'm really sorry to keep bugging you, Mike, but you may have the information that could set me free. It's not comfortable, sitting in the spot I'm in."

"Yeah. I know." Mike threw his arm around Peter's shoulders. "Tell you somethin', man, it ain't any too comfortable sittin' where I am neither. I see you getting close to nuts, and I wish to hell I could help, but I can't go back on my promise. I mean, a man's got to stand for something, and if I broke my promise—''

"I know, I know. I'm sorry. I won't bug you about it anymore.''

"It ain't that I'm mad at you, man, and it ain't that I'm mad at old Carl for dumpin' on me either. I'm just mad because I'm so fuckin' helpless!''

"It's okay.'' Peter got up. "See you around.''

"Yeah.''

Peter started to walk away, then turned back.

"By the way, I'm going up to Connecticut to see Marcy on Saturday.''

"Yeah?'' Mike's face brightened.

"She asked me to come. She's got something on her mind about the house.''

"Good. That sounds good, Pete.''

Peter caught the nine thirty train on Saturday morning as Marcy had suggested. He sat on the train and stared moodily out of the window as it rattled through Westchester County and over the line into Connecticut. He had constructed story after story in which a child might figure into the lives of Marcy and Carl, or even into his own life, to illuminate the message Vadim had received, but none of them seemed believable.

The train stopped at Greenwich, Stamford, and Norwalk. Only two more stops before Fairfield, and Marcy. He began to anticipate seeing her. Three weeks had never seemed so long, except when he was in the hospital. He had kept his promise to give her space, but God alone knew what it had accomplished. Now she'd asked him to come and see her. Perhaps she'd worked something out and felt it was all right for them to see one another now. On the other hand, she might have decided they should not see one another at all. No, that was unlikely; she would not ask him to come all the way up to Connecticut to tell him that. It wouldn't be like her at all.

Strangely enough, Jeannie had been on his mind a lot in the last few hours. Even though things were not the same between them now, he found himself remembering what it

199

had been like to have an uncomplicated life. Occasionally he missed her and felt tempted to call and invite her to dinner, but then he thought better of the impulse. It would be unfair to her, when he was still unsure of so many things.

The train stopped at Westport, then Southport, and he began to straighten his tie and comb his hair with his fingers to make himself presentable. Somehow he knew this was going to be one of the most important weekends of his life. The train started to slow down.

"Fairfield. Fairfield, next stop," the conductor called.

# Chapter Eighteen

"Peter!" It was Marcy running down the platform toward him. She was wearing a white tennis dress, and her blond hair was flying. It seemed to him that she had met him like this hundreds of times before.

"Marcy!" He waved and began to smile. The sight of her made him feel wonderfully happy. She stopped in front of him, and she was laughing and trying to get her breath, and he was struck again by her beauty.

"Oh, dear! I thought I'd never make it on time!"

"But you did."

"By the skin of my teeth." She laughed and their eyes met. It was an emotionally charged moment.

"I've missed you," he said softly.

"Yes." She looked away. "How are you?"

"Terrific now that I see you. But how are you?"

"Busy, and active—and why are we standing here?"

"I don't know."

"Come on, let's go." He picked up his overnight case and followed her to the car, a dark green Riley convertible with its top down. He could see that it was in mint condition.

"This is quite an automobile." He was something of a car buff himself, owning a 1969 Mercedes 190 SL sports model. He tossed his overnight bag into the back seat.

"It belonged to my uncle. He gave it to me when he

bought himself a new Bentley convertible.'' She slid behind the wheel, and he got in beside her.

"Quite a spectacular gift," he said.

"Wasn't it? But you see, I'd always loved it, and used to invent the most elaborate reasons to borrow it."

"All of which he saw through, of course."

"Of course. But he indulged me." She put the car into gear and they began to move.

"I should think that would be very easy to do—you being you."

"Thank you." She guided the car out of the parking area. "You don't mind if I take you by the back route out of the village, do you?"

"Certainly not."

"It's quicker." They drove alongside the tracks and then turned right under the railroad underpass.

"By the way, who won?"

"Won?"

"The tennis match."

"Oh." She laughed. "I'm afraid I did."

"Are you very good?"

"Oh—respectable." He suspected she was being modest.

"When my leg improves, how about giving me a match?"

"Are you good?"

"Oh—" he shrugged. "Respectable."

"It's likely to be a very square match with both of us being so respectable." She laughed, and he loved the sound.

"Oh, I don't know. There are several things I'm not so respectable about."

"Near side of, or far side of?" she asked, playing along.

"Oh, the far side. Decidedly so." They both laughed.

"This is the tiny crossroads of Greenfield Hill," she said as they came to a fork in the road. There was a neat white colonial Exxon station and a small food market and liquor store in the triangle. Behind that was what had undoubtedly been an attempt to reproduce a suitable version of Colonial architecture to blend with the surrounding countryside. The building housed several shops and a pharmacy.

"Would you like some cheese?" he asked. She turned and looked at him strangely.

"How did you know there was a cheese shop?"

"I read the sign."

202

"Oh." She slowed down to pass through the area. "No, I got some earlier."

"Anything else you need? I didn't have time to pick up wine or anything like that."

"No, not really." She veered to the right and started up the hill. "The area we live in is actually Greenfield Hill, although the post office is Fairfield." He noticed she said "we." To her Carl was still very much alive.

"Neat. Pretty," he remarked.

"Yes." She drove in silence for a moment. "This road is famous for its dogwood in the spring. People come great distances to see it."

"Seems to me I've heard about it."

"Do you know what's at the top of the hill?"

"Yes. A church," he replied without giving it a thought.

"Yes—a church." She turned to look at him, and he left butterflies in his stomach.

"All right. I don't know how I knew that."

"I wasn't going to ask," she said. "You may have seen a postcard at some time. There are lots of them around."

"Marcy, did you ask me up here to run a recognition check on me?"

"Yes and no." She pulled up before the church and switched off the engine, then turned to look at him. "It did cross my mind that it might somehow help you with your questions about Carl."

"How so?"

"Maybe you'll find out if what you're wondering is true or not."

"Suppose I find out it is, then what?" The anxiety had returned.

"Then you can get professional help with it. I mean, if you feel it's something you can't handle by yourself."

"To get rid of Carl, or submit to him?" he asked coolly. A troubled look came over her face.

"Whichever *you* want." Her voice was barely above a whisper.

"Which do *you* want, Marcy?"

"I want you to be at peace with yourself, Peter."

"That would be nice for a change." There was a firmness in his voice, and they did not speak for a few moments.

"I think we'd better go home," she said.

"Okay."

She started the car and they rode along in silence for a few miles. He wanted very much to know what she was thinking, but somehow he couldn't ask; he was afraid of what she might say. Suddenly she spoke again.

"Peter, I wanted to see you," she said. "These last three weeks have been difficult for me."

"Same here. I picked up the phone a dozen times to call you, then talked myself out of it."

"I know."

"So what did we prove?"

"That we have some willpower left, I guess." She laughed softly.

"Not much, speaking for myself. I still feel the same attraction."

"Do you know why I played tennis this morning?"

"No."

"Because I couldn't stand waiting for you to arrive."

"It ought to be an interesting weekend," he said.

She steered the car into Reading Road, and he looked at the neat, well cared for houses set back among the trees. He had grown up among just such surroundings, and there was a certain comforting familiarity about being here.

"What's been happening with you?" she asked.

"Oh, quite a lot, actually. I'll give you a blow by blow account later on."

"I'd like that."

"You know, this area reminds me of where I grew up."

"I know so little about you. Where did you grow up?"

"Wayland, Mass., near Boston."

"I know it well. I went to school at Wellesley."

"Right next door."

She took a sharp left turn into a side road, and slowed down for two riders on horseback.

"That's a handsome barn up ahead there," he said.

"That's an old one, too." She slowed down for him to get a good look at it.

"I've often thought of buying a barn and converting it into a spectacular weekend house for myself."

"Lovely old timbers in that one," she said.

"Is it for sale?"

"I don't think so, but you never know."

"Interesting house across the field there, too." The house looked to be built of raw spruce, and had tall glass panels spaced all along the side.

"A little change of pace from the white clapboard, shuttered Colonial styles around, isn't it?" She nodded. "Must belong to some independent, free spirit."

"It does," she replied.

They drove on past it, around a bend in the road where a clapboard and fieldstone house nestled into the curve of the road. Another handsome barn, painted white and not as interesting as the other one, was off to the side of the house.

"That's a nice barn too, but I think I prefer the other one," he said to make conversation.

"So do I."

They drove past fields, a large white Colonial house with black shutters, and came to another crossroads. She turned left and continued along a road that ran through fields where horses grazed. It seemed to him they were backtracking, but then Connecticut roads had always been like that.

"Amazing that this remains so rural, and yet it's only a little over an hour out of New York City."

"It takes me an hour and fifteen minutes to drive from New York," she said, making a left into a road which a small white signpost identified as Banks Road. They went along it for about a mile or so, until it ended at another crossroads. Almost dead ahead was the barn he'd admired and across the fields behind it, the house he'd liked. He turned to look at her and found her smiling at him.

"That's where you live, isn't it?"

"Yes."

"You're sneaky, Marcy." He laughed then, relieved that he hadn't recognized the house.

Marcy crossed Catamount Road and jogged left a few hundred feet to enter a lane which ran beside the barn. It was a long lane, bordered by a stone fence. None of it looked familiar to him. They pulled into the parking area of the spruce and glass house.

"Well, here we are." She got out, and a big golden retriever bounded toward her from the patio. Peter too got out of the car, and the dog saw him for the first time. She veered away from Marcy and began to bark and run around in circles, then, wagging her tail happily, threw herself at Peter, planting both paws in the middle of his chest and almost knocking him down.

"Hi, there," he said, taking hold of the two big paws.

"Cassey! Down, girl!" Marcy commanded as the dog began to lick Peter's hands, then to sniff his hands and his clothes. Suddenly she looked confused and jumped down. She backed away, showing her teeth and snarling. "Cassey," called Marcy, coming toward her. But the dog paid no attention to Marcy and continued to growl and show her teeth.

"Cassey!" Marcy caught her collar. "Down, girl! It's all right." Marcy stroked her head and talked quietly to her as she led her away, but the retriever kept looking back at Peter and growling; her confusion was obvious. "Cassey!" This time Marcy's voice was sharp with command. "Quiet, girl. It's okay, it's okay." Once she'd got the dog's attention away from Peter, her voice became quiet and soothing. Peter stayed where he was, uncertain what to do. Marcy looked up at him. "Come toward her very slowly and speak to her gently." Peter moved toward the dog extending his hand, palm up.

"What's the matter, Cassey?" he said quietly. "Don't know me, huh?" A low, guttural growl came from deep down in her throat, but Marcy held her tightly.

"Keep talking, Peter."

"Nice girl. Good girl," he said, approaching her slowly, his hand still extended. "I won't hurt you, girl, if you won't hurt me." Marcy reached out and took his hand, still holding onto Cassey's collar with the other hand.

"It's all right, Cassey, he's a friend." The dog looked up at him and he could see the confusion in her eyes. He knew that she'd thought he was Carl until she'd smelled his hands. "Kneel down, if you can," said Marcy, "and pat her on the head."

"I'm not sure that's such a good idea." But he knelt—with difficulty.

"She's really so gentle, I can't imagine what's got into her."

"Can't you?" Their eyes met.

"You think she thought you were—"

"Of course—until she smelled me. I didn't smell like Carl." At the mention of Carl's name, the dog looked up at

Peter and began to whine. Marcy let go of Peter's hand and hugged the dog close to her.

"It's all right, Cassey. It's all right, girl."

Peter got up and went back to the car to get his case. Marcy continued talking to the dog, and he went onto the patio where he put down his case and took a seat. He felt unnerved and weak-kneed. He watched the woman and the dog grieve and felt isolated and lonely.

Finally the dog was quiet, and Marcy picked up a stick and threw it out across the lawn. The dog bounded after it and brought it back to her. She threw it again, then came toward the patio.

"I'm sorry, Peter," she said. Her face was grave and tightly controlled. Their eyes met, and he knew she was holding back tears.

"Marcy—" He didn't know what to say so he reached out and put his arms around her.

"Oh, Peter," she said, and he gathered her close to him and held her. She clung to him as the tears finally came, then sobbed as though she would break apart. Guessing she had not allowed herself to cry very often in the three months since Carl's death, Peter held her close. She needed to cry it out.

When she was resting quietly in his arms, he took the handkerchief from his breast pocket and dried her eyes. Their eyes met, and he saw gratitude and hurt in them, and something else he could not make out. He took her face in his hands and kissed her wet lashes, and then lightly touched his lips to hers. She did not seem surprised, and made no effort to pull away from him. Suddenly he realized what the look he had not been able to fathom meant. He touched his lips again to hers, and tightened his arms about her. Her lips parted and her arms went around him. They kissed deeply, hungrily, passionately, as though unable to get enough of one another. Her body seemed to melt into his as reality slipped away from them.

It was the dog that finally brought them back: she had begun to howl. They broke apart and Marcy went to her. Peter watched, disturbed, as Marcy tried to quiet her.

"Peter, please go inside," Marcy said.

He picked up his bag and did as she asked. He entered a dining-sitting area with large brick fireplace, and eased down on the sofa; the starch had gone out of him. He sat there trying not to think, just feeling the excitement inside him.

Presently Marcy came in, but she did not look at him. She went in back of a long counter, behind which he saw the kitchen. He did not watch her, but closed his eyes and tried to relax. It was not easy to relax in a house that had been lived in by Marcy and Carl.

She came back into the room with drinks and sat down beside him. "Thought you might need this."

"Thanks. I do." He took the drink and sipped it in silence for a few moments, then carefully put it down on the table and reached for her hand. He held it tightly in his.

"Was it Carl or me?" he asked gently. She looked back at him, and they stared at one another in silence.

"I wanted to kiss *you*," she said finally.

"Just because I'm me?"

"I—I don't know. It was not a conscious thought, if it was Carl." Her eyes were clear and honest, and he believed her. But did she really know? He wondered if that question would always come back to haunt him.

"Look," he said, "I'm an idiot! I've wanted to kiss you since the night I saw you at the Plaza, and when it happens, I try to borrow trouble."

"Please try to put Carl out of your mind, Peter."

"I try every day, Marcy." Just talking about Carl now made him feel anxious. He got up and took a turn across the room, dug a cigarette out of his pocket, lit it, and paced quietly. "I go along for a little while, and I almost forget, and then something happens, and it hits me right in the gut again." She sat quietly listening, watching him pace; she could see how strung out he was. Mike had been right.

"Peter, I was having a very difficult time with this. I was suffering the same restless urgency you were, wanting to see you and feeling guilty about it; wondering if it was really you, yourself, I wanted to see and felt attracted to, or if it was that part of Carl in you. I was not handling it well at all, so yesterday I went to see Father Spencer. He's really Bishop Spencer now, but he used to be our minister, and he was a good friend of Carl's and mine. I had a long talk with him about—everything."

"What did he say?" He came back to her and sat down.

"He said a lot of things, but one of the things he was very clear about was that I had to let go of Carl and come back to myself, find my own center. He also reminded me that possessing a small physical part of Carl inside your body does not make you Carl; what makes Carl is his soul, and you can never have Carl's soul. He told me I should get better acquainted with my own spiritual center and replace my confusion with faith that God will help me find comfort—if I let him. He said answers would come to me through prayer and meditation.''

"Sounds good.''

"He also advised me to stop thinking of you in relation to Carl, and start seeing you as you. He told me to bury my dead.''

"Sounds like a very wise man, but I guess one has to have faith to make his advice work.''

"Not necessarily. But he also counseled me to stop accepting guilt imposed by convention. Again, he said I was being outer-directed instead of inner-directed. I had to ask myself what *I* felt, what I needed—separate the two of us from other people. He said when I had done that, if I felt good about my feelings for you, and at peace, I could trust my feelings.''

"Makes sense.''

"And—he said something else I want to pass on to you because I think it might help you, too.''

"Shoot.''

"I asked him about my feelings of being drawn to you, even before I left Paris, after Carl had—had died.''

"I didn't know.''

"Yes. I stayed on an extra day—I wanted to visit you after the operation, but I knew you wouldn't be able to see right away. So I went back to the hospital and asked Mike to let me know when you were able to see again.''

"And did he?''

"Yes.''

"He never told me.''

"No, he wouldn't. I told him I didn't want you to know.''

"What did Bishop Spencer say about you being drawn to me?''

"I told him that I sometimes wondered if Carl might be causing it. He said there could be psychological reasons why I might feel that, but to keep one thought in mind: if Carl were trying to reach me in some way, his motives would be for my spiritual well-being, and he would not be pushing me toward you if it were not in my best interest."

"Hmm, I have some questions about that myself. I'd like to talk with this man. What kind of bishop is he?"

"Episcopal."

"I was raised an Episcopalian."

"I thought you said you were. Well, if you're serious about talking to him, I'm sure he could find time for you."

"Yes, I think I really would like to. You know, three months ago I wouldn't have been very receptive to talk about God. Now I'm not so sure. Having been in a muddle of confusion for weeks now, the idea that there's a God who can help me straighten out my life seems an attractive idea."

"I know. I've always gone to church, but I don't know that I ever paid much serious attention to my spiritual development. I had a code of behavior, a set of values, that I tried to live by. But I sat up very late last night, examining my life in terms of the things Father Spencer talked about, and I realized that I didn't know anything about the exciting possibilities of having faith in God, and relying on him for guidance. Oh, I always believed in God, and I do now, but I didn't realize all the wonderful possibilities of that belief." Peter watched her lovely face as she talked, and he saw there the excitement of her discovery.

"Would you say you more or less got religion?" He spoke almost teasingly, but he was seriously interested in her answer to that.

"No. I didn't experience any spiritual transformation, or revelation, but I did discover what an exciting and compelling concept it is, having a close personal relationship with God."

"Well, let me share an experience of mine which is the antithesis of yours." He gave her an account of his two visits to Grandma Geranium Victoria, and Marcy listened with rapt attention, not once interrupting, or revealing that she already knew about the visits. When he'd finished, she shook her head sadly.

"Oh, Peter, why did you lay yourself open to something like that?"

"Sitting here talking to you, I wonder why, too, but that's how crazy I've been. Talk about confusion—I've been a walking jigsaw puzzle." She reached over and touched his face.

"You look so tired. Let's see if you can get some rest this weekend, and maybe find some peace."

"Do you really think that's possible in this house?"

"We can try. Come on, let me show you to your room so you can change. While you're doing that, I'm going to make us some lunch." He followed her up several steps into a spacious living room with a wide view of the out-of-doors through the glass panels he'd seen from the road. It was comfortably and attractively furnished with Oriental rugs, graceful contemporary sofas and chairs, indoor plants, bookcases full of books, and a fireplace in the corner. She led him through the living room and into another wing where there was a guest room and bath.

"This will be your quarters." She opened a sliding glass door. "This leads to the garden, and the pool is just back of the house. If you'd like a swim before lunch, go ahead."

"Yes, I might just do that."

"You'll find towels in the bathroom. Lunch will be in about forty-five minutes, and I'll serve it out by the pool. So if you'd like to lie in the sun after your swim and doze, please do."

"Thanks." Their eyes met and both were aware of the electricity between them, but neither of them made a move. Finally she excused herself and left.

# Chapter Nineteen

Marcy awoke suddenly. She had been dreaming that Carl was calling to her, and that she saw him standing by the skating pond in the woods. She sat up in bed, fully awake now, but she still heard his voice. It was strong, insistent, even urgent. She got out of bed and went to the bedroom window that overlooked the pool, and beyond it the woods. The night was bright with a moon and a few days on the wane from full, and she could see the woods quite clearly. How vivid the dream had been. Carl was standing by the old bench where they always sat to lace their skates.

She often dreamed of Carl, but this dream was different somehow, more vivid, more real in texture and sensation. Did Carl want her to go down to the pond? That was absurd; it was the middle of the night, and it had only been a dream. A cool breeze caused the curtains to billow out suddenly, and it made her shiver. She was naked, for she seldom slept in anything. She got back into bed and closed her eyes. She had sat up late talking with Peter; it was the first time they'd really had a chance to talk leisurely and without interruption. She found him an extremely interesting, complex, and sensitive man. The more she learned about him, the more she liked him. There was a gentle awareness about him that made him easy to be with. She knew he sensed certain things about her, but he was very careful to keep his thoughts to himself, and

her right to privacy. He was attentive and caring,
___ crowded her, or took advantage of the fact that
___ to him. Sometimes she was able to forget
___ part of Carl, and to see him for himself:
___ erudite, sensitive man who also happened
___ ompany. In fact he made her feel like an
___ woman again.

___ on falling asleep, but the dream kept
___, and she heard Carl's voice calling her again.
___ waiting for her by the pond. Finally she gave up
trying to sleep and sat up in bed. It was insane, of course, but
perhaps she should get up and go down to the pond just to get
the dream out of her mind. No—it really *was* insane to get out
of bed at this time of night and go traipsing through the
woods to the pond. On the other hand—why not? She couldn't
sleep, and if it would make her feel calmer, what was the
harm in it? Besides it would be a lovely walk to the pond in
the moonlight.

She got out of bed again and pulled on a warm shirt and
jeans. Her bedroom opened onto a balcony with stairs leading
to the patio and pool: she decided to go down that way and
not disturb Cassey who slept in the kitchen; the dog would
want to come with her, and would hunt out every little
creature sleeping in the woods. Marcy descended the stairs
quietly, crossed the patio, skirted the pool, and took the path
to the woods.

She heard the rustle of night creatures stirring in their
sleep, feeling the vibrations of her footsteps on the path. She
was startled by a baby rabbit who suddenly hopped into the
path, and seeing her, froze in his tracks. Knowing that rabbits
do not handle emergenices well, she stopped and waited for
him to collect himself. He gave her a quizzical look, hopped
a few steps, and cocked his head to look at her again, then
hopped rapidly into the cover of a bramble bush.

She resumed her journey with a slight sense of anxiety
beginning to insinuate itself. She tried to shake it off by
turning her attention to the shapes of the different trees which
were illuminated by the moonlight. She heard the splash of
the little waterfall at the end of the pond, and the gurgle of
the water which formed a brook below it and ran off down the
hill, through the woods, and out into the fields below.

The path curved around a large sycamore tree and the pond

lay ahead, tranquil and glassy in the moonlight. She approached it slowly, remembering how it had looked all frozen over in winter, and how she and Carl had skated happily on it, laughing at one another's antics. She headed for the old bench where she'd sit awhile and look at the pond before going back to bed. It had been a good idea to come—it was a lovely night. As she looked out over the pond in the distance, she nearly stumbled over a small branch which had fallen onto the path. She bent down to throw it out of the path, and as she straightened, she saw a man standing by the bench. Her heart jumped into her throat, and her hand went to her mouth. "Carl!" she whispered aloud. "Oh, my God!" She stretched out her arms and began to run toward him. He turned to look in her direction then, and seeing her, held out his arms to her. She ran into them, and he tightened them and brought her close against him.

"Marcy," he said huskily, and then they were kissing, wildly, passionately. They stayed like that, their bodies pressed together, their arms locked about one another. Then he was kissing her face, and her neck, and she arched her back as he pressed her into his groin. She hung there, balancing against his arms, and began to open her shirt to expose her bare breasts to him. His mouth was instantly upon them, kissing first one then the other, and she cried out with ecstasy as he too groaned with pleasure. Then his mouth was on hers again. Finally they broke apart, struggling for breath, and she saw his face.

"Peter!" she exclaimed, but she was not really surprised.

"Yes, didn't you know?" he asked, breathing hard.

"Why are you here?" she asked softly, not moving out of his arms. The fact was, she couldn't have moved if she'd wanted to; she was riveted to him with passion, and too weak to stand alone.

"I couldn't sleep," he said.

"How did you know to come here?"

"I don't know, I just came," he said. She made no reply, knowing already that they had not met by chance. Very well, so be it. She disengaged her arms and took his hand. They began to walk back up the path.

"Marcy—I—"

"Don't talk, please," she whispered. They walked back to the house in silence, and she held his hand tightly in hers all the way. She knew what she meant to do, and that brought a certain serenity.

When they got to the house, she led him around the pool and across the patio to his room. The sliding door stood ajar as he'd left it. They entered the room and she turned to face him, beginning to unbutton the rest of the buttons on her shirt. He began to unbutton his own shirt; the blood was pounding so hard in his temples he felt dizzy.

They stood a little apart, looking at one another. The passion they'd kindled at the pond was still on them, drawing them together like a magnet. He took a step toward her, and they rushed into each other's arms. The touch of his body, the feel of it against her, was wildly exciting. As they kissed, she felt his erection against her abdomen and wanted him with an almost unbearable ache.

They inched toward the bed, kissing at the same time, unable to let go of one another for a moment. He eased her gently onto the bed, and she reached her arms up for him. His body came over hers then, and his weight felt good pressing down on her, almost like an act of love in itself. She pulled his face toward her, and their mouths were together again, kissing deeper and deeper, their hands frantically exploring each other's bodies. This was not a time for leisurely loving; they wanted one another with an unbearable urgency. When he raised his body slightly, she understood and opened her legs. When he lowered himself, it was to come into her, and she cried out with the pleasure of receiving him.

They made love like two people who had loved one another long and well, moving in perfect rhythm and harmony into a shattering climax which made them cry out with abandonment. He made motions then to come out of her, but she didn't want to be separated from him, and she let him know by pressing her hands against the small of his back. He understood and buried his face in her neck. She held him tightly to her, feeling the throb of him in her, and waves of orgasmic ecstasy still rippled through her. Never in her life had she wanted a man more or felt a more complete and consuming orgasm. She did not understand why, but that didn't matter: she could not think about that now. She fell asleep locked in his arms.

She was awakened later by his hands caressing her body. She stretched with sexual tension and pulled him close to her.

"Your skin is beautiful," he whispered in her ear, and he began to kiss her neck, her breasts, her entire body. She writhed with the pleasure of his touch. When he kissed her between her legs, and teased her with his tongue, she moaned with the excruciating pleasure of it.

Then he flung himself over on his back and sighed heavily. "I cannot get enough of you," he said. "Every nerve in my body is alive with you."

"It's the same with me," she whispered.

Morning was beginning to cast a warm gray light over the room as she sat up and looked at Peter stretched out beside her. She touched his chest and began to run her hands over his entire body, then touched her lips to his chest, his abdomen. His penis was rigid in erection, and she felt a wild, uncontrollable impulse to take him into her mouth, something she had done with Carl, of course, but never with the wild abandon she felt now. She began to nibble at him with quick little kisses.

"Oh God! You're killing me!" he groaned.

"It's wonderful," she whispered and took him full into her mouth. But he lifted her face with his hands. "Let's have it together," he said, for he knew he was on the verge of climax already.

"Oh yes," she whispered as he came over her, and she guided him into her, crying with pleasure as he began to move in her. She felt herself slipping into total release, and submitted to it. They were both crying and yelling with joy as they reached climax.

He collapsed on top of her, exhausted, and did not move. She held him tightly in her arms and locked her long legs about his thighs. She felt the warm flow from him inside her, and welcomed it.

"I love you," he groaned. "Oh God, how I love you!" The words sounded beautiful to her. Yes, she wanted him to love her, she wanted it very much.

It was not the last time they made love that night, and each time it was with the same wild, all-consuming passion and fulfillment. It was true: neither of them could get enough of each other, she thought. Finally they fell asleep again from sheer exhaustion.

\* \* \*

When Peter awakened, the sun was pouring into the room, and he reached out to Marcy, but she was not there. He sat up and shaded his eyes against the sun to look at his watch: it was eleven thirty. He lay back on the pillow and thought about what had happened. What force had drawn him, last night, to a pond he didn't know existed? When he had left his room, he seemed to know exactly where he was going. And what had Marcy been doing there? Marcy—what an incredible woman! Not in his wildest imagination could he have guessed that the coolly beautiful woman he had seen at the Plaza, and the warm, friendly woman he had come to know later, could be the hotly passionate, loving, giving woman he had known in the night.

Just thinking about last night put him into a high state of excitement, and he flung himself over on his stomach and let out a groan. Peter Blanchard, he said to himself, you've met the woman of your life, and now what's going to happen? But he didn't have time to answer that, for the old torment was back, muddling up his brain. Carl! Was it Peter Blanchard Marcy had loved in the night, or Carl Morris? Had she given herself to him or to Carl? What had she been telling herself during those wild hours with him? There was no question in his mind now that he loved her—whether Carl had willed it or not didn't matter; the awareness of love had permeated his being. But if they were to have something together, would he always wonder whether her thoughts and feelings were for him or for Carl?

He tried to put the thought out of his mind and rolled over onto his side to get out of bed. He was not surprised to find himself erect again. He thought of putting on his robe and going to her. Would she be in her bed now—hers and Carl's? No, it would be a mistake to go to her in her own room, to make love to her in the bed she'd shared with Carl. He was certain that's why she'd led him back to his room last night instead of her own. He picked up a pillow and hurled it across the room. Goddamn Carl Morris! But the moment he'd thought it, he felt guilty; looking at the pillow lying against the bureau, he remembered that had it not been for Carl, he would be unable to see the pillow. But how long did he have to go on paying for what had been freely given?

He got out of bed and went into the shower. After he'd soaped down, he stood under the cold shower for several minutes to cool down his ardor. As he stood before the mirror later, shaving, he thought about Vadim and the riddle of the message he'd received from Carl. "Child." What did it mean? Did he dare talk to Marcy about it? Sooner or later he had to, especially after what had happened between them.

He dressed slowly, debating with himself about telling her. He decided to play it by ear, wait for a time which seemed right. When he'd finished dressing, he left the room and went down to the kitchen. It was empty. He went outside, but there was no sign of Marcy. It was a beautiful day, and the sun was warm and reassuring. He actually felt wonderful for the first time since before the accident. He put his hands into his pockets and strolled out across the lawn.

Off to the left he saw a neatly fenced garden and he walked over to explore it. There were neat rows of vegetables: string beans, squash, cucumbers, tomatoes, scallions, radishes, and corn. He entered the garden and picked a ripe tomato. He polished it until its bright red skin shone, then bit into it. The warm juice was wonderfully flavorful and took him back to his boyhood when he'd eaten the warm tomatoes in his grandfather's garden. A happy feeling came over him as he thought about the lazy summer days of his youth. He realized how much he'd been missing the country. Of course, he loved the city too—it's vitality and excitement—but one did get far away from the earth there; too far away from the basic, simple joys of life.

Roses lined the split-rail fencing around the garden, and he walked over to them and smelled their delicate fragrance. He picked a white one and strolled back to the house. Marcy's car was still in the driveway, so she must be there. Perhaps she was still asleep? No, he doubted that. Maybe she was out by the pool. He walked around the house and saw her lying on a chaise longue, her eyes closed. She was dressed in white linen slacks and a navy polka-dot blouse, and he had the feeling she'd been up for some time. He approached her quietly and sat down facing her. She opened her eyes and looked at him. He could not read the look, and so he said nothing, but he held out the rose to her. She smiled and took it, lifted it to her nose, then sat looking down at it without speaking for some time. He waited, her silence making him uneasy. Finally she looked up and their eyes met.

"I don't understand what has happened, but I knew what I

was doing,'' she said quietly, and there was sadness in her face.

His heart sank, but he said: "Thank you for that."

"I can imagine the questions that must be in your mind," she went on.

"Yes, there are questions, but I don't think the answers, if there are any, change what happened between us."

"No, they wouldn't."

"Can't we just accept what we felt and divorce that from anything else?"

"Perhaps." She looked down at the rose again and smelled it absently. "Peter, I'm not trying to take back what happened. Please understand that."

"I hope not," he said seriously, then grinned. "It would be a little hard to do."

"Yes." She chuckled softly and looked slightly embarrassed. "I guess it would at that."

"You're a beautiful woman in every way, Marcy."

"And you're a beautiful man, Peter. In fact, I think you're the most extraordinary man I've ever known."

"I'm glad you said that," he paused. "You know, sometimes a man wonders just what sort of person he *really* is—because he's different with different people, and he has levels of self that he shares. But the real man that lies at the core seldom dares to surface—it's too risky. That's the level you appeal to in me, and I'm not afraid to let you see it. It's the level I like most in myself, and so I like myself with you."

"I'm not sure I can say that about myself." She was quiet a moment, then went on. "I've been thinking about that this morning, and I'm not sure I like the person I'm turning out to be."

"I think you're a wonderful person, Marcy." He hesitated a moment. Should he tell her? Might as well admit it now and see how she reacted. "In fact, I've been thinking this morning, too, and do you know what I've been thinking?" He smiled softly.

"I'd like very much to know."

"I been thinking that you're the woman I've been looking for all my life."

"I'm deeply flattered, Peter. But it's not like boy meets girl, boy and girl fall in love, boy and girl live happily ever after. It's not that simple for us, is it?" She smiled sadly.

"Maybe it can be."

"No, my darling Peter, it isn't." She looked away. "I wish it could be, I really do."

"Do you, Marcy?"

"Yes. But there are ghosts."

"There won't always be."

"Perhaps, but the question now is, where do we go from here?"

"Do we have to *go* anywhere right now?"

"After last night, do you really think we could go back to being the way we were?" A surprised look came over her face.

"It would be difficult, but—" He let his sentence trail off, for he knew they couldn't.

"Of course we can't. Too much has happened. We know the power of what is between us." She looked at him for confirmation, and he nodded. "I don't know how it is with you, Peter, but I'm sitting here trying to stay away from you. I could go back to bed with you right now and stay there all day, and that surprises me about myself. I'm by no means a cold woman, but I never knew until last night the real depth of passion in me." She looked away. "That's a revealing admission, I know, and I probably shouldn't tell you that, but I don't see the point in being coy about it. I suspect you know anyway." She paused, then added, "I loved Carl deeply, and I loved being with him in bed, but I never felt the wild abandon I experienced with you last night."

"It's the same with me, Marcy. Last night was the ultimate experience of my life. I had never known total fulfillment."

Marcy nodded. "I left you this morning and went to my room because I knew that if you awakened with me there, it would start all over again, and I'd want it to. But sooner or later I'd have to come out into the sunlight and face up to the reality of my situation."

"I awakened ready for you." He grinned sheepishly, and she laughed softly.

"Yes. So did I, but I couldn't let it happen again. It took all the willpower I had to leave you."

"Do you want so badly to leave me, Marcy?"

"I don't know. I—I don't know what's best. I've been trying to reason it all out."

"I'm afraid it doesn't have much to do with reason, darling." He pulled out a package of cigarettes and lit one. "Do you feel bad about being with me?"

"No, I feel wonderful. At least, on one level I feel wonderful—and then there's the other—"

"Yes, I know."

"Peter, how did you happen to find the pond last night?"

"I couldn't sleep. I kept waking up. So I got up and went outside. I started to walk, and the direction I took was through the woods. I seemed to know where I was going, and suddenly I found myself at the pond."

"I never mentioned the pond in the woods, did I?"

"No."

"You see, there it is. So much I don't understand."

"How did you happen to go there?"

"I dreamed of Carl," she said and went on to describe the dream and to explain how she had been drawn there.

"You thought I was Carl, didn't you?"

"Yes. At least I think I did. But then, after you kissed me, I knew it was you."

"And later—in bed?"

"I didn't think. I just felt."

"But you weren't disturbed, you didn't feel strange with me, did you?"

"You know I didn't." She looked away. He got up and went to sit on the end of her chaise. He reached for her hand, but she hesitated for a moment before putting her hand in his. Her hand was cold, and he closed his fingers around it.

"Marcy, Carl is dead."

"Is he?"

"Unless you mean to keep him alive. Father Spencer told you to bury your dead."

"I know. But how about you? Can you bury him?"

"I've got to try. Life has to go on. And if we can find something good together—don't you think Carl would want us to have it?"

"It's not what Carl would want, Peter, it's what I can accept. And—it's just too soon." Her face showed the strain of her conflicting emotions.

"It seems to me that something, some force drew us both to the pond last night. If it was Carl, he obviously meant us to be together."

"Perhaps. But supposing he does want us to be together, he also stands between us. You don't know if I'm making love to you or to him, and I don't know if it's you I'm feeling this for, or the Carl in you. How can we have a relationship under those circumstances?" She shook her head.

"It is complicated, but is it any worse than the torment we go through trying to stay apart? I mean, sometimes I feel he is in me—driving—pushing—until I can't get any peace, or even function properly.

"Oh, I don't know! It's all so crazy!" She threw her head back and closed her eyes. "I don't know where I am half the time anymore." She pressed his hand with feeling, and he lifted her hand and gently touched his lips to it.

"Dearest Marcy." She opened her eyes. "I do love you."

"I don't want to lose you, Peter, but I don't know what to do. I don't want us to ruin it by rushing things." She sighed heavily.

"Would you feel the same about me if I no longer had these corneas?"

"I don't know." Her voice sounded frustrated and weary now. "That's my dilemma."

"You know something? Sometimes I'm so harassed and confused, I think of going to the eye bank and offering these corneas in exchange for someone else's—someone I don't know, never heard of!"

"Don't you dare!" she cried. "What a terrible thing to do to yourself." He saw a shudder go through her.

"To me, Marcy, or to Carl?" he retorted.

"To you, of course." She looked shocked.

"I wonder. Anyway, I think about it, and it seems worth it to get rid of him, to be my own person again—to know if it's me or the Carl in me that you care about."

"Peter, this kind of talk scares me."

"Know something? I'm scared most of the time now."

"Poor, dear Peter." She placed his hand against her cheek. "You didn't ask for any of this, did you?" She kissed his hand and held it in both of hers.

"No. But I wouldn't like to be blind either. If Carl hadn't given me his eyes, I'd never have known you, and I'd never have been able to see your lovely face."

"Oh, Peter, what are we going to do?" He heard her anguish.

"I drive myself crazy asking that question." He paused and looked down at her hand. "I want to tell you something, Marcy, and I hope you'll understand why I'm telling you."

"What is it?" She looked anxious.

"I've wanted to talk to you about it since I arrived, but I was waiting."

"What on earth is it?"

"Will you promise to reserve judgment on me for telling you?"

"Peter, what is it?" There was a faint trace of impatience in her voice now.

"Carl had some secret that was weighing so heavily on his conscience he had to tell Mike about it. But he made him promise never to tell anyone else. Have you any idea what that secret might have been?"

"None." Her voice was slightly cool, or was it fear he heard?

"You're sure? Think back over the last ten years?"

"If Mike promised not to tell, how do you know there was a secret?"

"I was in one of my crazier spells and Mike was trying to talk sense into me. It just slipped out, but he wouldn't tell me what the secret was."

"But why would you want to know? A man has a right to have a secret."

"I want to know because my intuition tells me it may have something to do with what's been happening to us. Somehow I think if I knew the secret—well, I think it would set us free."

"Oh, Peter." Her voice softened. "You're tilting at windmills."

"Maybe not. That's one reason I went to see Grandma Geranium Victoria, and crazy as she was, she also told me that Carl had a secret. That's why he wouldn't speak."

"I thought you said it was because his spirit was not in the other world."

"That's right, but then she went on to say it was hiding—hiding in that room—and it was hiding because it had a secret."

"But how did she know that?"

"You tell me. Anyway, that's why I went back to see her, but of course she wouldn't talk to me."

"That's strange, too. Why wouldn't she talk to you?"

"She got spooked because of my eyes." He lit another cigarette. "And Marcy, there's something else I haven't told you."

"Something else!"

"Yes. I went to see a psychic two days ago."

"You didn't."

"I'm afraid I did. I didn't know what to expect, but I was having nightmares that Carl was trying to take his eyes back—all sorts of things. I was afraid I was going to crack up. I knew I had to do something. So I got the name of this man from one of my writers."

"Peter, why didn't you come to me?" She pressed his hand against her heart.

"I'd promised to stay away from you, and I was afraid it might upset you. Anyway, I went to a man called Vadim in Scarsdale. He's a very dignified, tranquil kind of man, and there wasn't anything bizarre about him. He told me that he often gets messages from a departed spirit. He gets them through deep concentration—making himself open to receive any message that comes from the spirit of the departed person."

"Did he get a message from Carl?" He felt her hand begin to tremble.

"Yes."

"What was it?"

He took a deep breath and prayed he was doing the right thing. " 'Child.' That was all."

" 'Child?' "

" 'Child.' And, according to him the message was very clear."

"Was that Carl's secret?"

"Apparently. I told him I wanted to know two things: what Carl's secret was and what he wanted from me."

"I don't know what it means." She looked frightened.

"I thought you might be able to make something of it."

"No. Of course we wanted children, but you know all about that."

"Yes."

"How strange that Carl had a secret he had to tell Mike. I didn't think we had any secrets we couldn't share with one another." She looked hurt.

225

"He probably meant to tell you, but was afraid he'd die before—"

"Maybe that's it. But what could it have been?" She was quiet, and he knew she was trying to think back over their ten years together. "But if he'd meant to tell me, he wouldn't have made Mike promise not to tell anyone."

"Well, Mike will never tell. I'm certain of that."

"Obviously Carl didn't want me to know." She looked away. "Peter, why did you tell me this now?"

"Because of us. And—because there's something about a child that Carl wants me to know."

"But we don't know that that's the secret. If he'd wanted you to know, he wouldn't have made Mike promise not to tell."

"Maybe he's changed his mind now. Or maybe it's something that's so strongly on his mind, wherever he is, that Vadim picked it up."

"It's too disturbing. I don't understand it."

"Marcy—was Carl ever married before?"

"No. Our families had always known one another, and we were married when he was twenty-five. I'm sure he would have told me if he had been married before. It wouldn't have disturbed me."

"But what if there had been a child by marriage, or out of wedlock? Maybe he didn't tell you out of fear that it would upset you."

"If there had been a child, he would never have hidden it from me. He would have wanted the child to visit us. He loved children. He'd have known it wouldn't upset me."

"I keep thinking that maybe there's something about a child that he's guilty about, and he wants me to do something for him. Pay my debt for his eyes—something like that."

"I can't imagine . . ." her sentence trailed off.

"Marcy, could he have, at some time, had an af—"

"If you're going to say what I think you're going to say, don't." Her eyes confirmed the warning. But even though he knew he'd gone too far, he had to pursue it.

"But he wouldn't have told you about something like that while he was alive—because you hadn't conceived. Maybe he wants you to know it now because it's something left of him."

"Peter!" She dropped his hand, and anger flashed in her blue eyes.

"Marcy, don't—please. I'm not trying to destroy Carl's memory for you. I'm trying to figure out what the man wants from me, from us."

"How could something like that tell you what he wants from us?" Her eyes were reproachful, and it hurt him to see it, but more than ever he felt it was important to know the meaning of the message.

"Darling, Marcy, I know Carl feared leaving you alone. He told me so on the plane. And I also know that he loved you as much as a man can love a woman."

"I think you'd better stop playing with people like crazy old Grandma, and Vadim whoever-he-is, before you make both of us crazy!" She jumped up and started to run toward the front of the house. He ran after her and caught up to her as she was getting into the car.

"Marcy!" He grabbed her arm. "Where are you going?"

"To the beach to walk—*by myself!*"

"Marcy, please try to understand. I'm sorry if I hurt you, but we're in this together, and I thought I could talk to you. We've got to be honest with one another if we're going to survive."

"I know you didn't mean to hurt, but it does hurt that Carl kept a secret from me. It also hurts that you would suggest he was unfaithful to me."

"I didn't say that exactly, but accidents do happen sometimes. A chance meeting, a lonely time when traveling—but it doesn't mean anything in the relationship." He tried to put his arm around her shoulder but she sidestepped him.

"I'm going to walk along the Sound. There's coffee in the coffeemaker on the counter." She started the car and he stood aside and watched her go. Had he lost her by trying to find answers? He felt impotent and angry: he'd hurt the one person he didn't want to hurt. He turned back toward the house and shook his fist at it.

"Damn you, Carl Morris!" he shouted at the top of his voice. "Die! For God's sake die, and leave us alone!"

# Chapter Twenty

Peter went into the house in a black mood, and from the moment he crossed the doorstep, he felt a presence other than himself in the room. He poured himself a cup of coffee and found his hands were shaking. He spilled it on the counter and flew into a rage. He flung the cup into the sink and shattered it. "Goddamn you, you son of a bitch! Get out of my life!" he screamed, shaking his fist at the room at large. He ran out of the house and down the lane to the main road, and continued running until he'd worn himself out, then he turned around and started walking back toward the house.

"I'm really going off the deep end," he said aloud and felt more muddled than ever; having spent his anger, he was exhausted. How was he going to get rid of Carl? Had he lost Marcy? Lost her? He laughed unpleasantly. "I never had her to lose." He was talking aloud now as he walked down the lane, kicking at stones in his path. "She still belongs to the son of a bitch, no matter how much she loved me last night. And she did love me, damn it, I know she did!" And yet—she seemed to be telling him this morning that it was all a mistake, and she had doubts about any future for them. If Carl was trying to draw them together, he also seemed to be tearing them apart.

He kicked at a large stone and felt the pain in his toe, but he limped on, almost glad for the pain. One thing was certain:

he felt inadequate to manage his life. Jeannie was right, the Morrises had done a number on him. But Marcy—she couldn't have done that. But why had she slept with him and then denied her feelings? Could Marcy and Carl be playing a game on him? Or maybe Carl was trying to make him pay for his eyes, pay for being alive. Maybe he was pushing Marcy to punish him. "Oh Christ!" he groaned, "I really am crazy!" Jeannie was right—he needed a psychiatrist, someone to help him unscramble his mind. Jeannie—he missed her, missed the peace of their relationship as it had been before the accident. He had to see her when he got back to New York; maybe it wasn't too late to patch things up. Something had to be solid in his life, and he needed to be loved right now. Jeannie had loved him, perhaps she still did.

When he reached the house, he collapsed onto a chaise longue by the pool, and actually felt like crying, something he had seldom done since he was a boy. All the emotion had drained out of him, and he soon fell asleep, not only out of exhaustion, but out of the need to escape reality.

"Peter." He opened his eyes to see Marcy sitting beside him.

"Hi."

"Hi." She smiled. "I'm sorry for the temperament, but you unknowingly touched a sore spot."

"Marcy, I'm—" She laid her finger on his lips.

"Shush. Let me finish. I want you to understand this." She looked away for a moment, and he found himself fearing what she was going to say. "Can you imagine how a woman feels when she wants so much to have a child by the man she loves, and for years she fails?"

"But it wasn't your fault," he started to protest.

"That just made it worse. There was nothing wrong with me, and nothing wrong with Carl, and yet I was never able to conceive. Not once in all those years was there even a possibility that I might be pregnant. No matter how much medical science assures you you're okay, or how well adjusted and rational you may be, on some level you feel you've failed as a woman because you can't conceive."

"I am so stupid, Marcy. It never occurred to me you might feel that way."

"I know that, Peter."

"A man doesn't really understand those things about a woman—at least this man doesn't. Now that you tell me, I can see how you might feel you'd failed Carl."

"Failed myself, too. We women don't do everything just for the men in our lives, you know."

"I'm learning." He grinned. "I do want to understand."

"Of course part of that feeling is because of the conditioning we get as children. A woman's mission is to have children, and society looks down on a woman who doesn't. No matter what the reasons are for not having children, somehow you feel a little less a woman for not having had any."

"But you could. I mean, you can."

"But I didn't, Peter. Don't you see? I'm perfectly healthy and normal, and capable, but I *didn't!*" He saw her becoming upset just talking about it.

"Marcy, marry me." It came out spontaneously, prompted by an overwhelming flow of sympathy and affection.

"Peter, be serious."

"I am being serious," he protested. She smiled, but shook her head.

"Oh, Peter, I can't do that."

"Why not?"

"Because—because of things I said this morning, and because I don't understand the nature of my feelings. I have a lot of feeling for you. Otherwise what happened last night wouldn't have happened. But I don't know how much, or if it's love. Besides—" she paused, "we really don't know one another well enough to consider such a step yet." Her eyes pleaded for understanding, but he also saw a moment's indecision in them.

"Say yes," he urged and touched her face tenderly.

"Dearest Peter, I just can't. One part of me wants to, but I know it would be a mistake to rush it now."

"Will you think about it?"

"I already have thought about it." She grinned.

"You have?"

"Yes. I knew you would ask me sooner or later."

"How could you? I mean, I didn't even know."

"Didn't you?"

"Well, maybe I did and just hadn't put it into words for myself."

"Ask me again someday?"

"I will. There's only one thing I'm certain about, and it's the only thing right now—you're the woman I've been looking for."

"Because of last night?"

"No. I knew I wanted to spend the rest of my life with you the first evening I had dinner with you. As I said, I hadn't put it into words for myself, but I knew." He spoke from his heart, and he wanted her to be sure of that.

"Thank you." She leaned over and kissed him lightly on the mouth. He made no move to prolong the kiss. She got up and smiled down at him. "How about lunch?"

"Wonderful. I'm starving." He got up to follow her. "Can I help?"

"Sure." She reached for his hand, and he followed her toward the kitchen.

"Say, where's Cassey? I haven't seen her all morning."

"I took her over to a neighbor's house early this morning. She was whining at your door, and I thought it would be better to take her over there."

"Strange—the things animals pick up, isn't it?"

"Yes. I've never seen Cassey act this way. I don't understand it."

"You know, Marcy, sometimes I feel like we're sitting on some kind of time bomb. Things keep happening that are strange, irrational, inexplicable, and yet you and I are real, and what we shared last night was real, and tangible, and understandable."

"But the thing that brought us to it wasn't. Neither of us can really explain why we went to the pond." She turned around suddenly and threw her arms about him. "Hold me, Peter—" He held her close to him. "Sometimes I'm so scared."

"So am I." He held her until she was calm, and they went into the kitchen. She went to the sink to run water into the teakettle to make tea and saw the cup and saucer shattered there.

"What on earth happened here?" she said with surprise and turned to look at him. "There's a cup smashed in the sink."

"I know. I did it, Marcy." He felt embarrassed and ashamed.

"You?"

"Yes. I threw it?"

232

"You threw it!" Her eyes showed disbelief.

"I kind of went off the deep end after you left. I came back to the house, and I felt the presence of someone else in this room. I spilled the coffee, I was so unnerved. And then I got really crazy, and I threw the cup."

"Oh, Peter." There was sympathy in her face now.

"I'm terribly sorry, Marcy—and ashamed. I'll replace it."

"Oh, Peter, you've got to get some professional help." She came to him and put her arms about him. "Please, will you go and see someone? You just can't go on like this."

"Yes, I'll do something—when I get back to New York." She felt him tremble as she held him, and she stepped back to look at him.

"Will you do something for me, Peter?"

"Anything."

"Will you go and talk to Father Spencer?"

"Yes, if you think it will help."

"I think he can help you right now, today."

"Today?"

"Yes, why not? Let me call him and see if he has some time to see you this afternoon?" Again her eyes pleaded with him.

"Okay, if you want me to, I'll go. I'll try anything that will help me find some peace."

It was late in the afternoon when he took Marcy's car and drove to see Bishop Spencer. The bishop himself answered the door and ushered Peter into his study. He was right out of central casting, Peter thought: tall, handsome, patrician, distinguished, and elegant. His voice was warm and deeply resonant, and his manner was charming, cosmopolitan, and charismatic. He made one feel instantly at ease, and soon Peter was sipping sherry, feeling a great deal better just being there, telling his story: from the crash in France through the operation, his preoccupation with Carl, his restlessness, his confusion, and his feelings for Marcy. He also told the bishop about Carl's confession of a secret to Mike; his own visits to Grandma and Vadim, and his strange meeting with Marcy at the pond.

"That's quite a good deal for anyone to face alone, Mr. Blanchard. I'm not surprised you're feeling distressed."

"I'm badly in need of some intelligent counseling." He paused. "I've thought of consulting a psychiatrist."

"Might be extremely helpful. Have you seen a therapist before?"

"No, and I must say the idea of shopping around for one puts me off."

"Understandable." Father Spencer drew on his pipe thoughtfully. "Might I make a suggestion?"

"I wish you would, Bishop."

"Do call me Father. Bishop makes me think I ought to be dignified and ponderous."

"Okay, Father." Peter smiled, thinking the man was certainly dignified, and he hoped he wouldn't turn out to be ponderous as well.

"I wouldn't recommend any particular doctor, but I would suggest that you see someone trained in the Jungian discipline."

Peter nodded. He was familiar with the theories of the late Swiss psychiatrist, Dr. Carl Jung.

"Yes. I believe you can obtain the names of several well-qualified therapists from the C. G. Jung Foundation in New York."

"I'll look into that when I get back to New York. Thank you."

"I suggest the Jungians because I believe they deal most effectively with matters such as this. Jung himself was extremely interested in the occult, and incorporated into his methods an important awareness of the patient's psyche, and his spiritual being."

"Yes, I've read a good deal about Jung. An interesting man."

"But now you've come to me, and I will counsel you in spiritual terms, according to theology. That's my so-called expertise, if you will." He chuckled. "But first a brief word about psychics. I know of this man, Vadim, and apparently he is a sincere and gifted man. Whether or not he can, in fact, contact a departed person is not for me to say. Apparently phenomena do occur that seemingly have no explanation in terms of reality as we understand it. But whether they are imposed from without, or exist in the perception of the individual, I don't know. A person such as Vadim, with highly developed extrasensory perception, may very well receive

some *awareness* of a spirit's wish to communicate a message. But the idea that a departed spirit can manipulate people and events on earth—no, I do not believe that. Only God or Satan can influence people and events on earth.''

"God or Satan can influence events?" asked Peter.

"Certainly."

"How can we know which one it is?"

"That's an easy question to answer." Father Spencer smiled. "God wants us to attain the best possible state of being we can achieve. He is interested in our well-being, which is to say our total well-being. If something is going on which threatens our well-being, you can count on it being none of God's doing."

"Is it always that clear-cut? I mean, couldn't you be in doubt as to whether something will ultimately turn out to be good or bad for you?"

"Oh yes. You see, Satan is quite clever. Just remember that he knows what it's all about—he's been there, as it were. If you will remember, he was an archangel cast out of heaven for disobedience and pride. The Hebrew Talmund tells us the story."

"Of course, and Milton wrote about it in *Paradise Lost*."

"Exactly."

"To be quite candid, Father, I haven't heard anyone talk about God and Satan being in competition for man's soul since I was a child."

Father Spencer laughed heartily.

"It's not a popular subject. Never was a bestseller. In fact, it's *square* talk, to put it in the current idiom. The litany of Fundamentalists, Evangelists, and born-again Christians. But the fact of the matter is, good or evil, peace or torment, heaven or hell is the concept at the basis of all religions. There are two kingdoms, that of God and that of Satan." The bishop smiled and sipped his sherry; he was warming to his subject, and Peter's attention was thoroughly engaged.

"Do go on," Peter urged.

"I'd be delighted, but I must warn you that I will sound as simplistic as a Sunday-school teacher. That's the quickest route to square one."

"I asked for it."

"Very well. You see, Mr. Blanchard, God loves us, and he wants us to love him."

"Yes, I heard that at Sunday school."

"Yes, but did you learn why?"

"I can't remember that I did." Peter smiled apologetically.

"Another example of our failure." Father Spencer grinned. "But let me see if I can make up for it now. God wants us to love him, and wants us to know that he loves us, because through him lies peace and happiness. If you will remember, I said before that God wants us to attain the best possible state we can achieve. However, God gave us a free will to choose to love him or not to love him—to choose peace or torment, good or evil."

"Father, if God is all-powerful—just for the sake of argument—and if he is in charge of everything, why does he give us a choice? I've never understood that."

"Good question. One cannot love without a free will. You must know that from your own experience in life."

"I'm embarrassed to say that I haven't thought much about it. But, of course, you're right. Of course one can't love without a free will. Love can't grow in a rigid or crowded environment."

"Exactly!" Bishop Spencer smiled a wide, obviously delighted smile. "If you don't mind my saying so, Mr. Blanchard, you don't seem so muddled to me."

"Oh, my intellect works pretty well once in a while. The trouble is, lately I'm too anxious to think."

"Yes, I understand."

"But if I may—?"

"Please go on."

"It has always struck me—judging from the way the church presents the idea—that God looks like he has us poor mortals on trial. He wants us to love him, but he allows us not to love him, and then chastises us if we don't. That just doesn't seem very loving."

"Ah. I see what you mean." Father Spencer tapped his pipe into an ashtray and slowly began to refill it from his tobacco pouch. "God is hurt if we don't love him, because he does love us, but he does not level punishment on us. In fact, he wants to forgive us even when we deny him and hurt him, and he does forgive whatever we do, if we are truly sorry. All we have to do is ask forgiveness."

"Then all of life is staying in good with God?"

"I suppose so, if you want to put it that way. I'd put it a

little differently. God is the supreme mover, the all-powerful being, the center of the universe, the all there is. But God doesn't just want us to love him and please him for his own gratification.''

"Would you elaborate on that, Father?"

"With pleasure." Father Spencer sipped his sherry. "This is where things get a little more complex. You see, in God's grand design of creation, he created the creature man in *his own* image. The creature was complex, endowed with intellect, emotions, and a soul, if you will. He, of all God's creatures, had the potential to achieve a higher state of being, and the ability to direct his own life. God loved this creature and he wanted it to grow, and learn, and evolve, and be happy. Now that was the key—happiness. God didn't just thrust his creature into the wilderness to become lost.''

"No?"

"No, God watches over us, and is ready any time to help us if we stumble and fall, but like the good parent, he keeps hands off until asked in to help. You see, in my opinion God envisioned his relationship with man as one of partnership—God being the silent partner, keeping hands off unless asked to help. But he hopes we make the right choices, the choices that will make us happy. That's why he gave us intellect, judgment, the ability to attain understanding and wisdom. He tells us he is there to guide us if we ask him, but he hopes we will make the good choices because bad choices make us unhappy. For example: love makes us happier than hate, harmony makes us happier than disharmony. Would you agree to that, Mr. Blanchard?"

"Yes. I mean, how could one disagree with that?"

"Easily, if one is to judge by the unhappy people in the world. However, let's look at harmony—because that is the key to happiness. When we're in disharmony with ourselves, others, our society, we're not happy. Oh, we can find a lot of reasons why we think we're unhappy, but take it from me, we're unhappy because we're out of harmony with ourselves, and therefore with God.''

"Why God?"

"What do you mean?"

"I mean, there it is again—the power play. If we're in good with God, he lets us be happy; if we're not, he lets us flounder around and be unhappy.''

"I see what you mean. Let me see if I can explain it clearly." He pulled hard on his pipe. "You see, man—let's think of man with a capital m—man is not a meaningless being, he has intellect and spirituality—because, after all, he is the offspring of a heavenly father, the heir apparent to the kingdom of heaven. Every one of us is. Now, when God created man, he knew, having created so complex a creature, he would stumble. The experiment of life is not an easy one, and apprenticeship for the kingdom of heaven is no cinch either. But man has to attend to his own development, earn his happiness by making the right choices, and eventually he will attain spiritual harmony. God knows he can do it, for he gave him the tools. And God's always there to help if he's asked. But don't forget, God has faith in man, and he wants him to have faith in himself, too."

"God wants man to grow up to be like God?" Peter smiled; he was being partially facetious.

"If you want to put it that way." Father Spencer also smiled; he welcomed sparring. "You see, Mr. Blanchard, man gets into trouble when he forgets that about himself. When he sells himself short—gets off his center and out of harmony. That makes him restless, confused, lost, anxious, vulnerable. To put it in psychological terms: he becomes alienated, neurotic, even psychotic. To be uncentered is to be in a state of disharmony with oneself and God."

"Well, I can testify to the fact that such a state in inharmonious."

"Look at it this way: if we eat something that disagrees with us, our system gets out of sorts, rebels—we feel bad. Perhaps we've eaten or drunk something that is inharmonious with our physical machine, and the result is discomfort, sometimes even pain. The same thing is true of our spiritual mechanism. What makes us think we can stuff disagreeable ingredients into our spiritual system without discomfort and illness? We can't—it too rebels. Our well-being is threatened—we're in a state of disharmony."

But how do we know what is going to disagree with us? I mean, some things *seem* as though they will agree with us, even make us happy."

"God never expected us not to make mistakes. He gave us that free will, remember?" Peter nodded. "If we continue to feed ourselves a disagreeable diet, either physically or

238

spiritually, we will damage the mechanism and get ourselves into real trouble. It's like a disease that requires treatment: if we just let it go, we've got trouble sooner or later.''

"That seems very sensible, very logical—I can't disagree with you. But I do have problems with how one recognizes the dangerous food, and therefore avoids getting spiritually sick.''

"Let's talk about your specific problem, and bear in mind that there are but two powers, two kingdoms—the kingdom of God and the kingdom of Satan.''

"Yes, but I still have trouble with the concept that God and Satan are in competition for man's following.''

"God can't be in competition for us, Mr. Blanchard, he is *inseparable* from us. But let's talk about God's way and how to know that way.''

"How *does* one know? That's exactly what my question is.''

"God's way is the way of love and harmony. Christ brought the message of God's love. Before that message, God was perceived as a vengeful power. Christ told us that God loved us, and that we should love our neighbor as *ourselves*. Now, that was a revolutionary teaching in the light of the Old Testament. God loved us and wanted us to love ourselves— love thy neighbor as *thyself*. That told us God thought well of us, thought us worthy of love. For the first time the idea that God and man could have a partnership, a real relationship was introduced.'' Father Spencer smiled warmly. "Isn't that a comforting concept? God loves us, he wants us to love him, and love ourselves. That's a good bargain, don't you agree?''

"Yes, I would have to agree with that.''

"Well, here is the second teaching: we can't love anyone else, not even God, if we don't love ourselves. God wants us to love ourselves, the godliness in ourselves. If we do that, we love God, because we are an inseparable part of God. It's all hooked up together. Remember this passage: 'God so loved the world, that he gave his only begotten Son that, whosoever believeth in him should not perish, but have everlasting life'? Do you remember that?''

"Yes, I learned it at Sunday school.''

"Of course you did. And God sent us proof of his love with the cross. He let his beloved son be crucified for the

*239*

redemption of our sins. God bought us a clean bill of health, and wiped the slate clean with Christ's sacrifice.''

"I don't know that I've ever totally comprehended the significance of that sacrifice,'' said Peter.

"The crucifixion wiped out original sin and opened the way for a new era to begin. The theological significance of the crucifixion was that God forgave the primal Adam for succumbing to the temptation of Satan, and upsetting the grand design of the ideal existence in Eden. The crucifixion of Christ, and the forgiveness of man's sins ushered in the era of the second Adam—but I won't go into that now. If you're interested, I would be glad to talk more another time. What you need to remember now is simply this: God forgives us if we ask, and forgiveness is an act of love, and love is what it's all about. But we must love ourselves enough to forgive ourselves; only then can we forgive others. Now, how do we learn to love ourselves and forgive ourselves? We do it by letting go of our sins, turning them over to God, asking him to help us. But what are sins—that big catchall we hear so much about in church? Well, I think sin is when we do something that throws us off our spiritual balance; something that is self-destructive, unworthy of our likeness to God.''

"That is mind blowing, Father!'' Peter felt as if he'd been in a long tunnel most of his life, and he had just seen the light at the end of the tunnel.

"Isn't it?'' Father Spencer smiled broadly. "But, oh my, how reluctantly we let go of those destructive things. We just can't get used to the idea that it's all right to love ourselves, and that loving God is not somehow a privilege that has to be presided over by a priest. You see, man doesn't know how to love God because he doesn't understand his relationship to God.''

"Well, how can he, Father? No one ever puts it to him in terms he can understand.''

"Unfortunately you are right. I'm afraid it often suits the church to keep us in the dark. You see, I believe that loving God is the most natural thing in the world. God is good, fair, loving, forgiving. But we've been brainwashed by a church sometimes drunk on power, one that has subjugated man by making him believe he is evil and sinful. No wonder we don't love God—we've been led to believe that unless we are practically saintly, God doesn't love us. That leaves us painfully

vulnerable, unable to protect ourselves. So we don't love God because we believe we're unworthy of his love, and if he doesn't love us, we can't see any reason for loving ourselves. Lacking faith in our own spiritual worth, we have no rudder with which to steer our course. We're cast adrift in a sea of vulnerabilities, and we can be buffeted this way and that by any little storm that comes along. That's the kind of weather Satan finds clear sailing. He throws us a line and says, come on, I know the way, and off we go on a self-destructive route.''

"Father, all this talk about Satan and sin is a little overdramatic for me.''

"Satan is not so obvious, and sometimes neither is sin. Most of us are not thieves, or murderers, or wife beaters, or child abusers, but out of our ignorance, or confusion, or unawareness, we do things that are destructive of our spiritual balance. I see you frowning, so let's just say Satan's kingdom is that which is not of God's kingdom. That which is unharmonious and pulls us off our center.''

"I really hate to keep harping on this, Father, but I'm still not understanding how we know what choices to make. Sometimes the right choice for ourselves can have bad repercussions—for someone else.''

"Yes. All the more reason to stay in harmony with God, and seek his guidance. That is money in the bank, Peter, our secret weapon, if you will. We have first to try and maintain our own harmony, but if that disturbs other people, people close to us, then it becomes their problem with themselves. They are allowing themselves to be pulled off their center, and they have to find their own harmony.''

"This is all terribly interesting, Father, but I don't exactly see how it relates to my own special dilemma.''

"Actually it does, but I guess I have become a little too wordy. You see, it is very important that you understand man's relationship with God. I said in the beginning that a departed spirit does not have the power to manipulate people and events on this earth. But I do believe that a certain amount of communication can occur in the form of awareness through extrasensory perception. Perhaps it is possible that someone in the other world can concentrate so intensely on us that we acquire an awareness of them. But only God or Satan has the power to manipulate us. If the action we are seem-

ingly being pushed to take is harmonious with our being, and makes us happy, or at least not unhappy, it is of God's doing. If it doesn't, it is of Satan's doing. If we're in doubt, we must turn the problem over to God and pray for guidance. God will not whisper the answer in our ear, or speak to us out of a cloud, but if we are sincerely receptive, slowly the right course of action will come to us. We will know it is right because it *feels* right; we will feel relieved to have made the decision, or taken an action, or changed an attitude. When we've done it, we find peace and happiness. We are again in harmony with God and ourselves.''

"But, Father, why am I being tormented, if that's not too melodramatic a word, by Carl? Why do I feel he is trying to take me over?''

"It's not Carl. Carl Morris has no power to take you over. Remember?''

"Yes, only God or Satan has that power. Then you are saying that what I think is Carl, is actually Satan?''

"If you feel he is trying to take you over, you can be certain it is not the work of God. This thing that's happening, makes you feel confused, fearful, anxious—you're in disharmony with yourself. You've lost your centeredness.''

"I've lost my rudder, in other words?''

"Yes. And why? Why are you willing to accept the idea that another man's life is more valid than your own?''

"Well, I wouldn't exactly say I believe that.'' Peter was beginning to feel somewhat uncomfortable.

"But you are allowing yourself to be pulled off your center, to be buffeted this way and that. You said yourself that you feel incapable of managing your life, you're uncertain what your feelings are, you're confused, unhappy, out of harmony with yourself and God. You're not loving yourself, or God, Peter.''

"But what can I do, Father?''

"Come back to your own spiritual center and concentrate on Peter Blanchard. Love yourself, love God, believe that God loves you and will forgive you. Ask for forgiveness and guidance.''

"But what am I asking forgiveness *for?*''

"Not believing that God loves you and will help you. Forgetting to love yourself. Being destructive to yourself.''

"Yes, I suppose all that is true.''

242

"If God is in charge of your life, if you have an ongoing relationship or partnership with him, and hold to your spiritual center, asking God to help, you will end your torment."

"But how can I keep centered?" He felt like a little boy.

"Pray. Simple as that. Every time you feel yourself being pulled off-center, pray. When you begin to feel anxious or confused, when you experience spiritual disharmony or torment—stop and say to yourself: wait a minute there, Peter Blanchard. Then turn to God, ask his help, pray and meditate on what you must do to stop the disharmony, and get your centeredness back. If you really do that in all earnestness, the confusion and anxiety will pass and you can think clearly and act wisely. You will grow calm, and the torment will go away."

"It just seems so simple," said Peter, still feeling like a small boy sitting at the feet of his wise father.

"It is simple, Peter. It's simple in theory and in fact. The help is there—it lies in your partnership with God. In fact, God is the most powerful ally you can have. Just think of what an exciting prospect that is."

"Yes, it is."

"But if you ask, you must be prepared to accept what God gives you. You must trust him, and when you seek guidance, allow for the fact that what you ask for may not be God's will. He will help you in some way, though."

"It's sort of like having a Big Daddy at your beck and call," laughed Peter.

"Exactly. But you've got to work at it too, Peter. You've got to be ready to let go of willful and destructive behavior, and act on the decision God makes known to you. When you falter, or muddle things up again, then pray for guidance and get back on your center."

"It's a whale of a concept, Father!" Peter shook his head. "I just don't know if I can quite take it all in yet—and believe it."

"Don't accept it because I say so. Try it. But I can guarantee you it will work. I've tried it over and over, and I've seen it work for others over the years of my ministry. We make things harder for ourselves than we need to."

"You really believe that through prayer, letting go, and getting in touch with God, loving yourself and loving him, you can solve all the problems of life?"

243

"Yes, I do. They may not always work out exactly the way you want them to, but they will work out. The point is, you will not be floundering in helpless confusion. And just remember that everything we want is not good for us."

"Tell me, Father, why should such an idea infect me—like the idea that Carl is trying to—to possess me, I guess?"

"Oh, it seems to be in the air for one thing. The occult is enjoying a large and profitable popularity. But aside from that, there is a certain psychological reaction to receiving a part of someone else. I have read that some heart-transplant patients undergo tremendous psychological reactions. You have undoubtedly asked yourself why your life was spared when Carl's was taken." Bishop Spencer smiled gently.

"Yes, I have."

"You have your life because God chose to spare it. You have your sight because Carl gave it to you. But both things were God's will. Don't set yourself up to challenge God's decision. Accept it and be grateful."

"I am grateful," Peter replied.

"So grateful you're trying to pay for it by making the life God spared miserable?"

"Well—" Peter grinned sheepishly.

"God doesn't want that, you can be sure. You're not loving yourself, and you're not trusting God."

"Then there's also the matter of Marcy."

"Ah, yes. That's a little different. You're in love with her, and apparently she feels drawn to you."

"Yes."

"I would imagine you've told yourself that you're trying to take something else from Carl."

"Well, yes—sort of. I mean, it has occurred to me."

"Carl's dead. God took him, and by taking him, took him from Marcy. If it transpires that God wants you to love one another, he has a reason. Just relax and let it flow; leave it up to him."

"But both of us wonder if what we feel is really what we feel for one another, or because of Carl."

"Well, I can see how you both might wonder about that. Marcy may have a special feeling about you because you have a part of Carl, but that part is no longer Carl's. His physical self is no more. His corneas have become your corneas because your body contains them, your nerves and

muscles and blood operate them. That too was God's will."

"You know, you're right. They can't exist without me; I give them life now. Carl is not alive through them, because their life comes from my body now." Peter was smiling; it was a fine point, but it was giving him considerable comfort.

"You both have to accept it as God's will, and try not to tamper with it. As for your feelings for Marcy—I rather doubt your caring for her is paying a debt to Carl. Marcy's a beautiful, desirable, wonderful woman, quite easy to love in her own right, and deserving of love."

"Yes, I've never known any woman quite like her. In fact, I don't know how any man could keep from loving her."

"Think of it this way, Peter. If it's God's design that you love her, accept it and be grateful that you've found a woman you can love. If you have doubts, however, about the sincerity and substance of your love for her, then pray on it, seek guidance from God."

"I don't really doubt my love for her—at least I don't think I do. It's just that sometimes I get confused, and doubts and fears plague me."

"There you go again, allowing yourself to be pulled off your center. Of course it's healthy to examine one's feelings, but it is more important to examine one's motives for acting in a given way. Often that will help you arrive at the truth of the matter. But my advice to you there is still the same: return to your spiritual center. Ask yourself if loving her is causing you disharmony. If it is, try to understand why, and pray for guidance. If you still find that your harmony is disturbed, then pull away from her and see if you come back to your center. That will give you your answer." Father Spencer was silent then, and Peter wondered if he should go.

"I am very grateful to you, Father. You've given me a great deal to think about."

"It was my pleasure. It's always a joy for me to talk about the concept of being in harmony with God. I don't know why people are so reluctant to let go of unhappiness and disharmony—especially when the cure for it is there waiting to be taken." He rose and held out his hand. "I'm very glad to have met you, Peter, and I hope you will feel free to come again if you want to talk further about this."

"You've been a great help, Father. After I've digested it all, I'll try to practice it."

"We all have to practice constantly. Believe me, *I* know how easy it is to get pulled off that center."

"You, too, Father?" Peter asked with surprise.

"No one is immune to temptation, Peter. Christ himself was tempted."

# Chapter Twenty-One

When Peter returned from seeing Bishop Spencer, he found Marcy sitting on the patio, reading. She looked up at the sound of his footstep on the flagstone.

"Hello," she called, then got up and came to meet him. She wore white silk lounging pajamas with a haltered top all of one piece. The stark whiteness of the costume set off the golden brown hue of her skin, and the soft silk molded to her body with every movement.

"How did you like Father Spencer?" she asked.

"Very impressive, in fact, mind blowing."

"Isn't he? He makes God seem so real, and essential, and accessible you wonder how you ever got through life without him."

"Yes. Makes you feel rather foolish for not understanding before."

Marcy was moving toward the kitchen. "Would you like a drink before dinner?"

"Oh, maybe a sherry on the rocks? If you have it." He followed her.

"Of course I have it. Doesn't every *proper* household?" She laughed.

"*This* is a proper household?" he teased.

"Only because it has sherry." She smiled over her shoulder as she opened the door. He followed her into the kitchen.

"You know, I've never had a spiritual revelation about

God." Peter said. "I mean, I don't believe in God through any personal spiritual experience. I believe because I was taught to believe, and my intelligence tells me there has to be a master creator, a higher being."

"I know what you mean. It's been the same with me."

"But somehow Father Spencer made me believe in a different way. I found myself getting terribly excited, and hopeful. The idea that I can have a personal relationship with God, that he cares about me, and will help me, makes me feel less alone, less confused and isolated."

"Yes. Isn't it a wonderful comfort?"

"It really is. I know that I'll fall on my face a thousand times, but I feel like maybe I can get up again and he will help me."

"Yes, I've felt that way. Like maybe my life will not get away from me—I'll be able to see the danger signs and ask for help before it does." She dropped ice cubes into a glass and poured sherry over them, then handed him the glass. "Shall we take our drinks out by the pool?"

"I'd like that." He held the door for her to pass. "The lady of the house looks beautiful tonight. In fact she looks smashing."

"Thank you." They strolled toward the pool.

"In fact you'd better keep an eye on this thirty-six-year-old Caucasian male. He has designs on the lady." He laughed, but her face sobered almost instantly.

"I want to talk to you about that. I had plenty of time to think while you were gone."

"Sounds ominous." He sipped his sherry, but an alarm had gone off inside his head, and he knew she had made some decision regarding the two of them. He also had a feeling it was not going to be one that he would like. When they were seated, she turned to face him.

"I've decided to go up to Maine to see my sister for two or three weeks. I love fall up there, and it will give me time to sort things out."

"That's putting a lot of distance between us," he said quietly.

"I know it is, and I think it's important. I've felt the danger signs."

"Oh?"

"Yes. I know if I stay here, I'll be tempted to see you, but I know I must be by myself to come to terms with Carl's

248

death. I haven't really done that yet, and I must do it before I can think about you and me."

"I guess I know you're right, Marcy, but I can't help wishing you weren't going to be so far away."

"It's better for us, Peter."

"I'll probably be gone by the time you get back."

"Where are you going?"

"Germany. Going to the book fair in Frankfurt. It's an annual event and an important one in the book business. Publishers come from all over the world. A lot of business gets done there, both in selling American writers to foreign publishers, and buying foreign writers to publish here."

"I see. Will you be gone long?"

"Couple of weeks, maybe three. I'll be leaving just about the time you'll be coming back, so I guess we won't be seeing each other again for about a month." A feeling of loneliness and unrest began to creep over him, and he thought of Father Spencer's words.

"But that's good, Peter. Don't you see? I must accept the fact that Carl is gone, and learn to be alone before I can be with you, or anyone else." Her eyes begged his understanding. Both remained quiet for a time.

"Marcy?" he began finally.

"Yes?"

"I know what you said before, but I have to ask you again. You—uh, you don't regret last night, do you? I mean, that's not why you're going?"

"No." She looked away. "I don't regret what we shared, but I do wish it had happened later on."

"I don't want to sound indelicate, but I think last night showed us that we have strong feelings for one another."

"Of course it did. I won't deny it. But if they're real, they won't go away just because we're apart for a few weeks."

"No. I guess separation could intensify them." He realized that he was projecting what he hoped would happen.

"It's very important for us to find that out." She paused. "It's the only way for me, Peter."

"Would you like me to leave tonight?" He felt he should ask, but he hoped she wouldn't agree. She was silent for a few moments, and he knew she was debating with herself.

"I think it would be better if you took the train after dinner, don't you?"

"I guess so." He felt disappointed. Still, he reasoned, if he loved her, he had to honor her wishes.

"If you stayed tonight, I'm not certain the same thing might not happen that happened last night. The feelings are still fresh, and the attraction is still there. But it must not happen again until I'm more settled within myself. If I stayed with you tonight, I'd be in trouble with myself. It could ruin whatever we might have later on."

"Enough said. I'll catch the train after dinner." He looked away and they were both silent then, thinking their own private thoughts

"I'd better start dinner," she said finally.

"Why don't you let me take you out to dinner?"

"No, thank you. I'd planned dinner here."

"Okay, to be honest, I'd rather have the time alone with you."

"So would I." She smiled at him and both felt the urge toward one another. She looked away to keep her feelings from showing, but he didn't need to see her face to know; he felt the same way.

"When will you leave for Maine?" he asked to relieve the tension.

"Tomorrow. I talked with Adam earlier, and it's all right with him. In fact he suggested that I go away earlier."

"I gather he and Carl were close friends as well as partners."

"Almost like brothers. They grew up together, went to law school together. Adam was very broken up over Carl's death." She got up suddenly. "I'm going to start dinner. Would you like another sherry?"

"No. I've been drinking too much; I'm going to cut down. Maybe I'll stop altogether. I think I can handle my head better without it."

"Anybody can. I've been very careful about that since Carl died. It really doesn't help."

"Can I give you a hand with dinner?"

"Sure. Come on."

Peter had been back in New York a couple of days and was finding it difficult not to think of Marcy. At times he was angry at her for leading them into the intimacy they'd experienced in Connecticut, and at times he seriously wondered if she would ever get over Carl. Somehow it was easier to be

certain of where he stood with her when they were together. But he kept trying to practice what Father Spencer had taught him, and he found that praying did ease his anxiety.

He sat in his apartment now, working at the desk in the living room, still trying to catch up on the work that had backed up when he was in the hospital, and trying to clear things away so he could go to Frankfurt with a clear mind. A lot was expected of him in Frankfurt, and he had every intention of coming back with some good contracts. He only hoped the books he found over there were worth buying; for he had found he was much more selective now than he'd been before the accident. When the doorbell rang, he glanced at his watch. It was nine o'clock, and he wondered who would arrive unexpectedly at his door at this hour. He got up and went to the door.

"Hello." Jeannie stood there smiling at him.

"Well, hello." He was happy to see her.

"I know it's déclassé to just appear at a gentleman's door without warning, but I was afraid you might not want to see me and would put me off if I telephoned first."

"How could you imagine I wouldn't want to see you?" He held the door open wide. "Please, do come in." She walked into the room and stood somewhat ill at ease, he thought.

"You're working?" She had seen the pile of papers on the desk.

"Yes, but it can wait. Sit down. Can I get you something?"

"I think I could use a Scotch."

"Coming up." He went to the bar and poured her a drink, but poured himself a plain soda. "Here you are." She had seated herself on the sofa. He took a chair beside the sofa.

"How have you been?" she asked.

"Pretty good. Busy. And you?"

"Okay, busy." There was a silence in which both of them felt acutely uncomfortable.

"Been going out to Southampton?"

"Yes." She put the glass down on the table and turned to face him. "Peter, I've missed you terribly, and I came to see you to tell you that I'm afraid I was not very understanding with you. I think I was impatient and unreasonable. I really didn't give you a chance."

"Jeannie—"

"No, let me finish. They say confession is good for the soul, and I've got some confessing to do."

"Okay, if it makes you feel better, but it isn't necessary. I don't think you were unreasonable."

"Yes, I was, Peter. I acted like a self-indulgent, spoiled brat, which I've discovered I am anyway."

"Don't you think you're being rather hard on yourself?"

"No. I've discovered what I am, and I want to talk about it."

"Go ahead then."

"I know I was neither understanding nor supportive when you most needed it. I was too intent on what I wanted, because I've always gotten what I wanted. I've been spoiled since I was a baby, so naturally I expected everything to go my way. No tragedy ever touched my life, Peter. I've skimmed by on the surface of life. And I've been selfish and demanding."

"I don't think you were selfish and demanding, Jeannie."

"That's because you're one of the sweetest, kindest men in the world. But don't you see, that was part of it, too. Nothing has ever been asked of me before, everything has come to me. My parents, my friends, the men I've known have all made things easy for me. Then you were injured, and I wanted to come to France to be with you, but you wouldn't let me. Now I understand why, but I didn't at the time, and I was very hurt."

"I'm sorry, Jeannie, but I couldn't have handled it then."

"Yes, I see that now, but I wish you hadn't just assumed that I wouldn't be able to cope, that I would freak out, or something, when I found you were blind."

"I'm afraid I was thinking more about myself than about you then, and the problem was that *I* couldn't handle your knowing."

"Well, in either case, the point I'm trying to make is, nothing has ever been asked of me before. I wanted that chance to help you, and I was hurt that I didn't get it. Again, I guess I wanted my way." She took a cigarette from the cigarette box on the coffee table and Peter got up to light it for her. "Thanks." She was still nervous. "So you came home, and you were in a bad way, but I expected to be greeted with open arms. I expected you to be as thrilled to see me as I was to see you, but you had your own problems, and they were about all you could handle. You didn't have room to worry about me and my feelings. In fact you hardly

seemed to know I was alive. I panicked, and began to imagine you didn't love me anymore, and maybe you hadn't wanted me to come over to France because of that. I even imagined that you had fallen in love with Mrs. Morris.''

''Jeannie—'' Peter wanted her to stop talking because he was beginning to feel guilty.

''Peter, please let me talk it out.'' She got up and began to pace the room. ''I needed reassurance that you still loved me, and I thought the only way to prove that you did was for you to make love to me. I was determined to make you want me. Again, selfish Jeannie wanted her own way. Instead of understanding the trauma you'd been through, and what it might do to you mentally as well as physically, I was impatient and demanding. You were asking my understanding, and for me to be patient with you, but I was too wrapped up in my own needs. I'd always wanted to be needed, and to do something for someone else, but when I got the chance, I struck out.''

''You did try, Jeannie. You were very patient with me for quite a time.''

''Yes, but I expected too much too soon, I know that now. That wasn't very loving of me, and certainly not supportive. I've come to realize, since we stopped seeing one another, that I'm not very mature. If I loved you as I thought I did, I should have been supportive, instead of demanding that my needs be gratified.''

''Perhaps all love is selfish, Jeannie.'' Peter didn't know what to say to her, but he could see that she'd been going through a bad time, and that it was very hard for her to come to him and say the things she had just said.

''What I'm trying to say is—I know that I love you, and that I've let you down. I want to ask you if—if you can forgive me.''

''Of course I forgive you, Jeannie. You didn't mean to let me down, I know that. And I know that your life hasn't exactly prepared you for patience and sacrifice, but I don't hold that against you.'' Peter didn't know what else to say, and he was beginning to feel very anxious. She came to stand in front of him and then knelt so she could look into his eyes.

''Peter, can we start over again? I mean, can we try to take the good things we've had and build on those? I think I've learned a lot in the past few weeks, and I think I'm finally growing up. I want—I want a second chance, Peter. Can we

try?'' Tears stood in her eyes, and he had never found her more appealing.

"Oh, Jeannie, honey.'' He ran his hand over his face and closed his eyes. He was very moved by what she'd said, and all the more so because he knew how difficult it had been for her to say it. But what could he say to her? He knew there was still feeling in him for her, but there was also strong feeling for Marcy.

"Peter?''

"Yes?'' He opened his eyes and looked at her upturned face. What was he going to say to her? What did he want to say to her? And whatever he said, would it be fair to her?

"Can't you say something to me? Don't leave me hanging like this.''

"I don't know what to say, Jeannie. I'm so uncertain about my own feelings at this point. I'm by no means out of the woods on the Morris matter. I still have nightmares, and I still have problems reconciling my feelings about the transplants.''

"But I understnad that now, and I can be patient and supportive.''

"I believe you, and I am very touched by your coming here and saying these things. I know how hard it must have been for you. But I guess what I have to say is, I need time alone to think things out. I've changed a lot, too, Jeannie, and I've got some adjusting to do. In a way I'm getting to know myself all over again.''

"Peter, do you still care for me?'' She looked very vulnerable as she awaited his answer, and suddenly he wanted to run. He was being pressed for answers he wasn't ready to give.

"Yes—I care for you, Jeannie, but I don't know yet how much.'' A look of hurt came into her eyes, and he felt miserable. "If you can give me some time to think it out, maybe let us see one another casually from time to time, with no expectations, or demands on one another, I can find out where I am.''

"Yes, I can do that, Peter. I know now that I love you enough to be patient.''

"If you really mean that, I'd like to be able to see you, but not if you're going to be hurt by my lack of sexual interest right now—I mean, if it continues that way. I can't bear to

254

hurt you, Jeannie. I'd rather not see you than put you through a relationship that makes you feel unwanted—as a woman, I mean."

"I know what you mean." She tried to smile reassuringly. "I think I can handle it now. I know that I want our relationship to work out. I want us to get back together, Peter."

"I can't guarantee that, Jeannie, I want you to know that." He spoke gently, taking her hand in his.

"Tell me one thing, Peter?"

"If I can?"

"Do you have feelings for Marcy Morris?" There it was, and she deserved an answer, but he resented the question; he had a right to his own private feelings. But she had a right to know the truth as well.

"Yes, I do have. I'm sorry, Jeannie, but if we're to have any kind of relationship at all, we've got to be honest with one another." There was pain in her eyes at his answer, but he also saw the stiffening of her back. The thoroughbred in her was rising to the challenge.

"Thank you for telling me the truth this time," she said in a choked voice.

"I didn't lie to you before, Jeannie. I didn't know how I felt about Marcy then."

"Is there a chance we can get back together, Peter?"

"Perhaps. I don't know, and that's the truth."

"But you're willing to explore the idea?"

"Yes. If we can see one another the way I suggested." He took out a cigarette. "I'm going to Frankfurt in a couple of weeks, and I'll be gone two or three weeks. It will give me time to think things over."

"Are you seeing Marcy, too?" She was crowding him again, and he felt the same resentment rising.

"No. She needs time to grieve for her husband." He didn't want to talk about Marcy, and it was actually none of Jeannie's business. He had told her a little to satisfy her, but that was all he was going to say.

"I guess it serves me right." She sat down, and a dejected look crossed her face. "I don't want to lose you, Peter."

"If it's right, and meant to be between us, we won't lose each other, Jeannie. But let's not try to rush things."

"You seem so different, Peter. Almost like a different person from the man who left my apartment that disastrous

255

night. I mean, you were different when you came back from Paris, but you're even more different now. Has something important happened?''

"A lot of things have happened. I've just about run the gamut of emotions. I've been down in the depths of despair; I've been terrified by nightmares; I've been almost incapacitated by anxieties; and occasionally I've been excited and happy. It had been a very uncertain and unsettled existence, and I guess I'm a different person in many ways. But I think—I hope to God—I am on my way out of it.'' He didn't feel like going into an explanation of what he'd learned from Father Spencer and how it had begun to help him. He found that he didn't really want to talk about it, and he wasn't exactly certain she would understand anyway. Perhaps he was underestimating her, but the important thing was, he didn't want to share it right now.

"I hope you're coming out of it, too. But if I can help, will you let me? I mean, don't cut me out this time, Peter, please?''

"Yes, I'll share things with you more openly, but I don't feel like talking about anything tonight.''

"I understand.'' She got up and took her glass into the kitchen. He did not protest because he realized she found comfort in doing something familiar and possessive. He stood in the doorway and watched her rinse out the glass and put it in the drainer.

"You look relaxed in there,'' he said lightly.

"Feels good.'' She dried her hands and walked past him and on to the front door. He followed. She paused at the door, her hand on the knob. "Will you call me?''

"Yes. And I appreciate your coming tonight.''

She reached up and kissed him on the cheek. He put his arm around her waist and held her close to him for a moment. "Take care, darling. I'll be in touch,'' she said, and left.

With Jeannie gone he went back to his desk and tried to concentrate on the work she'd interrupted. But it was no use; his mind would not be organized. He threw down the pencil and got up. Here we go again, confusion and anxiety—but, am I being a fool to let Jeannie go? Could we reestablish our relationship, and could it work? Would it be the best thing for everybody in the long run? Marcy was still so uncertain, and he had no guarantee that she'd ever be any more certain. Yet

256

he knew that he loved her, and no matter what happened, he would not stop loving her. "Damn it, I'm letting myself get pulled off-center again," he said aloud to the room. "About time I tried talking to my partner."

Peter boarded the plane at Kennedy Airport with feelings of trepidation. When he'd flown back to New York after the accident, he'd been so heavily sedated and tranquilized against the pain in his back and leg he'd hardly been aware of flying. Today, however, he was on his own and resolved to make the flight without the help of whiskey. He had quit drinking after the weekend in Connecticut. And while his preoccupation with Carl had not completely disappeared, he'd been better able to keep it under control with the help of Father Spencer's lessons. Prayer did help, but it was hard work, and took a gread deal of discipline and concentration.

He folded his trench coat and placed it in the bin above the seat, and stowed his attaché case under the seat. He sat down and fastened his seat belt. He had been careful this time to sit in the rear section, it ostensibly being the safest position in case of crash. But he felt butterflies in his stomach all the same. He leaned his head back against the seat, closed his eyes, and began to pray. He prayed continually as they taxied down the runway, for he had experienced a moment of panic when the door had been closed and he had known there was no escape.

The big plane turned on the runway, and the pilot revved the engines until it vibrated violently with restrained power. The brakes were released and the plane shot forward, hurling itself down the tarmac. Peter gripped the armrests as the plane lifted off and was airborn. Once in the air he began to try and relax. He was wet with the perspiration of fear, but he told himself that God would surely not have spared him before only to let him die four months later.

He unfastened his seat belt and glanced for the first time at the man seated next to him. Carl Morris! A shock went through him like an electric current. No, it couldn't be. Carl was dead! Peter closed his eyes, hoping the image would go away, but each time he opened them, the image was still there—Carl Morris, calmly reading a magazine. He felt his heart thudding against his ribs, and he began to pray once again, that God would help him control the panic.

"Excuse me." Peter opened his eyes. The man he had imagined to be Carl Morris was standing, looking down at him. "Could I get past you, please?" Peter almost laughed, for the man did not look at all like Carl. He got up and the man moved past him and went down the aisle toward the rest room. Had he imagined that the man looked like Carl? Why would he do that? Was he feeling guilty for being alive again, punishing himself by imagining Carl sitting next to him as he had been on the plane to Paris? Whatever the reason, he was feeling anxious and getting pulled out of his center.

"Okay, God, I've got the warning," he said aloud. "What am I up to anyway, allowing this to happen? Am I doubting you? Please don't let me doubt now."

On his second day in Frankfurt Peter was approached by a German publisher with the English translation of a book which was fast becoming a best seller in Germany. Parthenon Publishing Company was his first choice of American publishers. Peter was flattered and promised to try and read the book and give him an answer within a few days.

After dining with a British and a Dutch editor that evening, Peter begged off from a tour of the Frankfurt night spots and went back to his room to read the manuscript. It was an easy book to get into, and he liked the writing. It was about a man who had died and come back to earth as Satan's emissary to spread the message that God had been conquered by Satan.

According to the emissary, one Dimitri Luxor, God had been a hoax to start with: Satan had been the real power in the contest. The book then detailed the battle between Satan and God, and told how God's power had proved inferior to Satan's. But the real clincher, according to Luxor, was the fact that when they had totaled up the number of followers each had been able to acquire on earth, Satan had unquestionably been the winner. The majority carried the day, and the emissary had come to set up Satan's kingdom on earth. His job was to gather disciples and spread the word of Satan. He was, in a word, the Satanic Messiah, and while some right-thinking folk opposed his take-over, all perished before his awesome power.

The book was cleverly conceived and quite seriously written. It was not a satire on the coming of Christ; it was, as nearly as Peter could determine, written by someone who unabashedly believed in Satan. When he put the book down,

he felt quite literally frightened. He sat for some time considering the horrifying aspects of such an idea. According to Dimitri's concept man was utterly meaningless, a human robot in the hands of Satan. Every decent sensibility in Peter rejected the idea, but the businessman in him knew the book would become a best seller in the U.S.; a lot of Americans loved to scare themselves nearly to death with the idea of impending danger. Could he take a pragmatic position on something so demoralizing to the human spirit?

He thought back over his conversation with Bishop Spencer, and about the comfort he had derived from his as yet faltering relationship with God, and he knew he could not publish the book. He was certain that another American publisher would, however—and do well with it, at that. Professionally it would be in his best interest, and in the best economic interest of his publisher, to buy the book, but he could not bring himself to do it. Tomorrow he would reject it, and that was that. He snapped off the light and went to sleep.

Unfortunately that was not that, for the German publisher was determined that Parthenon would publish the book, and he had already sent a copy of it to Parthenon's president in New York. Before the week was out, Peter received a call from the president instructing him to buy the book. Peter refused, mounting a convincing argument for why it was not a good investment for Parthenon. The president insisted, and Peter continued to refuse. The argument raged over the trans-Atlantic telephone wires for two days, with both men adamant about their positions. Finally the president announced that he was flying over, and Peter should book him a suite and be available to meet with him at two o'clock the following day.

R. Preston Sheffield was an imposing figure of a man, six feet three inches tall, silver haired, patrician in features, and a former quarterback from Princeton, class of 1946; the latter was a fact which he never let anyone forget. He was awesome when he was in a fighting mood. And he was in a fighting mood when he arrived in Frankfurt.

"What in the name of all that's holy have you got up your ass, Blanchard?" were his first words to Peter.

"How are you, R. P.?" asked Peter, calmly ignoring the question.

"I'm madder than hell, that's how I am!"

"Sorry to hear it. Have a nice flight over?"

"No, I didn't. A totally unnecessary expense caused by your unreasonable attitude toward this goddamned book."

"I agree the expense was unnecessary, R. P. I've already given you my valid reasons for not buying this book, and I have not changed my mind." Peter spoke quietly.

"Do you mean to stand there and tell me that you don't think the book will sell like hotcakes in the U.S.?"

"It may and it may not. There's a very good chance that it may offend a lot of people and get the church community down on us."

"Hell, Peter, you're a pro. You know that's like money in the bank! Why, any idiot knows that free press like that is something a publisher prays for." Sheffield was striding up and down the room now, waving his cigar recklessly in the air, spreading ashes from one end of the expensive rug to the other.

"And what if organized religion brings suit against Parthenon to force us to remove it from the market? And we're not just talking about the Catholic Church, we're talking about the entire Protestant community as well."

"Let 'em! All those good church people will line up to buy the book while the fuss is going on."

"And if we lose the case?"

"Don't think we will, Pete. But if we do, we'll already have sold enough books to come out on top! You know legal things don't move that fast, and we'll print two-hundred-fifty-thousand copies first crack, and be ready to print another one-hundred to one-hundred-fifty-thousand right on top of that."

"In my opinion it's too risky, and I wouldn't like to see Parthenon do it." Peter had remained calm, sitting in a chair, watching Sheffield pace the floor, and he had used logical arguments that he thought Sheffield would comprehend, for he was always screaming economics. However, those were not the reasons he didn't want to publish the book; his reasons would be less acceptable to Sheffield.

"I don't get you, Blanchard. If ever there was an imaginative and audacious promoter, you're it. I don't know another man in publishing with your business savvy. Why, you've always been able to smell a best seller, and here you are giving me these weak, damn near timid arguments against

what in my opinion is a sure thing. What the hell has got into you? That plane crash addle your brain?''

"Look, R. P., I happen to think this deal could backfire on us for reasons I've already enumerated, but there's something else to consider as well.''

"What in God's name is that?'' Sheffield stopped pacing and stood frowning at Peter.

"Well, R. P., there is such a thing as social responsibility, and I think it would be irresponsible of Parthenon to publish this book. It's flying in the face of some of the most basic beliefs of the American people, and I don't think it will make any friends for us in the long run.''

"Son of a bitch! I don't believe what I'm hearing. Big Deal Blanchard of Publishers Row is not only passing up the deal of the year, but reading me a fucking Sunday-school lesson to boot!'' R. P.'s face was getting red, and Peter knew the explosion was not far behind, but he'd come to the meeting prepared for a showdown.

"Well, it may surprise you to know that Big Deal Blanchard has a set of values along with his business savvy, and this book doesn't meet them.'' Peter was still speaking calmly.

"Shit! Do you mean to tell me you're turning this book down on moral grounds, too?''

"Yes, that's exactly what I'm telling you, R. P.''

"You've either lost your marbles or got religion, and neither one goes down with me. I want this book, Peter, and I mean to have it. Now, you get your ass out of here and buy it, and that's an order!'' Sheffield was shouting now.

"I'm really sorry, R. P. but I can't do it.''

"I don't think you heard me, Blanchard, I just gave you an order!''

"If you insist on that position, Sheffield, you leave me no alternative but to resign.''

Sheffield's face registered shock. "Peter, use your head, man.'' Sheffield's voice had lowered.

Peter had momentarily taken the wind out of his sails, but he knew that Sheffield would no more back down on his position that he would on his own "I've thought it over very carefully, R. P., and that's my position.''

"Look, I'm only asking you to buy one goddamned book. You may not be crazy about it, but it's not worth throwing

away a career on. Why don't you sleep on it, and we'll discuss it in the morning."

"I'm not going to see it any differently in the morning."

"Come on, Pete, this nonsense has gone far enough. Jesus Christ, it can't be that important to you!"

"Oh, but it is. I do not want to be associated with the book."

"Look, you don't have to. I'll buy the fucking thing, and I'll give it out that I bought it over your opposition. All you have to do is direct the promotion of it."

"I don't think you quite understand. I don't want this book published at all. I know I can't stop it, and another publisher will undoubtedly pick it up if you don't, but I will do nothing to aid in this book's publication." Peter had finally lost his patience with the subject, and his voice left no room for doubt that he meant what he said.

"Holy shit! You've really gone 'round the bend! And come to think of it, you've been acting weird ever since that damned plane crash. I think you better see a doctor, sonny boy!" Sheffield's tone was disdainful and patronizing, but Peter knew that he had surprised the man with his unmovable position; it always confused Sheffield when he didn't get his way, or he made a miscalculation. He had thought that by coming to Frankfurt and bullying him, he would cave in; now that the tactic hadn't worked, Sheffield didn't know what else to do but bluster.

"You'll have my resignation in the morning." Peter got up. "Sorry it had to come to this, R. P., but nothing lasts forever, does it?" Peter smiled and put out his hand. Sheffield eyed him for a moment and shook his head.

"Goddamn it! I don't know you anymore. You're just not the same man I've worked with all these years."

"I'm the same man, R. P., I'm just a little more my own man, that's all." Peter removed his hand from Sheffield's.

"Bullshit! You were always your own man!"

"Let's just say I expect a little more of myself that I once did."

"What the hell does that mean?"

"For one thing it means that I won't publish this kind of book." Peter walked to the door and turned to look back at the big man. "Sorry I can't wish you luck with the book, R. P., but I do wish you luck with Parthenon."

"If you change your mind, I'll be here for a couple of days."

"I won't change it. But thanks anyway. So long, R. P."

Peter went quickly out the door and heaved a sigh of relief. Well, that was that!

Peter returned to New York jobless, but thoroughly convinced he had made the right decision, and the only decision he could live with. And he'd hardly set foot off the plane when his telephone started to ring off the wall. The trade press had gotten hold of the story in Frankfurt, and the wire service had picked it up. Now the working press wanted the inside story of his resignation. He finally agreed to an interview, and told them that his resignation had been based on moral grounds; he believed that a publisher had a responsibility to society. He had decided against buying the book because he could not in good conscience do it. Since Mr. Sheffield disagreed with him, obviously both could not win; therefore he had offered his resignation.

The reaction to the newspaper stories was varied: some people thought he'd turned into a religious fanatic, others applauded his courage of conviction. Bishop Spencer read the story and wrote Peter a warm letter in which he stated his respect and admiration. It was very gratifying to learn that some of his colleagues respected his position as well. Nevertheless he was sorry to leave Parthenon. He'd put in ten years with them, and a lot of his energy and hopes. He was concerned how the decision would affect his future in publishing, but he wasn't going to worry about it. He'd done what he had to do, and he knew he'd do it all over again if the decision was put to him again.

Jeannie called, congratulating him on his decision but offering condolences for the job. She wanted to see him, and he promised to call her for dinner in a few days. There was no word from Marcy, and that depressed him, but he did not try to contact her. Perhaps she was still in Maine and hadn't seen the story.

After two weeks of unemployment Peter felt at loose ends and painfully conscious of how difficult it was to stand up for one's beliefs in a commercially minded world. While it was exhilarating to know one could not be intimidated by commercialism, it wasn't an ideal solution to paying the bills. He

wondered if he would have made the same decision had the book been offered to him before his exposure to Bishop Spencer, and he decided he would have bought the book without much debate. "Well, God," he said aloud, "see what you got me into? Now I need your help more than ever."

He began to put out feelers to other publishers, and the response was somewhat cool. By the end of three weeks of uncertainty he was beginning to feel depressed. He told himself that he'd been foolish, grandstanding his high principles when some other publisher would no doubt pick up the book. In fact all the fuss that had been made over his refusal to buy it would only increase the interest in it, and the sales at the bookstores.

By the end of the month, however, he was surprised by a call from the president of Strouk & Grange, one of the oldest and most prestigious publishing houses in the country. The president asked him to lunch, and during the luncheon he told Peter that he admired his courage and integrity. He wound up offering him the executive editorship of his company. Peter accepted on the spot; it was a position for which any editor would give his eyeteeth.

Overjoyed by his good fortune, and more convinced than ever that God did work in strange and mysterious ways, Peter tried to call Marcy to share the news with her, but she was not to be found either in her office or at home in Connecticut. Determined to give her the time she'd asked for, he had not tried to contact her since the weekend in Connecticut, but now it had been almost seven weeks since he'd seen her, and in view of all that had happened to him, he felt he could justifiably contact her. But no one seemed to know where she was. She'd simply disappeared—or had she? Perhaps she was trying to avoid him? No, that would not be Marcy's style; she was too sensitive and straightforward for that. If she had decided she didn't want to see him again, she would have told him to his face. But where was she, and why did everyone else seem to be in the dark, too?

# Chapter Twenty-Two

"Marcy, are you not feeling well?" Marcy's sister Jane was seated across from her at the breakfast table.

"What makes you ask?" Marcy replied absently.

"Oh—you just haven't seemed like yourself for several days now."

"No, I feel fine." She continued buttering toast. "Physically I feel fine."

"Memories crowding in on you, huh?"

"Not exactly," Marcy replied rather too casually, signaling Jane that something was indeed wrong. She carefully put down her coffee cup and fixed Marcy with a sympathetic look.

"Want to talk about it?" The two sisters had always been close and able to share their thoughts.

"Oh, I don't know. It's probably nothing. Just a passing thing." Marcy bit into the toast and suddenly didn't want it anymore.

"I'd hardly call moping around several days a passing thing. I know something is bothering you, so do I have to pull it out of you, or are you going to tell me about it?"

"I think I'm making a mountain out of a molehill, that's all." Marcy put the toast down and began to stir her coffee.

"Will you stop being so cryptic!" Jane smiled and Marcy laughed.

"Yes, I guess I do sound cryptic, but I really think I'm getting myself worked up over nothing."

"There you go again! Either tell me it's none of my business, or spill it!"

"Well, I'm a little embarrassed to talk about it—"

"Embarrassed? You? Since when?"

"Oh, I guess I might as well tell you." Marcy sighed heavily.

"Good. I really don't enjoy guessing games."

"You shouldn't be so curious." Marcy smiled and wagged her finger. "Mother was right, you do have a Sherlock Holmes complex." Both women laughed.

"Yes, I know, but in this case I'm trying to be a good friend and loving sister. So, spill it!"

"Well—I'm almost three weeks late getting my period." Marcy dropped her eyes.

"Come on, Marcy, be serious." Jane was getting slightly impatient.

"I *am* serious," replied Marcy, meeting her sister's eyes.

"You are?"

"Yes." Marcy went on looking at her.

"Oh." Jane picked up her coffee cup. "Well, so what?"

"I've never been late for my period in my life."

"Well, do you think something's wrong? I mean, maybe the shock of Carl's death and all?"

"Carl's been dead almost five months now, and it hasn't affected me that way once." The two women went on staring at one another.

"Are you trying to tell me that you're pregnant?"

"Of course not!"

"But you're wondering, aren't you?"

"It has crossed my mind." Marcy looked out the window to avoid Jane's eyes. She didn't want to see her put two and two together.

"But, if Carl's been dead almost five months—" The words came out slowly as the realization dawned.

"I know," Marcy said calmly, feeling anything but calm inside.

"Oh—"

"Before you ask, the answer is yes. It is possible." Marcy made herself meet her sister's eyes.

"I didn't know. I mean, you didn't say anything." Jane

toyed with her spoon. "Well, I didn't know there was any-body." Jane ran out of steam, and Marcy was wishing she hadn't raised the subject, because now she didn't know what to say.

"I guess I owe you an explanation."

"No. No, you don't have to tell me anything. That's your business."

"Stop it, Jane. There isn't anything to tell, really." Jane was looking uncomfortable. How to tell her about Peter? She had to tell her, because to leave her wondering was worse. "Look, this isn't going to be easy, and you're going to think I'm getting crazy when I do tell you."

"Try me."

Marcy began to tell her about Peter, starting with the transplants in France. As she talked, she realized how strange it all must sound to someone not involved. In fact it began to seem to Marcy that she was telling a story about someone else. When she finished, Jane remained silent for a moment.

"Wow! Big sister—that's some story!"

"I know it sounds unreal, but—"

"It sounds a little strange—but wonderful!"

"It didn't seem so strange as it was happening."

"Obviously not." Jane lit a cigarette. "And you're not on the pill?"

"Janie, I tried to get pregnant for ten years, remember?"

"Yeah, that's right."

"Besides I never meant that to happen with Peter."

"But only one night—I mean, the chances of your getting pregnant, especially since you didn't in all those years—"

"That's what I keep telling myself."

"Must have been some night!" Jane grinned sheepishly.

"Jane, please—"

"Okay, sorry."

"It just isn't possible; it can't be."

"Then there's got to be another reason you haven't gotten your period, and you ought to see a doctor—find out."

"I'll wait a few days and see." The two sisters fell silent again.

"Marcy?"

"Yes?"

"Supposing you are, then what?"

"I can't be—that's all."

267

"But just suppose," Jane persisted.

"No. I can't think about that now." But Marcy had thought about it for over two weeks now; in fact she'd thought of almost nothing else.

"But you've got to know what you're going to do, Marcy."

"I'll cross that bridge when, and if, I come to it. Right now I don't want to think about it." Marcy jumped up and grabbed her sweater. "I'm going sailing."

"Wait up, I'll come with you," Jane called. Marcy stopped and turned back.

"Please, Janie, if you don't mind, I'd like to go alone."

"No problem. I understand."

"Thanks, Sis." Marcy smiled apologetically and ran out of the room.

Two weeks later, and one week late on her second missed period, Marcy had to face up to the fact that either she was pregnant or something was very much wrong. Whichever was the case, she did not feel well and obviously had to see a doctor. She would have preferred going home to Connecticut to see her own gynecologist, but she'd purposely stayed on in Maine to make it easier to stay away from Peter, and it was probably just as well that she went to a doctor she didn't know. In fact she and Jane had decided to avoid Jane's doctor in Bar Harbor, and had gotten the name of a Dr. Johnston in Bangor.

Early one morning she drove into Bangor to see Dr. Johnston, and after the examination he announced that he was of the opinion she was pregnant. By afternoon the results of the pregnancy test proved him right. She was, in fact, five weeks pregnant. Of course she had faced up to that possibility, but it did not really come home to her until the doctor had put it into words:

"Mrs. Morris, you are pregnant, and I would say about five weeks along." He spoke with the Down Easter's customary economy of words.

"Are you sure, Doctor?" she had asked.

"No doubt about it, Mrs. Morris," he replied and began to advise her on diet, and other things she supposed doctors told women who became pregnant for the first time, but she really did not take much of it in. All she could think of was the irony of her situation: for ten years she had wanted a child, and now she was going to have one, and she didn't want it.

It was not an easy drive back to Bar Harbor. She kept asking herself how it could be that she could conceive a child after one night with Peter, and not in ten years with Carl. How she had longed to become pregnant, how she had prayed each month that she'd be late with her period, but she'd been right on time every month.

At last she was carrying life inside her, and suddenly the reality of it hit her. "How wonderful!" she said aloud. "I am really going to have a child at last—my very own, living, breathing child!" She began to laugh and cry as the car sped along the highway. "I am really capable of conceiving. I'm all right!"

But after the first wave of elation had run its course, she came down hard. It wasn't just her child, it was Peter Blanchard's child, too. Peter Blanchard, father of her child—not Carl Morris, her husband. But Carl was gone, and gone forever. Did he know she was pregnant? Did the dead know things that happened to their loved ones left on earth? Had Carl, for example, been there with her and heard the doctor say she was pregnant? Was he looking down on her now, and if so, what was he feeling? Was he hurt that she'd conceived by another man? Then another thought occurred to her: had Carl known when she lay with Peter? "Oh, God!" she said aloud. The thought was so devastating that she had to pull the car off the road.

When she'd come to a stop, she dropped her head down on the steering wheel and gripped the wheel with both hands. "Oh God, no, no, no! Let it not be so!" she cried aloud. "Oh, my darling, Carl, if you know, please try to understand how it happened—and forgive me. Please forgive me."

After a time she felt calmer and began to reason. Perhaps Carl could forgive her being with Peter—it had been something of an accident—but what about the child? Wouldn't he be asking himself how it happened that she became pregnant with Peter and not with him? Would he be feeling that she hadn't wanted a child by him? Surely he would know that was not true. And yet, how to explain why she hadn't conceived by Carl? How hurt and angry he must feel. Oh, why had she given in to her desire that night? Why hadn't she resisted? Because it had been *her* decision to be with Peter; he had not seduced her into being with him. The guilt was hers, and hers alone, and the result was a new life now growing in

her. A life she had not wished for, and didn't want. No! That was not really true. It was true that she had not wished for "*this child,*" but she had wished so often for "*a child,*" and she did want the child. The excitement she'd experienced a few miles back—that was real. Didn't that tell her that she wanted the child? It didn't matter, it couldn't matter, that Peter was its father. What would his reaction be when he knew? Even knowing him so brief a time, she knew that he would be happy about the child, but she also knew that she couldn't think of him knowing. It seemed, somehow, a further betrayal of Carl for Peter to know. But did he have to know? Of course he had to know; it would be cruel and dishonest to keep it from him. He didn't have to know now, however; he could know sometime later, perhaps after the baby was born.

Finally feeling calm enough to go on, she maneuvered the car back onto the highway, but her mind continued churning with turmoil. She began to examine her feelings about Peter's knowing. Why didn't she want him to know? Was it because she knew he would want to marry her, and she didn't want to be tempted to marry him for the wrong reasons? After all, it would not be the easiest thing in the world to be an unmarried mother, and it wasn't as though she didn't care for Peter. But how much did she care for him? She didn't know. She did know, however, that she could not think of marriage so soon after Carl's death. There was still too much grief for there to be room for love, the kind of love one needed for a marriage.

Carl, if only she knew what he was feeling about the child, she would know better what to do. Perhaps he was angry, perhaps he resented it. She could hardly blame him if he did. But why, why had she not been able to have a child by him when it had been so easy with Peter? She had been truly in love with Carl, but not with Peter. Could there have been some deeply buried psychological reason, a reason unknown to her, that had kept her from conceiving? Why, why, why? So many questions and no answers!

And now— the child. She not only had to rethink her life without Carl, she had to rethink it in terms of carrying the child eight more months—alone, giving birth to it alone, raising it alone. Suddenly she realized that she was thinking of herself as always being alone, but that wasn't true. Someday she might remarry. Then the child would have a father,

and a child needed a father. What was the matter with her anyway? The child already had a father. Why did she want to ignore Peter? Was she resenting him because he had given her what Carl had not? Was she even blaming him for her hurting Carl? That was not only unfair, it was crazy! She couldn't push her guilt onto Peter, and she had no right to deny him his child either. Denying him his child could not make it up to Carl. What was happening to her? She wasn't that kind of person. She had to stop thinking like that; it was dishonest, neurotic thinking, and it sickened her.

But thoughts of Carl would not go away—the feeling that wherever he was, he knew about the child and was angry with her. He must feel that she had not only let him down all those years, but she had betrayed his memory by being with Peter. What would he want of her? How could she make amends? Could she make it right by denying Peter knowledge of his child, cutting him out of her life forever, never seeing him again? Perhaps she could pay that price, and perhaps Peter could, but the child shouldn't have to.

"Wait a minute, Marcy Morris," she said aloud to herself. "There's another way out of this." The thought had come from nowhere and insinuated itself into her mind without her being conscious of it at all. She didn't have to keep the child! Yes, perhaps that was the answer. It would solve so many problems, perhaps even make it right with Carl. No! Even the thought of giving up the child brought with it a terrible feeling of loss. She'd only been certain for a little over an hour that she was going to have a child, and yet she had experienced the excitement and joy of its existence, and a sense of no longer being alone. Could she give it up now? A new anguish had entered her already overtaxed mind and emotions, and her head was beginning to ache unbearably.

Jane was waiting for her when she got back to the house, and she did not need to be told the verdict. Marcy knew that one look at her face told the whole story.

"Well, I guess I'd better start knitting booties," Jane said with a grin.

"You can't knit worth a damn and you know it." Marcy dropped into a chair.

"True. Well, I'll think of something *auntlike* to do."

"Oh, Janie, I didn't need this." The two sisters looked at one another a long moment.

271

"How about a drink?" Jane asked.

"It's too early."

"Coffee on the rocks?"

"I'd love it."

"Stay where you are; you look beat."

"I am."

"Be back in a flash."

Marcy leaned back in the chair and closed her eyes. She'd have to make a decision about the child, and very soon, but did she have the right to decide to get rid of it without talking to Peter? Of course she did! After all, she would be the one to carry it, and raise it—alone. Because she'd slept with him under dramatic circumstances, and by chance conceived, did not give him rights in a decision which concerned her body and her future life. It had simply been by an act of circumstance that she happened to be involved in it at all.

"Here we are." Jane handed her a glass of iced coffee and took a seat. "Well, where do we go from here, big sister?"

"I guess I have to decide whether or not to have the child, don't I?"

"Yeah. You've got a choice, but it's a toughie. If you decide to have it, will you marry Peter?"

"No."

"Why not? He's the father, and you said yourself you *are* attracted to him, you do care for him on some level, and he wants to marry you already."

"Yes, Janie, but you know I'm suspicious of the reasons for that attraction." Marcy sipped her coffee. "I just don't think an accidental happening is good enough reason to marry someone. And even if it were, I'm not ready. Carl is too much a part of me still—and maybe always will be. It wouldn't be fair to anyone else."

"Oh come on, Marcy! You've got your whole life ahead of you yet. Surely you're not thinking of being alone forever."

"No, probably not. But right now I just can't think any other way."

"Well, if you do decide to have the child and you don't marry Peter, you've got a rough road ahead. Being an unwed mother, if you'll pardon the expression, is not an easy role."

"I know."

"Let's take our mother for starters. She's really going to *love* being a grandmother to a—"

"Bastard?" Marcy broke in.

"I was going to be a little more genteel and say 'fatherless' child."

"Sorry, Jane, I'm really on edge."

"You'd be inhuman if you weren't. I wouldn't like to be in your shoes right now, I can tell you that. In fact I think you're doing remarkably well under the circumstances."

"What do you think I should do?"

"Ohhh, no, big sister. You're going to have to decide that one for yourself."

"Of course I am, but can't you tell me what you'd do in my predicament?"

"No. And I don't think anyone else really could either. No one knows what they'd do until they're faced with it."

"I guess not."

"But I will tell you one thing—"

"What?"

"I kinda feel sorry for Peter. In a way he's an innocent bystander in it all. And he is in love with you."

"I know what you mean."

"I don't think he should be involved in your decision, but I guess he does deserve to know."

"I don't know, Janie. Maybe it's better he doesn't know, because if he doesn't know, he can't be hurt, whatever I decide to do."

"Well, that's true." The two women fell silent again.

"You know what keeps haunting me?" said Marcy.

"What?"

"I'm wondering if Carl knows."

"Oh, Marcy! You're borrowing trouble!"

"But we don't know! Maybe they know what goes on down here. I keep feeling Carl knows—and that he's hurt and angry."

"Because you slept with Peter or because you're pregnant"

"Both. He must be asking himself why I never gave him a child, and now I can't help feeling that somehow I let him down."

"But you wanted to get pregnant, you tried and tried. You have no reason to be reproaching yourself. How can you say you let him down?"

"Because I can't explain why I didn't get pregnant."

"I guess you and Carl just didn't have the right combina-

273

tion of those little reproductive goodies." Jane shrugged. "How do I know?"

"Do you think I could have had some kind of psychological block that could have prevented me from conceiving?"

"What is this anyway? Are you building up some kind of guilt trip?"

"I guess I am feeling kind of guilty. I just don't understand why it was so easy with Peter."

"How do we get ourselves into such deep water?"

"I don't know, but I just wish I weren't pregnant—and I wish I didn't feel that Carl was hurt and angry at me."

"Women!" Jane threw up her hands. "You know we're really crazy. Next thing I'm going to hear is that you're going to give up the child and Peter, to make something up to Carl that doesn't need to be made up."

"You know me very well. The thought has occurred to me."

"God, Marcy! You've always been the sane one of us, but at this rate you're going to make yourself good and crazy!"

"Okay. I'll stop talking about it."

"I don't mind listening to rational, constructive thoughts. I don't even mind a little guilt trip, but I don't want to hear any more of this morbid self-flagellation."

"I'm really sorry, Janie."

"Marcy, hasn't it occurred to you that Carl might have let you down?"

"Let me down? How on earth could he have done that?"

"When a woman doesn't conceive by a man she's nuts about for years, and then conceives by another man without half trying, it looks a little suspicious for the first man."

"What are you saying?" Marcy sat up very straight and stared at her sister.

"I wouldn't be at all surprised if Carl were sterile."

"What?" Marcy looked shocked.

"You heard me. I'd put my money on it."

"Look, I know you're trying to make me feel better, but that's a really terrible accusation to make. You know that the doctors said we were both all right."

"Well, we know now that you are, but how do we really know Carl was?"

"Because the doctor said so."

"Did the doctor tell you?"

"No." Marcy answered carefully. "Carl told me—when he got the results of the tests."

"Could Carl have lied to you?" Janie asked softly, carefully.

"Jane!" Marcy suddenly exploded. "How dare you make such a suggestion?" Marcy's eyes flashed with anger now.

"Because it just doesn't make sense that you should suddenly get pregnant after all these years. You've said so yourself. You don't understand how it could happen with Peter after just one night."

"I may not understand it, but I know Carl would never lie to me. Why should he?"

"Because he might seem less of a man to you."

"That's absurd!"

"No. Men are very strange when it comes to their virility. It's also possible that he could have lied to you out of the best of intentions. He might not have wanted to depress you. And knowing that you couldn't have children would have depressed you—you know it would."

"Carl would never lie to me about a thing like that. I wanted children, yes, and I wanted them by him, but if he had been sterile, we could have adopted." Marcy was defensive.

"Did you ever talk about adopting?"

"Yes. A couple of times. But we kept hoping we'd be lucky and I'd get pregnant." Marcy seemed near tears and Jane got up and went to her.

"Marcy, darling, I'm not trying to hurt you." Jane took her sister's hands in hers. "But I don't want to see you agonize like this and blame yourself for something that may not have been your fault."

"I know, but please don't tell me again that Carl lied to me. You know he'd never do that."

"Okay, okay. I'm sorry I brought it up." Jane smiled reassuringly, but she was not at all certain that Carl wouldn't have lied to Marcy; she hadn't forgot that Marcy nearly didn't marry Carl because of Clive McAllister. But the important thing now was to keep Marcy from falling into a state of guilt and depression. "Honey, you were a wonderful wife to Carl," continued Jane, "and I know he was a happy man."

"He really was, wasn't he?"

"Yes, he was. But he's gone now, and your life has to go

275

on. You've got all you can handle, to decide what you're going to do about this baby.''

Marcy got up and went to the window to look out at the sea. ''I know.'' Marcy felt tears in her throat again. Janie was right; she had to make a decision about the baby, and it had to be the best decision for herself. If only she could get rid of the feeling that Carl was hurt and angry, she could think more clearly what she *wanted* to do. But what had made Janie suggest that maybe Carl had been sterile? It wasn't like Jane to say something to be hurtful, so she really must think that Carl could have lied. Then again, maybe she had just been trying to keep her from feeling guilty. Whatever Janie's reason had been, it was well-intentioned, but Marcy had known Carl better than anyone else, and she knew he wouldn't have lied to her. Dear as Jane was, she had always somewhat resented Carl because she preferred Clive. In fact the whole family had preferred Clive.

But she had made the decision in favor of Carl, and she'd never regretted it. Their relationship had been everything she had wanted, except for the lack of children, and there had always been openness and honesty between them, even when it was occasionally hurtful. No, Carl would not have lied to her; it would have been difficult for him to tell her, had he been sterile, because he would have hated disappointing her, but he would never lie to her. No matter what anyone said, she'd never believe that. But what about the secret Peter had mentioned? The secret Carl had confessed to Mike in Paris. She'd always thought there was nothing they couldn't tell one another, and yet Carl had kept a secret from her, one he couldn't even tell her when he was dying. What had that secret been? Would Mike tell her? No, if it was something Carl had not wanted her to know, it would not be right for her to ask Mike to tell her now that Carl was dead. It wouldn't be fair to put Mike in that position either.

Suddenly she had a terrible headache and felt more confused than ever. Why wouldn't people leave her alone? Why did they have to voice their opinions when they hadn't been asked? Couldn't they just allow her to grieve for her husband? Since when was it neurotic to grieve for one's husband?

# Chapter Twenty-Three

After several days of trying unsuccessfully to contact Marcy, Peter telephoned Bishop Spencer, but he had no idea of Marcy's whereabouts either. Peter was beginning to worry, and a few nights later he took a cab up to the bar on 125th Street on the hunch that Mike might know something.

"Hey there, Pete!" Mike called out from the bandstand when he saw Peter come in. Peter waved and took a seat at the bar to wait for Mike's break. He ordered a plain seltzer with bitters and settled down to listen to the good rock sound of the group. Normally he did not care for rock, but he liked the unique sound of Mike's group. He only had to wait a few minutes, however, for the set to be over, and then Mike was beside him, punching his shoulder and grinning broadly.

"Mike, how are you?"

"Good, good." Mike climbed on the stool beside him. "Say, you been makin' waves in the scribe world out there, huh?"

"Sort of," Peter grinned.

"You got balls, I'll say that for you! But I sure would like to get a look at that big, bad book!"

"You and a lot of other people! I think I did them a favor."

"Whatcha doing for bread?"

"Got another job. A better one."

"No jive?"

"Yeah, integrity hasn't completely gone out of style."

"Say, that's great!" Mike laughed. "Now I don't have to offer a *small* loan."

"No, but I sure appreciate the thought."

"So what else is happening?"

"Have you seen Marcy? I've been looking for her, but can't locate her. Thought maybe you'd know where she was."

"Yeah, saw her a couple of weeks ago." Mike's face turned serious, and he was silent for a moment. "She wanted to know about the secret Carl told me."

"She what?" Peter set his glass down hard on the bar.

"You heard me. I figured you're the one that spilled the beans."

"Yes, I asked her if she could think of anything that Carl might not have wanted her to know. It was up in Connecticut, the weekend I went up there. A lot happened that weekend. We did a lot of talking."

"Yeah, she told me."

"She did?"

"Yeah."

"How much did she tell you?"

"Enough." Mike smiled, man to man, but Peter did not comment.

"You didn't tell her the secret?"

"No." Mike's face had sobered again.

"Do you know where she is now?"

"You mean you ain't seen her?"

"No. She needed some time to think things out. Then, I went to Germany—and—anyway, I haven't seen her for weeks."

"Shit, Pete, can't help you there. Sorry." Mike looked thoughtful.

"Damn it, I was hoping you might know where she is."

"Nope, but if I was you, I'd get my ass moving and find her."

"Mike, is something wrong with Marcy?" Peter was getting a strong feeling that Mike knew something he wasn't telling him.

"Yeah, in a way—yeah, something is wrong."

278

"What?" Peter grabbed Mike's arm. "For God's sake, tell me, what's wrong with her?"

"Well—" Mike looked uncomfortable.

"Jesus, Mike, you got to tell me! What is it?"

"Well—" Mike's hesitation made Peter more nervous. "Marcy's got trouble, Pete. I mean it's heavy."

"Oh, my God, what is it?" Peter was on the verge of panic.

"I don't think I'm the one ought to tell you, Pete. But she's in a bad way." Mike saw Peter's stricken face. "Now, just cool it, man. I mean, she's okay physically, she ain't got no fatal disease or anything like that. But—uh—she needs you, whether she knows it or not."

"If I just knew where to find her, I'd be there in a minute, but I don't. There's no answer at her place in Connecticut; Father Spencer—that's a friend of hers—he doesn't know where she is; they don't know where she is in her office, or if they do, they're not telling me; and there's no answer at her apartment here."

"Yeah, well, she must have gone somewhere."

"Maybe she doesn't want to see me." Peter stared at Mike's face in the mirror behind the bar, but it revealed nothing.

"I doubt that, Pete. Like I said, the lady's in a bad way, but I think you're the one who can help. You just find her."

"If I have to put missing persons on it, I'll find her, because I'm in love with that woman, and I want to marry her."

"Am I invited to the wedding?" Mike grinned.

"Is there going to be one?"

"How do I know?" Mike shrugged. "All I know is, the man says he wants to marry the chick. I don't argue with the man."

"In your opinion, will she marry the man?"

"There you go askin' questions I can't answer."

"If it ever happens, I expect you to be my best man, how's that?"

"Dynamite!"

The following morning Peter made another try at Marcy's office, but got nowhere. He asked for Adam Newhouse and was told that he was abroad on a business trip and would not

be back for at least two weeks. On his lunch hour he hopped a taxi and went to Marcy's apartment building. The doorman informed him that Mrs. Morris was not in. Peter asked if she was away, but the man would not give him any further information, and, in fact, regarded him suspiciously. Peter gave up and decided to try the night doorman, who might remember him. He went back to his office feeling frustrated and more worried than ever.

He had meetings most of the afternoon, but before he left the office, he remembered that Marcy had a brother in New York. The only trouble with that was he did not know Marcy's maiden name and therefore could hardly look him up. He put through another call to Father Spencer and told him his dilemma. Father Spencer did not remember her maiden name, but since she had been married in the church, promised to look into the church records and find the record of her marriage ten years before. Peter thanked him and decided to go home and wait for Father Spencer's call.

Around nine that evening Father Spencer called back with her maiden name: it was Dunbar. Peter thanked him and began to feel somewhat less helpless. He then got out the New York telephone book and looked up Dunbar; there were only two in the East Eighties, which he thought was where Marcy had once mentioned her brother lived. At the first number he tried, he got no answer; at the second number a maid said she didn't know anything about a sister of Mr. Dunbar's named Morris, and when he pressed her to be certain, she informed him that she'd worked for the Dunbars for twenty-five years, and she certainly did know that Mr. Dunbar had no such sister. At that she hung up on him, and Peter put the phone down and felt defeated again. Where could Marcy be, and what was happening to her? He began to hope for guidance in finding her, and that she was all right wherever she was.

It was shortly before eleven that night when he walked up to the night doorman at Marcy's building.

"Hello, remember me?" he asked the doorman.

"Yeah, you look kinda familiar; can't place your name though."

"Blanchard, Peter Blanchard. I'm a friend of Mrs. Morris."

"Oh, yeah, remember you coming 'round late one night. I was working the twelve to seven shift. Remember you bring-

ing her home couple of nights when I was on this shift, too."

"That's right."

"You looking for Mrs. Morris?"

"No, actually I'm looking for some information. I've been away in Europe, and I've been calling Mrs. Morris since I got back, but I don't get any answer here or up in the country."

"Oh yes, Mrs. Morris, she's away."

"That's what I figured. But I need to get in touch with her, and I thought maybe you could tell me where to find her." Peter was playing it very casual.

"Jeez, I can't. She's been gone quite a spell, and the super said something about her not being back for several months."

"Maybe she left a forwarding address for mail?"

"Might, but I wouldn't know anything about that. You'd have to ask the super that."

"Could you give me his name and telephone number so I can call him in the morning?"

"Sure."

Peter took out his address book and wrote down the name and telephone number.

"Thanks a lot—"

"George."

"Thanks very much, George." Peter reached into his pocket and pulled out his money clip. He chose a five-dollar bill and handed it to the man.

"Jeez, thanks, Mr. Blanchard. Anything else you need to know?"

"I don't think so. Good night, George." George tipped his cap, and Peter put his hands into his pockets and walked briskly away.

Unfortunately Peter was no more successful the next morning when he telephoned Marcy's superintendent. The man said Mrs. Morris had probably left a forwarding address with the post office because she hadn't left one with him, and no mail had arrived for her. Peter asked him if he knew when she would be back and explained that he needed to get in touch with her. The super said that judging by the instructions she'd left with him, he'd got the idea she meant to be gone several months. Peter thanked him and hung up feeling terribly depressed. How could she just disappear, and why had she? Obviously something had happened, something serious

enough for Mike to advise him to find her. Find her he would, but how? He had no leads. The first Dunbar phone number he'd tried still was unanswered.

At lunchtime he walked over to St. Thomas's Church at Fifty-third Street and Fifth Avenue and went inside. He sat down in one of the back pews and stayed there, quietly trying to think of a way to find her. Now and then he would pray that God would help him find her, and then pray that she was all right, wherever she was. He had prayed for the same thing repeatedly since Mike had advised him to find her, and while no answers had been forthcoming, at least it helped somewhat to ease his mind about her well-being and gave him hope that he would find her. As he sat there in the church, he began to think of Carl; God had helped him to become less preoccupied with Carl, but he was still aware of the fact that he had a part of the man, and he still felt a strange awareness of his presence. That awareness, however, did not create the same anxiety and confusion it had before. He still wondered, though, what Carl had wanted from him, and what he still might want from him. If he had wanted to draw him and Marcy together, why didn't he help him to find her now? Did he know where she was? And was it Carl that Marcy was disturbed over? If not that, what could it be? And why wouldn't Mike tell him? He had said she should be the one to tell him—what did that mean? Peter put his head down on his arm, which rested on the pew in front of him, and prayed that he would be able to keep calm and think rationally.

Feeling more hopeful, he left the church and strolled back toward his office. The streets were full of rushing people, and he looked at the faces of passersby and wondered what turmoil might be going on inside them. As he passed a travel agency, he saw a poster in the window extolling the advantages of vacationing in Florida. It pictured an inviting strip of beach with a couple walking hand in hand. He stopped and stared at the poster, and a strange sense of knowing came over him; he knew that Marcy was somewhere near water and a wide sandy beach. He closed his eyes, and he saw her, in his mind's eye, walking alone on a beach. He went into the travel agency and inquired where the picture on the poster had been taken. The travel agent didn't know, but when he insisted that he needed to know, the agent suggested that he telephone the Florida Chamber of Commerce in Tallahassee, or the

Florida State Tourist Commission, if there was such a thing. Peter thanked him and hurried out of the agency. He practically ran back to his office and instructed Grace—who had come over from Parthenon—to get hold of the Florida Chamber of Commerce. In a few moments Grace buzzed; she had a man from the Chamber in Tallahassee on the phone. After much description and prodding, Peter found out that the photograph had been taken by a photographer in Miami, and the location had been in, or near, Palm Beach. But if Mr. Blanchard would call back in an hour or so the man would be able to give him the name of the photographer, who would undoubtedly be able to tell him the exact location.

Peter was beginning to feel excited; this was the first lead he'd had, and although it was only a hunch, he was inclined to trust that sense of knowing he'd experienced on seeing the poster. It was as if his prayers had been answered, and God, or Carl, or some force was pointing him in the direction of Marcy.

He reached the photographer in Miami shortly before he left the office for the day, and the photographer pinpointed the location of the photograph as just south of Palm Beach, in a private area owned by several wealthy families. As soon as Peter hung up, he asked Grace to book him on a flight to Palm Beach on Saturday morning. If Marcy was in Palm Beach, she could, of course, be anywhere, but at least he had a location to start with.

Peter boarded a nonstop flight to Palm Beach at nine twenty on Saturday morning and arrived at the West Palm Beach International Airport at noon. He rented a car and drove through West Palm Beach to the Royal Palm Way Bridge over Lake Worth, which separated West Palm Beach from Palm Beach. On the Palm Beach side of the bridge he turned left onto South Country Road, vaguely remembering that he'd seen a very nice motel down near Worth Avenue on his last trip to the area. South Country Road ran parallel to South Ocean Boulevard where the larger homes were located and the beach area where the photograph had been taken.

He found the motel with no difficulty, and checked in, then changed into white slacks and a navy Lacoste shirt and sneakers. After a light lunch he set out for South Ocean Boulevard. He drove past the Bath and Tennis Club, and on to the area he thought the photographer had been talking about. He pulled

his car off the road and got out to walk. There was no access to the beach except through the grounds of the estates, and he wasn't sure he wanted to chance that. Yet, that was the only way to the beach. He picked a house which had no car in the driveway, no gardener working on the grounds, no sign of life at all. He cut across the grounds and headed for the beach, looking neither to the right or left. He had decided that if he were stopped, he would say he was looking for Mrs. Carl Morris, which was the truth, and if they knew her, so much the better. How she would feel about his surprising her, he didn't know, but he knew he had to find her, and his intuition told him he had come to the right place. On the flight down he had felt again a strong awareness of Carl, and he sensed that Carl wanted him to find her. Well, if that were true, he could do his stuff now; he needed all the help he could get.

"Hey, you there, where you going?" He had been wrong; there was a gardener working at the front of the house. He was a rather elderly black man, and he didn't look angry, only curious.

"I'm looking for Mrs. Carl Morris," said Peter with all the casual innocence he could muster.

"Ain't no Morris here. This here is Burblingers' residence, and they ain't home."

"Oh, I'm sorry. Guess I must have misunderstood the directions."

"Reckon you did."

"Maybe you can help me anyway." Peter walked closer to the gardener.

"Maybe."

"Have you seen a very tall, very beautiful blond lady around here? She doesn't really live here, she would have come for a visit within the last couple of weeks."

"Umm. Don't know the name of the folks she's visiting?"

"No."

"Well, sir, you're lost in more ways than one, ain't you?" The man laughed softly, and Peter joined in.

"Seems that way. Kind of embarrassing, you know, to go barging into the wrong house."

"Yeah. This lady, she know you're coming?"

"No, I wanted to surprise her. I flew down from New York this morning."

"Always wanted to go to New York City. Don't reckon I ever will, though." He removed his hat and scratched his head thoughtfully.

"Why not?"

"Oh, gettin' too old, and things is way yonder too expensive up there for the likes of me."

"You're certainly right about prices being high, but I don't for a minute think you're too old." The gardener chuckled and Peter's mind was back on Marcy. "Listen, Mr.——" Peter appealed to him for his name.

"Lucius, name's Lucius, just plain Lucius."

"Well, I was wondering if you might help me find my lady."

"Be glad to do anything I can."

"I'm almost certain she's staying along here somewhere, and I want to know where."

"Then you don't actually know the house, is that it?"

"That's it, Lucius." Peter smiled sheepishly. "I was bluffing you before."

"Run off from you, did she?"

"Not exactly—not from me, that is."

"Have a spat?"

"No. I've been away on a business trip, and when I got back, I couldn't find her. We aren't married, I mean, not yet—but I hope to marry her."

"And that's why you want to find her, you want to ask her?"

"I've already asked her once."

"She turn you down?"

"In a way, yes. You see, she's been recently widowed, and she's just not ready to get married yet. She's thinking about it. But a friend of mine saw her while I was away, and he thinks she needs me. He told me to find her."

"My woman died awhile back. Five years it is now, and I ain't got over it yet. Sure lonesome without her."

"Yeah, I guess it takes a long time."

"Uh-huh." Lucius settled his hat back on his head. "Tell you what I'm gonna do, Mr. Blanchard, I'm gonna nose around some, see what I can find out."

"That would be great, Lucius. In the meantime, do you think I could get onto the beach here and just take a little walk? See if I could spot her?"

"Don't see no reason why not. My people is gone, won't be back for couple of months yet. Not 'til it gets cold, you know."

"Thanks, Lucius. I'll be back after awhile." Peter ran across the lawn and onto the beach. He stopped and pulled off his sneakers, set them on the wall, and started walking. The sand felt good on his feet, and there was almost no one on the beach; here and there he would see mothers and children on the beach in front of their houses and an occasional group of teen-agers lying faceup to the sun. He walked a mile or more down the beach, not paying too much attention to the houses, but on the way back he scrutinized every house for any sign of Marcy. He saw no one who vaguely resembled her, but he had an intuitive feeling that she was somewhere near.

When he got back to where he'd left Lucius, he found the old man seated in the shade of a palm tree.

"Didn't have no luck, huh?" he asked.

"No. How about you?" asked Peter.

"No. But young Billy Jo Moore chauffeurs down to the Farnsworth place—knows everything. If there's a beautiful blond lady visiting around, he'll know about her. Stop there on my way home."

"That would be wonderful, Lucius."

"Stop around here tomorrow morning 'bout ten. Likely as not I'll know something by that time."

"I'll do that." Peter offered his hand and Lucius shook it. "See you around ten in the morning."

Peter went back to the motel and left his car, then walked down County Road to Worth Avenue, and strolled along looking at the elegant shops. He was really hoping to run into Marcy, and he searched every face that went past him, and looked over the heads of others, hoping to catch sight of her blond head. As he approached the Everglades Club, he saw a tall blond woman come out, and he stepped up his pace to catch up to her, but as he came near her, he saw that it wasn't Marcy. Disappointed, he turned around and walked back up Worth Avenue.

Late in the afternoon, just before sunset, he went back to the house where he'd met Lucius. He parked his car in the driveway and went down to the beach. He began to walk again, this time watching every house for some sign of her,

286

but the beach was deserted, and people seemed to be busy inside their houses. About a mile down the beach, however, he saw what looked like a garden cocktail party in progress. He walked nonchalantly up the steps, into the garden, and mixed in with the people. Many of them were casually dressed, and he'd kept his sneakers on this time, so he did not look unduly out of place. He made his way to the bar and asked for a soda and bitters. The bartender looked at him for a moment, then grinned.

"Light or heavy on the bitters?" he asked.

"Light. I don't want to get bombed so early in the evening."

"On the wagon?"

"No, just practicing in case I ever have to go to AA," replied Peter. The bartender laughed, dashed a few drops of bitters into the glass, and stirred it into the soda.

"Where's our hostess, anyway?" asked Peter.

"Mrs. Stonington?"

"Yeah."

"Over there, talking to the little Arab prince."

"The tall blond?"

"Don't know her, huh?"

"Nope, never saw her before in my life. What's her first name?

"Margot." The bartender eyed him with a grin still on his face.

"Pronounced Margo, my good man."

"Somebody bring you here?"

"Nope, just walking along the beach, and it looked like a good party."

"You're putting me on?"

"No way."

"Aren't you afraid I'll tell?"

"No. You won't."

"What makes you think I won't?"

"Because you could use a good laugh, and I'm about to go and kiss Margot, and make a lot of fuss over her and she's going to pretend she knows me because she's got good manners, and you're going to get a good laugh out of it."

"Know something?"

"A few things."

287

"You're right. I've always wanted to do something like that, but I don't have the balls."

"Well, I may not have any if they find out I washed up off the beach." Peter laughed. The idea appealed to him—he was just frustrated and desperate enough to act outrageously. At least it would take his mind off Marcy and help to kill time until tomorrow morning.

"Let me clue you about Margot," said the bartender softly.

"Shoot."

"She's one hell of a nice lady. Flirts a lot, but don't take her up on it. I've been bartending for them a long time, and to my knowledge the lady's strictly straight."

"Jealous husband?"

"He plays around."

"Where is the gentleman?"

"Over there, feeling up the chick half his age." The bartender indicated a suave, iron-gray-haired man dressed in a white silk shirt opened to show a lot of gray chest hair, and white trousers tightly tailored to accentuate his slim hips and large genitals.

"Regular sex symbol, isn't he?"

"If you believe the advertising," replied the bartender.

"What's his name?"

"Paul."

"Okay. Got all the facts. Don't go away, I'll be back." Peter sauntered over to where Margot stood with the Arab. "Pardon me, Prince, but I just had to tell Margot how extraordinary she looks tonight." Margot Stonington turned to look at him and he saw the lack of recognition in her eyes, but only for a moment. Then she smiled warmly.

"Darling, how are you?" She had a slight foreign accent which he identified as upper-class, educated German. He kissed her on the cheek and stood away to admire her.

"You're looking lovelier than ever. I keep asking myself if I'd found you before Paul did, whether our lives might have been different?" He smiled his boyish smile, and her eyes told him that she was used to such compliments; she appreciated them, but did not take them seriously. In fact he also saw kindness and vulnerability in her face, and it made him feel slightly ashamed of himself. He had a feeling that he would like Margot Stonington; there was something very appealing about her.

288

"I see that you are old friends," the prince said and started to move away. "I'll just get a drink while you talk."

"Don't let me drive you away," Peter said.

"Don't worry, I shall be back," the prince smiled.

"Are we old friends?" Margot asked with a disarmingly wise smile.

"No, but I wish we were," he replied and meant it.

"One should always have room for new friends, real friends," she replied.

"My name is Peter Blanchard, and I'm applying for the position of new friend."

"I believe you mean that," she said, turning her head slightly to one side and meeting his eyes directly.

"I'm banking on intuition, and I hope I'm not being pushy."

"I very much doubt that you could be," she said and linked her arm through his, beginning to walk him away from the path of the oncoming prince. "I would hardly know how to conduct my life without my intuition."

"Would you believe that I'm in Palm Beach tonight looking for someone that my intuition tells me is here?"

"This person must be very important to you."

"Very."

"A woman?"

"Yes."

"Ah, then you are also a romantic."

"I plead guilty to the charge."

"You know, I do not believe that our intuition is as strong or as reliable when our emotions are not involved. Do you not agree?" She had walked him away from the crowd, and they stood looking out toward the sea, still arm in arm. He felt very close to her, but not in a sexual way.

"Yes, I think I do agree. However, I intuitively feel very close to you, and I am not involved emotionally with you. How do you explain that?"

"You are a sensitive and sympathetic man, and you know that I am feeling a little bit hurt tonight. Therefore your emotions are involved in the way a caring friend's emotions would be involved."

"You know, you are right. I crashed this party. I was walking along the beach feeling pretty alone and worried, and when I saw your party, I decided to crash it, do something outrageous to take my mind off myself. When I spoke to you,

I was being a smart ass—taking a dare. But when I saw the niceness, the kindness, and vulnerability in your face, I liked you, and I felt ashamed.''

"Yes, I saw it. And believe it or not, I realized I didn't know you. But I also saw something in your face that intrigued me, that engaged my sympathies. You have experienced a great agony, perhaps you are still experiencing it. Is that not so?''

"You are amazing! Does it show that much?''

"To me it is very clear.''

"And you—is it your husband's attention to other women that hurts you?''

"You saw?''

"I'm afraid so.''

"Not that he has the need to make conquests—I know him very well, and I know that he loves me, but he cannot help himself. He feels age threatening him, and like an animal storing for the long winter months, Paul is trying to have everything he can now.''

"You don't mind that he has other women?''

"Yes, I mind, but I know the man. It is his fear and his pain that drive him on. It is because he is indiscreet that I hurt.''

"Isn't he afraid you will leave him?''

"He knows that I will not.''

"Why not?''

"Because I love him, and because he would not survive without me.''

"Is he so dependent?''

"I'm afraid so. When it first began, I threatened to leave him, before I understood how it was with him, and he threatened to kill himself if I left.''

"Many people threaten, if I may say so.''

"Paul would do it. He is terrified of being alone, and he trusts no one but me, not even himself. Least of all himself.''

"That's a very heavy responsibility for you.''

"Not if you love someone.''

"Yes, I suppose not.''

"Now, about you. You have come to find a woman that you believe to be here?''

"Yes. My intuition tells me that she is.'' She guided him to an empty table and chairs and they sat down. He told her

most of the story, and she listened intently, and occasionally put her hand on his arm to convey her understanding and sympathy.

"Yes, you have certainly had your agony." Suddenly he saw her expression change from one of sympathy and feeling to one of excitement. "Your Marcy, she is very tall?"

"Yes."

"And blond—with blue eyes—and quite beautiful?"

"Yes." Peter was beginning to pick up her excitement.

"There is such a woman near here. I saw her the other day, walking along the beach alone. She seemed troubled and sad. I was touched by her aloneness. In fact I asked my cook about her—the servants know everything. And the woman I saw is staying at the Dunbar place—"

"Dunbar!" Peter shouted. "Did you say Dunbar?"

"Yes. Mrs. Dunbar is a widow, has quite a lovely house about a quarter of a mile down the beach."

"Margot, that's it! Marcy's maiden name was Dunbar."

"Oh, my God! I think we've found her, Peter! Because my cook tells me this woman is Mrs. Dunbar's daughter, and she is visiting from Connecticut."

"Oh God, oh, God! It's Marcy!" Peter felt as if he might cry, but he fought back the tears. Margot sensed his emotion, and took his hand in hers, but did not speak. She held his hand until he had gotten himself under control. "Thanks, Margot, thank you, thank you." He raised her hand to his lips and kissed it tenderly. "Some power directed me to you, I know that now. You were meant to help me find Marcy, that's why we were drawn to one another so quickly."

"And you were here to help me through Paul's making a spectacle of himself with that young woman."

"And we have become friends," he said, wanting to hug Margot.

"When will you go to see her?"

"I'll try to see her in the morning. I'll be on the beach early and hope she goes walking. If I can't find her that way, I'll telephone or go to the house."

"Oh, Peter, do try to meet her on the beach—by accident, of course. She will not be prepared for you, and the surprise at seeing you—ah, that could reveal much about her feelings for you. Yes, it should be by accident, definitely." Margot's

eyes were shining. "Besides, darling, it is quite romantic, and sooo Hollywood."

"It is a little, isn't it?" He chuckled.

"You must telephone me after you've seen her, and let me know if all is well, if it is not, come, and I shall commiserate with you."

Peter spent an extremely restless night, haunted by anxiety dreams. He had stayed late at the party and finally had supper with Margot. She had insisted that he stay; Paul had gone off with the young woman. He awakened early, before dawn, and got up. The excitement of knowing Marcy was near made it impossible to stay in bed. He dressed and drove out South Ocean Boulevard to Margot's, where he left his car in her driveway, by prearrangement. He went down to the beach, walked toward the Dunbar place, and picked out a spot where he could watch the house. He sat down and said a quick prayer that Marcy would come onto the beach and that she would be glad to see him.

# Chapter Twenty-Four

The sun came up slowly over the Atlantic, timidly edging its rim over the horizon and spreading a fan of color over the eastern sky. The new day came on, fresh and clean and bright, and Peter hoped it would be the day that light came into his life; that Marcy would be all right, and that she might finally be able to see a life for them. Until Mike had told him she was in a bad way, he had been somewhat ambivalent about them, wondering if he were being foolish in hoping that she might be able to come to him. Then having second thoughts about Jeannie, especially after her surprise visit to his apartment just after he'd come back from Connecticut.

But when Mike told him that all was not well with Marcy, he realized how deeply his emotions were involved with her, and that he had to go the long road. She would have to make a decision, and soon, about them, and he hoped and prayed it would be the one he wanted.

Suddenly he caught sight of a figure coming onto the beach in front of what he thought was the Dunbar house. His pulse quickened. If only it would be Marcy. The figure hesitated, looking up the beach and then down, and he held his breath, hoping that whoever it was would come in his direction. But unfortunately the figure turned and started down the beach in the opposite direction.

"Oh, Marcy, please, don't go that way," he groaned aloud, and almost as if she'd heard him, she stopped, turned, and started up the beach in his direction. His pulse raced

wildly, and he found he could not move. He waited, watching her approach then finally he felt secure enough to get up and walk toward her; he had seen that it was a woman, and he was pretty sure it was Marcy.

He did not walk directly toward her, but kept off to the side for fear she might not want to encounter anyone. As they drew nearer, the sun climbed higher, and its rays caught the gold of the woman's hair, and he knew it was Marcy. "Oh, God be with me now," he prayed aloud and quickened his step slightly.

Marcy was looking down at the sand as she walked, her bare feet leaving footprints in the wet sand. She wore jeans and a loose shirt, and she seemed lonely and solitary. Everything about her body language told him something was wrong; this was not the Marcy he knew. She seemed to sense his presence then, for she looked up and he could see even in the dim light that she looked thin and drawn.

"Marcy—" he called out to her softly, and she looked in his direction. She stopped, and a quizzical expression crossed her face, then she saw who he was.

"Peter?"

"Yes." He started running toward her, and he saw her face light up, and she came toward him then. He caught her in his arms and held her tightly against him. "Oh, Marcy, darling, how I've missed you," he whispered. She clung to him, and he could feel her trembling all over. He kissed her hair, her check and tried to kiss her mouth, but she buried her head in his shoulder.

"Oh, Peter, don't, please don't. Just hold me." He held her until she had stopped trembling, then she disengaged herself from his arms and stepped away from him.

"How did this happen? Why are you here?"

"I had to come. I was worried when I couldn't find you."

"How did you find me?" Her voice was strange.

"I'll tell you later. Just tell me how you are."

"I—I don't know." She looked away from him.

"Marcy, what's wrong?" She did not answer him, and he was suddenly frightened. "Darling, please, what is it?"

"You don't know?"

"No. I only see that you're in trouble."

"Can't you guess?" She looked back at him then, her face closed.

"No. I'm afraid I can't think of anything that could make you like this. Please tell me."

"I'm—I'm pregnant, Peter." The words hit him like a blow to his chest, and it took him several minutes to register what she'd actually said.

"You're—pregnant?" he stammered. Her eyes had not left his.

"Yes. I'm carrying your child." She smiled sadly then, and he started to take her in his arms again.

"No, Peter. Please."

"But, but this is wonderful news!"

"Is it?" There was a note of bitterness in her voice now. Her eyes, the way she looked at him, told him that she did not think it was wonderful.

"You don't want the child?" The shock of the realization made him feel weak in the knees.

"I want the child," she replied matter-of-factly.

"But—you don't want it to be mine, is that it?" He felt as if the world had stopped turning on its axis and would momentarily come to an end.

"I'm glad it's yours." There was no joy, however, in her voice or her face.

"I don't understand." He covered his eyes with his hand. The emotion inside him was suffocating. She wanted the child, was glad it was his, and yet there was no joy in her. In fact she looked as if she'd been suffering some deep trauma.

"Of course you don't understand." There was still no hint of emotion in her voice. "My poor Peter, I *am* sorry. It's not a nice way to find out you're going to be a father."

"I'd feel better if I saw some sign that you were just a little bit happy about it."

"How can I be?" He heard the anguish in her then and saw it. She had deep emotions about it after all.

"Why not?" he asked gently.

"In ten years I never became pregnant by Carl, and now I'm pregnant after one night with you. Can you explain that to me?" Her eyes challenged his, and he started to speak but didn't know what to say. He held out his hands, palms up, then dropped them in a sign of resignation.

"No, I can't," he said. "But does it matter why?"

"It does to me. The question haunts me night and day."

"It just didn't happen for you and Carl, that's all."

295

"I've been wondering if I didn't want to become pregnant by Carl."

"But that's nonsense. I know that you did." She looked pale now despite her deep suntan, and he thought that she was weak as well. He took her hands. "Come, let's sit over here." She allowed him to lead her to a log that lay half buried in the sand, and they sat down side by side. He held one of her hands in both of his. "Try to talk about it, Marcy."

"I thought I wanted to become pregnant by Carl more than anything, but I can't explain why I didn't. It—it was so easy to become pregnant by you. Now I ask myself if subconsciously I didn't want to have a child by Carl. I've also been wondering if I didn't love him enough."

"But, Marcy, he knew—everyone knew—how much you loved him."

"But did I? I keep thinking that I failed him, and I think that he knows."

"How can you say you failed him?"

"If I loved him so much, how could I be with you so soon after his death? And become pregnant so easily?"

"Marcy—"

"What kind of woman am I, Peter?"

"Marcy, these things are not always in our hands. There's a higher power, and—maybe you just weren't meant to have a child by Carl." She seemed not to be listening now, and intuitively he knew she was close to cracking. What he said to her now was very important and could determine their future. He felt totally inadequate to handle the situation, but somehow he had to try.

"Darling, you are a woman, not a saint. You're a woman with needs and a woman's heart. You loved Carl as much as a woman can love a man, I'm as sure of that as I am of being a man. But we are not always in control of everything that happens to us. God has a hand in it. You wanted me to go and see Bishop Spencer, and I did, and he helped me to understand how God works in our lives. It was obviously not God's will that you conceive by Carl, but it apparently was his will that you have a child. Perhaps I was the means to that. Perhaps it is his way of showing us that we should be together."

"But to become pregnant after one night." He heard the misery of her guilt over that night.

"Marcy, that night had been in the making for weeks. We

296

both felt the attraction. It was not a passing thing; there was feeling and meaning in it for both of us.''

"Peter," she sighed heavily. "I don't feel the child was conceived in a sordid way. I wanted to be with you, and yes, the feeling was there. And, I'm glad you're the father—but what I don't understand and can't reconcile myself to, is the fact that I conceived so easily." She was growing agitated, and her normally quiet, pleasant voice was tight and tremulous. "I always thought I wanted a child—I prayed for a child." She was staring out to sea now. "Did I secretly not want a child? Why, why, why? That question screams at me!" She covered her ears with her hands as if to shut out the sound of the words. Peter clenched and unclenched his fists, fighting back the urge to hold her and try to soothe away the suffering.

"Darling, don't do this to yourself. You're a sensible, rational woman—this morbid sense of guilt is not like you."

"I don't know what I'm like anymore." She sounded so desperate, he felt her pain throughout his own being. "I can't escape from the feeling that I let Carl down." Peter sensed that she was near hysterics, and he tried to speak gently, soothingly.

"You didn't let Carl down, Marcy. You wanted a child, and you tried, and tried, and tried. What more could you have done?"

"But subconsciously—subconsciously! The question won't go away. I have nightmares—" She broke off and lapsed into silence.

He wanted to be quietly logical with her, make her see how irrational her thoughts were, but he kept feeling inadequate and frustrated. He couldn't seem to reach her. No matter what he said, she went right on asking the same question. "Listen, Marcy—remember when we talked about me feeling guilty because I was alive and Carl had died, leaving you alone?" She didn't answer and he went on. "You told me then that it was Carl's time, and you felt no resentment toward me for being alive." She finally nodded, and he knew he had her attention. "Well, your being pregnant now is no different. You just were not meant to be pregnant by Carl, and apparently you were by me. Can't you accept that?" Again she made no answer. "It can't be wrong to bring a child you want into the world. God has given us the child. God took Carl away from you, and he gave you a child. I'm happy that you will have what you wanted, can't you be?"

She turned frightened eyes on him. "You think Carl is happy about this child?"

"Yes, I think so—if he loved you, and I know he did, he would be happy for you."

"I don't think he's happy. I think he's hurt and furious at me. I never gave *him* a child." She stopped talking and he knew she was about to cry. "I—I dream of his soul crying out in agony and rage." She began to shake, and he could restrain himself no longer. He put his arm about her.

"No! You must not touch me!" she cried, and there was a look of terror in her eyes. He knelt in front of her.

"Marcy, I love you. I want to hold you and comfort you."

"No! You cannot, you must not!"

"But, darling, why not? I want to marry you, be with you during this time."

"That can never be."

"Never be?" Her words cut into him. "But why? I'm the child's father. I know you cared for me. What happened?"

"It just can't be, that's all." She looked down at him, and he felt that she wanted desperately to be comforted. Why then was she holding him off?

"Marcy, this is going to be *our* child. *We* are its parents. The child deserves a chance, too."

"Peter, it just can't be. I'm—I'm terrified."

"Terrified? Of what?"

"Of—Carl."

"Carl!" He stared at her in disbelief, but the terror in her eyes left no room for doubt. Suddenly he began to understand. Because Carl was hurt, she would deprive herself of him, and him of their child. She was appeasing Carl, doing penance for being with him, for becoming pregnant. Suddenly he was more frightened than he'd been since before he went to see Father Spencer, but he was not afraid of Carl now; he was afraid of what she might do to herself.

"Marcy, darling, don't be afraid of Carl. He wouldn't do anything to you, he loved you deeply."

"Not to me, Peter—"

"Then—?" He stopped, afraid even to voice what he was thinking.

"Yes, to the child. He might do something to the child. It is not his child, he does not love it."

"Oh, my God!" How stupid he had been not to realize

why she was afraid. "Listen, listen to me, Marcy. Carl cannot hurt the child. Father Spencer says a departed spirit does not have the power to influence people and events on earth. Only God and Satan can do that; they're the only force with that kind of power."

"Do you really believe that?" She looked accusing now.

"Yes, I do."

"Then why have you been afraid Carl was trying to possess you?"

"I don't think that anymore. Not since my talk with Father Spencer. I was doing it to myself. I've learned that when we get confused and pulled off our center, in disharmony with God, we're wide open for Satan to step in and help us muddle up our lives. I've learned to trust God and to ask his help against destructive influences. That's why I'm not really afraid of Carl anymore."

"Carl's leaving you alone because he's angry at me."

"Oh, Marcy, darling, you don't, you simply can't, believe that. Carl loved you much too much to harm you, or anything you loved."

"But I let him down, and I hurt him. It's your child I'm having, not his!" He realized then that she was too frightened and too confused to hear anything he might say. But how did such paralyzing guilt get hold of a woman like her?

"Marcy, come back to New York with me. Talk to Father Spencer."

"No. I'm going to stay here. No one will know."

"Then what? You can't keep the child secluded forever. And I *am* its father."

"Peter, don't. This is what I want to do."

"But you've got to get some help. You're making yourself sick. This can't be good for the child." He felt frantic, and he knew he had to get hold of himself if he was to help her.

"I have to work it out for myself." She touched his face and smiled softly. "Go back to New York, darling, and forget about me for a while."

"How can I do that? I want to be with you." He took her hand. "Marcy, I love you—you know that, and I'm thrilled about the child. Please come home with me." He pleaded, but she pulled her hand away and averted her eyes.

"I can't, and you know why. Please go and leave me alone."

"All right, I'll go, but I'll be back. I'm not going to let

you do this. There are three of us now—not just you and me."

"Stay out of it, Peter. If you love me, and care about the child, you'll stay away."

"But, Marcy, please believe me. Carl cannot harm the child. He hasn't got that kind of power, don't you understand?" He heard the frustration and fear in his own voice then, and he knew that was not going to help her.

"I can't take the chance." She got up then. "I'm very tired now, Peter. Please go home." She started to walk away from him, but he followed.

"Marcy, please—" She kept on walking and he stopped. He'd said all he could say now. There had to be some other way to reach her, to help her. He shoved his hands into his pockets and turned to walk back up the beach. Are we never going to be free of Carl Morris? he asked bitterly.

Marcy reached her steps and turned to look back at his retreating figure. She hated to let him go like that for she knew he was deeply hurt. It wasn't fair, and it wasn't kind, and she didn't like herself for sending him away. If only he could know how much she wanted him to stay; how much she needed him, needed his strength and comfort. But she knew him, and she knew that if he'd gotten the slightest hint of how she felt, he would have insisted on staying in Palm Beach, and she couldn't take that chance. The nightmares about the baby and Carl had grown more horrifying and more frequent. They came almost every night now, dreams that the child was born with some terrible deformity; she was afraid to sleep for fear of the dreams. As a result she'd become too tired to think straight. Somehow she felt if she could just hold on until the child was born, it would be all right. She only hoped that Peter would understand and forgive her then for what she had to do to him now.

No, I must not think these thoughts. Carl will know them, she cautioned herself. She was afraid now that Carl knew her every thought as well as her every action. In fact she felt totally exposed, without privacy, and as possessed as Peter had ever felt. In her more lucid moments she tried to think what it was Carl wanted from her, but each time she drew a blank. At one time she thought he wanted her to get rid of the child, but she knew she couldn't do it. She wanted the child, although she knew now that she had wanted a child during their married years because it would have been a symbol of

their love, a part of each of them. She had not longed for a child for the sake of having a child. And she had defied what she believed Carl wanted, and kept the child of Peter's—not only because she now wanted a child, but because she was responsible for its existence. And from the moment she had made the decision to keep the child, she had begun to fear for it. Then the dreams had begun, and she'd had no peace since then.

She looked again at Peter's retreating figure, and wanted to call him back, to tell him not to despair, to tell him to wait until the child was born, that she would not keep him from seeing it, or knowing it. But she was afraid to do it. Strangely enough, though, it was reassuring to see him there, walking on the same beach and as the distance between them grew, she wanted to run after him, but he was too far away now. She sat down heavily on the steps. She felt isolated and alone again.

"Oh, Peter, I know you're going with a heavy heart, and mine is heavy, too." She felt the sunshine warming her skin, and she welcomed it; everything was cold and black in her life now.


"Who was that you were talking to on the beach?" asked Jane, sitting beside her now. Jane had arrived a few days earlier, and Marcy was certain her mother had asked Jane to come.

"Peter Blanchard," answered Marcy.

"Peter Blanchard! Well, thank God." Janie turned to look at her questioningly. "I hope you told him."

"Yes, I told him."

"And—?"

"He was delighted. Asked me to marry him again, as I knew he would."

"And what did you say?"

"I said no."

"And you sent him away?"

"Yes."

"Oh, Marcy, for God's sake, why?" Janie was getting impatient with her sister because she would do nothing to help herself, and she was becoming more and more worried about Marcy.

"We've been through all that before, Jane."

"Yes, I know—you're afraid of Carl, afraid for the baby. But you know what I think?"

301

"I've a pretty good idea, but I'm sure you're going to tell me anyway."

"Damn right I am! You're getting really crazy—and you know why?"

"Oh, Janie, please." Marcy started to get up.

"Wait a minute, Marcy, it's about time you faced up to the truth! All this shit about keeping Peter away because of Carl's anger and vengeance, and fear of what he'll do to the child, is pure smoke screen. You can't face up to the fact that you like Peter Blanchard and want to be with him because you think it's too soon after Carl's death. It doesn't fit your nice tidy image of yourself. Neither does the fact that the child you wanted by Carl is Peter's. You're killing yourself with guilt because it's easier than accepting the fact that you just may be in love with Peter Blanchard. I happen to think that you are, and you'd better wake up before it's too late!"

"You might be right, Jane—I don't know—but I can't take the chance that you're not." Marcy pulled herself wearily to her feet and started for the house.

"Marcy, please get some help. Go to Peter, or go to a therapist—but do something! Don't just sit here until you're so sick and weak you'll crack up, and maybe lose the baby."

"Maybe that's what I'm trying to do. That would fit right in with your theories about my neurotic state."

"Yes, well, you are in a neurotic state. But don't you know my concern is because I love you? I'm badgering you to do something because I got the shock of my life when I saw you three days ago. Can't you see what you're doing to yourself?"

"I'm doing the only thing I know to do, Jane." Marcy sat back down suddenly on one of the chaises on the patio and dropped her head into her hands. "If you love me, help me to find a little peace and quiet, and don't yell at me." The tears came then, and Jane was beside her at once, holding Marcy's shaking body, talking to her quietly. Jane was afraid now, too, but not of Carl; she was also afraid of what Marcy was doing to herself. Somehow the spell of self-destruction had to be broken, and soon.

# Chapter Twenty-Five

Peter had been back in New York only a few days when Mike called late one evening.

"Hey, Pete—wondered if you went to see Marcy?"

"Yes, I did. Came back a couple of days ago."

"How is she?"

"Like you said, in a bad way."

"Uh-huh. Find out anything interesting?"

"Yes, that I'm going to be a father. Did you know that?"

"Yeah, yeah I knew. Didn't think it was my place to tell you. I mean, that's something she ought to lay on you herself."

"Well, she did," Peter said somewhat grimly.

"You're some cool cat. You don't sound very happy about it."

"I'm happy about it, but I'm worried out of my mind about her."

"Say, whatcha doing?"

"Worrying."

"Well, come on uptown and get your mind off it for a while."

"Well—" He hesitated because he had work to do. Getting into the new job was hard enough without having his mind in turmoil at the same time.

"Come on, Pete. Do you good. Besides, with my superior brain maybe we can think of some way to help her."

"Okay. Maybe it is a good idea. Be up in a little while."

Sam was tending bar that night, and he recognized Peter when he walked in.

"Hey there, Pete. How you doin'?"

"Pretty good. How about you?"

"Can't complain, can't complain. Whatcha drinkin'?"

"Oh—got something like a Coke?"

"Sure. You on the wagon or something?"

"Just don't feel like drinking, Sam."

"Okay. One Coke coming up!" He put a bottled Coke and a glass of ice in front of Peter.

"Hey, Pete!" Mike slid onto the barstool beside Peter. "Can I buy the daddy-to-be a drink?"

"You can pay for my Coke if you like." Peter grinned.

"Coke! Man, you sick or something? That stuff'll eat your insides out."

"Just don't feel like drinking, Mike."

"How many of them you gonna drink?"

"Not many."

"In that case, guess I can afford it."

"What's happening with the group?" asked Peter.

"Got a tour booked. Gonna try the Paris scene again."

"Terrific!"

"Yeah. Hope we make it this time."

"You will."

"Bother you—flying again, I mean?"

"At first. Then I calmed down."

"Man, I want to tell you I was spooked when I come home from ole Paree. Got on that kite, and bang! I got a case of the shakes you wouldn't believe. Course after I poured a few gins in, nothing bothered me the rest of the way over."

"Want to hear something weird?"

"Sure, lay it on me."

"This guy sitting next to me on the way over to Frankfurt—well, he looked a little like Carl."

"No shit!"

"Truth."

"That's hairy."

"Telling me! I damned near panicked. But when I got a good look at him head on, he didn't look so much like him."

"Can't get rid of that cat, can you?"

"Doesn't look like it."

"Time, man, time." Mike sipped his grin. "But tell me about Marcy."

"Mike, she's scared to death, and she looks awful. I'm really worried about her."

"Still feeling guilty about being pregnant, huh?"

"Yes, and confused about why she got pregnant after one night with me, and never did with Carl." Peter sipped his Coke, and sighed. "She's even got it into her head that she let him down—I mean purposely—by not getting pregnant."

"Heavy! Bet it's rough on her."

"That doesn't worry me as much as something else." Peter made sweat rings on the bar with his glass.

"What's that?"

"She thinks Carl is angry at her over the baby."

"Oh man! What a bummer!"

"It's worse than that! She's afraid he's going to harm the child."

"Oh shit!" Mike set his glass down with a bang. "That's one sensible lady, but she's going bonkers!"

"And she won't marry me either. In fact she won't even let me get near her."

"No wonder you're half out of your gourd." Mike shook his head.

"She told me straight out to stay away from her and keep out of it."

"That doesn't sound like our Marcy."

"I've got to think of some way to help her, Mike, but I don't know how." He was silent a few moments. Mike said nothing. "She just looks awful, and if she goes on this way, I'm afraid she's going to crack up."

"Listen, Pete. Did you ever find out anything more about what that spook told you?"

"Which one?"

"The cat that told you the message he got from Carl was 'child.' "

"I ran up against a stone wall. It didn't mean anything to Marcy, or to Father Spencer. I just spun my wheels over it—nothing made any sense."

"Why don't you talk to some of Carl's friends? Maybe they might know something."

"I don't know any."

"Well shit, man, ask around. Find out who they were."

"Mike, I'm getting a strong feeling that you're trying to tell me something. Am I right?"

"Maybe." Mike stared into his glass, and Peter felt a sudden rebirth of hope.

"It does mean something, doesn't it?"

"I said *maybe*."

"Mike, Marcy's sanity and our future is at stake here. If I can't get her off this kick, I don't know what might happen to her, or to the child. I mean, this can't be good for it."

"Now, Peter, lay off. I'm not saying any more than I already said."

"You are one hardheaded, stubborn son of a bitch!" Peter was on the verge of getting angry.

"True!" Mike grinned. "But instead of trashin' me, get out there and do some detective work. If you can get something on ole Carl, you might break that guilt trip she's on."

"You know, you might have something there!"

Peter went home determined to find out the meaning of the message Vadim had received. He prayed for help, and kept on praying until he was exhausted, but nothing would come. He finally went to bed and fell into an exhausted and troubled sleep. He dreamed that Marcy was lost in a barren desert, and was running away from something. She was carrying a tiny baby in her arms, and crying out for help. Then he saw that Carl was running after her, and behind Carl, heavy-footed and slow, came himself, desperately trying to reach Marcy before Carl did. His feet kept sinking down into the sand, and he could make no progress. Carl was fast gaining on her, and the baby was crying. Peter began to scream at Carl, ordering him to stop, but Carl ignored him. Suddenly a man stepped into Carl's path, barring his way. He had come from nowhere, and he was dressed in a surgeon's mask and gown, and had a stethoscope hanging around his neck. The doctor shook his head and wagged his finger at Carl, as a parent might when correcting a bad child. Carl hung his head in contrition.

"Thou shalt not lie!" said the doctor, and Carl began to disappear into the haze of the sun, and with him went the doctor's image. Peter began to run again, and then Marcy turned and saw him, and came back toward him, running and smiling.

Peter awakened drenched in sweat and with his heart still pounding. He sat up in bed and stared into the darkness. He knew the dream was in answer to his prayers, but what *was* that answer? Marcy was obviously running to save the child from Carl, that was clear, and he was running to help her. But what was the significance of the doctor? He had stepped between Carl and Marcy, and Carl had stopped at the sight of him. Then he had begun to disappear when the doctor scolded him and said "thou shalt not lie." Had Carl lied about something important, and if so what?

He kept going back over the dream, and then suddenly it hit him like a bolt of lightning! Of course, it was so obvious, so idiotically simple! Carl had lied about himself. He had been sterile! Carl couldn't catch Marcy and the child because he was sterile. That was the significance of the doctor, too! He knew Carl was sterile, and he prevented him catching up to them because he had lied. Only the doctor knew the truth. That was why Marcy had never become pregnant! Yes, it was conjecture, of course, but he was clutching at straws, any straw. Yet intuitively he knew he was right, just as he had known Marcy was in Florida when he had seen the poster in the travel agency window.

He switched on the light and looked at the clock. It was only six A.M., too early to call anyone. But then, who would he call? If that *had* been Carl's secret, Mike wouldn't confirm it, and he was the only one who really knew. He got out of bed and began to pace the floor. He would have to prove that Carl had been sterile, of course. Just because he'd had a dream and believed in his bones that Carl had been sterile would not be enough to convince Marcy. God had answered his prayers, he was certain of it, but now he had to prove it. Vadim's message no longer seemed obscure, it was the *right* clue. No wonder Carl had confessed his secret to Mike, and no wonder Carl's soul was troubled and could not rest. It was a terrible secret to take to the grave.

He'd have to find out the name of Carl's doctor, but how? He couldn't ask Marcy. Mike wouldn't know. Who else was there? Adam Newhouse, Carl's partner! Maybe, just maybe he knew the truth and maybe he'd tell him. If only it were true that Carl was sterile, and if he could find a way to prove it, it would set her free. It would take something that shocking to break the spell of her guilt. One thing was certain—he

would leave no stone unturned until he found the truth! For the first time in months he felt like his own man, and he knew that God had helped him, and would help him *if* he believed and prayed for guidance.

Peter was received in Newhouse's office at two thirty that afternoon. Adam had been busy, and wanted to put him off to the end of the week; he'd just come back from a business trip and was swamped. But when Peter explained that the visit concerned Marcy, and that only Newhouse could help her, he had agreed to see him.

"Mr. Newhouse, I apologize for insisting on this appointment, but it is a matter of great importance to me, and to Marcy."

"I'm afraid I don't understand, Mr. Blanchard." Newhouse looked slightly annoyed and began to shuffle papers on his desk.

"What I have to tell you is very personal, but I believe you are Marcy's friend, and care about her welfare."

"That's true, but could you come to the point? Is something wrong with Marcy?"

"You've not seen her recently?"

"No. She's taken a leave of absence. A wise move, considering all she's been through."

"Well, I've seen her—a few days ago in Palm Beach, and I can tell you that she's in a very bad way."

"What's wrong?" Newhouse was attentive now.

"For one thing she's pregnant." Peter had said it matter-of-factly.

"Pregnant?" Newhouse's face was a study in perplexity. "But—but Carl's been dead six months."

"I'm the father of the child, Mr. Newhouse."

"You! But—but—" Newhouse began to sputter.

"It's a long story, how it happened—but it had a lot to do with the fact that a part of Carl is ostensibly still alive in me: his corneas. You see, Marcy felt drawn to me, and I to her." Peter paused momentarily as he saw Newhouse's craggy face crease into a disapproving frown, but he continued anyway. "We've not been carrying on an affair, if that's what you're thinking."

"I doubt that it makes any difference what I think."

"No, it really doesn't, but I know you and Carl were close

friends, and I don't want you to think less of Marcy—"

"I'm not a moral prig, Mr. Blanchard. Marcy's a grown woman, and quite capable of running her own life. How she does it is none of my business!" Despite the words he used, Newhouse sounded pompous, and Peter was finding him damned hard to talk to.

"On principle I quite agree; it is none of your business, and I'm not in the habit of discussing my personal life with strangers either, but I have very little choice if I want to help Marcy."

"Accepted. Please go on."

"A lot of very peculiar things have been happening since I received the transplants, things that have drawn Marcy and me closer together. It was because of this that Marcy and I happened to get together one night—and only one night. In fact we hadn't seen one another in two months, not until I went to see her the other day. That's when I found out that she was pregnant."

"I suppose you will come to the point before the afternoon is over, Mr. Blanchard?" Newhouse looked at his watch and Peter wanted to punch him in the nose.

"Yes, I will come to the point, but I wanted to give you a little background for Marcy's sake. You see, she has become deeply disturbed over her pregnancy."

"That's hardly surprising, under the circumstances."

"Yes, well, she feels guilty because she became pregnant from being with me one night—and didn't become pregnant by Carl in ten years' time."

"I suppose that makes you some kind of superpotent stud?" Newhouse smiled unpleasantly, and Peter started to get out of his chair, then sat back down. He couldn't afford to punch Newhouse; he was his only hope of finding out who Carl's doctor had been.

"No, it makes me a worried man. You see, I happen to be in love with Marcy, and she's in trouble with herself. Because she became pregnant by me, she feels she failed Carl in some way—and that he's hurt and angry at her."

"Carl Morris was not that kind of man," Newhouse said curtly.

"I don't think so either, but Marcy's afraid of him."

"That's absurd!"

"Remember she's not thinking very clearly. As I said, I'm

afraid she's going to crack up, and that's why I've come to you."

"All right, what is it you want from me?" Newhouse sounded a little less impatient now.

"I want to know the name of Carl's doctor."

"What on earth for?"

"I have good reason to believe that Carl was sterile."

"That's pure nonsense!" Newhouse finally exploded. "You're a very dangerous man, Blanchard!"

"And you're an insufferable prig! I came here to try and get help for Marcy, and so far all you've done is make sarcastic remarks, and behave as if I'm a schoolboy confessing some sordid indiscretion. That woman is going through hell feeling guilty for conceiving a child by me—a child which she wants, by the way—and tormenting herself because she thinks she let Carl down. She very well may crack, Newhouse, because she's so disturbed she's afraid Carl will harm the child in some way." Newhouse looked embarrassed and started to say something, but Peter cut him off. "Oh yes, I know Carl is dead! But things have happened to both of us that could suggest that his spirit may be at work. Yes, I know that sounds crazy, too, but just take my word for it. At any rate Marcy believes it at this point, and because she believes he's angry at her for letting him down, she's terrified for the child she's carrying."

"This is the craziest thing I've ever heard," said Newhouse, but he didn't sound quite as arrogant as he had before.

"Crazy or not, if Carl was sterile—and as I said, I've good reason to believe he was—Marcy's suffering a torment she could be freed from with the truth." Peter stared hard at Newhouse, who was surprisingly quiet all of a sudden.

"But, Carl told me several times that nothing was *wrong* with either one of them."

"Yes. He told me the same thing. But to put it bluntly, I think he was lying. For what reason, I don't know—and don't care. All I care about right now is Marcy, and keeping her from cracking up."

"Marcy is one of the sanest people I've ever known."

"I agree, but as I said before, there are circumstances, and a woman in grief, and suffering guilt and fear during pregnancy, especially during pregnancy, can become very emotional. And remember, she is frightened for the child she's

310

carrying. All that stress could throw the healthiest woman.''

"Yes. Well, perhaps you're right. But I just can't believe Carl would lie all those years—especially to Marcy. I mean, he was crazy about her.''

"Maybe that's why he lied. But it's a pretty cruel lie. If he lied, however, it will be easy enough to prove if you'll just tell me the name of his doctor.''

"I doubt he'll tell you anything. A person's medical records are protected by law.''

"Screw the law! Carl Morris is dead and Marcy's alive—and her sanity, and the welfare of an unborn child are at stake. He'll tell me all right!''

"Mr. Blanchard, what do you do for a living?'' The question was so unexpected and offhand Peter was speechless for a moment.

"I'm executive editor at Strouk and Grange. Why?''

"Are you the man who refused to buy that German best seller?''

"Yes.''

"Maybe you aren't so crazy after all. Strouk and Grange, huh? Didn't take you long to get a better job, did it?''

"Some people still regard integrity as an asset in a man.''

"Yes, well—congratulations.'' Newhouse took out a pad and pencil and started to write. "Here's the name and address of Carl's doctor. On the one hand I hope you're wrong, and on the other I hope you're right. In any event, I'd appreciate knowing the truth. And, I don't mind telling you I don't envy you having to tell Marcy that Carl lied—if he did.'' He handed the sheet of paper across the desk to Peter.

"I don't look forward to it either. It will hurt her, and she'll probably hate me for a while, but it will free her. I have to take that chance.''

"You've got guts, I'll say that for you.'' Newhouse thawed a bit more.

"Sure you can spare that?'' asked Peter and walked to the door. Newhouse followed him and stuck out his hand. Peter took it.

"You going to marry Marcy?''

"Make an honest woman of her and give the child a name?''

"Now wait a minute—'' Newhouse got the point only too quickly and looked embarrassed.

"Yes. When she gets over hating me, if she'll have me. I asked her before I spent the night with her, and I asked her again three days ago. She said no both times."

"Because of Carl?"

"Yes. For your information I fell in love with her the night I met the two of you coming out of the Plaza Hotel."

"Oh yes. I remember that night very well. We went to the ballet."

"Well, thanks for the name of the doctor."

"Quite all right. Don't forget to let me know—and keep me posted about Marcy, will you?"

"Yes, I will."

"Good luck, Blanchard."

"Thanks, I'm going to need it."

Dr. William Larkin sat behind his desk and looked formidable behind his gold-rimmed glasses. Peter knew he was going to be a tough old bird to crack, but crack him he would, somehow.

"Well, what is the complaint that couldn't wait, Mr. Blanchard?"

"First let me say that I very much appreciate your being kind enough to see me. I know how busy you doctors are." Peter paused, but Larkin said nothing. So, he wasn't susceptible to flattery. "I'm told you were Carl Morris's doctor."

"Yes. Carl was my patient for many years. Very sad about his death."

"Yes. I was on that same plane, and in fact, I was sitting right next to him."

"That so?"

"I am much indebted to Carl. He left me his corneas when he died. Mine were damaged as a result of the accident. I had transplants over there."

"Successful, I take it?"

"Yes. I see very well. But I am not here about myself, Doctor. I'm here because of Carl's wife. I believe she is on the verge of an emotional breakdown."

"Marcy?" Dr. Larkin leaned back in his chair. "That surprises me. Marcy was not my patient, but I did know her father, and I've seen her from time to time over the years. I expected her to take Carl's death hard, but I wouldn't have

thought it would be that bad. She always impressed me as a strong, sensible woman.''

"There are reasons, sir, and they don't really have much to do with Carl's death—not directly, anyway." Peter then told Dr. Larkin the same story he'd told Adam Newhouse. When he'd finished, the doctor reached for the telephone and asked his secretary to bring in Carl Morris's records.

"Quite frankly I cannot remember if Carl Morris was sterile or not. I've not seen him for some time. But you realize that a patient's medical record is confidential information.''

"Even when the patient is dead, and another person is in emotional trouble because he has lied to her?''

"Well, that does put something of a different light on the matter." The secretary came in and handed the file to the doctor. When she had left, Dr. Larkin stared at the file for a moment and then opened it. Peter sat on the edge of his chair, waiting. He knew the doctor would find that Carl had been sterile, but whether or not he would tell him so, he couldn't be sure. Dr. Larkin read through several sheets of paper, then closed the file. He swiveled his chair around to look out the window behind his desk.

"It isn't only Marcy I'm afraid for, Dr. Larkin, it's also the child. If Marcy has a breakdown, it can't do the child she's carrying any good. The guilt she's suffering is bad enough, but her fear that Carl will harm the child could be the thing that will drive her over the edge.''

"You're certain that he told her he was all right?''

"Yes, he did. He also told me, and his law partner, Adam Newhouse, the same thing.''

"Do you happen to know how long Carl and Marcy were married?''

"Ten years, I believe.''

"You realize that I am in a difficult position?'' Dr. Larkin turned back to face Peter.

"Yes, sir, I do. But I haven't any choice. You're the only person who can tell me the truth—and I feel that the truth is the only thing that's going to save Marcy, and possibly the child.''

"Umm, there may be some truth in that.''

"If she knows he was sterile, she will stop blaming herself for failing him, and stop being afraid for the child. If Carl

was sterile, he can't possibly be angry because she did not give him a child.''

"Umm." Dr. Larkin rubbed his chin thoughtfully. "In view of the fact that the patient is dead, and that a woman and her expected child could be in danger, I suppose it would be ethical to reveal medical information. A doctor's commitment is to saving lives.''

"Are you saying that Carl Morris was sterile, sir?'' Peter held his breath and prayed silently.

"Yes. I'm afraid he was." Dr. Larkin did not look comfortable.

Peter sank back in his chair. "You don't know what you've done for Marcy and me, Doctor.''

"I think I do." He smiled briefly. "I would, however, like you to know that there is another factor which worked in your favor.''

"Oh? What was it?''

"Carl Morris was sterile before he married Marcy, and he knew it.''

"My God!'' Peter stared at Dr. Larkin in disbelief.

"When I read that, I decided to tell you what you wanted to know.''

"How could he have married her without telling her?''

"I'm not a psychiatrist, Mr. Blanchard, but it isn't very hard to figure out. He was undoubtedly afraid she might not marry him.''

"But to lie to her all those years!''

"Regrettable." Dr. Larkin arose and extended his hand. "It will be a hard thing to tell her.''

"I don't look forward to it—but I really haven't any choice.''

"Good luck.''

Peter left the doctor's office and started walking down Fifth Avenue. How could Carl do that to her, loving her as he did? He thought he knew Marcy pretty well, and he was certain she would have married Carl anyway. But for him to lie to her all those years? That must have been hard for him to live with. And since he hadn't told her before the marriage, it would have been harder to tell her afterward. Still it was pretty despicable to let her go on trying to have a child, and hoping, and constantly being disappointed. No wonder he had to confess to Mike, and to make him promise not to tell. It

wasn't the kind of thing a man would want his wife to know when he was dying. It would be a bitter thing to leave her with, because there was no way to try and make it up to her, or to explain why he had been driven to lie to her.

Peter had only been home from the office a short time when the house phone buzzed: it was the doorman asking if a Mr. Mike Fuller could come up. Peter assured him it was all right.

"Good," he said to himself as he went to the liquor cabinet. "Just the person I wanted to see." He poured a gin for Mike and went to the door to wait for him.

"Don't ever say you don't get service around here," said Peter, opening the door and handing Mike the glass.

"Hey, man, *that's* hospitality!"

"Come on in," laughed Peter. Mike came in and flopped on the couch.

"Man, am I bushed."

"How did you get that way?"

"Worrying."

"You! What about?"

"You and Marcy—and that little youngen."

"Oh?"

"Yeah." Mike sipped his drink. Peter said nothing. "I mean, you laid a trip on me with that news flash, man!"

"What news flash was that?"

"Listen, Pete, you know I think they don't make 'em any better than Marcy, and it's buggin' the shit out of me thinking maybe she's going nuts with the guilt shit. I mean, even being spooked about the kid. Man, that is heavy shit!" Mike stirred restlessly and Peter knew what he was about to do.

"Stop right there, Mike. I can spare you a conscience trip. I know Carl was sterile."

"You do?" Mike's eyes opened wide.

"Yes, I do. I figured it out—with a little help from the big man in the sky. It was the only thing that made any sense. So with a little arm twisting, I got the name of his doctor and I went to see him. With some coaxing, he loosened up and told me Carl was sterile."

"Man, that takes a load off me! I been walking around with that secret sticking in my craw too long. It was bad enough when I saw the two of you having trouble, but when Marcy got pregnant, and all that guilt come down on her—"

"Well, it's over now. I know about it," Peter said. Mike shook his head and then began to laugh.

"Oh, man! What a relief!"

"I can understand now why Carl didn't want to take that with him."

"Yeah, he was really hurtin'. But he had to take it with him anyway, didn't he?"

"Yes." Peter shook his head. "You know, I really can't understand why he didn't tell her the truth. They could have at least adopted a child. But to let her go on for years hoping they'd get lucky when he knew they never would!"

"It was the one big character defect in ole Carl. He just couldn't admit to her that he didn't have the juice."

"But why? They had a good relationship."

"Afraid he'd seem less of a man to her, maybe."

"God! He lived with her for ten years and he didn't know the kind of woman she was. She really loved him."

"Yeah, I know. But that was what he was afraid of all the same. There was this other cat before she married Carl, and I guess she had a hard time making up her mind. Old Carl didn't feel too secure about that, I don't think. So he lied, and he lived with it a long time. But the weird thing is, he meant to tell her when he got home from Paris. Course the plane changed all that. When he knew he was gonna check out—well, he had to dump it. By then he didn't want her to know because he was afraid it might make her bitter—hurt her too much."

"And spoil her perfect memory of him?"

"You guessed it. But he was man enough to take it with him—do without her forgiveness. That was heavy, Peter."

"Did he also tell you that he knew he was sterile before he married Marcy?"

"Yeah. Holy, goddamn fuckin' shit—that was the hardest part for me to hear."

"My sentiments exactly!"

"Jesus, it's no wonder that cat's soul can't find no peace."

"And I'm the one who's got to tell her the truth."

"Do you have to?"

"I'm convinced it's the only way to help her."

"Yeah, I guess she's got to know. It's the only way she'll get off that trip."

"I just hope she doesn't wind up hating me for telling her."

"It's a lot to swallow, man. But once she gets used to it—I mean, Marcy's too fair to hold it against you permanently. She'll know you had to tell her for her own good."

"I sure hope you're right."

"When you leaving for Palm Beach?"

"Tomorrow or the next day. As soon as I can get away from the office."

"Well, I better get out of here and let you get your beauty sleep." Mike got up. "I'll sure keep my fingers crossed for you."

"Thanks." Peter walked him to the elevator. "And— Mike, thanks for coming down here to tell me." Peter grinned. "I know that was hard for you, too."

"Yeah." Mike grinned. "Thanks for telling me before I shot my mouth off. Oh shit! We sound like two old biddies making polite. See you around, whitey!" Mike punched him playfully.

# Chapter Twenty-Six

Peter ordered a radio taxi to take him to Kennedy Airport for the flight to Palm Beach so that he would be certain to get there in good time for the flight. Taxis were sometimes difficult to find in the early morning in Manhattan. By eight fifteen the taxi had not arrived and his flight was at nine twenty; normally it took a good hour to get to Kennedy. He got on the telephone and to his surprise found that the taxi company, usually so reliable, had lost the order slip on his taxi. He shouted, they apologized and promised to have a taxi at his door in five minutes. It was more like ten when the taxi finally arrived; he was waiting in front of his building for it.

The driver gave him the option of the route via the Fifty-ninth Street Bridge, which was short but could be slow because of the rush-hour traffic through Queens, or the Triborough Bridge, which was a little longer in mileage, but might pay off in time. He opted for the Triborough, which turned out to be a mistake because they ran into a traffic tie-up on the FDR Drive. They sat and waited, Peter got more agitated by the moment; it was beginning to look as if he might very well miss the flight.

As they got moving again, Peter began to think of how he was going to tell Marcy about Carl, but instead found himself thinking of Carl. He had wanted so badly to keep his secret from Marcy, but it had come back to threaten her welfare

now. Did Carl know that the truth was about to come out? Was he aware that he, Peter, was now on his way to tell her what he had tried to keep from her? The thought was suddenly unnerving: what if Carl did know? Was he somewhere watching right now, hoping that he would miss the flight? Or maybe—no, that was muddled thinking again. Carl could not prevent his going to Palm Beach!

"Looks like we got trouble, Mr. Blanchard," the driver said as he guided the car, which was riding rough now, out of the fast traffic lane into the far right lane, and pulled to the side of an exit ramp.

"What's wrong?" asked Peter.

"Feels like the right front tire to me." The driver climbed out of the car amidst honking horns and rushing traffic.

"I don't believe this!" Peter looked at his watch. "If that tire's flat, I've had it!"

"Practically a brand-new tire!" The driver got back into the car and reached for his microphone. "Car 407 on the Van Wyck Expressway."

"Yeah, 407, what's up?"

"Got a tire going down fast, and a passenger bound for Kennedy."

"Where are you on Van Wyck?"

"Just south of the Kew Gardens interchange."

"What time's your flight?"

"Nine twenty," said Peter, leaning over the seat, listening to the exchange.

"Nine twenty, Herb."

"See what I got. Hang on."

"Oh, Jesus, this is all I need." Peter dug in his pocket for a cigarette.

"Sure sorry, Mr. Blanchard. Can't understand why that tire would go down, unless the night man picked up a nail, or something."

"Four oh seven, you there?"

"Yeah, Herb."

"Got nothing in the immediate area now. Take about ten to fifteen minutes to get somebody to you—don't think your passenger could make the flight. See if you can flag a cab, any cab, to get your passenger to Kennedy."

"Got you."

"And, George—"

"Yeah?"

"No charge on the passenger."

"Right."

"If you don't get a cabbie to take him, I'll route a man to pick up your passenger, and get the repair truck out to you right away."

"Right, Herb."

"Ask your dispatcher to notify the airline I'm going to be late. They probably won't do anything about it, but it's worth a try."

"Right." The cabbie took the flight information from Peter, and radioed it to his dispatcher. Then he got out of the car and stood on the edge of the expressway, his arm in the air, looking up and down the roadway. Every taxi light was out, indicating they had a fare. Peter was seething in frustration and anger.

"This just cannot be happening!" he said aloud. "I've never missed a plane in my life!" Just then a taxi pulled alongside, heading up the ramp.

"Where you going, Mac?" asked the driver.

"Kennedy. Got a passenger for a nine twenty flight."

"Umm." The driver looked at his watch and whistled. "Man, that's close, but I got a fare to let off about five blocks from here. If your passenger is willing to try, I'll hightail it back and get him."

"That's stupid! Take him with you now. Go on from there. Be a hell of a lot quicker," said Peter's driver.

"Yeah, good idea, if the lady don't mind."

"Well, ask her. All right with you, Mr. Blanchard?"

"Sure."

"The lady says it's okay," said the other driver. Peter jumped out of the taxi and climbed into the back seat with an elderly woman wearing a pair of large blue sunglasses studded with rhinestones.

"I really do appreciate this," Peter said.

"Don't mention it," she said in a colorfully husky voice. "We should help one another out, don't you think?"

"Yes, I do," replied Peter, hoping she would not continue. Fortunately there was not time, for the taxi soon pulled in front of a row of two-family houses, and the woman in the blue glasses got out. Peter thanked her, and the taxi pulled away from the house as the old woman went up the walk.

Peter looked at his watch, it was five minutes past nine.

"Think you can make it?" he asked the driver.

"Know a short-cut. If you're game, I am."

"Let's go," replied Peter.

"Hold onto your seat, it's gonna be a hairy ride!"

"Just get me there in one piece."

Peter sat back, braced himself, and closed his eyes. He tried to think calming thoughts and said a short prayer that he might make the flight on time. The driver hadn't been exaggerating when he said it would be a hairy ride—it was all that, and then some—but it kept Peter's mind off missing the flight. It was all he could do to keep himself from winding up on the floor of the taxi.

When the cab pulled in front of the airline building, Peter didn't even bother to look at his watch; he simply stuffed money into the driver's hand, grabbed his small case, and ran.

As he approached the departure desk, he saw that it was deserted, but a uniformed employee was still at the desk. He looked up as Peter reached him.

"Mr. Blanchard?"

"Yes."

"I'm really sorry, we held the flight a few moments for you, but the captain is a stickler for schedule."

"Has it taken off?"

"No, but it's on the runway waiting for clearance."

"Any chance of holding it there and getting me out to it?"

"Oh, I'm afraid not, sir. It's really too dangerous, and once the plane's engines are revved up and waiting for takeoff, they don't like to cut them. They'd have to do that for you to board."

"Damn it! I really needed to get on that flight!"

"Well, it could be worse. We have a plane leaving from La Guardia at ten ten, making one stop, and arriving West Palm at—"

"Never mind, one mad cab ride is enough for me today. Can't you get me on something that leaves here this morning?"

The clerk picked up the phone, and Peter took out his handkerchief and wiped the sweat off his face. It was a few moments before the clerk announced that there was a flight leaving from another terminal at ten o'clock, and another five

minutes until Peter's reservation on the other airline was confirmed and his ticket rewritten. He dashed out of the terminal, and when he at last reached the departure gate for his new flight, he found a chair and fell exhausted into it. He felt totally frazzled already, but as he sat there, he felt an anxiety beginning in the pit of his stomach. Too many things had happened, too many obstacles placed in his way, for them all to be coincidental. Nonsense! Of course they were coincidental. What else could it be? Carl? There was the demon again. No, you don't! He told himself. You're not going to be spooked by these events, you're going to get on this flight, and have a nice, peaceful, *safe* trip to Palm Beach. He talked calmly to himself and turned it all over to God.

The loudspeaker called flight number 83 for West Palm Beach and Peter got up automatically and started toward the boarding gate. He presented his ticket at the gate to the ramp and started down the narrow corridor to the plane. Suddenly panic seized him, and he wanted to run back up the corridor. Come on, Blanchard, this is absurd! You know nothing is going to happen. Please, God, go with me now, don't let me get pulled off my center. I know I'm doing the right thing for Marcy, and the child. Please, if it be thy will, give me courage now not to be afraid.

He continued to walk woodenly, fighting down the panic. He reached the door to the plane, and the flight attendant smiled at him. She was pretty, a green-eyed brunette, and her smile was warm and welcoming. It helped.

The only way to describe the two-hour-thirty-three-minute flight to West Palm's International Airport was horrifying! Peter was in a panic most of the way, despite his prayers, and when the drink cart was brought around just before lunch was served, he ordered a straight Scotch, and no lunch. He knew it would be disastrous to eat. The Scotch anesthetized him somewhat by making him slightly sleepy. He had not been drinking for a couple of months, and the liquor hit him harder than it normally would have. Still he listened to every revolution of the engines and continually fought down his fear.

When the approach was announced for West Palm Beach, he gripped the armrests and prayed, and only when he finally set foot on the ground in West Palm Beach did the panic subside. It didn't matter why, he was only grateful that it had. As he walked to the telephone to look up the number for

Dunbar, he found he was weak in the knees and unsteady on his feet. He found the number and dialed it. A maid answered the phone and finally Marcy came on.

"Marcy, it's Peter. I'm here in Palm Beach, and I need to talk to you for a few minutes."

"Peter!" For a moment her voice sounded excited, then the elation was gone as quickly as it had come. "Well, I don't know. I really don't think it would be a very good idea for us to meet right now, Peter."

"Marcy, for God's sake!" He heard the annoyance in his voice and immediately regretted it. "Look, I came down here to tell you something of great importance to us, and I must see you. It won't take long."

"Are you sure it's necessary, Peter?"

"Damn it, yes—it's of vital importance to both of us." She had never heard him angry before, and it surprised her; in a way it also pleased her, because his anger took from her some of the responsibility for giving in.

"All right. Come out to the house in a hour."

"Thanks, I'll be there."

"Miss Marcy, honey, a Mr. Blanchard is here to see you."

"Oh, yes, Miami, it's all right. Ask him to wait in the drawing room."

"Already done that, honey."

"I'll be right down." She needed a few more minutes to compose herself before seeing him. She glanced at herself in the mirror, and wished that she didn't look quite so awful. She smiled to herself, realizing that there was still a spark of vanity left in her. It would have been nice to look good for him, to see admiration in his eyes. *His* eyes? How odd, she had forgotten that they had once been Carl's.

Peter sat in the drawing room waiting for her with butterflies fluttering wildly in his stomach. He wanted desperately to see her, but he realized that he was scared as well. He fully realized that what he had to tell her might be the end of their relationship. Knowing that, however, had not once made him consider not telling her. Whatever the results, he knew he had to tell her for her own sake and that of the baby. And, as for Carl Morris, well, in a few moments, unless he dropped dead on the spot, the secret would be out, and maybe they could try to put their lives back together. He heard footsteps on the

marble hallway and hoped it would be her. He said a quick prayer that he would be able to handle the scene well and that she might not hate him.

"Peter." He opened his eyes to see her standing in the doorway. He jumped to his feet and went to her. It had been a shock seeing how she'd changed on his first visit, but it was an even greater one now. She looked totally exhausted, and had grown even thinner. She was not yet showing her pregnancy much, but she moved slowly, almost lifelessly, as she came toward him.

"Marcy, how are you?"

"A little tired and worried, but otherwise well. How are you?" She would not look directly at him.

"More than a little worried about you."

"Well, don't be." She sat down, and he sat opposite her. "You shouldn't have come, you know."

"It was very important that I come." He paused and took a deep breath. "I had to come to tell you that you're wrong about Carl being angry with you. Believe me, he is not angry, and there is no danger to the baby."

"Oh, Peter, really." Her voice was impatient. "I know you mean well, but *you're* wrong."

"No, I am not wrong. I know that you did not let Carl down."

"And who told you that? Vadim—or maybe crazy old Grandma Victoria, whatever her name is?" There was a note of disdain in her voice.

"I've not seen either of them."

"I suppose you've been talking to Father Spencer again."

"Wrong. I've been talking to a medical doctor." He kept his voice calm and gentle; it was important to go carefully now. She was already agitated, and he couldn't help seeing her extreme nervousness.

"A medical doctor? What on earth does a medical doctor have to do with this?"

"Quite a lot, darling. Does the name Dr. William Larkin mean anything to you?"

"Dr. Larkin? Yes, he's Carl's doctor."

"That's right."

"You've been talking to him?"

"Yes."

"I can't imagine why." She looked annoyed again.

325

"Will you promise to hear me out? Because what I have to tell you is not easy."

"Well, I don't know. It depends on what you have to say, but if you're going to rehash the situation, I don't think it's going to help either of us."

"Just take my word for it that what I have to tell you can make all the difference in the world to you and the baby, and to us."

"All right. What is it?"

"Well, I also found it difficult to explain why you got pregnant so easily by me and never with Carl. It just didn't make sense. I kept telling myself there had to be some logical reason. So the other night I went over everything that's happened, and everything that's been said. I thought of Vadim's message—'child'—which we couldn't find any significance in. But I was always sure it had some significance, so I began to pray for some clue to its meaning, some way to help you. I had a dream, Marcy, a dream that seemed to offer an explanation. I won't go into the details of the dream—it isn't important, except to know that out of it came an idea that I had to pursue. I was grasping at any straw that might lead to an answer; I was desperate to try and help you." He paused, hoping to read how she was accepting what he had said thus far; he saw that she seemed to be listening with more interest. If only he could put it in a way that wouldn't hurt too much.

"What was your idea?" she prompted. That was a good sign.

"That Carl was sterile." She stared at him for several minutes, and when she finally spoke, it was with unmasked disdain.

"I never thought you'd stoop so low, Peter. I want to believe you're trying to help me, but that's a very insensitive way of doing it." She got up suddenly.

"Marcy. Wait a moment—please. Hear me out."

"You've said quite enough already." She started across the room.

"Marcy, Carl *was* sterile! Dr. Larkin confirmed it." She turned, and their eyes met. She looked at him for several moments, and he met her gaze steadily, his heart pounding. "You know that I wouldn't lie to you about something like that. I've been afraid to tell you ever since I found out because I knew how much it would hurt—" He saw her

waver and put a hand out toward a chair to steady herself. He rushed to her and helped her into the chair. He knelt in front of her. "I've been worried out of my mind about you. I had to take the chance of your hating me if I told you the truth—I had to do it to free you, Marcy. I know the torment you've been through."

"I don't believe you." Her voice was barely above a whisper, but it was cold as ice, and her face was deathly pale, despite her tan.

"It's true, Marcy. If you won't believe me, call Dr. Larkin. Or call Mike. When I told him what Dr. Larkin told me, he confirmed it. That was the secret Carl told him before he died."

"But why didn't he tell me?" Tears came into her eyes. He wanted desperately to take her in his arms.

"He was ashamed. He thought he'd seem less of a man. And—he was afraid of losing you."

"Oh, God—" She covered her face and began to sob. He stayed beside her and let her cry it out, aching to hold her. Finally she grew quiet, and the eyes she turned to him were full of bewilderment, or what seemed like bewilderment to him. "He didn't know me at all, did he?" she whispered.

"I think he did. It was *his* block, *his* problem. He just couldn't accept the fact that he was sterile—and that was his own personal problem."

"Poor Carl." She looked down at her hands. "I still failed him, Peter. I didn't make him feel my love enough for him to trust me with his secret."

"Marcy, don't. It would have been the same with any woman. It came out of his doubts about his own masculinity."

"But if he'd felt secure in my love, he'd have known he could tell me. Why wasn't I able, in all those years, to make him feel he could trust me?" The tears ran down her face, and Peter was feeling scared again. Was she now going to blame herself for Carl's problem? Was there no end to it? Well, he hadn't meant to tell her the most hurtful part, but perhaps that was the shock that would finally bring her to her senses.

"Marcy, you did not fail Carl in any way." He paused. "I hadn't meant to tell you this, but if you're going to go on punishing yourself for something that was not your fault, you may as well know all of it."

327

"There couldn't be more." She looked frightened.

"Yes, there is more. You see, Marcy, Carl knew he was sterile before he married you."

"No, oh no! Don't tell me that!" she cried out in pain.

"He did know you loved him enough to hear the truth, because Mike told me that Carl had planned to tell you the truth when he got back from Paris. But when he knew he was going to die, he decided you shouldn't know. He hoped that some day you would remarry and have children. And—who knows? Maybe he did hope that we might get together. Maybe that's one of the reasons he gave me his eyes."

"To think he carried that secret all those years. How he must have suffered." Her eyes met his then, and he saw the deep compassion in them. What a truly remarkable woman she was. She could find it in her heart to forgive him the lie, and to feel for his agony. Could she also forgive him for telling her?

"I have always understood why any man would love you, Marcy, and now I understand why Carl loved you so much," he said softly. She went on looking at him, and he did not understand the look in her eyes. "I just hope you can understand why I had to tell you. After I saw you before, I was afraid you'd taken all you could. I had to find a way to help you—"

"I'm sorry I accused you of lying about Carl," she said.

"It was a normal reaction. You didn't want to believe it, I can understand that. Naturally I hoped you'd understand why I had to tell you, and forgive me sometime—for hurting you. But I hope I'm prepared for the fact that you may not be able to forgive me."

"You took a big chance, Peter."

"I didn't have a choice. I love you too much to sit by and watch you doing what you've been doing to yourself. And—I was concerned for the baby."

"I'm grateful." She paused and turned away. "Would you mind leaving me alone now?"

"Of course. I understand."

"Will you go back to New York right away?"

"Yes. I have a new job, and I can't stay away too long."

"Did you change jobs?"

"Yes." He told her then what had happened over the German book.

"That took a great deal of courage, Peter.'

"Well, fortunately it all worked out okay for me." He got up to leave. "Will you be all right?"

"I think so. It will take me awhile to understand, and—and to get over the hurt. I—I have to think about what you've told me, and try to put it into perspective. My relationship with Carl was obviously not what I thought it was." She got up.

"I know." He kissed her tenderly on the cheek. "I love you, and I want to marry you. Will you please think about that, too?"

"I have a lot of thinking to do, Peter. I just don't know anything right now. I'm not thinking very clearly, lately."

"Well, you know where to find me."

"Yes." She walked to the door, and they stood looking at one another.

"Be well, darling," he whispered.

"Don't worry about me, please."

"I'll try not to, but promise me that you'll try to get out of this morbid state and get some rest. Try to find some peace, Marcy."

"Yes, I'll try." She smiled sadly, and he kissed her once more on the cheek and went out the door.

Marcy started upstairs and met her sister coming down. "You were right about Carl," she said coldly.

"What about him?" asked Janie.

"He was sterile." The two sisters faced one another, Janie regretting the truth, Marcy being defensive.

"I'm sorry," said Jane softly.

"Why didn't I believe you?"

"Because you loved him and trusted him."

"Yes, and I was wrong, wasn't I?"

# Chapter Twenty-Seven

After Peter's return to New York, he threw himself into his work. He tried not to think whether or not Marcy would marry him, but the nagging fear that she would not was always there in the back of his mind. Three weeks had passed, and no word had come from her. He kept reminding himself it had been necessary to tell her the truth, but he couldn't help wondering if by doing so he had signed his own death warrant.

The first snowfall of the season covered New York with a thin layer of white, and he took to walking in Central Park on his lunch hours. It was difficult to be confined indoors, he felt so confined and restless within himself. Even in the park he found reminders of his situation. Mothers and nannies pushing perambulators with pink-cheeked babies seemed to be everywhere. This brought thoughts of Marcy and the baby growing inside her—his baby, a baby he might never be able to help care for, or watch grow into a little person.

He was feeling very low and depressed when Jeannie called one day and asked him to dinner. He accepted, needing a little admiring attention to boost his morale, but he felt slightly guilty about his selfishness. She'd probably expected him to call her weeks ago. Was he taking advantage of her now? No, she had asked him, and he supposed she felt able to handle it, or she wouldn't have done so. He had to stop feeling guilty

about everything; it had never been a problem of his until recently, but then he had seldom examined his motives so closely in the past. Perhaps his introspectiveness made him a nicer person, but it wasn't easier to live with.

He arrived at Jeannie's with flowers and a bottle of wine. She answered the door, looking happy and attractive, and he felt his spirits pick up at once. It was nice to see a happy face around for a change.

"Peter, how lovely! Flowers and wine—are we celebrating something?"

"Maybe Halloween past, or Veteran's Day coming?"

"Let's celebrate Halloween. I adore goblins, ghosts, and witches!"

"I've had the spooks, Jeannie. Maybe we should just celebrate being alive."

"Oh, we are in a grim mood, aren't we?" she teased.

"Maybe a little, yeah." He laughed at himself then, and determined to enjoy himself tonight.

"You need cheering, darling. Why don't you mix us one of your super martinis?"

"God, I haven't had a martini in six months."

"Neither have I. Not since the last one you mixed for me."

"Well, let's remedy that right now." He pulled off his jacket and hung it over a dining room chair as he passed through on his way to the kitchen. He opened the refrigerator and looked for lemons, found one, and began shaving off the peel. He opened the freezer and saw that two glasses stood there, frosted and ready. Just like old times, and there was something comforting about the familiarity.

"And here we have the ice bucket—filled." Jeannie put it down on the counter and removed the top.

"Thank you." He took a tall glass out of the cabinet, poured a generous splash of cold Russian vodka into it, then opened two cabinets looking for the vermouth.

"Looking for this?" Jeannie stood in the doorway, holding the bottle of vermouth.

"Yeah, where you hiding it lately?"

"On the bar cart."

"Thanks, love." He took the bottle and dashed a few drops into the vodka, then added several ice cubes and began to stir. "Jeannie?" She had disappeared again.

"Yes?" she answered from some other part of the house.

"How many times do I stir the martinis?"

"Sixty-five."

"That's right." He continued to stir until he'd swirled it sixty-five times, no more, no less. Then he removed the frosted glasses from the freezer and rubbed the rims with lemon peel, and twisted two peels and dropped them into the glasses. Finally he poured the liquid into the glasses, picked them up, and carried them into the living room.

"Where are you, anyway?"

"Coming."

"Don't let this get tepid. I've outdone myself this time."

"Here I am."

"And here's your Blanchard special." He handed her the glass.

"Here's to living," she said, raising her glass, looking at him over its rim, her eyes laughing at him.

"Here's to living." He sipped the martini and found it just right.

"Umm, the superest super!" she said, sipping hers.

"Not bad if I do say so myself." He sat down in the chair he'd chosen as his when they had first started seeing one another, and she draped herself on the sofa.

"Bought any good books lately?"

"Yeah. Matter of fact, bought one today I really like."

"By whom and about what?"

"About a fifty-four-year-old woman trying to find herself."

"I thought May Sarton had the corner on that market."

"Apparently not. But I guess most of us have thought teen-agers and undergraduates had the corner on the market, but every day now we learn that no age has a monopoly on it."

"The women's movement certainly blew the subject wide open."

"Yeah. I don't know if it's the spirit of the times, or what it is, but people seem to me much more introspective, more in search of answers, determined to come to terms with life. Those are all great big general terms, I know, but people just don't sail through life, skimming along the surface, and get away with it like they once did. It's as though people have suddenly awakened to the fact that life is a very serious

business, and the ones who can't measure up are losers. Nobody gets a free ride either economically, intellectually, or spiritually any more. You've got to be *responsible* for yourself today."

"I've been one of those skimmers most of my life. Selfish, irresponsible, superficial, and willful!"

"Well, I think you're exaggerating, but how did you come to those conclusions?"

"By losing you. When I asked myself why, I had to take a good hard look at myself, and I didn't measure up very well. You were different—you'd outgrown me through facing death; surviving when others had died; being blind and getting your sight back; and fighting to keep your own identity when you were threatened by Morris and his eyes. You came back a different person, and instead of trying to get to know that person, and understanding him, I played the same game I'd always played. My game. Give me what *I* want."

"I don't think it was quite that bad."

"Yes, it was. It took me a little while to realize that I was out of my league, and that there was a bond between you and Marcy Morris that I couldn't break. You were the grown-ups dealing with agonies of the mind and spirit that I'd only read about and didn't understand too well when I did."

"And now?" he asked gently.

"I'm trying to grow up. A little late, I'll grant you, but maybe I won't blow it the second time around."

"The thing of it is, Jeannie, the process doesn't stop. We keep on moving—and getting to the point where we have to take the next giant step."

"How're you doing, Peter?"

"I'm in pretty good shape. I think I've got the business of my eyes under control. Oddly enough, it came about by my realizing that I needed a power higher than myself to help me. Actually I was persuaded by an Episcopal bishop into turning to God for help. My anxieties are greatly reduced, and I seem to be in charge of my life now."

"I'm so glad. You really scared me there for a while."

"I was scared to death myself."

"And—what about us, Peter? Is there a chance for us now?"

"Oh, Jeannie, so much has happened to me." He wished she hadn't asked; it had been nice to be familiar, and relaxed

and comfortable. To be accepted as he was, without conflicts or tensions. But the question had been asked, and she deserved an answer. Was he going to give her an honest answer, be an honorable and responsible adult? Or was he going to hedge, play it safe, leave the door open in case things didn't pan out with him and Marcy?

"Are you with me, Peter?"

"Yes. I'm just trying to think how to answer that question honestly, Jeannie. You see, it isn't so much a question of you and me, it's a question of me and Marcy. There is a bond between us, you're right about that. It began with Carl, and the cornea transplants."

"I know it's none of my business, but are you having an affair with her?"

Why was it that people had to define a relationship in sexual terms?

"An affair? No, not really. It's very difficult to have an affair with someone who is grieving for a husband whom She loved. But I do love her."

"I was afraid you did." Jeannie was trying to be adult about Marcy, but he saw the look in her eyes.

"I'm afraid I'm committed to her, Jeannie. I'm sorry, but I want to be honest with you."

"I'm glad you are."

"Probably I wouldn't have told you tonight if you hadn't asked me. I was feeling very comfortable, and relaxed. After all, we had some good years together, and I still have a great deal of feeling for you. I've realized that tonight. But as I said, I'm committed to Marcy—because there is another bond between us now."

"Oh?"

"A more important one. Marcy is carrying my child." That was the hardest part to tell her, and he saw that it came as a blow she could not disguise.

"But—but you just said—"

"Yes, I said we were not having an affair, and we're not."

"But the woman is pregnant!"

"Obviously we've been together, it's not an immaculate conception. I spent a weekend with her in Connecticut, but neither of us planned for it to happen. It just did. We were attracted to one another from the beginning, but it was so

complicated with Carl's eyes, and his death, and so many things. So we were not having an affair."

"Are you going to marry her?" Jeannie sounded confused, and he couldn't blame her; his explanation did sound strange, but he wasn't going into all the complications.

"I hope she is going to marry me; it's up to her."

"But does she love you, Peter?"

"Yes, I think she does. But right now she doesn't know how she feels, and there are a lot of things she has to reconcile herself."

"But she is going to have the child?"

"Oh, yes. No question about that."

"What if she doesn't marry you?"

"That will make it difficult."

"If I couldn't break the bond over Carl, I certainly can't break this one, can I?" she asked simply, trying to conceal her emotions.

"I don't know what's going to happen, Jeannie, but I had to tell you the truth. I expect it will all be decided within a few weeks, and I may still be a bachelor, looking for a good home-cooked meal."

"But you are in love with her?"

"Yes. I'm afraid so."

"I really blew it, didn't I?" She reached for a cigarette, and he got up to light it. He saw tears in her eyes as she avoided his.

"No. Circumstances over which we had no control intervened. And, as you said, I came back a different person."

"Are you hungry?" She was changing the subject.

"Starved." he replied, grateful for her style.

"Come on, I'll feed a hungry bachelor, if he'll help me cook."

"Love to." He relaxed and followed her to the kitchen.

Just before Thanksgiving, when he was feeling most depressed and hopeless, Peter received a call early one evening from Marcy. She was back in New York and wanted to see him.

In the taxi on the way uptown to her apartment, he tried to contain a building excitement, and to imagine what she would say. He prayed that she might be ready to say yes to him, but if not, he prayed that he might handle himself well.

When Marcy opened the door to him, she was smiling, and looked more like her old self. His impulse, as always, was to take her into his arms, but he restrained himself, uncertain of his ground.

"Hello," he said.

"Hello. Come in." She held open the door and he walked into the room.

"Sit down," she said pleasantly, sounding like herself again. "Would you like a drink?"

"Maybe a Scotch?" He hadn't been drinking, but tonight he thought he could use one. He watched her move across the room and noticed that she was showing her pregnancy. It gave him a thrill to see it, and to know that the child was theirs. She came back with the drinks and sat down opposite him.

"How are you?" he asked and marveled that he felt shy, almost like a young man on his first date, and yet he had slept with this woman, and she was carrying his child. How really strange and unpredictable the human emotional mechanism was. A perfectly secure and self-assured person could become insecure and self-conscious when uncertain of his acceptance by someone he loved and wanted.

"Peter? Are you all right?" she asked.

"What?"

"I was speaking to you, but you didn't seem to hear me."

"Oh—I was thinking about something. You didn't say how you are."

"I feel much, much better. How are you?"

"Scared," he laughed uneasily.

"I've given you a hard time, haven't I?"

"Not really."

"I went to see Father Spencer today."

"Oh?"

"Yes. I wanted to talk about us." She paused and he waited for her to go on. "He sent you his regards."

"I must go to see him. I want him to know how much he helped me."

"Well, he helped me a lot today. And—that's what I want to talk to you about." She lit a cigarette, and then leaned forward, meeting his eyes. "It's so difficult to know the right thing to do."

"Don't I know it."

337

"I'm not sure if I'm in love with you, Peter. I think I may be, but my emotions are in such a tangle right now. At first I thought my feelings for you were due to the living part of Carl in you, and later I felt certain that was all there was to it. Then you came to Connecticut, and my feelings were once again thrown into confusion by what happened between us." She sipped her drink, and he lit a cigarette. The tension inside him was building. She continued. "When I had time to think back on our time together while I was in Maine, I thought I probably was in love with you. Otherwise how could it have seemed so right with you? Then I found out I was pregnant." She paused, and he started to speak, but she held up her hand to stop him. "Let me get it all out, Peter."

"I'm sorry."

"When I found I was pregnant, I was almost paralyzed with guilt, and there wasn't room for any other feelings. I became totally confused then, and frightened. I didn't want to be alone. That's why I went to my mother's."

"I knew that, Marcy, I really did."

"When you came to see me, I was at my lowest. I was terrified, and I didn't want to see you again. I was so disturbed, I thought your very presence was dangerous. And—I resented you. In my confusion I blamed you for what I had convinced myself was my betrayal of Carl." She smiled apologetically.

"And then I showed up again," he said.

"Yes. And I'm terribly glad you did. After you'd gone, I realized how much you cared. You came to tell me the truth, even realizing that it might turn me against you permanently. It must have been a very difficult thing for you to do."

"It was. I was afraid you'd never want to see me again, and I came home with the same fear."

"I shouldn't have let you go like that, but I couldn't do anything else. After you left, I began to get myself together. You were right—the truth did free me finally. Of course I was hurt, and I had to try and work out my feelings about Carl's lie. I went through a period of feeling sorry for myself, and being angry at Carl for all those years I had felt inadequate. But thinking back on my feelings of inadequacy made me realize the inadequacy he must have felt in being sterile. Slowly I began to heal, but I still had to sort out my feelings for you—and the child."

"Have you done that now, Marcy?"

"I think so. I believe that I love you, and the feeling grows as I begin to love the child I'm going to have. I also had to be certain that my feelings for you were not motivated by the fact that you were the child's father. Just as I was afraid my original feelings for you were because of Carl's eyes. So, finally I can admit that it is love I feel for you, yourself. I think maybe I always did. And I love you more as I love our child. There are times when I still have doubts, but it seems to me we have quite a lot more than just the child between us."

"Of course we do." Hope had begun to rise in him.

"Is that enough for you? I mean, do you think we have enough to build a good marriage?"

"Do you?"

"I'm beginning to think so."

"Are you saying you *will* marry me, Marcy?"

"Yes. If you still want me." She smiled a warm, open smile; the smile he loved so much. Suddenly he felt wonderfully happy and excited. He moved to sit beside her on the sofa and took her hand in his.

"Yes, my beautiful, lovely Marcy, I want you. And—I think we can have a beautiful marriage."

"I think so, too. There's a lot I don't know about my feelings yet, but I have a feeling of rightness about us. She looked directly into his eyes now. "Please kiss me, Peter," she said. He felt as if his emotions would burst out of his chest as he gathered her in his arms. They kissed, and the old excitement rushed back, the same kind of wild, passionate excitement they'd experienced in Connecticut.

Lying beside her in bed later on, he placed his hand gently on her slightly protruding abdomen and held it there.

"What a good feeling it is to know that a child is growing inside you, and that it's part of me, too."

"I was so frightened for it—before."

"But you're not anymore?"

"No. Now that I know about Carl, I don't think he would harm it. Perhaps it's wrong to feel this way, but somehow I feel he owes me this child." Peter bent over and kissed her abdomen.

"I love you, little baby," he said softly. Then, raising himself on his elbow, he looked into her eyes. "Marcy, I

never felt anything like this before. I didn't know what it felt like to really be *in* love."

"I'm a lucky woman," she said. "You've been so loving and patient with me." She took his face in her hands and pulled his mouth down to hers. She kissed him tenderly, then they were kissing passionately, their bodies reaching out with an urgency to be joined. They were joined, and gave of themselves fully, without hesitation or restraint.

They were married in a quiet ceremony in Connecticut with Bishop Spencer presiding, and held a small reception for a few friends and family at Marcy's house.

They were extremely happy in the weeks and months following the wedding. They gave up their apartments and got a bigger one on Fifth Avenue, overlooking the sailboat pond in Central Park. They went to Connecticut on weekends, redecorated the house to make it theirs, and played tennis until Marcy got too far along to play comfortably. In fact they did all the things they both loved to do, and their relationship deepened and grew, and they found that they were beautifully companionable. Life was good, and promised to be even better when the baby arrived.

The biggest uncertainty in their lives was what to name the baby. The doctor had told her it would be a boy, and they made list after list of names. Marcy favored old-fashioned names, and Peter announced that he would be satisfied with anything she chose so long as it could not be shortened into a nickname. He had hated being called Pete, and he didn't want his son saddled with the same problem.

"How about something like Grant?" he asked. "You can't do much with that."

"Grant Blanchard—not bad," she tested. "No, that's not bad." She wrote it down on the list and began to chew on the pencil. "Or, how about Seth?"

"I like it. Sounds old-fashioned, all right." He kissed her on the cheek. "Sure you wouldn't prefer Ahab?"

"Very funny." She got up and sat on his lap and put her arms around his neck.

"Know something?" he asked.

"What?"

"You're getting heavy."

"The baby is going to be a giant."

"I do hope it won't be green and jolly."

"No, he'll be dark and handsome like his father."

"I'd rather he were blond and beautiful like his mother. Is it true that blonds have more fun?"

"They do!"

"Do they really?"

"This one is having fun being married to you."

"Then it isn't true, because this dark-haired man is having more fun that he's ever had in his life."

"Umm." She kissed him on the mouth.

"You're seducing me again—and if you don't let me get dressed I'll never get to work and little Seth Blanchard will never have the advantages he deserves."

"But he'll have a happy home because his mother and father are in love."

"True. Maybe I'll just stay home today. After all, it's more important to be happy."

"On second thought, he is going to have to go to college, and things like that. Maybe you'd better get dressed."

"Damn, you built me up and let me down!" He laughed softly.

"True. But I've got things to do to get ready for little Seth's appearance."

"Are you feeling anything?" He looked concerned.

"He's making noises like he's thinking of putting in an appearance soon."

"Really?" He felt excited. "Are you sure?"

"Well, Dr. Bondurant says it could be any day now."

"Maybe I should stay home?"

"Nonsense! Go to work, Peter Blanchard."

"You'll call me the minute you feel anything positive?"

"Of course."

After he had gone to the office, Marcy made herself busy. She hadn't wanted to say anything to worry Peter, but as her time drew near, she found the old nagging fear for the child cropping up. Each time it came to the surface, she dismissed it, but it still lurked in the back of her mind, and she became more and more concerned that it should be there at all.

It was two days later, in midafternoon, that Peter got the call. Marcy announced calmly that she thought she was going into labor and was on her way to New York Hospital. Peter

panicked and tore out of the office, telling his secretary to cancel everything: his son was on the way!

He arrived at the hospital just as Marcy was checking in and was able to go through the procedure with her. By the time they got to her room, Dr. Bondurant had arrived, and assured them both that everything was perfectly normal and going according to schedule. Although Marcy was calmer than he was, he could tell that something was on her mind.

"Marcy, is something wrong?" he asked.

"Labor pains are lots of fun, didn't you know?" She chuckled. "Just hold my hand." He held her hand and suffered through every spasm of pain. When the spasms got closer and closer together, Dr. Bondurant decided it was time to take her to the delivery room. As they wheeled her out, he walked along beside her, holding her hand. When they got to the elevator, she smiled up at him despite the pain.

"Go do whatever expectant fathers do," she said. "And—Peter—"

"Yes, darling?"

"Whatever happens, please remember that I love you, and I'm very happy that I married you."

"Same here," he said and kissed her forehead.

"See you in a little while," she said as they wheeled her into the elevator.

When the door closed, he felt a terrible sense of separation, and stood looking at the closed door. He felt cut off from her, and uneasy. What had she meant by that "whatever happens"? Was she afraid of something going wrong? He walked back to her room feeling troubled. He lit a cigarette and sat down to wait, but found that he literally couldn't sit still. He got up and began to pace the floor. Was Marcy secretly still afraid for the child, still afraid of Carl? "Oh God, please don't let anything happen to the baby," he prayed. "And please, please let us finally be free of this man." He went to the window and looked out on the East River. He knew he would spend the rest of the time praying for little Seth and Marcy.

It was about two hours later that a groggy Marcy was wheeled back into the room. She smiled wearily at him. "We have a son," she said. He leaned over and kissed her lightly.

"Thank you," he said, and she smiled and squeezed his hand. He stayed like that, holding her hand and feeling

wonderfully happy as she drifted in and out of sleep. Late in the afternoon she awakened and looked up at him.

"Hello, Papa Blanchard," she said weakly.

"Hi, Momma Blanchard. How do you feel?"

"A little tired, but happy."

"Me, too."

"Guess we have to decide on a name."

"Shall we call him Seth? I've been kinda thinking of him that way."

"Would you mind?"

"I'd love it. How about Seth Dunbar Blanchard?"

"Sounds wonderful."

"I like the idea of his having your maiden name too. I don't think it's fair that a child should only bear the surname of the father. After all, it's the mother's child, too."

"Well—I see our new mother is awake," said Dr. Bondurant, coming into the room. "How do you feel?" He came to the bed and felt her pulse.

"Wonderful, but a little tired."

"Odd if you didn't." He chuckled easily.

"Is the baby all right?" she asked, and Peter detected the fear in her voice.

"Hale and hardy! A fine, healthy, eight-pound boy," replied the doctor, and Peter saw the relief come into her face at the doctor's words.

"Can we see him?" she asked.

"Yes, in a little while. Now, what do you want to call him? I have to make out his birth certificate."

"Seth Dunbar Blanchard," replied Peter.

"Nice name," said Dr. Bondurant. "If you'll just come with me, Mr. Blanchard, and make certain I get all the facts straight, I'll fill out the certificate now."

"Okay." Peter got up.

"I'll look in on you a little later, Marcy," said the doctor, patting her arm reassuringly. "You're doing just fine."

Peter followed Dr. Bondurant out and down the hall to a small office at the end of the corridor. When he had given the doctor all the information he needed, he got up to leave.

"Uh, Dr. Bondurant?"

"Yes?" The doctor looked up from the form he was still filling out.

"Are you quite sure that little Seth is all right?"

"Quite. Never seen a healthier specimen." Dr. Bondurant smiled, and Peter breathed easier. He wanted to be absolutely certain about Seth so he could reassure Marcy, because he knew she'd been afraid, and even though she'd said nothing, there was still some apprehension in her mind.

"Everything is perfectly normal, is that right?"

"What is this, anyway? I told you both. Seth is healthy, normal, and I might add—damned beautiful!"

"His eyes, are they okay?"

"His eyes? Why, yes, they're fine. I put the birth drops in myself."

"Thanks, Doctor. I'm sorry to be such a nuisance, but his mother has been somewhat apprehensive, and I just wanted to be able to reassure her that our son is fine."

"I don't understand, Mr. Blanchard. Was there some reason to believe Seth wouldn't be all right?" Dr. Bondurant looked curious now.

"Let's just say this child is very important to my wife, to both of us."

"Oh. Well, it's an understandable concern, I guess. A lot of mothers have it." Dr. Bondurant smiled. "But I'm happy to be able to reassure you both that there's no need to be concerned about Seth. He's A-number-one!"

When Peter got back to Marcy's room, it was a radiant Marcy who smiled up at him, for little Seth nestled warmly beside her.

"Look what the nurse brought me."

"Umm. Where did she get it, F.A.O. Schwarz?"

"Peter Blanchard, you ought to be ashamed of yourself. Not even F.A.O. could make a toy so beautiful as little Seth." Peter touched the baby's little clenched fist, and he opened his eyes and looked up at his father. Peter felt a rush of happiness welling up inside him. This was his *son*, a part of himself, and a part of Marcy. He took the little fist in both his hands.

"Hello, son," he whispered. Little Seth gurgled happily.

"Isn't he beautiful, Peter?"

"The most beautiful thing I've ever seen in my life—except his mother."

"Beautiful and healthy. We're very lucky, aren't we?"

"Very." Peter caught her eye. "You were still a little afraid of Carl, weren't you?"

"Oh—" She looked away. "Maybe just a little. But I will never be afraid of Carl again, and you shouldn't either. That's all over now." There was a strange note in her voice that he didn't understand.

"I'm sure it is," he replied.

"Do you know how I know?" she asked.

"How do you know?"

"Well, after you left with Dr. Bondurant, the nurse brought little Seth to me, and I was holding him, just as I am now, and I guess I must have dozed off—or maybe I was having a waking fantasy, but I saw Carl enter the room as clearly as I see you now."

"Marcy—" Peter was alarmed.

"No, no, it's all right, darling." She smiled reassuringly and took his hand. "Listen to me."

"Okay."

"Well, Carl walked up to the bed and looked down at Seth, and touched his little hand, as you did just now, and then he looked at me and smiled. And do you know what he said?"

"No. What did he say, Marcy?" He was still feeling uneasy, but she was smiling and relaxed.

"He said, 'I just wanted to see your son. He's very beautiful.' And, I said, yes, isn't he? And he said: 'I'm contented now.' Then he turned to leave, and he stood by the door and said: 'Tell Peter good-bye. I won't be bothering him anymore. Be happy.' And then he left." Her eyes held his.

"Was it a dream?"

"Perhaps. It doesn't matter. I know that's how he feels."

"I hope he is at peace. Somehow I think he may be—now that you have little Seth."

"We have a lot to be grateful to him for."

"Yes, and I am grateful." They were both quiet, looking at little Seth sleeping soundly. "I think Seth may be a very lucky little boy. I just have a feeling he's going to have someone up there looking out for him."

"Yes." Tears came into her eyes. "I do love you, Peter Blanchard," she said.